LULLABY
ROAD

LULLABY ROAD

A Novel

JAMES ANDERSON

CROWN
NEW YORK

This is a work of fiction. Names, characters, places, and incidents
either are the product of the author's imagination or are used
fictitiously. Any resemblance to actual persons, living or dead,
events, or locales is entirely coincidental.

Grateful acknowledgment is made to Gary Miranda for permission
to reprint an excerpt of "First Elegy" from *Duino Elegies* by
Rainer Maria Rilke, translated by Gary Miranda and published by
Tavern Books in Portland, Oregon. Translation copyright © 1981,
1996, 2013 by Gary Miranda.

Library of Congress Cataloging-in-Publication data is available
upon request.

ISBN 978-1-101-90654-5
Ebook ISBN 978-1-101-90656-9

PRINTED IN THE UNITED STATES OF AMERICA

Book design by Andrea Lau
Jacket design by Michael Morris
Jacket images: (snow) Christy Chaloux/Aurora/Getty Images;
(road) RJW/Stone/Getty Images

10 9 8 7 6 5 4 3 2 1

First Edition

Dedicated to my enduring
role models, warriors and heroines all:
Louisa Michaela Cabezut, grandmother;
Helen Zuur, mother; Eileen Bernard, aunt;
Louise Anderson, sister; Cheryl Zuur, cousin

In my life there are many silences.

—JUAN RULFO

What angel, if I called out, would hear me?
And even if one of them impulsively embraced me,
I'd be crushed by its strength. For beauty
Is just the beginning of a terror we can barely stand:
We admire it because it calmly refuses to crush us.
Every angel terrifies. And so I control myself,
Choking back the dark impulse to cry.

—*Duino Elegies*, RAINER MARIA RILKE, TRANSLATED
FROM THE GERMAN BY GARY MIRANDA

LULLABY
ROAD

1

A momentary silence was all that marked the passing of summer into winter. After living most of my almost forty years in the high desert of Utah, twenty driving a truck, I had come to the conclusion there were really only two seasons: hot and windy and cold and windy. Everything else was just a variation on those two.

Late in the evening I lay half-awake in my single bed and knew the silence meant the season had changed. I like to think maybe I know a thing or two about silence. Real silence is more than the absence of sound: it is something you feel. A few heartbeats earlier a steady wind scattered the leftover sounds from evening—a car passing, neighbors talking from behind closed doors, somewhere a dog barking—all the usual muffled racket of nearby lives. Then there was nothing, nothing at all, as if the desert and everyone in it had vanished and left nothing behind but an indifferent starless light.

By four a.m., when I begin my workday, winter was on its hind legs and waiting. It took longer than usual to get to the transfer station and load my truck. The time was well after five o'clock when I finally got under way, driving cautiously through the light snow and ice in the predawn darkness. My heater was blowing full blast and the bitter, dry cold hijacked the warmth from my body and cracked my skin into something akin to a hardpan lakebed. My last routine stop was to take on diesel. I had missed the morning fueling rush, if there had been one, by being either a few minutes early or a few minutes late. All of the pump islands were empty.

Cecil Boone was the manager of the Stop 'n' Gone Truck Stop on US 191 just outside of Price, Utah. The Stop 'n' Gone was a cheapo independent, stuck out alone in a patch of sand and broken rock, with the rundown look of a place that must have low prices because it didn't have much of anything else. Cecil was a stubby, sour man in his fifties. We were inside the small convenience store and Cecil was behind the register. In the eight or so years I had been buying my diesel there, nearly every weekday, I had never seen the man smile before that snowy October morning.

There are probably lots of reasons to smile. Most folks do it every day. In my line of work I don't see many smiles and I probably don't give many, not even to myself. That was the way it should be. No one wants to glance up and see a truck driver grinning. My sense is that such a sight is bound to have an unsettling effect on the ordinary driver. I was quickly sorting through the reasons people smile—humor, warmth, trivial annoyance—and coming up short. It was just Cecil and me—and Cecil's smile.

I paid for my diesel.

"Someone left something for you on Island 8," he said.

I asked him what.

"None of my business. Just make sure you take it with you when you leave."

Cecil walked back toward the door of his cluttered office. "Eight," he said over his shoulder. I thought I heard a small laugh before he closed the door. It might have been gas.

My tractor-trailer rig was parked at Island 2. Eight was on the far west side of the truck stop. I stood for a minute and looked out the window at the blowing snow. Not much accumulation. Ice beneath a thin dusting of white. The fine flakes eddied around the high arc lights of the truck stop like a scene from a low-rent snow globe. Outside I paused and glanced in the direction of Island 8. Nothing I could see.

The inside of my cab was warming up. I was in favor of getting on the road and starting my day. Who would leave something for me at a truck stop? It couldn't be that important or valuable or it wouldn't have been left outside. Maybe this was a joke. I could take a joke. Anytime. Later. Cecil's smile floated in and out of the restless snow beyond my windshield. That smile, if that's what you wanted to call it, seemed to dare me to swing by Island 8 and take a peek. No matter what Cecil said, I felt no obligation to take it with me.

I jockeyed my twenty-eight-foot tractor-trailer rig in a wide turn and slowly approached Island 8. What looked like a short pile of clothes was stacked against a battered trash can—nothing that couldn't wait, or be ignored entirely. I began to pull through the cluster of canopied fuel pumps and kept an eye on my side mirror to be sure I cleared the concrete stanchions that protected the pumps from idiots in motorhomes and U-Hauls and once, years ago, when I was hungover, me. The clothes stirred and launched a small wisp of snow into the wind.

I set the brakes and jogged back toward the island, slipping on the ice a couple times and barely managing to stay upright. A large white dog was tightly curled into itself and raised its long nose up an inch or two as I approached. Its pink eyes followed me and then settled intently between my shoulders and head—my neck. No growl or bared teeth. This was a dog that meant business—and it knew its business well. I stopped several feet away and the two of us discussed the situation in silence.

Our conversation ended when the dog uncurled and stood, stretched, and shook the powdery snow off its fur. Its thick coat was still white. Not just white, an impossible luminous white that made the animal almost a blurred white shadow floating inside the blowing snow. The dog was also larger than I first thought, an indeterminate mix of husky and German shepherd, with maybe a little timber wolf thrown in for good measure.

A pair of black, almond-shaped eyes rose like timid fish to the surface of the furry white lake. They stared at me from behind the dog's back. A small child.

I fell twice in my hurried march back to the building. The soles of my old Ariat roper boots were as thin as paper and just as smooth. Leaving a little kid out in a snowstorm was just the sort of thing that would draw a smile from Cecil. This was his idea of a joke. A five-car pile-up on the interstate or a grisly hit-and-run might give him laughing fits. I was limping badly when I reached the door. It was locked.

A hastily written sign was taped at eye-level, my eye-level, about six foot four in boots. BACK IN TEN MINUTES. Somehow I doubted Cecil would be back until I was well down the road. I had a schedule to keep. He knew I wouldn't wait, not ten minutes. Not even five.

After pounding on the door and yelling Cecil's name, I kicked at the bottom of the heavy glass. My reward was another fall. If Cecil was inside he was determined not to show himself. I walked carefully back to Island 8. The dog hadn't moved; the kid still huddled behind it. The dog moved aside and fully revealed the child, a young boy. This was permission to move closer.

I guessed the boy's age at five or six, brown complexion and straight, black hair cut in the shape of a bowl. He was dressed only in jeans and a short-sleeved white collared shirt. His tennis shoes looked new, the kind with blinking red lights in the heels. A piece of paper was pinned to his shirt.

I took a step closer without taking my eyes off either the dog or the boy. Neither seemed afraid, though they keenly gauged my progress. The boy never took his dark eyes from mine, not even when I reached down and gently unpinned what I assumed was a note.

PLEASE, BEN. BAD TROUBLE. MY SON. TAKE HIM TODAY. HIS
NAME IS JUAN. TRUST YOU ONLY. TELL NO ONE. PEDRO

The note was printed in block letters with a black marker that
had bled through the flimsy paper. It was a cash register receipt.
There was no mention of the dog, without which the boy might
well have frozen to death. I read through it several times.

Pedro was the tire man at the truck stop. The tire shop was in
an old metal building hunched behind the truck stop where the
crumbling concrete turned to gravel. We were friendly in the way
strangers who infrequently came in contact with each other were
friendly: I knew his name and he knew mine. Not much else.

The month before I had bought new tires. They gave me a hell
of a deal on brand-name rubber. Pedro and I engaged in the usual
bullshit banter. He had never mentioned he had a son. I hadn't
felt shortchanged by not knowing much about him. Why he would
turn to me when he was in trouble, any kind of trouble, especially
entrusting me with his son, didn't make any sense. I did not feel
particularly honored by his trust.

My options were limited. Call the local cops or take him with
me. If I called the police I'd have to wait for them to arrive. When
they arrived there would be questions, most of which I wouldn't be
able to answer and Cecil wouldn't be much help, if he showed up
at all. When you tell cops "I don't know," all they ever hear is "I
won't tell you," which in my experience always made for long and
frustrating conversations.

Leaving the boy with Cecil was not an option. My guess was
that Pedro had left him inside and Cecil, the sick asshole, put the
kid and his dog outside in a snowstorm just for giggles. The second option had only a single downside, and it was a big one—I just
didn't want to babysit a damned little kid in my truck all day—or
his dog, which I wasn't going to take under any circumstances.

I jerked a long-handled squeegee out of its canister and flung it through the snow in the general direction of the office. It was a pathetic gesture. The squeegee fell way short of hitting the side of the building. The icy apron of Island 6 took it without a sound.

I cautiously picked up the boy and carried him to my cab and opened the door. The dog scampered past me and quickly made itself comfortable on the warm floorboard. I sat the boy on my passenger seat and grabbed two big handfuls of white fur and readied myself to yank the animal out of my cab. I would have done just that if not for those pink eyes. Those eyes asked me one simple question: *How badly do you want to keep your hands?* I answered by letting loose of the fur and slamming the door.

2

It took some fiddling to get Juan's tiny frame secured in a seat belt made for adults. He stared ahead and made no effort to resist or speak. At his age I suspected I was the same way—a half-breed orphan always being shuttled from one place to another. There were always different faces, different rooms, and different vehicles. You learned to go with life and always keep yourself inside, protected—untouchable. Juan's steady, unemotional attitude toward me—toward the ice and snow and wind—made me wonder about his brief life, and about a father who would leave his child alone at a truck stop.

The dog's ears perked. He lifted his big head.

A few seconds later Ginny's old Nissan skidded to a stop in front of my truck. She and her three-month-old infant, Belle, occupied the other side of my shabby duplex. Just barely eighteen, unmarried and alone, Ginny worked two jobs and took business classes part-time at the local community college, and still found time to help me with my bookkeeping. A few months earlier she had saved my tiny trucking company, and me. As usual, she was on a mission, always late and moving fast.

She hopped out of her car while I wondered what in the hell could be so important she would race across town to intercept me. Her spiked red-and-purple hair was even more spiked than usual. I rolled down my window and asked her what was up. She ignored me and pulled the infant seat out of the passenger side. I'm rarely the smartest guy in the room unless I'm alone, which fortunately for me was usually the case. No one needed to draw a diagram for me to guess what her intentions were.

I flung my door open. "No!"

Ginny ignored me. She approached with the infant carrier dangling from one hand and a large pink bag in the other. She was still dressed in her black flannel pajamas decorated with Day-Glo white skulls. Under the lights of the truck stop the skulls danced on her arms and legs. Random flashes glinted off the silver rings in her nose, lower lip, and eyebrow.

I climbed down from the cab and put my arms up to wave her away. "I can't."

Ginny made quick use of my arms. She hung the pink baby bag on my left arm and threaded the handle of the infant seat over my right.

"You have to," she said.

For the first time in our friendship I swore at her. "Goddammit, Ginny. I can't take a baby out on 117! I won't. Not in this weather." I nodded toward the open door of the cab.

I started to object again and thought better of it, at least for the moment, as every man does or should before arguing with a woman, especially someone as important to him as Ginny was to me. We were friends, and only friends, and that meant something special to me, as perhaps it does to any orphan. But friends didn't begin to cover it.

In a few short months Ginny had become my family, though there were always dirty little minds that worked overtime suggesting a different kind of relationship. When I heard such talk, usually punctuated with a sly wink or worse, my fuse got lit, though more for her than for me.

In her own way, Ginny was an orphan herself. You had to know her mother, Nadine, to know why. I'd dated Nadine for a brief time maybe ten years earlier. Ginny was only a little girl then. My time with Nadine was not brief enough and I was half-relieved early one morning to catch her and a UPS driver in the cab of my truck. Considering the cramped quarters, what they were managing to do belonged in a pornographic circus or *Ripley's Believe It or Not.*

Then, by accident, my path crossed with Ginny's in the dead of night where she was working the nightshift at the twenty-four-hour Walmart in Price. That had been May. She was seventeen, seven months pregnant, and living in her car. She asked me to help her find a second job so she could have a place to live when the baby came. She'd been abandoned by her mother and kicked out of high school and had promptly gotten her GED and was already taking a class at the University of Utah extension.

I'd never met anyone with Ginny's kind of sand. In the middle of all that she put herself and her body piercing and unborn child in harm's way for me. If that wasn't family, I didn't know what was. I was more than grateful. I admired her and in my own way I was protective, though neither one of us was comfortable thinking about just what we meant to each other, or what we felt.

I thought maybe if I calmly reasoned with her. "Look around you, Ginny," I said. "I'm headed out into the desert in this shit. Not exactly a safe place for a baby."

"I've got two tests this morning and the sitter just called. She's sick. My shift at Walmart starts at two. You can and you will. Belle is safer with you on 117 than in her crib."

I was between a rock and a hard place, and it was obvious that between the two, Ginny was the rock.

"I have no choice. You have no choice," she said, and walked back to her car.

Few things pissed me off more than hearing the phrase "You have no choice." I'd heard it in one form or another all my life, sometimes from someone explaining a self-inflicted tragedy after making a bad choice. Usually it had been served up to me as a last resort in someone's effort to convince me a crap sandwich was better than no sandwich at all.

"Please don't do this, Ginny," I shouted. "There is always another choice."

"Then you make it. I don't have time to argue."

Pure Ginny. Nothing I could say was going to change her mind. It was up to me to stand up or stand down to the occasion. Ginny was in a bind and she needed me. Knowing her, just coming to me for a favor, to anyone, was an act of courage. How she managed school and work and the baby, plus the bookkeeping for me, and all of it at eighteen and alone, was both a mystery and a miracle. She had never asked for help. And despite the sharpness of her manner, she was asking. I'd never heard a complaint from her. One way or the other, I would deliver. I owed her, and more. She was a friend. She was family, or as close to one as I was ever likely to have. I was her first, best, and only choice and any man with a brain and worth his salt should welcome the privilege.

Ginny revved the old Nissan's tired engine and the pistons knocked loudly in protest and puked blue smoke into the air. The car didn't move. I watched as she sat behind the wheel. When she opened the door she sat a long moment and stared at me before getting out. She left her car idling and walked slowly back to me and gave me a tired smile.

"I don't know what to do, Ben." She rested her chin on my chest. "I'm so exhausted I can't think."

This was a side of her I knew had to exist, though I'd just never seen it before. She didn't let me see it. She didn't let anyone see it, even herself. That was her way. The way she did it all. Eyes straight ahead. No prisoners. No quarter given and none asked for.

"Are you asking for advice?"

Her head didn't move from my chest and she let out a deep sigh into my flannel shirt. "I fell asleep at work the other night.

Facedown and snoring like a pig on a clearance counter I was supposed to be stocking. When I woke up some of the older women
were standing around me so the manager couldn't see me. I would
have been fired. They had just been letting me sleep for as long as
they could. I was so embarrassed."

"Do what you have to do," I said. I might have tried to hug her,
but I didn't.

She pulled her head back from my chest and stared up at me.
"Okay, then," she said. "Suck it up, cowboy."

She sped away and left me draped in a baby and pink diaper
bag like a daycare scarecrow in a concrete field.

I was reviewing my very short list of alternate choices when a
gas tanker made the left-hand turn off US 191 into the truck stop.
Davey Owens drove between Salt Lake City and Moab. He was a
decent-enough, hardworking man with a wife and three kids at
home. Davey inched his big rig to a stop near the spot where Ginny
had been and rolled down his window. He leaned on his bare left
arm and studied me for a few seconds.

"I sense there has been a change for Price's most eligible
bachelor."

I was busy choosing the right words for my response. Davey
was a straight arrow, a recovering alcoholic and born-again Christian. All the words that came to mind consisted of four letters and
graphic instructions.

"You okay?" he asked.

I said I was.

"Then you best get your new family out of this cold."

His rig began to move forward again. As he rolled up his window I could see him shaking his head. I know I was shaking mine,
in frustration or disbelief I couldn't have said—probably a bit of
both, followed quickly by resignation.

From where I stood the empty highway stretched a couple hundred feet in the general direction of Moab before disappearing
into a wall of shifting white embraced by darkness, like a tunnel

probably leading to more than a hundred miles of the same. Maybe not. Probably not.

There was a small jump seat behind the passenger seat and the boy and the dog watched patiently as I wrestled with the car seat in back of them until I got it anchored as best I could with its one lap belt. For her part, Annabelle stared up at me with her round white face and blue eyes and, or so it seemed to me, a wry smile of both comfort and victory. Somewhere I'd read an observation by a writer and it came to mind as I tucked a blanket around the baby: *It is rare to see the promise of a man in a young boy but you'll always see the spirit of a woman in a little girl.* Annabelle was damn sure her mother's daughter.

Once again I thought of the road ahead, and the weather. A smarter man with less experience might have checked the weather conditions on the road ahead. I knew better. In all likelihood I knew I would need at least a hundred different weather reports, one for every mile of two-lane blacktop, and a hundred more for the return. I'd probably see a little of everything the road and sky had to offer—snow, ice, rain, freezing rain interspersed with sunlight and clouds, low and high, dark and bright, and sometimes everything all at once. Hell, somewhere along the way it might even turn nice—for a minute or two.

My route along State Highway 117 took me through the heart of a hundred miles of nowhere before dead-ending at the dying former coal-mining town of Rockmuse, population 2,344. I climbed up on the driver's side running board and tried to bore a hole through the blowing snow to guess what the day might bring, which was as futile an exercise as trying to tell the future. I was stalling and I knew it, hoping a solution to my predicament might present itself. It didn't. Go to work or turn around and call it a day? The soft vibration of the diesel engine rose through my feet and the nearby air was tinged with oddly sweet exhaust fumes trapped by the snow and cold air.

I did a quick inventory of cargo and the schedule of deliveries to determine if any of them were absolutely necessary. A couple ranchers and a desert rat needed the fifty-gallon plastic drums of water I was hauling. Those fifty-gallon containers of water might be life or death. I didn't know. Then there was the mail. The mail was the least important cargo.

A couple months earlier I had been fortunate to secure the contract to take the US Mail to the Rockmuse Post Office—not that there was ever very much of it or anyone particularly cared. The postmaster, Calvin Harper, was a short, affable guy in his late fifties or more. He was locally famous for the model airplanes he built and which were dangled on wire from every spare inch of ceiling space of the tiny post office. He had that kind of time on his hands. Water. Mail. Ten cases of bulk oil. Parts to repair an old windmill. Fresh vegetables for the Rockmuse Mercantile Grocery. There were other miscellaneous odds and ends. It came down to the water, as it often did.

Do my job or turn around and go home? Ginny knew damn well I'd head out into the desert, no matter the weather, with or without Annabelle. She didn't even ask me to cancel my workday. I doubted it even crossed her mind. As for the boy's father, who knew what in the hell he'd been thinking? Call it work ethic or habit, or necessity, or just a nasty stubborn streak. I would go out to do what I had done five days a week for half my life—drive the desert.

I got inside the warm cab and turned to my passengers. "Weather," I said, "is my only prediction."

Belle gurgled and the boy Juan stared ahead through the windshield and into the rhythmic swing and flap of the wipers. The dog angled his big head in my direction and briefly cast his pink eyes on my throat again before burying his nose back into his fur. Maybe he was either too cozy or too lazy to act? Or going after me just wasn't worth the effort. Maybe he was curious about what would happen if he let me live. So was I—and I surrendered the four of us to the road and announced our departure with a whispered *shit* as I dropped into first gear and cautiously pulled out onto an ice-varnished US 191. At best it would be a long day, and at worst, a long dangerous day that wouldn't have us back in Price until late evening, if we made it back at all.

3

Being primarily a day driver and not a long-haul operator my truck didn't carry a sleeper; I couldn't afford the cost, space, or the weight and, as a general rule, I didn't need one. There were exceptions. During winters I always spent a handful of uncomfortable nights, sometimes a day or two, with my boots on the dashboard waiting for the weather to break. Ginny and Pedro might spend a long night full of anxiety waiting for me to return their damn kids. There was no happiness in that thought for me.

My truck pulled the steep grade out of town at a steady and safe thirty miles per hour and then tiptoed down the ice rink on the other side in low gear before dropping onto the desert floor and a straight stretch of five miles, not that I could see it. Visibility was less than a quarter mile. One touch of the brakes could mean trouble. The wind began to gust and buffeted the sides of my trailer like they were sheet-metal sails. A couple times the truck and trailer scooted sideways all of a piece as if pushed by unseen hands.

Up ahead I could just make out the red taillights of another truck and I kept pace with his lights a safe distance behind. Every few minutes I took my eyes off the road and checked on my crew, all of whom seemed serenely unconcerned, which was good, since I was concerned enough for all of us.

There were no headlights behind me. Not one vehicle approached from the opposite direction. A tardy dawn began to send slanted needles of soft red light down through the snowy canopy of darkness. Instead of helping visibility the broken and shifting light made the distance even trickier to penetrate.

The junction of US 191 and State Highway 117 came at about the halfway mark of the five-mile straightaway with no flashing yellow warning light and only a small, unlighted sign—and not so much as an extra foot of a turn lane. It was usually a dangerous left-hand dodge considering traffic behind picking up speed off the hill and a string of oncoming trucks getting a run at the coming 7 percent grade.

The fact that the road seemed empty did nothing to make me feel easier. Some of the worst accidents happened at that junction, at least one a year, and though none of them had ever involved me, a few times I'd come upon the fresh wreckage minutes ahead of the Utah Highway Patrol. Someone, often more than one, was always dead or dying and there was never a damn thing I could do about it except comfort the injured and dying and string flares up and down the highway in both directions.

Juan turned and stared at me as if he might be reading my mind, maybe seeing the collage of horrors I had witnessed over the years. I hoped not. Those were memories even I didn't want. I slowed to barely a crawl and checked my side mirrors again and again. Nothing. For a long, quiet minute the only sound was the crunch of hard ice beneath the tires. Nothing up ahead. Satisfied we were alone on the highway, I committed the truck to the turn and began to cross the oncoming lane.

I couldn't see the low headlights of the semi. The red running lights strung across the roof of its cab jumped into my peripheral vision and sliced through the scattered pink palisades of dawn and shadow. In that terrible second of realization Juan smiled up at me. The inside of my cab filled with the rushing bright glow of the truck's dual headlamps as the distance between us rapidly closed.

Assuming the driver saw us in front of him it was still too late to avoid a collision by swerving around us into the southbound lane. One touch of his brakes would send his trailer sideways making it and his tractor into a twenty-ton, hundred-foot-wide snowplow sweeping away everything in its path.

My fear-pounding impulse was to accelerate. I wanted to push the pedal to the floor. It would have only made the inevitable worse. I couldn't speed up without spinning my drive wheels. Doing that would only slow us down and make the odds even better that he'd hit us dead square on the passenger side. Annabelle's side. Juan's side. There was only one thing either of us could do—come ahead and try to reduce the point of impact to just the rear of my trailer. I white-knuckled the few seconds as we crept ahead and the semi bore down on us.

One second. Two seconds.

Our cab filled with blinding white light. The impact was deafening. Shudders of stressed aluminum screamed the length of my rig as the trailer lurched sideways and tipped upward. For a few seconds we hung in the air, balanced on one side of tires. The tractor and trailer righted itself with a jarring bounce. We were rubber-side-down and still moving slowly ahead onto Highway 117, though at an odd angle. Our headlights pointed not at the road but north, into the swirling snow and silence of the jagged darkness of the desert shoulder of 117. I slipped the transmission into neutral and let the tractor ease itself to a complete stop.

I relaxed and let my body slump forward, resting my forehead against the steering wheel. All the breath I had been holding escaped at once. From beneath my right arm I cast a one-eyed glance at the boy. Juan was rigid in his seat with a wide, snaggle-toothed grin that suggested anything but joy or amusement, like a silent scream sucked inward and held. The dog was sitting up looking at the boy. I am no authority on dogs, or children. My guess was that the dog was expressing concern—a concern for the boy alone.

I straightened up in my seat and forced what I hoped was a reassuring laugh. In the dim light of the cab I checked Belle. She was still secure in her car cradle, awake and quiet and appearing vaguely entertained, as if she had experienced nothing more than a gentle rocking.

"How about we all check our diapers?" I said. The expressions on the faces of the dog and the boy did not change. Opening my door, I added, "Okay, then, you'll excuse me while I check mine." Almost as an afterthought I set the brakes and flipped on the emergency flashers before stepping down onto the running board.

The sun had finally made up its mind to rise in earnest. Well out of view of the boy, I leaned in against the side of the trailer with my palms against the cold metal. Then I spent a well-earned minute swearing, mostly at myself. I did have choices at the truck stop and just like some of the people who pissed me off in the past, I made the easier one, the wrong one, because I refused to make the choice between hard and harder. The harder choice would have been to call it a day and go home. Sure, I'd thought about it. Like a good many people, when faced with a hard decision, most of my thinking involved trying to come up with a good excuse not to do what I knew I should do. The refrain of *woulda-shoulda-coulda* repeated itself over and over in my head.

I walked around to the rear of the trailer as another northbound semi split the creeping dawn. An inspection of my hydraulic lift gate and trailer door indicated no damage—none at all. But I knew we had been hit, and hit hard. Then I saw it, up high on the right rear corner of the trailer—a souvenir of our near-death misadventure. Half-buried in the aluminum skin of the trailer, like a chromed artillery round, was the side mirror from the semi. My legs quivered with the inescapable proof of just how close we had come to an ugly end. The difference between life and death had come down to weight and speed, and less than an inch. Experience will help you make the right decision. And when you make the wrong decision anyway, it might save your sorry, stupid ass.

The other driver hadn't stopped after our trucks made contact. It would have been dangerous to even try. Maybe he was speeding. Maybe not. I doubted he was going all that fast. The visibility and road conditions only made his speed seem fast. He'd lost a mirror and that was all. Down the road, probably at the Stop 'n' Gone, he'd pull over and assess the damage. And think. And maybe change his underwear. At some point I'd have to get a ladder and surgically remove the mirror. For the time being, it would have to stay where it was.

I walked out to the front of the truck and paused to watch the sun come up over the desert. In less than a minute the snow stopped and the wind dropped to barely a whisper as wide patches of blue opened up between the clouds overhead. Even as I watched, the white expanse of snow-covered ground began to stretch out before me farther and farther until the sheer cliff face of the red, mica-flaked mesa a hundred miles distant was revealed, its flat top still obscured by clouds and behind them the first piercing rays of sunlight. As forbidding as the desert might be in summer, it was nothing compared to the silent and cold emptiness of winter.

Even as I stood there surveying the vastness of it all I was drawn toward it, into it, like it was some crazy lover forever promising passion and never love. Yet it was always there, beckoning, and sometimes I thought it was that constancy that drew me, that simple need to know what I could never know in a place, from a landscape, that didn't care either way. And Utah 117 ran straight through its bloodless heart. Driving it was my job. In rare, charitable moments I thought what I did might be important. I'd been doing the job for so long I didn't know anything else. And maybe I didn't want to.

I turned and looked up at the windshield of the truck and

thought of my passengers. Maybe Ginny had a point. Belle was safer with me on 117 than in her crib, or just as safe. For all I knew the same was true of the boy. I knew it was true for me. I felt safer in a natural world no matter how treacherous and unforgiving, without promises or illusions, than at home in my crib.

4

Except for random patches of ice, the ten miles to The Well-Known Desert Diner were trouble-free. The locals had long ago nicknamed the place The Never-Open Desert Diner. The diner was always my first stop, and sometimes my last, even when I had nothing to deliver to Walt Butterfield, its owner. As usual, I parked my rig on the gravel apron. The Closed sign hung from the front door and the place, while never open, seemed more closed these days than in times past. The two antique glass bubble pumps were just homeless old men who had run out of conversation. A frozen lace of spiderweb reached across one corner of the door. It was a beautiful and lonely addition, caught as it was in the early sunlight.

If Walt was still Walt he'd been up for hours and was already tending to his collection of vintage motorcycles in the 50 × 100-foot Quonset hut behind the diner. He knew I had arrived. Even at eighty years old that extra sense of his that alerted him to the presence of visitors was just as keen as ever, which only served to give him warning there was someone around who might require ignoring, or dismissal. It occurred to me on the drive, during a moment of irresponsible cowardice and desperation, to ask Walt if he would take care of Belle for the day. Most likely I wouldn't, no matter what excuses I came up with. The probability Walt would say yes was the textbook definition of a long shot. Walt could be full of surprises and there was always a chance he might surprise me and not be an asshole.

With Belle swinging from her car seat and the diaper bag slung over my shoulder I walked across the gravel toward the diner. A little gust of wind kicked up and fluttered the spiderweb and swept some dry snow off the roof. Call it habit or superstition, I always peered through the window for the little taste of reassurance or, since Claire died, the sad welcome, provided by the interior of the diner.

It was all there in its timeless glory, as it must have been when the diner was first built in 1929. Back then it was the Oasis Café. Walt and Bernice, his Korean War bride, bought the place in 1953 and changed the name. She chose the name Bernice. He was only twenty. She was just sixteen and spoke no English.

I let my eyes wander and linger over the spit-polished lino-leum tiles and chrome-lined counter, lime-green vinyl chairs, and stools. My heart missed a beat or two as my eyes settled on the old Wurlitzer jukebox against the far wall. Only a handful of months earlier, on a spring evening in late May, I'd come upon Walt and Claire dancing in front of that jukebox. I just stood there as I had that night and watched them dance the tender never-ending dance between a father and daughter, though neither one ever acknowl-edged that blood connection.

For me, the diner held them unchanged just as surely as it en-folded the tables and chairs, the lone ticket from the last meal prepared for a paying guest in 1987 and, I supposed, also Claire's mother, Bernice, her rape and gradual mute death along with Walt's grisly vengeance. In its own way, The Never-Open Desert Diner was always open, if only to memories and ghosts.

I'd seen Walt the previous day, a Sunday and the last day of September. I was working at the solitary house in Desert Home and tending to the graves in the little grotto nestled into the hill-side behind the house. It was still summer and hot, with no sign cold had ever touched the parched ground or that it ever would

again. The sky was a deep yawning blue and cloudless all the way
to the red mesa.

Desert Home was an abandoned housing development a mile
down the road from the diner. It had once been Bernice's dream,
and that dream died with her in 1972. The modest model home was
the only structure ever built in Desert Home, though the empty,
sand-swept streets were there and continued to make promises.
Walt had given the house to Claire and me when he thought, and I
hoped, we would be married. After Claire died I began maintaining it even though no one lived there and probably never would.

I worked hard all day on the house and graves with the sun
pounding me. When I took a break to wipe the sweat from my
eyes I searched the horizon for the imaginary sound of Claire's
cello or her smile and listened for her voice calling after me as I
trudged up the slope toward the arched entrance. I sometimes sat
on the porch in the green chair and squinted at the wind in the
eaves of the house and heard only what one ghost might whisper
to another.

Late in the afternoon I stood with my back to the grotto and
watched as the trail of dust and sand cut like a rusty scratch across
the roadless beige expanse to the south. No sound, only the bleeding powdery line that marked the motorcycle's steady path toward
me. I knew Walt would veer away at the last moment just as he had
for the past few months. It wasn't just me he was avoiding; it was
the house and the graves—Claire's grave, Bernice's grave. He might
have dodged the desert itself, the desert all three of them loved, if
he could have. Eventually, he angled away and took the back way
to Utah 117 and his eternally closed roadside diner. How long I
stood there afterward I couldn't have said. Walt had long since disappeared when the iron shadows of approaching dusk began their
creeping journey across the desert floor.

Belle began to squirm in her car seat to remind me she was
there. The powdery snow had been swept off the wide flagstone
patio separating the rear of the diner from the Quonset. I knocked

on the Quonset door only once. Knocking twice was overdoing it in Walt's opinion. My jaw still ached on occasion from the last time he expressed his opinion. If he wanted to come to the door he would come to the door. Belle and I waited as the cold continued its work.

When I turned to leave I saw something I'd never seen before. The back door to the diner was ajar. The sight startled me. A lot of things were possible. The one thing that wasn't possible was that Walt had simply forgotten to close it. That door led to the kitchen. I tightened my grip on the car seat and slowly shouldered the door until it swung open enough to allow us through. The kitchen was in shadow and from what I could see nothing was out of place. It was church quiet. Walt's tiny bedroom, which had once been used for storage, was just to my right. That door was ajar as well. I used the toe of my boot to inch it open.

5

It wasn't that I expected to find Walt dead. He was the healthiest eighty-year-old on the planet, tall and ramrod straight, a head of thick white hair and the lean muscle of a young man. Of course, I knew Walt had to die one day, even if he didn't, but none of us youngers would probably live long enough to see it. What I couldn't understand was what kept him going, day in and night out, all alone with a life to remember that most people would choose to forget if they could. For that matter, I sometimes wondered what kept any of us going. It was a line of thought I didn't want to follow too far.

Walt lay fully clothed on top of the single bed, his arms folded behind his head, with just a little light from the one high small window on the outer wall. I couldn't tell if Walt's eyes were open or closed.

"Did you think I missed your knock?"

I told him I didn't. "The back door was open."

"You think an open door is an invitation to enter a man's home?"

Walt had made no effort to move. It was cold enough in the small room our words sent small bursts of white breath into the air. I didn't answer his question, mostly because we both knew the answer and I sure as hell wasn't going to say I was concerned about him. He might acknowledge my concern with his opinion.

"What the hell, Ben. Are you driving a school bus now?"

"Ginny stuck me with her baby today. An emergency."

Walt lay motionless with his arms still behind his head while I waited for him to speak and the room began to lighten as the sun found the back of the diner. Ginny and Walt had met briefly and only once not long after Claire died. He knew who she was and I had mentioned her a few times, about the baby and college, and renting her the other side of my duplex at a greatly reduced price in exchange for bookkeeping. The two hadn't said a word to each other and the conversation that passed between them was more like two fighters circling each other in the ring. If those two ever got into it I wouldn't know who to bet on.

Walt swung his long legs off the bed and set the soles of his steel-toed boots on the bare floor. "I know whose baby that is." He nodded in my direction, downward to my right.

The boy Juan had gotten out of the truck and stood just beside me. The dog pushed his big nose forward between the boy and my leg. There wasn't any use in being upset. The truth was I had forgotten about him.

"It's a long story," I said, though it wasn't. "Jesus, Walt, it's freezing in here."

Walt ignored my observation. "Well, I'm sure you'll find someone who wants to hear it," he said as he stood.

The revolver had been on the nightstand. In the dusky room I hadn't seen it until he picked it up. The boy grabbed my leg and when I looked down at him he had that same strange grin, though his eyes told a different story. That poor little kid had seen a gun before and knew what it could do and had enough sense to be frightened. I was pretty sure Walt wasn't going to shoot us, though with Walt you couldn't be certain of anything. Some relationships are like that. For one thing, he was cradling the gun in his cupped palms, like water, or a wounded bird. It was an odd moment. It was the same revolver he had given to Claire to protect herself from wild animals, though we all knew he meant the kind of animals that walked on two feet—and the same gun she had returned to him the day before Dennis, her ex-husband, strangled her and took off across the desert.

Staring at the gun in his hands, Walt said, "I wonder sometimes if Claire had kept this if she'd be alive today."

It wasn't a question I could answer. Neither one of us were there. Probably not. It must have happened so quickly, and Claire returned it not because she was afraid of her former husband—she returned it because she was afraid of herself, her temper. She was so convinced Dennis wasn't the violent type. I knew better. Walt knew better. Every type was the violent type given the right provocation and moment, maybe especially the ones who believed they weren't the violent kind. Except for Walt and me, no one knew what had happened to Claire, or her cello, and up until that moment, though several months had passed, neither one of us had spoken to the other about her or even mentioned her name.

Walt put the gun back on the nightstand and took the two short steps to where I stood. Both the dog and the boy backed up. He carefully pulled the blanket back from Belle's face and the two of them were blue eyes to blue eyes. It was almost a whisper. "You're a fool, Ben."

The words were out of my mouth before I knew I'd said them. "I had no choice."

Walt didn't respond, not that he needed to. He glanced at the boy and the dog and said, "The furnace is broken." He pushed by us and out the back door. I heard the door to the Quonset open and close.

The furnace kicked on and blew warm air on us from a vent above our heads. I marched my little parade out of the diner and left the door open and paused for a few seconds near the door of the Quonset and considered the man behind it, the gun, the diner and the obviously functioning furnace. A few seconds was too damn long. Walt was still a mystery and some mysteries didn't need solving, couldn't ever be solved, and the best thing you could do was just accept them.

Out of the corner of my eye I noticed the dog was also staring at the Quonset door. I gently mussed Juan's hair with my free hand and said to the dog, "You sure backed your furry ass up in a hurry." For a moment it seemed to me the dog wore a slightly embarrassed expression before he lowered his head.

Walt and I had an unspoken agreement never to speak of Claire. That had changed and I didn't know how I felt about it except that I didn't want to think about it. We shared her and our loss in silence, bound by memories only the two of us had of her, and of her misleading headstone on the grave next to her mother, Bernice, less than a half mile away. Walt calling me a fool could cover a lot of territory. For years he'd been telling me driving a truck to deliver necessities to the desert rats and eccentric exiles who lived along Highway 117 was nothing more than suckling losers. Of course, there was never any mention of the fact that The Well-Known Desert Diner and Walt himself lived on 117. He was the King of 117 and the Emperor of Solitude, a man apart in ways even I couldn't understand—and maybe in a desert of losers, depending on what was lost, he was the undisputed champion.

Once I got Belle's car seat belted back into place I motioned for Juan and the dog to climb inside the cab. The dog complied. Juan pointed to his crotch. Clear enough. He had to pee. The way the morning had gone so far had cut down on my usual coffee consumption but I still needed to water the desert myself. I walked across the empty highway and motioned to Juan and the dog to follow.

The dog sniffed at a scrub juniper and then got down to business. Juan looked up at me and then at the dog and pulled down his jeans while I made a note to myself to find him a coat or a sweater somewhere. Though I was standing several feet from Juan

I respectfully turned away and began to unbuckle while I enjoyed the southern vista.

It was the first time I had heard the dog make any sound and the two sharp barks echoed across the desert floor. Juan was squatting and my first thought was that I had misunderstood what he had meant. The dog barked again and the pee began to cascade to the frozen ground in a cloud of steam. What was happening still took a moment to register. When it did I instinctively averted my eyes—Juan was a little girl. Juan was a little girl? I didn't know much about women and even less about little girls, but I knew enough to run across the road to the truck to grab some toilet tissue. I handed it to her with my head turned. Not much had changed, and I felt as if everything had changed.

I didn't know how long she had been holding it. Judging from the steady stream I heard it had to have been quite a while. Babysitting a little boy was one thing and somehow babysitting a little girl, the daughter of a stranger, was something else entirely. Maybe women felt the same way. I didn't know.

She brought me the roll of toilet paper and held out the damp piece between her thumb and forefinger in an almost ladylike gesture. I scuffed up a little hole in the gravel and after she dropped in the used tissue, I covered it over while she watched.

Lowering myself on one knee, I softly asked her name. The dog was sitting next to her, his head almost even with hers. Maybe this was all news to him as well, though I couldn't imagine why. She didn't answer and simply turned her large dark eyes out toward the desert.

She began walking at a fast pace down the rutted trail, a shortcut that led to the graves and the model home. The dog did not follow her. She was sure-footed and quick and gathered speed until it was almost a run, each step taken with purpose as if she had made the hike all her life and knew exactly where she was headed, which of course she couldn't have. There was nothing down that way but a dead dream and forty years of memories that had nothing to do with her.

In a few strides I caught up to her and gently lifted her into my arms and carried her back up the trail and across 117 to the truck.

I knew damn well I hadn't misread Pedro's note—it had said "son." Juan—a boy's name. And now I was well down a road in the middle of nowhere on my way to no place with a little girl. Pedro had said "bad trouble" and I couldn't begin to imagine the level of shitstorm it would take to leave your little daughter alone in the hands of a stranger—a male stranger at that. I was reasonably certain I wasn't a pervert and marginally if not reliably responsible, but Pedro couldn't have known that. It was a toss-up between anger and fear and when the anger subsided I knew I would be left with only fear—for the girl, and with enough extra for Pedro as well.

6

My next stop, about twenty-five miles down 117 from the diner, was Dan Brew's place, which had originally been a dirt house, or a sod house, as they were called on the prairies, dug out of the ground with a roof of wild grass. Dan's had been made by a settler before the turn of the last century and he hadn't added much except a metal carport and a cheap solar array. He had tunneled back into a rocky hillside to add a couple rooms.

No indoor facilities, which meant an outdoor privy and no running water. He kept a cistern to catch rainwater. There had once been a seasonal well but it had gone dry over a year ago. Cool in the summer and warm in the winter, a dirt house was about as basic as you could get in the desert. There was smoke chugging out of his chimney pipe that I could see for most of the half mile of rutted road that wound itself around two low hills before ending up at his front door.

Like most people who lived off 117, Dan probably wouldn't notice or care much if the world ended. He'd been married and divorced several times since I had first met him, and last I knew he was working on number seven, or maybe eight. He was the kind of man who seemed to prefer to share his loneliness with a partner and while there apparently was a never-ending supply of women, usually from big cities, who saw a certain romance in the beauty and solitude of his lifestyle, sooner or later the daily diet of beauty and silence always wore thin. It usually started with the missus wanting to go to town more often and ended one day when she went to town and failed to return.

I knew more about Dan than most of the people I delivered to on 117. In fact, I knew more than I cared to know, courtesy of accidentally coming upon a meeting of the Dan Brew ex-wives club. I had heard that a few liked the area enough they wanted to stick around the desert, though just not around Dan's Happy Acres. There were three of them, ranging in age from late thirties to late forties, sitting around an outside table at a restaurant on a sunny weekend in downtown Price. Unfortunately, I happened to walk by. I hesitated to accept their invitation to join them, and after I did I knew why and wished like hell I had kept walking. Every sentence began with "I loved Dan, but—"

Years before in a bar I'd heard a WWII vet who had been in the Normandy invasion describing what a grand thing it was and how proud he was to be an American and what a bloody mess it was. When he finally ran out of war stories he finished with "It was a million-dollar experience that I wouldn't pay a nickel to do again." Each one of the wives had survived Normandy, and listening to those three for five minutes was the longest day of my life. Somehow I managed to feel sorry for all of them, including Dan and his dirt house. Dan might not have been a Nazi, but at least for those three women sharing his life in the Utah desert, it was a beachhead of sorts.

Dan was waiting for me in his open doorway wearing a dirty bathrobe with no drawstring, no shirt, and nothing but a pair of tighty-whiteys, that weren't all that tight and far from white—and worn cowboy boots that had seen better days twenty years ago. I'm not exactly a fashion icon myself, but underwear, bare legs, and cowboy boots was never a look I much cared for, though I'd seen it a few times, and not just on men, I'm sorry to say. As a manner of dress, even in the desert, it seemed to make a quiet statement about life that made you afraid to get too close for fear of attitude contamination, and your own good hygiene. It wasn't a look I'd seen on Dan before, and while I guessed his age in his late forties, his attire made him timeless in the worst way.

With perhaps a bit more conviction and an earnest *please* I told the girl and the dog to stay inside. Dan had been expecting me and stood his ground in the doorway as I walked up to him. "It's a little cold for sunbathing, isn't it?"

He ignored me. "I wasn't sure you'd make it," he said. "I could use that drum of water."

I bit my tongue. He did need to use some water, preferably hot and soapy. "I usually make it."

Dan offered to give me a hand and together we strolled across the frozen ground to the rear of the trailer, his robe flapping in the breeze. The power lift gate worked fine. Fifty-gallon plastic drums of water were damn heavy, right at five hundred pounds, and I kept a manual forklift jack in the trailer for such loads. Maneuvering the drums onto the lift was a chore and his help was welcome. I stood on the raised lift gate and yanked at the sliding door strap and damn near tore my arm off. It didn't budge. My first thought was ice on the interior door tracks. I kicked around the edges to loosen it up and pulled again. Same result.

At that moment I knew what the problem was. Before I could say anything Dan pointed to the offending shrapnel left by the semi and announced he saw the problem and went off to get a ladder. I took the opportunity to look in on my road crew and satisfied they were doing okay I went back and waited for Dan. As he hiked toward me I couldn't help thinking that I wished the ladder covered up more of him.

He slapped the ladder against my trailer and scampered up. "What in the hell is this?"

"Just what it looks like," I said.

He gave it a bit of thought and suggested he could knock it loose with a sledgehammer and drive it through to the inside. How the mirror got embedded in the side of my trailer was a matter of indifference to Dan. Indifference was a currency almost all my customers traded in, and so did I, though I chose to think of it as minding my own business which, in the Utah desert, greatly contributes to continued survival.

I gave Dan's suggestion a minute of consideration. While I stood there with my hand on the ladder I looked up at his beefy legs and a breeze blew the robe aside and exposed his soiled, threadbare underwear. When I said, "Hell no," I was commenting as much on the view as I was about his solution. "I'm not going to tear up my trailer."

"I need my water. What's your plan?"

The day was already headed for shot and I had two very valuable pieces of cargo. The jury was still out on the dog. If I couldn't deliver to Dan it meant I couldn't make any of my other deliveries either. My only choice was to drive straight to Rockmuse and see if I could get Toby, the elderly widower who owned the Rockmuse Collision Center, to pry the offending mirror out and get my sliding door working again, preferably with as little damage as possible and quickly. Toby had to have a more delicate approach and better tools than Dan and a sledgehammer. I wasn't certain of this, but I was hopeful. Like most rigs, including trailer, mine was leased and a gaping hole in the side did not fall under the description of "normal wear," meaning it would cost me plenty when my lease was up.

I offered Dan the two five-gallon water containers I kept behind the driver's seat and told him my plan. "That should hold you until I get back this way later today."

"Well, it won't."

I rarely had sharp discussions with my customers. I rarely had discussions at all. Silence joined with indifference to keep conversations to nods and shrugs. Sometimes it almost compensated for how long it took some of them to pay me. If Dan and I had words it wouldn't be the first time. A couple years back when it was all I could do to eat and pay for diesel, Dan owed me several hundred dollars, which he kept promising to pay. Then one day I saw him driving a brand-new Chevrolet pickup with all the bells and whistles. When I confronted him he pulled out a wad of hundred-dollar bills and begrudgingly paid his bill. He'd stayed current since.

"It will damn well have to," I said. "I'll stop on my way back to Price."

Dan tried to stare me down for a few seconds and gave up and stomped into his house and slammed the door so hard a chunk of sod broke loose and fell to the ground. I took out one of the five-gallon containers and put it near his door. I thought for a minute and then went back and got the second one and put it next to the other. I'm usually not an asshole if I take a minute to think it over. Sometimes I need more than a minute.

I pulled out of Dan's place in low gear. As my rig crawled up the hill I began thinking how he was no different from most of my customers when it came to an income, which, if they had one, was as lowly and fragile as their desert existence. As far as I knew, which wasn't far, some ran a few cattle, or horses, or scraped by one way or another with small gardens or crafts or, in a few cases, a few dollars in savings from another, nearly forgotten, life or relative. I was completely in the dark when it came to Dan. His means were a mystery and, to hear them tell it, a mystery to the three wives I had met.

Once, on a long ago April 15, I commented to Cal, the Rockmuse postmaster, that he should probably be getting a lot of traffic during business hours as folks pushed the deadline to file. We both had a good laugh. Then he brought out a big box of envelopes, all with various government return addresses, including the Internal Revenue Service and Social Security Administration.

Cal told me it was one box of almost sixty going back since before he became postmaster. "If you make a ton of money you pay no taxes. If you make no money you don't even bother to file. Hell, an IRS agent comes by here at least once a year. They always send a different new young guy all buttoned down full of himself." He pointed out toward the desert just beyond the low buildings of

Main Street. "I tell every one of them the answer to their question is out there, which is pretty much what rich people and corporations tell the government, though I'm sure they have accountants and lawyers do the talking.

"Sure, sometimes someone's boat comes in." He tapped one of the model airplanes swinging from a wire above his head and watched as it gently swung back and forth. "It's usually about the same size as this."

We both watched the little P-38 model and Cal said, "You remember Karl and Wilhelmina ... hell, I can't recall their last name." When I said I remembered them, they had both passed a few years earlier, Cal said: "They had that little sand and rock patch out off 117 where they raised a few ponies.

"An IRS agent came in one day and asked me if I knew where to find them. I did my point and shrug show for him and he left. But I ran into Karl a couple days later and told him an agent from the IRS was looking for him. 'Is that so?' he said. 'I gave a kidney and three fingers in WWII. I gave my son to Vietnam. You see that fellow again, you tell him I'm paid in full.' Karl and Wilhelmina both died not long after that. They'd been dead a month out there until someone found them—next to each other in bed, or so I heard."

I remembered. I had been the one who found them. Either Karl or Wilhelmina had put a note on the door: "Ben—come in. We're waiting on you." They'd ordered a new wood-burning stove and asked me to deliver it when it arrived. Six weeks later it had and I did. I thought the note was a little strange, since they had no idea when I would deliver the stove, though if I stopped to consider every strange thing that happened during an average day I wouldn't ever get through my route on schedule. Cal heard right. That's how I'd found them.

Cal had said, "You know the difference between you and the US Postal Service?" I waited for him to answer his own question. "You only deliver what people ask for."

I guessed that was true enough, which was why most people

on 117 chose to forgo addresses and mailboxes so almost all US mail on 117 was sent General Delivery, Rockmuse, Utah—which they usually ignored and refused to pick up, sometimes for years. They'd rather sacrifice and pay me to deliver even little stuff the US Postal Service would have delivered at little charge or for free. When I showed up they knew exactly what they were getting and nothing else. I didn't entirely understand it, but I was thankful for the mystery.

But that damn new Chevy pickup of Dan's set my teeth against each other. Whatever Dan's ship, it had been a sight bigger than a model airplane. By the time I'd pulled onto 117 I realized I hadn't seen his pickup out in front of his place where it was usually parked. In fact, I hadn't seen it in a long while, nor the soon-to-be new Mrs. Dan Brew. Maybe that's why Dan was in such a state, though whether it was the loss of the pickup or the loss of his bride, or both, was no concern of mine. Dan's ship had gone out to sea again, maybe with his truck and probably his fiancée, and for all I knew his pants as well.

7

I followed 117 southeast toward Rockmuse, which was a good
sixty-plus miles, figuring if I got my door repaired in a decent
amount of time I could get through all my deliveries, including the water to Dan, and back to Price before dark. The sun-
brightened miles slipped by as the towering granite mesa loomed
larger on the horizon and the girl and the dog dozed off and on
lulled by the low, steady hum of the engine and high whine of the
tires.

For the first time since leaving the Stop 'n' Gone I felt as I usually did heading out on 117, like I was going home, or as close to
a home as I had ever known. Maybe home was too strong a word.
Once I was on 117 the asphalt wound out ahead of me and I always
felt a little better. The desert was a familiar unknown and I was
properly respectful, filled with purpose and just damn glad to see
what I had been seeing for twenty years, and seeing it new every
day, always the same but different.

The sun glared up off a patch of ice as I came over a small rise
and when it cleared I saw the cross bobbing along the shoulder
maybe a mile ahead. With all the excitement of the morning I'd
forgotten about John and the life-size crucifixion cross he hauled
up and down 117 from late spring to winter. Given that winter
came on so quickly and early it made sense the weather caught
him out on the road.

John, or Preach, as everyone else called him, was a dependable mystery. No one knew his last name or exactly when he had arrived, though sometime after the coal mine had closed almost twenty years earlier. His church, if you wanted to call it that, was the First Church of the Desert Cross, denomination unknown and unimportant. Located in what was once a True Value Hardware store in downtown Rockmuse, it consisted of a handful of deck chairs on a scarred wooden plank floor and not much else. When John was in town he preached up a storm to the congregation of empty deck chairs. He slept on a surplus army cot behind a makeshift pulpit, which was really only a couple of plastic milk crates that had been duct-taped together.

Infrequently one or a few people would show up, I assumed on purpose, which wasn't how I'd met him. I had been unaware that the hardware store had closed, and I was in search of a half-inch socket drive to repair my truck. Once inside the door I was too embarrassed to leave, so I sat through most of an entire fire-and-brimstone sermon. When he finished, well over two hours later, my heathen ass had gone to sleep. Even though I was the only one there, he stood at the door as if there were a long line behind me and shook my hand and thanked me for coming.

It wasn't until some time later, out on 117, that I explained why I had been at his church. He took the news with measured joy, noting that in God's plan there were no accidents. "Jesus sent you to his house," he said. "The socket drive was just the burning bush."

Over the years I'd often pull over and converse with John, if I had time and he was on schedule and we were both so inclined. He managed to travel about ten miles a day. In the evening he would camp at one of his unofficial Stations of the Cross campsites along 117. He had attached a bracket and a rubber tire from a wheelbarrow to the road-end and strapped a pack with some camping supplies to the cross. Other than that, his was a pure stocker of a cross, right down to the hand-hewn hardwood and dimensions, and damn heavy.

I passed John and pulled over a couple hundred feet in front of him. It was still cold out, though there was very little snow along the shoulder. He didn't drink coffee, or anything but water, which I usually carried. I set the brakes and requested everyone stay put. The baby was asleep. It seemed best to keep them both where it was warm and where the girl and the dog would be safe from traffic, if there was any. Though it was only John, I figured keeping the girl's presence a secret was probably a smart move. My roadside visits with John never lasted very long.

I hopped out and waited for him with a thermos of water. He'd been at it for a while, probably since before dawn, and his tattered old down parka hung over the tip of the cross like a khaki surrender flag. I could see the sheen of sweat on his face as he approached.

John lowered the cross from his back, stretched his fingertips to prod the sky, and took the thermos from me and gulped down the water, careful as always not to waste even a drop into his white beard. He handed me the thermos. "Praise the Lord."

"Got caught with your skivvies down out here, didn't you?"

"Depends," he said.

"On what?" I asked, both curious and a little afraid to hear his answer.

"On what you mean by 'out here.' The Lord has a plan," he said, "and when you give yourself to it, you're always ready. To my way of thinking, there is no 'out here' only *here*. God's plan unfolds everywhere."

"Is that so?" I said, pointing above us to the mirror embedded in my trailer. "Tell me that was God's plan. And I thought I was ready."

John was quick on the uptake and guessed what was lodged in the side of my trailer and exactly how it got there. He nodded solemnly keeping his eyes on the damaged trailer. "The Lord was watching out for you, Ben. His plan shall be revealed."

"This little break of good weather will change, John." I almost always called him by his first name, though many in the desert either didn't know it or didn't care. To them his name was Wacko or Wingnut or, at best, Preach. "Don't you think God's plan might be for you to use the brains he gave you to get the hell off this road and come in from the cold?"

John seldom smiled, and when he did his long white beard seemed to dance. "Maybe," he said. "But God gave me this road and the glory of the day. Seems a little ungrateful to leave it because of bad weather." He stared up at the blue sky and bent his tall body over and touched his toes. "That felt good," he said. "I got a new pouch of tobacco."

This was my cue. "I've got some fire."

Both of us had quit smoking years before but somehow we had set upon a ritual of pretending to have a smoke during our roadside meetings. John pulled imaginary papers and pouch from the lapel of his denim work shirt and went about rolling a cigarette, never taking a shortcut, every motion and detail exact.

John put the cigarette between his lips and leaned forward. I struck a Diamond match against my beard, which was as nonexistent as the match itself. Part of God's plan was for me to not have much of a beard, owing maybe to my mixed heritage. The match head popped to life and we could smell the acrid sulfur in the air between us. John inhaled and let the smoke ease out into the desert breeze.

John handed me the cigarette. "I know it's a sin, but I do enjoy a good smoke. The Lord has forgiven me so much." He winked at me. "I like to think he'll forgive me for allowing this poison into his temple."

John had his back to approaching traffic and didn't see the Utah Highway Patrol cruiser crest the hill behind him. "We've got company."

8

John turned and we both watched as the vehicle slowed and pulled over behind my truck. We both knew the trooper, Andy Smith, who seemed to be the only real law that ever made it down Highway 117, and only rarely at that. He'd been on the Utah Highway Patrol for about ten years, all of it out in the southeastern desert region. Most of his time was spent on US 191 between Price and Green River. Andy wasn't exactly a friend, but he was more than an acquaintance. I liked him and our meetings; most of them had not been official.

I waited to see if Andy would put on his hat. If it was official, troopers always put on their hats. No hat this time. He waved as he walked toward us. The wind caught some strands of his fine blond hair and stood them at attention like a Mormon Mohawk. "Morning, gentlemen."

John and I both said our good mornings. John was acquainted with Andy, though never officially, as far as I knew. I knew for a fact Andy from time to time would cruise a part of 117 just to check on John. There was no question that John was a bona fide crazy, but the general consensus was that he was *our* crazy and as such some of us allowed for a certain acceptance and communal guardianship. Also, out in the desert, John had some serious competition in the crazy sweepstakes that sometimes almost made him and his cross seem pleasantly ordinary.

Andy's stop might have been just courtesy and yet he seemed to have something on his mind. I passed the cigarette back to John and Andy, knowing of this ritual, watched the cigarette go from John's hand to his lips.

"Can I get a hit of that?"

"Can you get a 'hit'?"

Even John seemed startled and more than a little amused. He started to hand over our imaginary cigarette. "Hold up there a second," I said. "I don't think John and I want to be involved in contributing to the delinquency of a Mormon."

Andy opened a good-natured smile. "I'm confident we'll all be forgiven. After all," he added, "it's not real."

"Well," I said, warming to the moment, "I'm no Christian, Andy—and maybe John will help me out with this—but doesn't the thought count? A sin in the mind is still a sin."

Andy took the cigarette and began a long, slow draw. John nodded and started to speak. Blowing smoke with his words, Andy said, "Don't encourage him, John." He returned the cigarette to me. "Have you seen anything unusual out here in the last week?"

We both did our best not to let our eyes drift over to John and his cross. I drew on the cigarette and handed it to John.

"Could you narrow that down a bit, Andy?"

"A vehicle."

John took a puff and looked toward the mesa and shook his head.

"Now that you mention it," I said, "last week I saw a Prius with a gun rack."

Andy sighed. "Ben, don't make me go get my hat."

"Nope," I said. Andy was like all cops asking questions, careful not to lead. "What's this about?"

"Not much, probably. Since I want you to keep a lookout, I'll tell you."

John offered Andy the cigarette. Andy declined so John handed it back to me.

"You know that Utah Entry weigh station as you come down that steep grade on 191 from Soldier Summit coming into Price?" When I said I did he continued: "Last Wednesday a truck dodged it."

"That all?" I said.

"It would be except that he'd done it before—always early in the morning, before dawn. Moving fast on that downgrade. Last Wednesday I took a nightshift as a favor and I was on US 191 north of Green River. I had plenty of time to intercept him. A Price officer was investigating a prowler and saw the truck and trailer going south at a high rate of speed. Then the rig just disappeared."

Andy didn't need to spell that out for me. The driver didn't want to be stopped and inspected and he was willing to risk it all. "You figure he turned down 117?"

"I do. Only turn he could have made. And that scares me. For him to reach the turnoff for 117 ahead of me he had to be traveling at least a hundred miles per hour, maybe one twenty or better. I don't have to tell you a truck going that fast is dangerous in the extreme. Felony reckless endangerment. You get time, not just a ticket. Your vehicle is impounded. Your CDL will get jerked in a heartbeat. To risk that you're not just stupid, you're either high or—"

He didn't need to finish his thought. "A lot of trucks out here, though not so many on 117. You got any kind of description?"

"I've got color and a little more. You know those old cab-over White Freightliners from the 1960s and early '70s? Flat-nosed monsters?"

I did. In their own way they were legendary. Blowers. Some ranging up to 800 horsepower. "Kinda rare," I said.

"This one was freshly painted candy-apple red."

"Subtle," I volunteered.

"Some words in block letters. 'Red' something. Begins with an *h* maybe 'Hell.'"

That got John's attention. "Red Hell?"

"You've seen it?"

"No. If I did, I'd remember." John appeared relieved to say he hadn't seen it, as if it were more than just a truck speeding through the desert night.

"If you do, just let the Highway Patrol know as soon as possible, okay? Don't either of you try to approach the truck or driver." The concern in his voice was unmistakable, especially for John. "You see him coming, get well off the shoulder. You listening to me, John?"

John said he heard loud and clear.

For a moment I thought about mentioning the semi that had clipped me earlier and just as quickly dismissed the idea. As far as I knew it wasn't a cab-over, though it might have been. I was too damn busy, half-blinded, and pointed in the wrong direction to notice its color. Its driver came at me fast, but his actual speed was difficult to judge. I decided against mentioning it because all I could really tell Andy was that I'd seen a truck.

Out of habit, I dropped our imaginary cigarette to the ground and rubbed it out with my boot. "You got a vintage red truck with maybe the words 'Red Hell' painted on it going over a hundred miles an hour. That's a neon-blazing crazy. Anything else?"

"The trailer. Also relatively rare. Either a side-dumper or a live bottom, though he could change trailers."

Both trailers were specialty jobs, used mostly for road construction or sometimes agriculture, at least as far as I knew. They were long trailers usually pulled by a three-axle tractor that unloaded to the side or had an opening beneath them that unloaded waste or aggregate of some kind. Either one was designed for a quick release and go and to keep the load from getting in the way of their tires or impeding traffic at a construction site. Unless you were on a highway where roadwork was being done or on a construction site the odds were you might never see one during daylight. Seeing one under way past dark was damn unusual no matter where you were.

Andy wished John and me a good and safe day and walked back to the white Ford F-150 pickup that served as his cruiser.

I followed him and leaned over and waited for him to open his window. When he did, I said, "I've never seen or heard of you pulling your service weapon, Andy, but you pull that truck over I suggest you have it drawn."

After a grim nod, Andy said, "You know I still see that county deputy around. That scar on his face is hard to miss. And there's more than a few more officers around wearing similar souvenirs you gave them. I never thought I'd live to see the day Ben Jones would warn a cop to be careful."

"You still haven't," I said. "For the record, remember, that county jerk-off punched me in the gut while I was handcuffed. It wasn't an intentional head butt no matter what he said. My attorney made it clear it was simply a reflex in response to his punch. Besides, that was a long time ago. And I was drunk. I'm a changed man."

"Sure," Andy said. "A reflex. Of course it was. Though I'll wager it seems just like yesterday to him every time he looks in the mirror. He probably doesn't care much about you changing. Even I wonder how changed you are, Ben. No matter how much time goes by a volcano is still a volcano."

"What are you getting at, Andy?"

"I'm not getting at anything, really. Just making an observation. Like you, I have a lot of time to think. I had coffee with Captain Dunphy a few weeks after his retirement. He'd been doing some thinking too. There were a lot of questions that weren't asked a few months ago when that woman and her million-dollar cello disappeared. Part of the reason they weren't asked is because the insurance company wouldn't file a report. Maybe the biggest reason is that insurance investigator PO'd the captain."

Though Andy said he was just thinking, I didn't care for where his thinking was taking our conversation. "That asshole pissed me off too," I said.

"Did you know they found tire prints out there near where they found that rented SUV? You remember, don't you? The one that got caught in the flash flood and killed that woman's ex-husband? The one you flagged for Search and Rescue?"

"I remember. So?"

"Tire prints from a motorcycle."

I waited.

"Dunlops. Just like the ones on Walt's vintage Vincent Black Shadow."

"Walt rides that Vincent all over this desert. And all of his other motorcycles too. And I'm sure there are other bikers." I wasn't sure about the last. It sounded plausible enough.

"Walt sure does get around, that's for sure."

We could have gone on pretending I didn't know what he was doing, but I didn't have the patience and I didn't want the conversation to continue. "You wearing an invisible hat, Andy?"

We watched each other's faces. "No," he said. "When I put on my hat it won't be invisible and it would be a big mistake if you failed to see it."

"Come on, Andy. You saying Walt and maybe me had something to do with that woman and her cello disappearing?"

Walt and I were the only two people who knew the whole story of Claire and her cello. As far as Andy and the rest of the world were concerned, particularly the law, she and the cello had vanished into the desert with no connection to us—just an old man and a truck driver. Now Claire and her twenty-million-dollar del Gesu cello were on an eternal tour with Elvis. I wanted to keep it that way. I needed to keep it that way, though if pressed I might not have been able to come up with a logical explanation. Sure, some of what we had done was illegal, but not criminal—not to my mind anyway. Claire might not have been the cello's legal owner, but she was sure as hell its rightful owner and it belonged where it was—in her grave.

"I'm saying that the couple times my path crossed with you and

Walt since all that happened, you two have seemed a little—" He took a breath. "Different. That's all. It's got me to thinking about how rare it is for a man to actually change."

"Who are we really talking about? Me or Walt?"

"I don't know. It doesn't really have to be one or the other, does it?"

Though it happened a long time ago, if you kill three men with a butcher knife like Walt had, no matter what the circumstances, people, especially law-enforcement types, will always wonder what you're capable of in the future. No charges were ever filed against Walt for killing Bernice's three rapists, and no one but me knew about the fourth—and as Walt said, he didn't kill the guy, he just didn't save him. It was a fine line to be sure, and only I knew where that body was buried.

"Well, if that's what keeps your time occupied, then you go on thinking all you like."

"I will. Just don't go off the reservation, Ben."

I'd heard that saying a lot in my life as a way of generally warning someone not to get crazy. I never liked it much. "How come people say that about Indians and never about Jews? I've never heard of anyone saying, 'Just don't go off the kibbutz.'"

"You're right. So here it is for both sides of your heritage: Don't go off the kibbutz, Ben. You stay a changed man. You know anything more about that truck?"

"No," I said. "But you and I know that driver is trouble. If I knew anything, I'd tell you. Just for the record, I'm not warning a cop. I'm warning you. My guess is that the driver didn't go far down 117. Probably just far enough and waited long enough to think it was safe to get back out on 191. He's long gone by now."

"Probably," he said. "By the way, have you seen Dan Brew lately? Particularly his new bride, or latest fiancée?"

I told Andy I'd just seen Brew.

"The woman?"

I shook my head. "Not lately. I can't even remember the new

one's name. Maybe I didn't ever hear it. Not that I care either way."

"She hasn't been in touch with her family back east for a while. They're concerned. I was asked to drive out there and check on her. You were just there?"

"An hour or so ago."

"There was no one there when I stopped by. If you see her or Dan, tell Didi to phone home."

I laughed. "Didi?"

Andy put on his hat and pulled the brim snug against his head. "Shut up, Ben. And don't forget what I said about the kibbutz."

He spun his tires on the gravel shoulder and turned around and disappeared back the way he had come.

9

John had begun to feel the cold again and was putting on his coat when I returned. "Seemed like you and Trooper Smith were having quite a conversation."

I ignored his observation and wished I could do the same for my own. John stretched again and cocked his head at an odd angle. "I think I'm spending too much time out here."

"You think?"

"I'm beginning to hear things."

This was mildly concerning to me, though truth be told it didn't surprise me. "Is God speaking to you?"

"No," he said. "And yes. He speaks to all of us all the time if we're listening. This time it's just the wind."

Eager to be on my way, I asked a question without much interest in hearing the answer. "And what's the wind saying?"

"Not saying anything, exactly. Just sounds to me like a baby crying."

John recoiled a half step from the startled expression on my face. I'd forgotten all about my passengers. It was only a few steps to the door of my cab and I covered them in record time. The dog was sitting up and looking at the girl, who was cradling the baby in her arms. She smiled at me and gently rocked Annabelle, which quieted her a bit until she got her next breath and then she let loose with an ear-piercing scream. I caught a whiff of the problem.

John had come up behind me and I felt his presence at my shoulder. "Well, well," he said, "I think you have a chore ahead of you."

He seemed content, at least for the moment, to keep any questions he might have to himself. I took Annabelle and motioned for the girl to scoot over onto the driver's side. She complied. The dog squeezed over the center console and resumed his position at her feet, though his attention was now on me.

Like a carpenter unpacking his toolbox I laid Annabelle on the seat and grabbed the baby bag and dumped its contents on the floor of the cab. She let out another wail while I considered my next move.

I was embarrassed and angry with myself. How could I just forget about them? My excuse was simple. I had spent five days a week for twenty years driving the desert alone. Suddenly having children as passengers was a steep and dangerous learning curve.

As I stood there surveying the new tools of child care, John said, "It's been a long time, Ben, but I'd appreciate it if you'd let me do this. I used to be good at it."

"I can do it!" I barked.

He put his big hand on my shoulder and said, "I know you can. I'm just saying this brings to mind such sweet memories. I'd consider it a favor if you let me."

I always knew John had a story, everyone did, though his dead-ended on a Utah desert road. Whatever his former life, it wasn't something I thought much about, and it always struck an unsettled nerve in me when he infrequently referred to some ordinary fact as if an ordinary life could somehow land your aging old ass in the middle of nowhere hauling a cross.

"Since you put it that way," I said. The two of us exchanged places on the running board.

We watched him go to work—by "we" I mean the girl and the dog, and me—first washing his large, callused hands with a wipe before touching the baby. If Annabelle had been imaginary he couldn't have done a better job. No wasted movement, almost rhythmic the way his hands moved, firm and gentle at the same time. He had her out of her little jumpsuit in a flash even as she squirmed and complained.

I noticed the pink flannel suit was covered with a pattern of green Day-Glo skulls with pacifiers in their bony mouths, surrounded with happy little flying black bats. I idly wondered where in the hell Ginny found all of her grim crap. Maybe there was a Halloween Baby Gap tucked away somewhere in Price. I stopped asking myself the "why" of her fascination months ago. I knew it would be the kind of answer that only made sense to the young. To anyone of serious years the symbols of death meant something a bit more personal than a fashion statement. If I ever saw a nose or lip ring near Annabelle, Ginny and I would have a holy roller come-to-Jesus meeting, or a come-to-Halloween meeting. I didn't care which it was.

John paused and admired his fresh handiwork while the baby reached for a handful of his white beard. He turned and winked proudly at me. "Praise the Lord. Muscle memory."

I complimented his work just as Annabelle went all out with a new wail that burst past us in a warm cloud into a quickly cooling breeze. John and I exchanged our clueless masculine befuddlement. We might have puzzled a while longer if not for the girl. She scooted off the seat and lifted one of the full bottles out of the side pocket of the baby bag and offered it to John.

Bottle in hand he dabbed a bit of liquid on his wrist and then confessed he didn't know if it was warm enough.

"Try it," I said. "If she doesn't find it to her liking I'm betting she'll let us know in short order."

John wrapped the baby in a blanket and held her close to him, out of the rising wind. It might not have been just right, but it was right enough. There on the side of the road as the sky darkened she took the nipple and drank with the abandon of a man dying of thirst. I didn't know such a little thing could consume that much liquid so quickly. John lifted her to his shoulder and patted for a minute or two and the ensuing burp brought a bit of laughter from both of us.

John put her down on the passenger seat again, swaddled and full and already drifting, and tipped a corner of the blanket across her face. A breeze blew the blanket back and the girl and John both reached at the same time to replace it. Their hands touched above the baby's head. From behind John all I could see were the girl's steady black eyes and their hands, her tiny dirty fingers across his clean, huge wind-burned paw. The seconds ticked into a minute, maybe longer, and neither one removed their hand.

The weather worsened around us. When the first small snowflakes began to skitter across my face I tugged at John's jacket and their hands separated. Together John and I resettled Annabelle into her car seat and strapped her in and the girl and the dog resumed their positions on the passenger side.

I closed the door. "Seems like you and my other passenger were having quite a conversation yourselves."

John took his time responding, though it wasn't really a question that required an answer. He zipped and buttoned his jacket all the way to the top and pulled a threadbare gray scarf from a pocket and wrapped it twice around his head before tying the ends in a bow beneath his long white beard. He extracted a pair of old deerskin work gloves from another pocket, and as he put them on he said, "Ben—" That was as far as he got.

He looked over to the cab and started again. "Ben, that girl . . ."

"Her father is an acquaintance," I said by way of unnecessary explanation. "He's in trouble of some kind and asked me to watch her for the day. If I had to guess, I'd say it's an immigration thing."

"Maybe," he said. "Except that particular conversation was one of the most sorrowful I've ever had, man, woman, or child. Satan is always at work."

Getting a sense that John was sinking into one of his crazy religious holes, and not wanting him to drag me along unless I could bring a snack and something to read, I decided to try one more time to get him to accept a ride into town.

He shook his gray-scarfed head and lifted the cross to his shoulder with a grunt.

"Staying out here is stupid, John. You're two days from town. I'll even come back later and get your cross and deliver it right to your door."

He turned and gave me a raggedy smile. "Thank you, but this cross doesn't accept rides and neither do I. You just take care of that little girl. Hell's black water is rising faster all the time."

With that and a handful of steps he and his cross began to dissolve into a veil of blowing snow. For a few seconds I stared after him as I listened to the squeaking axle of the wheelbarrow tire as it labored under the weight of the cross.

A short time later we were under way again and creeping up to a safe speed of thirty miles an hour. I kept a lookout for John along the shoulder. The snow was thickening while a milky fog seemed to be settling into the spaces between the flakes. The girl was curled in a ball on the seat and the dog was curled on the floor and both were dozing, warm and apparently content. It occurred to me that it might have been a good long while since the girl had eaten. Somewhere behind my seat was a brown paper bag that held a banana and a peanut butter and jelly sandwich.

The girl? I didn't think I'd mentioned to John that the child was a girl. Maybe I had. Maybe she had told him in the silent conversation I'd overheard. Within five minutes I knew I had somehow driven past John without seeing him and that made me think again about how dangerous it was for him trudging along the shoulder. There weren't ever many vehicles on 117, though a few times I had been surprised to come upon the only two cars in five hundred square miles of desert that had managed to collide with each other like estranged lovers in a dark barroom.

10

I enjoyed driving through the snow while everyone else slept. From time to time the dog would raise his hoary snout and survey the cab for a moment to make certain, or so I assumed, that all was well in our warm tin can. Once, he rested his long nose on the seat and just stared at the girl as she slept, contemplating her as if trying to see into her dreams and considering if he should enter and check them out. Maybe he decided there were places he shouldn't go. After a minute he was curled again into his own furry dreams.

Someone's dreams, perhaps especially a child's, are a country best avoided. Most adults would probably be terrified. There's something about keeping company with a kid that makes you think of when you were that age. I thought of my own childhood and my dreams and often wondered which was which. Here she was, so young, separated from her family, and she showed no fear. She didn't seem frightened of the tall old man with the wild pale eyes and long white beard. There had been a few times in the past when he sure as hell frightened me. Maybe when compared to what she had known, John didn't bounce the needle on her fear gauge? If that was the case it told me something I didn't want to know and I was surely scared for her.

I knew from my own experience that for such children fear was as normal as breathing, a part of you, like an internal sky. I knew all about that. What was inside and outside were the same.

At the Indian School, I couldn't have been much more than four or five, I made the mistake of telling some older boys in the cafeteria I could fly. I flew in my dreams all the time back then, except I didn't know they were dreams. When the laughter stopped they took me to the second story roof of the dormitory and pushed me toward the edge and dared me to fly.

There on the edge, my backside teetering above the schoolyard, a big kid pushed me. I didn't like being pushed. Still don't. He was enough taller than I was that my head came to just above his waist. I wrapped my arms around his legs and tore at his groin with my teeth like a coyote ripping fresh meat. He screamed and I let loose. He dropped to his knees crying. The rest of them went silent and backed away. I turned, arms stretched, and off I went, probably flapping like crazy and absolutely certain I could fly until the moment my little body hit the hard dirt. Even then, in the pain, I didn't know I couldn't fly. I just thought I hadn't done it exactly right. I needed practice. I made a promise to myself to pay more attention when I flew at night.

How many times did I jump from that roof? And each time I expected to fly. I winced just thinking of hitting that ground. Somehow I convinced myself I was making progress. No loop-de-loops, but maybe slowing, maybe a touch of a soar. Stubborn little SOB. Maybe the years hadn't changed me all that much. At some point they started locking the door to the roof. I responded by simply changing perches.

We descended a slow, easy grade and the snow suddenly stopped as a straight stretch of a few miles opened before us. I cracked my window and guessed that within a hundred feet the temperature warmed twenty or thirty degrees. It was crystal clear and almost balmy. Flat desert reached to the horizons on both sides of the highway and the random clumps of prairie grasses and big sages bent and sprung and whipped in the crosswinds scattering fireworks of purple, pink, and white flower petals into the wild air.

A pair of headlights gleamed in my side mirror before bursting out of the white soup behind us. I was gaining speed on the sunny flat and still the vehicle was rapidly overtaking us. My first thought was the rogue White Freightliner Andy was searching for. I wondered if the driver even saw my truck ahead. I touched my brakes a couple times to signal him with my brake lights. On he came, not slowing at all.

Highway 117 is narrow and its shoulders can be soft and treacherous, especially for heavy vehicles. It wasn't the Freightliner. I inched my tractor-trailer as close to the shoulder as I dared just as the pickup passed. It was a rich man's circus train. The new pickup was towing what looked like a new Airstream. Attached to the rear of the Airstream was a chromed flatbed carrying two camo-colored ATVs. Even the pickup bed was loaded to the top of the cab. A gust of wind sent the trailer with the ATVs so near to my cab I cringed and let my right-side tires grab a ribbon of shoulder to put a few more inches between us.

The driver whipped his trailers into the lane in front of us with only a few feet to spare. His ATV caboose might have clipped my fender if I hadn't hit the brakes. Down the road he went at a speed maybe in excess of eighty miles per hour while the crosswinds lashed his trailers across both lanes like a ten-pound tail wagging a two-pound dog. He was out the other end of the straightaway in less than a minute.

The dog was the only one of my passengers disturbed by my sharp braking, and his eyes seemed to register a warning for me to knock it the hell off. By way of explanation I pointed my finger toward the road ahead and the idiot who had just passed us. The dog wasn't interested in excuses and let his warning stand a few seconds before lowering his head.

The wind slapped against the cab and I recalled John's words about the black waters of hell rising. It seemed to me that John pretty much thought those waters were always rising. Maybe they were. For him, the girl, or everyone? Maybe that's why he walked the desert with his cross like he did, though being a freelance heathen it didn't seem to me to be doing him any good unless he planned to eventually float on those dark waters strapped to his cross.

The last time I tried to fly I had gone to the highest building at the Indian School—three stories. If being an orphan and unaffiliated with a tribe wasn't enough to make me a full-time pariah, the staff and other children cut me an even wider berth after I started jumping. Taking a bite out of that boy's groin probably also had something to do with it.

My plan, as I remembered it, was to give myself just a little more height and time to get my wings working properly. The pain didn't stop me; it was always temporary, and a small price to pay for my practice sessions. Nothing was ever broken. The rest of the school seemed relieved that I spent so much time in the infirmary and away from them.

I awoke on the ground surrounded by some teachers and kids, and an Indian man I'd never seen before. He was kneeling over me and smiling—not laughing—just an easy, amused smile. The teachers were telling him I was crazy, suicidal, and "unclaimed," which is the word they often used to describe my orphan status. "No people. He's not right in the head," as if the two were connected.

The man's hair was long, to his shoulders, and so black it seemed blue in the sun. "Why do you jump?" he asked while he gently felt the bones in my arms and legs.

No one had ever asked me that before.

"I'm not jumping," I answered. "I'm flying."

There was a low collective moan from the crowd.

"I can fly at night but not in the day."

He knew. He understood. I could see it on his face. He brought his mouth close to my ear and whispered, "Me too, little one. I think we come from the same people. We fly only at night. That's our secret."

He carried me to the school infirmary. As usual, nothing was broken. I never saw him again. Not long after that began a string of foster homes. For a while I believed the man was my father, or wanted to believe. A teacher told me he was just a drunk, a day hire, brought in with other men to collect and haul away garbage.

I whispered to the sleeping girl, "I hope you're flying, little one."

11

A warm sun stayed with us the rest of the way to town and it was a welcome companion. About a mile out, before the Rockmuse City Limits sign, we passed the old Subaru station wagon that signaled 50 percent of the two-person population boom that occurred over the summer. It had been abandoned though not forgotten on the shoulder and was ornamented by Andy in the red Highway Patrol stickers warning that it would be towed. It hadn't been yet and probably wouldn't be because the Highway Patrol would have to pay the towing charge all the way to the impound lot in Price. It was covered in dust and the words JUST DIVORCED were written in white across the back window. The lone woman who had been driving it had since taken up residence in a closed movie theater down a little and across the street from John's True Value First Church of the Desert Cross.

The Shell station is the first place you come to as you pull into Rockmuse and the circus train was stretched out alongside a row of pumps. There was a small convenience store inside the station and I decided to get the girl something to drink with her sandwich. As we wound around the lot she awoke and immediately pushed her face against the window. I parked in front of the doors as I always did, the cab pointed toward the highway in order to make it easier to get back onto the highway.

I checked the dates on the pint carton of milk. Eckhardt, the owner, didn't pay much attention to expiration dates, especially when winter came on and customers got few and far between. Sometimes I delivered to him and it had been at least a couple weeks. I'd heard a rumor once that someone chipped a tooth on one of his Twinkies. The milk was past its date and I opened it and took a whiff and a sip. It was okay. Eckhardt watched me, none too pleased, and took my money without a word of hello or goodbye.

The girl took the milk and banana and sandwich and attacked. I stood outside the cab and surveyed the circus train and what I assumed was its engineer, a guy about my age, late thirties, in jeans and a tight sleeveless camo T-shirt that showcased his muscled arms and chest. His head was not quite shaved, barely a stubble of hair. He wore a sidearm in a holster high on his right hip.

The glistening black pickup was a brand-new Ford Super Duty F-450 XLT dually with the 6.7 liter Powerstroke diesel. It was quite a rig and I did feel a twinge of envy for a truck I couldn't afford at a tenth the price, which didn't stop me from dropping by the Ford dealership from time to time to dream and kick tires. You could buy a damn nice home in Price for less than the cost of that pickup. My guess was it had every factory available bell and whistle, including the manual Turbocharger, plus some aftermarket goodies. With the Airstream and the chromed flatbed with the ATVs the cost of the whole outfit had to push a quarter of a million dollars. The truth was I didn't really have a clear idea of what the circus train cost. For me, it was like estimating the distance from one star to another with a wooden ruler. I was the ruler.

Only thirty or so feet separated us and he saw me appraising his circus train. We raised our chins to each other in acknowledgment and I started walking in his direction knowing damn well I should have gotten back in my truck with the girls and got on with my day. The little voice telling me to do just that yammered in my ear with every step I took in his direction.

He was the first to speak. "Fuck me, you see the price of diesel in this shithole?"

Eckhardt's Shell was the only place to get fuel within a hundred miles. He didn't gouge, really, owing to the fact he didn't get a lot of business and he paid more to get deliveries so far off the main routes. I also knew he gave locals a discount, which he didn't have to do. I didn't comment, though the voice telling me to walk away had turned into a chanting crowd. He had a couple hundred thousand or more in his rig and he was complaining about the price of diesel?

I turned my attention to the Airstream and noticed it had a damn satellite dish folded onto its roof next to an air-conditioning unit. The pickup bed held two dirt bikes, one a miniature of the other, and a Honda generator. Maybe $300,000 was a better estimate.

I whistled. "Quite an outfit," I said. "A little late in the season."

He kept his hand on the nozzle while the pump numbers spun like a roulette wheel. "Thought I'd take the brat camping. This was the only time I had. My blood-sucking ex has me working almost three sixty-five." He waved at a blond boy that was maybe nine or ten sitting in his cab.

The boy didn't wave back. He was looking at the girl in my truck whose head rose just above the bottom of the window.

Considering what he had spent on what was lined up in front of us, a couple thoughts came to mind. The first was that the blood-sucking ex he mentioned still had a long way to go, and I hoped she got the last goddamned drop. The second was maybe he wouldn't have to work so hard and long and might have more time to spend with his son if he backed away from the Ford and Airstream dealerships.

"Camping?" I said. "Looks more like resorting."

He didn't like the sound of that. "Can I do something for you?"

"You were going a bit fast back there. The crosswinds out here can be tricky. They will flip you in a heartbeat. Just a heads-up."

Our eyes met for the first time and then he gazed past me at the side of my trailer. It's a distinctive yellow logo against black, a helicopter with a cargo net beneath a full moon and the name of my company, Ben's Desert Moon Delivery Service.

He read the name out loud. "You must be Ben."

I nodded.

"So you're a truck driver. Are you also the sheriff in these parts, Ben?"

I didn't say anything. I could barely hear my own thoughts above the football stadium screaming in my head. I glanced up at his kid. My girl was waving at him. She was actually smiling. He returned her wave with his middle finger.

"Just some well-intended advice," I said.

The pump clicked off with a thump, which he ignored. "I've lived in Utah my whole life. I've got some advice for you."

I started to say something and then thought better of it.

"Are you thinking of giving me trouble?" He rested his hand over his holster.

"Nope," I said. "I see you brought enough with you."

Then I finally did what I should have done in the beginning. As I was walking I was muttering to Andy. *See, Andy, I stayed on the kibbutz.* But I knew I sure as hell had just stood on the border. I was a slow learner but little by little I had discovered that you can beat the brains out of someone but it's almost impossible to beat any brains in.

I paused for a moment inside the cab. The girl had peanut butter around her mouth and a dab of jelly on her nose. It suddenly occurred to me that maybe she had a name if I asked in my lousy Spanish. *"Cómo se llama?"*

She lowered her head below the window so the boy couldn't see her. No response.

I wiped off the remnants of her lunch with a tissue and she raised her chin to help me. "My name is Ben," I said, and repeated my name and pointed to my chest. No answer except her black eyes into mine and out of nowhere I felt a sadness enter me like a knife. It took everything I had to look away and when I did I saw the dog staring up at me. I couldn't read his thoughts and I was praying to all the gods within earshot that he couldn't read mine.

Pedro's note had said "Juan." I was compelled to give her a name, even if it wasn't her real name, anything that made her a person, both to her and to me, even if it was only temporary.

When I was at Indian School someone had told me our ancestors had a special word for everything, and nothing was real, nothing truly lived, unless there was a word for it. I remembered myself at that age. I did have a special word for everything. One word. Actually two words, though the second was just to guide the one word to its target. She needed a name. The obvious choice was Juanita. I tried it and received no response. Was the wrong name better than no name? Juanita just didn't feel right to me and I resolved to give it some more thought.

I gripped the wheel and released the brake while my heart chugged in beats I could feel through my chest. "Next stop, Rockmuse Collision Center." I spoke with a cheerfulness that sounded hollow and forced, even to me. Already I was thinking hard about where I could leave the girl and the dog, and maybe Annabelle too—just for a few hours, just so they were safe. Or so I told myself.

12

The sunlight ricocheted off the surface of the empty streets of Rockmuse—the town that wouldn't die. Toby, the aging proprietor and sole employee of the Rockmuse Collision Center, had lost his wife to cancer fifteen years earlier and as far as I knew he kept active, though not busy, maintaining the two postal delivery vehicles and the Rockmuse school bus, which was so old it was the same bus that ferried some of the current students' grandparents. There weren't many collisions these days and the damages resulting from the few that did occur were left alone to rust and scar like all the other ordinary tragedies you saw on the faces of a small-town population. Nearing the corner building that housed the collision center I got an idea and turned off on a side street that led to the countess's ranch a couple miles out of town to the north.

Phyllis Bradford wasn't a real countess, and no one ever called her that to her face, but she was close enough, being that she was foreign, that is, from the east, and had a certain assured bearing, tall and slender with short blond hair, blue eyes, and high cheekbones. She had shown up driving a silver Rolls-Royce not long after the coal mine closed and the smart folks were leaving town as fast as they could and property was cheap and getting cheaper by the day. She was alone except for the two small children with her, a boy and a girl, who turned out to be her grandchildren, though she was only in her early forties at the time. No one at the time thought she was any kind of desperado, and she paid cash for a nice turn-of-the-century two-story ranch house and a hundred acres.

Rich people have no goddamned clue when it comes to hiding from the law. They go right on with their privilege and wealth in some backwater and nine times out of ten that's how they got into trouble in the first place, though the countess was the exception. She must have thought she'd arrived safely on Mars and not a soul in Rockmuse would notice and she and her grandkids would never be found. It took less than three months. Considering who she was and where she'd come from, and what she'd done, you'd think the FBI had been asleep for the first ten weeks.

Her private road was graveled and long, a quarter mile or so, lined on both sides by white ranch fencing with horses in the meadow, which wasn't a meadow unless you counted the tufts of prairie grass floating like tiny green islands in the brown sand and rock. I pulled up in the circular drive in front of the house. She kept it freshly painted white with turquoise blue trim. The barn was turquoise too. Turquoise must have been her favorite color because it was also the color she chose for the Rolls that had long since been transformed into the damnedest looking pickup anyone had ever seen. The conversion had been done by Toby at the Rockmuse Collision Center. Could have been that was what had made me think of her.

I sat in my truck and listened to it idle and waited, as is the custom in the desert country, to announce a visit. The low wraparound porch slanted forward from the years of foot traffic and foundation settling. It was an eastern-facing porch and as such looked straight into the maw of the mesa, so close and tight that standing on the porch you couldn't see the top of its 2,000-foot plateau—a little claustrophobic for my taste. I'd been at her place a few times in the late afternoon when the sun was getting low in the west and the combination of heat and light reflecting off the red stone and mica radiated and pulsed pink until you were disoriented and floating and damn near blind.

Phyllis opened the door and stepped out onto the porch. During her first three-month residence she was a sight around Rockmuse with her high heels and fashionable dresses, never without pearls or diamonds. After prison, when she returned, without the diamonds and pearls, she slipped easily into the native garb of cowboy boots, jeans, or sometimes a long ranch dress and western checked blouse. Today it was jeans and boots and western blouse. On her, somehow, the ranch clothes still reminded me of the little black dress and pearls.

She raised her hand to shield her eyes. "Ben?"

I opened my door and confessed to my name.

"Am I getting so old I forgot I ordered something?"

I told her it was a social call, sort of, and asked if I might come in for a moment.

"I've never known Ben Jones to make social calls." She waved me in the open door. "Not that I am complaining. It's a pleasure, Ben."

It was agreeably warm inside. I sat down on the sofa. She made herself comfortable in a wingback chair, body upright, shoulders straight, soles of her boots flat on the hardwood floor, her hands folded on her lap. The October sunlight filtered in through lace curtains behind me. There were streaks of gray in the blond these days and a few wrinkles here and there. Overall, she hadn't given much away to age, still trim with the jawline of a young woman. She possessed a kind of calm, natural confidence that took over and in that way the countess was as close to class as you could get in Rockmuse.

There was a tall glass with brown liquid and ice on a table next to her. Without a word she got up and returned with a glass for me. "Long Island iced tea."

I assumed Long Island tea meant that it was imported from Long Island. I swallowed a sip and it burned my mouth and then proceeded to light a fire all the way down my throat. I coughed and my eyes started to water.

Phyllis sprang up and began patting my back and apologizing. "It has a touch of gin in it."

I didn't say it, but I was thinking that what it had a touch of was tea. The other thing I was thinking was how her hand had stopped patting me on the back and was now just resting warm and soft on my neck. She must have noticed too, and returned to her chair.

She apologized again and punctuated her apology with a clear ripple of laughter. "I'm afraid to admit since turning sixty I have joined the 'It Must Be Five o'Clock Somewhere' club. You said this was a social call?"

"A favor," I said, and quickly explained about the girl and the baby, and the dog and the accident. "I just need someone to watch them for a few hours until I get my trailer door repaired."

"Of course," she said. She didn't stand, so neither did I. "Are you seeing anyone these days?"

The visit seemed to be turning a bit more social than I anticipated. I thought of Claire, of her above me laughing as we made love at the model house in Desert Home and then her dying next to me in my old Toyota pickup as we bumped across the desert. And of her secret grave next to her mother, Bernice, Walt's wife.

"No," I said. It was true but it felt like a lie.

Phyllis raised her eyebrows. "Let me share something with you, Ben. I was going to suggest an arrangement. To be candid, I've been thinking about you for a long time. Yes, there is an age difference. There are many differences. I've practiced this speech many times. I wanted it to sound vaguely salacious, hopefully witty and playful. Something like, 'How about an older woman? Half the responsibility and all the fun.' I realize that's just not who I am." She sipped from her tea. "Perhaps it's been a game for me. Nothing more. Then out of the blue you show up on my doorstep today. And I realized something else. It's not who you are, either."

"You're very pretty," I said, and meant it.

"Yes," she said, "I am." There wasn't a hint of brag in her voice, only the quiet truth. "And I miss the company of a man. Not just in the bedroom—in my life. What's left of it."

I started to speak and she placed her index finger over her lips. "Just listen, please. I'll be happy to watch your charges. I don't ever want us to speak of this subject again. Your word as a gentleman, please?"

"If that's the way you want it. You have my word."

"Good. I trust you. When I asked you if you were seeing anyone, you said no. If there is one thing a woman—a real woman, an honest, discerning woman with an open heart—knows, it is the shadow of another woman on the face of a man in whom she's interested. Maybe it's the gin. Or the years. This empty house. The desert. But I know this: whoever she was, she wasn't just a woman, not to you. You love her. If I were still rich and beautiful and young, I still wouldn't have a chance. And somehow, dearest Ben, that makes me feel better. Now, let's go get those lovelies of yours."

Phyllis greeted the girl with a hug and I couldn't help notice that there was more than shyness in the way she stood, arms to her sides, inside herself. I explained I didn't know her name. Phyllis got on one knee in front of the girl and asked her name in Spanish. Not my Spanish. Formal, lilting Spanish. She got the same response I did. I remarked on her Spanish. Phyllis replied that her Spanish was still good, but her Italian and French were far from what they once were.

Phyllis smiled at the girl and then at me. "You two look enough alike you could be related."

Thinking Phyllis was finding a roundabout way to suggest the girl might be my daughter, I said, with a bit more sharpness than I intended, "Well, we're not."

"Relax, Ben," she said. "I meant like a little sister or niece."

I could maybe see it. Same dark eyes and thick, coarse black hair. That was about it. There was something else about the girl, the way she kept herself inside, and I recalled how she had set me to thinking back to my own childhood before I was adopted.

The girl took tentative steps across the porch, her head swiveling, taking the place in, overcome with awe, like Dorothy entering the gates of Oz. She suddenly stopped and turned and stared at me. The dog, who had dutifully followed her, turned and stared at me as well.

Phyllis said, "Tell her you'll be back soon."

"I don't think she'll understand me."

"Say it, Ben. She'll understand just fine."

I said the words and the girl stood on the porch and watched me get in the truck. An idea came to me as I released the brake. I beckoned Phyllis to come over.

"What's 'little sister' in Spanish?"

"Formally, you'd say *la hermana menor.*"

I didn't care for it. Back to the drawing board.

I thanked Phyllis and she began to walk back to the porch. She turned and said, "There's another word. Casual. Affectionate, though. *Manita.* I might be wrong, but I think it also is used for the Mexican hand-flower."

I liked it and tried the word on my tongue a few times. I looked at the girl standing on the porch and liked it even better. "Is it a pretty flower?"

"Very."

"Think she'd mind if I called her Manita?"

"I think she'd like it just fine, Ben."

I drove away with an eye on the girl and Phyllis. The dog watched too, though with an amused indifference to whether I was going to ever return or going permanently to hell. Halfway down the drive I checked my review mirror and she was still standing on the porch, not waving. *Manita.* Though I doubted she could see me, I waved.

13

Toby was good enough to take his feet off the desk and come out and take a look at my trailer. He'd gained a fair amount of weight. In his stained foul-weather overalls he bore a strong resemblance to a Carhartt summer sausage. I told him I hoped he could get to it soon and he said he was booked solid through December. And winked.

"Give me an hour," he said. "Maybe two." He backed up and held his thumb in front of him like a painter getting perspective. He seemed to be analyzing the angle of impact. "Jesus Christ, Ben. You are one lucky son of a bitch."

I agreed with him.

It was nearing noon and the lunch I'd packed was riding in the belly of the girl. The Rockmuse Mercantile was four blocks away and it had a deli with decent fresh food that didn't require an expiration date. My other option was to sit in Toby's waiting room and read ancient copies of magazines about once-famous people who were long dead and forgotten, or soon would be, or should be.

The Rockmuse Mercantile sounds like it would be larger than it is, and it once was. The shrinking town meant everything in it shrunk as well, including most of the aging residents, with the possible exception of Toby. The upstairs was empty. Some of the tall windows had been broken and boards had been nailed over them. Sometimes the wind howled through the plywood and across its floors so loudly people had to shout to be heard in the grocery below. It was a small store now, with the deli and one aisle of clothes, mostly jeans and underwear, and a few aisles of canned goods and sundries. A little bit of everything. A very little bit.

As soon as I walked in, the idea of going hungry while reading back issues of *Mechanics Illustrated* and *People* magazines seemed like the smarter choice. A few picnic tables lined a far wall near the deli counter and a combined meeting of the Rockmuse Chamber of Commerce and Town Council was in full session. The two groups were composed of the same people and did not officially exist, meaning it was a revolving attendance of six or seven people, mostly men, who had nothing better to do than talk. I'd witnessed this once or twice a week as I made deliveries to the store and always pleaded being short of time when I was invited to pull up a bench. With no delivery rig and therefore no excuse, I felt defenseless to fend off their good-natured offer. I ordered an egg-salad sandwich and coffee from Peggy, half of the older couple who owned the Mercantile, and sat down.

"We need to be the gateway to something."

There were nods all around.

"Gateway to what? To the end of the road?"

"It doesn't matter. Something to draw in tourists, like Moab does. Those fuckers think they're the only damn gateway in Utah."

Peggy didn't allow swearing, and a sharp rebuke rang out from behind the deli counter. "Byron! You know the rules."

Another man spoke up. "Moab has prettier rocks. And they're bigger."

Byron hunched low over his coffee as if dodging an incoming punch. "Maybe we can talk some Indian tribe into building a casino here. What do you think, Ben?"

All eyes were on me, the Indian, when it suited them. "Yeah, sure," I said. "I'll have my Indian people call their Indian people. It might take a while with the smoke signals and all."

There was a round of quiet laughter and a minute filled with collective thinking and gusts of wind spitting against the building.

There had been some rumors of such a thing for a long time. I envisioned acres and acres of RVs, buses, and travel trailers, a fountain and valet parking, and a goddamn golf course rolling endlessly green into the horizon. Water. Lots and lots of water. But like it or not, Utah was run by Mormons and to my knowledge there wasn't a gambling casino anywhere in the state and as long as the angel Moroni and the ghost of Joseph Smith were running things there wouldn't be, and that suited me just fine.

A number of new ideas started to pop from the group. Peggy brought my sandwich and coffee and I began to eat my lunch. Quickly. Next up was a weeklong biker rally, along the lines of Sturgis. Then came something called Mesa Days, which, as near as I could figure, involved nothing more than getting a whole lot of people to come and just stare at the mesa. I kind of liked that one.

One of the guys had a Eureka moment with "Desert Gay Days." There would be a celebration of homosexual contributions to the Old West and a gay rodeo finale. The lone woman at the table wondered if there could be a part of the wingding devoted just to lesbians. Oddly, this seemed to put a damper on the general idea for a few seconds. A voice at the end of the table said, "Well, I like it. Those people have money and they love parties."

Peggy and Joe, her husband, had a nephew who had come to help them a couple years earlier. He was a nice kid in his twenties, hard worker, who had graduated from BYU. He had been stocking a shelf on the other side of an aisle near the picnic tables and listening to the conversation. The most recent comment compelled him to surreptitiously raise his head just above the aisle until he made eye contact with me. He wiggled his brows at me and I smiled. He mouthed the words *those people.* We shared a secret.

A year earlier, during a rare trip into Salt Lake City, I had run into him and his boyfriend holding hands in a coffee shop near the university. When he saw me the blood drained from his face. His parents didn't know and neither did his aunt and uncle. There was nothing I could say to settle him down. I took hold of his right hand and maneuvered the fingers into the well-known hand gesture. "Screw 'em, Lenny," I said. "Your business is your business. Who you love is none of mine." I meant it, not just for him, but for everyone. Since then he always nodded when he saw me and flashed me a smile and low middle-finger salute.

The next ideas to be floated involved a hybrid of sorts, a gay biker parade and swap meet, a quilting extravaganza, and my personal favorite, "The Mesa Marathon." Runners would be sent out into the July desert with no water until they finished the race, which ended in Rockmuse where water would be sold at an outrageous price. This, in fact, was not an original idea. It seemed to me that corporations around the world had already put this sick plan into operation, perfecting this idea as they went by buying up public water and making millions if not billions off of thirsty poor folks.

I'd had enough. "Not to change the subject," I said, hoping to do exactly that, "most of you know Andy Smith, don't you? The Utah state trooper?" There were nods around the table. "Andy is looking for a truck that might have found its way down 117. It's an old White Freightliner painted candy-apple red."

"What's he done?"

"Speeding. Dodging scales," I said. "Maybe more. Any of you seen a truck like that around here?"

A minute of welcome and thoughtful quiet ensued before everyone agreed, all with some obvious regret, they hadn't seen it.

Roy Cuthbert was sitting at the other end of the table. I knew him a little better than the rest. He leaned back and took out a .45 caliber revolver from his holster and put it on the table. "Speeding. Evading a trooper. Dodging scales. Sounds like there's a lot more to 'maybe more.' Like trouble."

I suddenly wished I hadn't changed the subject. "It's Andy's trouble," I said. "Let him handle it. That's his job."

"Andy doesn't get down this way too often. We never see a county deputy and Rockmuse hasn't had its own cop since—" There was a long pause while everyone remembered the young guy the town hired part-time who had disappeared in Rockmuse's 1997 battered gray Ford Fiesta police unit, taking the best young teacher in the school with him.

Roy slowly spun his revolver with his finger. "Someone brings trouble to town, if necessary we bring trouble to him."

"Or her," said the lone woman.

Roy loved his gun. He would have liked to own more than one. That's when the final contribution to the "how to save Rockmuse" meeting occurred. Roy said, with predictable enthusiasm, "What about 'Second Amendment Days'? With a huge gun show and fast-draw competition?"

"Gotta go," I said, and excused myself, dropped my plate and mug in the plastic tub, and waved to Peggy and Joe and Lenny on my way out. I had just cleared the door when Roy caught up to me.

"What do you think that trucker is up to?" he asked.

"I don't know. Maybe nothing."

"Yeah, well there's a lot of nothing between here and Price."

There was enough sadness to go around in Rockmuse, and even though I kind of liked Roy, he was among the saddest. At somewhere over fifty he still wore the silver belt buckle he won in the Rockmuse High School rodeo, back when there was a high school, and a rodeo. Now the school was everything from kinder-garten through high school, and small at that. The buckle was still on the same belt that still cinched around his slim hips. For all I knew the black Stetson he wore might have dated from the same period.

Roy had worked at the coal mine as a yard driver since he graduated from high school. Not long after it closed his wife, a high school sweetheart, left him. The company hired him as a night watchman to keep an eye on the abandoned pit and leftover machinery and junk they'd left behind. After a year his checks, at minimum wage, stopped coming, but no termination notice. He was an honest and loyal man and kept working while month after month he called and got the runaround from the company, the usual—clerical, computer glitch. Then one day he managed to get a VP on the line, who just laughed at him and said, "Sue us" and hung up. He stayed drunk for five years after that and though he was sober now, he lived in someone's garage and survived by doing odd jobs. The jobs rarely involved money because no one had much. Usually he was paid in food and patience, if not kindness.

I started walking and he followed. "You think that truck maybe has to do with drugs? That's been tried, you know. Bad people think there's no one out here in the desert. Or if they discover there are a few people here they think we don't give a shit—or we don't matter."

The reference was inescapable. A group took over an abandoned homestead way out on 117. Some said they had been cooking meth. Maybe they were. In the end they were the ones who got cooked. By the time the cops got around to investigating all they found were charred corpses—and a lot of locals who didn't know a thing about it.

Roy wasn't done with me, and I began to walk faster. "Ben, you're out on 117 every day almost. Chances are you're going to be the one to run across that red truck. You got a gun, don't you?"

"Nope," I said. "I run like a gazelle."

"Well, you should. I'm never without mine."

I stopped and faced him. "Is that so?"

"Damn straight," he said, and put his hand on the empty holster. "Goddamn!" he shouted. "I left it at Mercantile!" He took off back down the sidewalk, trying to manage a wobbly run in his cowboy boots.

I didn't run to the Rockmuse Collision Repair Center, but I sure as hell didn't dawdle either. I did own a gun. It was in the cab of my truck, tucked into a zipped bag attached by Velcro underneath my seat. It was the same gun a man used to try to rob me. He blew a clean hole through a love handle with it before I took it away from him. I emptied the chamber into him and he lived. Since then it's never been out of its bag and I often thought of getting rid of it. I'm an okay shot with a pistol, but I was so damn blind mad at the time that my single-minded intention to beat him to death with the gun threw off my aim.

Roy Cuthbert broke my goddamn heart. He hadn't always worn a gun. To my knowledge, this was his first handgun, though he'd owned a hunting rifle in the past. He pawned it. The .45 and its holster were traded to him a few years earlier for some labor he did. I was afraid he might shoot someone someday, maybe himself, and maybe on purpose.

From what I could tell, when folks started drowning, from debt or grief, loneliness, losing power over their lives or whatever, they often grabbed for the first life preserver they thought of, and too damn often a gun seemed like a life preserver. I believed there were times when a gun might come in handy for defense, but that wasn't how guns were generally used. I considered them a tool and unless you were a cop or a soldier, carrying one around all day was like putting a wrench in your pocket in case one of your nuts came loose. In my experience it seemed that once you started carrying that wrench you started suspecting everyone's nuts were loose except your own. Roy didn't care what that driver and his truck were up to, not really. He just wanted to shoot someone and feel like his championship belt buckle fit him again.

14

I was way early when I stepped into Toby's shop. It didn't matter because he had just finished and was wiping his hands on a rag. The ragged hole where the mirror had been was more or less repaired, the metal straightened and flattened and a similar if not matching piece screwed down over the wound.

"That'll have to do," he said. "You'll need to order a new panel. As for the door, I got it working but not for long. The inside track is busted to shit."

I thanked him while he pulled up the sliding trailer door.

"See up there? I heated it up and bent it into shape as best I could so the rollers stay in the track. The door still sticks some. I called into Johnson's Commercial in Price and they'll have a new section of door track waiting for you tomorrow morning. Won't take long to install."

I thanked him again and took out my wallet.

"No charge, Ben," he said. "Remember when I told you what a lucky man you were?" He walked around the trailer to the patch. "Just getting to tell this story is payment enough." He took a mangled piece of metal off a nearby worktable and handed it to me. "I thought at first this was an M2 mirror off a medium duty. It's not. Jesus, Ben, you got hit by maybe the only kind of rig that wouldn't have spread your guts and bullshit all over Utah and halfway to eternity."

I had a funny feeling. "What are you saying?"

"Almost all of the big road rigs these days are long-snouted front-engine designs. The Peterbilts and Freightliners and so on. Their fenders and fairings come out far enough that what happened here just couldn't happen without making structural contact. You had to be hit by an older rig, practically a ghost these days."

"Like a cab-over? Maybe an old White?"

"That's it," he said. "Jesus was riding shotgun with you on this one. What are the odds?"

"Yeah," I said. "What are the odds."

I put the remnants of the mirror back on the worktable thinking of my conversation with Trooper Smith and wishing I had mentioned the truck I'd made contact with early that morning. If I knew then what Toby was telling me I sure as hell would have. But I didn't. Now that I did, I would, first chance I got. It might not be the truck Andy was searching for and then again, it just might be. That driver would be looking to replace his side mirror as soon as he could. There weren't that many places in the area he could go to get that particular mirror and have it installed. At least it gave Andy and the Utah Highway Patrol a place to start.

"Again, I'm no expert in accident investigation, but I have over fifty years of experience. The way that mirror was planted in your trailer that cab-over was doing at least eighty. Probably more, judging from the way the metals fused from the impact."

Toby opened the bay doors and I thanked him again as I drove out into the street. I set the brake and hopped out and walked back to where he was standing. "I was just wondering," I said. "Any chips or indication what color that truck was?"

He shook his head. "There might have been some on the anchors for the extender brackets but those got blown to hell on impact. Can't help you."

"Do me a favor, Toby?" He nodded, and I said, "Keep this story to yourself for a while?"

He nodded again.

"But not from the Highway Patrol. Put that mirror in a clean bag and give them a call in Price. Tell them everything you told me. And make sure you mention I told you to call. Make sure they let Trooper Smith know. Tell them I'll come by as soon as I can and file a report."

Toby said he'd get to it and pushed the button that closed the bay doors. I stood next to my truck thinking. Roy's voice startled me. "Found my gun," he said. "Right there on the picnic table where I left it."

"Good for you," I said.

Roy's mode of transportation these days was a 1970s kid's bike, a Schwinn Stingray with a banana seat and handlebar risers. Pride and embarrassment are sometimes expressed in the oddest of ways, especially, or so it seemed to me, by men. For a long while Roy drove a pretty nice pickup, nothing grand, but decent and newer. Finally his inability to make the payments caught up with him, along with the repo man, and one day it just disappeared. Rather than tell folks his truck was repossessed by the finance company, which everyone knew anyway, he told everyone he'd gotten a DUI and he lost his license and his truck was impounded.

People are usually generous when it comes to a lie so boldly told, and no one disputed Roy's story—not to his face, anyway. Since then he'd taken to riding his bicycle. He was a tall man, and with his cowboy boots and black hat and damn holster and gun, he had become an odd but accepted fixture pedaling around Rockmuse. A lot of people had sunk damn low and my guess was that seeing Roy on that bike somehow made a lot of others feel better about themselves, maybe even a little superior. Waves and pleasantries were exchanged when Roy would ride by, and without so much as a grin. At least not a grin he might see.

Roy was sitting on his Schwinn with his legs splayed out for balance. "Hey, Ben, you got a few minutes?"

I was still thinking about the mirror and the odds and wondering just how many cab-overs might be still running around on America's highways. Five hundred? A thousand? Maybe. I started to tell Roy how I was short on time and then I saw him there on his bicycle with his Stetson pushed back on his forehead. I couldn't say no.

"A few," I said. "We'll have to make it quick. What's up?"

From his wide smile you would have thought I'd just given him a Christmas present. Maybe I had.

He began pedaling and gave me a high "Westward Ho" come-along wave. "Follow me!"

He rode through town and I stayed behind him driving slowly in first gear. We passed the First Church of the Desert Cross and Ginger's Glass, Whatnots, Handmade Soap & Ballroom Dance Emporium. Ginger had been the one driving the Subaru abandoned over the summer on the outskirts of Price. She'd wasted no time in starting over and setting up her shop in the former movie theater across the street from John's church. Small-town businesses have a way of combining their products and services and Ginger's store was a prime example. Others included Harvey's Barbershop/Ranch Supply and the Rockmuse Toys and Liquor Mart, which, if you know drunks at all, kind of makes sense. You can buy a bottle and an apology gift for later all in one stop.

Ginger was outside up on a ladder adding a new service in black plastic letters to the theater marquis when Roy pedaled by. She was almost six feet tall with red hair that reached nearly to the small of her back. My guess was she was pushing fifty and a little on the heavyset side, and the round, kind face she wore into town was a breath of fresh air, always smiling and upbeat in her long bright dresses and hippie-dippy ways. I'd never spoken to her. She and Roy waved to each other and even at a distance I could see the dark patches on her back where the perspiration had come through her blouse.

Out to the south side of town, past shuttered storefronts and empty strip malls, we turned onto a dirt road and came to an old house that backed up against miles of unbroken desert. I parked in the drive while Roy unfolded the kickstand with a boot tip and dismounted. He lifted the garage door to his home. If I owned a wristwatch I would have been checking it.

As I stepped down from the cab onto the running board, Roy shouted, "I'm like you, I'm an entrepreneur!"

The inside of the garage was overflowing with what looked to me like junk. Somewhere I supposed there was a bed of some kind, though I couldn't see it. An acrid stench of burning rubber rolled out of the open garage door. Everything was covered in black dust. Old mattresses had been stuffed between the studs of the wall for insulation. Several long tables held wires and electronics and baskets hung from the rafters spilling over with various hand tools. Toward the back of the garage were a drill press, band saw, lathe and jigsaw, plus what appeared to be a molding press of some kind. Several rough drawings and diagrams on white copy paper had been thumbtacked to some of the mattresses.

I had yet to see a bed but I did see a microwave and a hot plate. He gave me the nickel tour and I noticed a broken-down easy chair covered with crap. In front of that was an old portable Sony television sitting on a TV tray that held a VCR with three movies next to it: *The Wild One, Breakfast at Tiffany's,* and *Cool Hand Luke.* I approved, except maybe for *Breakfast at Tiffany's.*

"Congratulations," I said, and hoped a little sincerity trickled through. "What have you got here, Roy?"

"The doghouse of the future!"

15

I continued to survey the contents of the garage, somewhat disgusted and certainly mystified, and bided my time while I thought of something to say that was decently laudatory if not strictly genuine. Such a remark refused to present itself. After a minute Roy led me through the labyrinth and out the back door into a small room he'd made out of metal curtain rods over which he had stretched clear sheets of plastic. It was more like a big square tent.

"It's a doghouse made from recycled tires," he said. "I'm still perfecting this prototype."

Inside was a construction that with an imagination and a case of beer a blind man might recognize as a doghouse—pieces of tires of various thicknesses, their worn treads crisscrossed in a jigsaw way, loosely interlocking with one another. I didn't know if it was the doghouse of the future but I was damn glad at least it was a doghouse, or might be mistaken for one.

He pointed to some empty square holes in the doghouse roof. "This is where the solar panels will fit. They'll provide some heat and maybe a cooling fan." Like a proud papa he rested one hand on the roof as if posing for a photo. The structure moved ominously under the weight and I half expected it to topple over, taking Roy with it. "It all comes apart and can be assembled in thirty minutes or less."

I assumed this statement was a hope and not a fact, as was what he said next.

"It even has a little doggy reading light and I'm working on a basic water purification system that recirculates so Fido always has fresh water to drink. Also solar powered. I'm going to sell them on the Internet."

For the moment I set aside the image of a dog reading.

"Do you have a computer?" I asked.

"Not yet. I still have some things to work out. But I'll get one and I'll figure it out. I been working on this for a couple years now."

"A couple years," I said. "Imagine that."

His enthusiasm was almost contagious.

Trying to show interest, I asked, "Where did you get all the electrical stuff?"

"I found some of it and I got a lot for practically nothing when the Radio Shack went out of business. The rest came from garage sales. Some I got just because people were moving and left it behind. I traded work for most of the power tools."

"What happens when you run out of tires?"

Roy asked me to follow him through another plastic curtain out the back of the plastic room. There was a stack of eight tires of varying sizes. "That's not going to last me. I need your help. I'll pay you."

"You want me to pick up used tires in Price and bring them to you?"

"No need," he said. "I found some. I just need some help getting 'em in from the desert. Not far."

I couldn't refuse him. The day was already shot and an hour or so wouldn't change that much. He got in my truck and we backtracked down his street a quarter of a mile and turned down an alleyway separating houses that had been foreclosed upon and stood empty, some falling into themselves. I asked him why he didn't move into the house next to the garage. The old woman who had lived there was in a nursing home in Price.

"Never been invited," he answered. "I'm not a squatter, Ben." He said this with a grim conviction, as much to himself as to me.

The way he said it straightened my spine a little and I took note. Roy was a man who had hit upon hard times and was doing his best to fight his way back. He deserved my respect, not my pity. For him there was a damn important distinction between living in a garage and being a squatter and until he pointed it out I wouldn't have noticed. Maybe, just maybe, I was one of the people who felt superior in the presence of his misfortune. The truth was my life was almost as close to the bone as his. If not for Ginny's resource-fulness a few months earlier, who knew where I might have ended up? Maybe riding a bike and living in a garage. If I got down off on my short high horse I might see that Roy was damned smart and he'd been resourceful, hardworking, determined, even ingenious, getting as far as he had with his doghouse of the future. I resolved to show him the respect he deserved, if only by keeping my damn mouth shut.

Roy went on to explain his situation. The family lawyer paid the electricity bill every month and in return Roy kept an eye on things, including keeping the yard up the best he could. That was the understanding until the old woman died or the family figured something else out.

The alley spilled onto a dirt road and from there out northwest into the desert paralleling but gradually moving away from the mesa cliffs. There were all kinds of roads in the desert like the one we were on, intersecting, converging, winding, occasionally circling back on one another, and all of them eventually leading nowhere. Who made them, where they thought they were going and why weren't even memories anymore, lost and gone like the people who created them.

We bumped and rattled along. The road was becoming less like a road and more like a rutted trail, much like the ones I used every day to deliver necessities and occasional luxuries to the desert rats, hardscrabble ranchers, and other assorted exiles who chose to live off 117. The snow and rain hadn't softened the surface but I was watchful and cautious. I asked him how much farther and he answered not far. After five miles I asked Roy, "What were you doing all the way out here?"

He shrugged. "Sometimes I like to just go for a drive."

I guess in his mind pedaling his bike was a drive, or he preferred to think he was driving. Maybe he just misspoke. It didn't matter. I continued to drive for a while and then said out loud what I had been thinking. "You rode your bike all the way out here?"

"Yep," he said. "I got ahold of an old wheelchair and made myself a plywood wagon to pull behind the bike. It doesn't hold much. The big wheels make covering this terrain easier because they roll so good and the weight is more evenly distributed. It takes ten tires to make a doghouse. All I can haul in a trip is three or four."

I did the math in round trips. "Takes a lot of work to be an entrepreneur," I observed.

And a lot of time, of which he had plenty. I didn't think for a minute he had a chance in hell of getting his solar doghouse business off the ground, so to speak. Still, it provided something for him to do and if I couldn't exactly cheer him on at least I would do all in my power to refrain from saying anything that even remotely sounded like I was pissing on his dream. You can take pride in a dream, even if it never comes true, as long as you work at it, and Roy was sure enough working at it.

"Just over that hill," he said.

It was a short incline, but steep. I thought of him on his bike sweating and grunting in the desert wind and sun as he stood on the pedals to reach the top. We crested the hill and what lay before us took my breath. I was expecting a few old tires left behind by a rancher. What I saw were low, snakelike mountains of tires in row after row extending the length of a small canyon. It put me in mind of the spore from a fleet of Goodyear blimps.

Roy saw an entirely other view that filled him with excitement. "A lifetime supply of doghouses. And all free!"

I was excited too. I tend to get excited when I'm pissed off and, as we drove down the hill and in among the mountains of tires, my mood went from excited to stunned and mutely sickened.

It didn't take long to load up twenty tires. There was room for more in the back of my trailer, but twenty was all I could stand. We had to be careful. Rattlesnakes had apparently assumed the tires were a fancy subdivision and moved in. Since winter hadn't officially come on they hadn't begun to hibernate and they took agitated exception to us disturbing them. Their rattles, from maybe hundreds of snakes, seemed to be coming in from every direction and together they made an undulating hissing sound like a convention of cicadas blasted over a loudspeaker.

At the end of the canyon was a commercial trailer. Before we left I walked down and took a look at it. The tires were flat, the rims half buried in the sand. The whole thing was crusted over with dirt. It had obviously been abandoned there for a long time, probably years. No plates. The coal mine was maybe ten or fifteen miles away to the north, a huge open-pit affair that covered a couple square miles or more.

If I had to guess, the tires came from the coal company over a long period of time. It occurred to me that Roy didn't just stumble upon the dump; he knew about it, even contributed to it when he was a driver for the coal company. I didn't say anything. No point. What did interest me was the style of trailer it was—a side dumper, like one of the possible trailers being towed by the rogue old White Freightliner Andy was looking for. I stewed on that all the way back to Roy's place.

Roy and I didn't say a word to each other on the return. Conversation wasn't on my menu and he was smart to realize that. I angrily threw his tires in front of his garage and made a beeline straight for the Rockmuse Mercantile to drop off their vegetables and use their phone. The phone first.

I hit the old door so hard it almost flew off its hinges. There was only one phone call I wanted to make. The place was empty of customers and Peggy and Joe stood close together, as though they had been in the middle of a serious and private conversation. Lenny was nowhere to be seen, not that I cared. I demanded the phone, which they set on top of the deli counter, while they tried to talk to me. I wasn't having any of it. One look from me and they went silent and backed away, though still staying close.

The Highway Patrol patched me through to Andy, who was on 191. As soon as he heard my voice, he said, "I know. I'm en route, but it's snowing hard on this end. Might not get through—"

I cut him off. "How in the hell would you know? I just got back in to the Mercantile to phone you. Goddammit, Andy, you wouldn't believe the fucking mountains of tires I found."

Peggy caught my eye and I was about to apologize for the ob-scenities when she rested her hand on my arm. "Preach has been hit out on 117."

I lowered the receiver a few inches from my ear. I could hear Andy saying something along the lines of what Peggy had just told me.

"You already call Life Flight?" I asked Andy.

I guessed what he was going to say before he said it. The Mur-phy's Law of 117. Help is rarely on the way. The one helicopter was already on its way to an accident on US 6 on the western side of Soldier Summit. By the time the injured were stabilized and loaded and the helicopter returned to the hospital in Price and refueled, the approaching weather would be too bad for the crew to take off again. Andy must have made the turn onto 117 where radio reception was spotty at best and usually nonexistent. The receiver filled with static and then the connection was severed.

I had only one question. Peggy or John could answer it better than Andy. "Is he alive or dead?"

16

T he two of them glanced at each other before Joe answered my question. "I heard he was alive, though just barely. Some desert rat brought him in laid out across the hood of his old Willys jeep. He wanted Preach's spine and neck to stay as straight as possible and not jar him around too much."

I was already headed toward the door, assuming John had been taken to his storefront church. Peggy must have guessed. "He's not at his church," she said. "He's at Ginger's, the old movie theater."

I thanked her and she reached out and caught my arm. "Ben, I heard he's in bad shape. Broken and bloody from head to toe. It was a hit-and-run."

Instead of driving I walked the few blocks to Ginger's as quickly as I could. Such an accident was long overdue, assuming it was an accident. What certainly wasn't an accident was the fact that he had been hit, and hit hard, and whoever had done it knew what had happened—and then just left John there on the side of the road like so much roadkill. Then what?

John was traveling southeast and the vehicle that hit him probably came from behind, meaning it was going east as well—likely all the way into Rockmuse, though before town there were a few small ranches and desert rats holed up in mobile homes and stone cabins off the highway. I knew them all, and they all knew John, if only, as is said, in passing. I just couldn't see any of them hitting him and then driving off. The inescapable truth was that whoever had hit John was probably in Rockmuse and maybe lived there. Or had come into Rockmuse from the desert to run errands or get supplies. Chances were that I either knew the person or knew of them. Then there was the circus train and the candy-apple cab-over. The cab-over seemed only to be spotted at night. The circus train was headed into the desert for what the idiot wagon master had called "camping."

The rusted old Willys that had delivered John was parked askew at the curb in front of Ginger's place. There were dried rivulets of blood on its hood. A small group was gathered in front of the theater ticket window talking quietly. They nodded at me and I at them as I pulled open the door and entered the empty lobby. It was dark inside, lit only by the light in the glass display case that once held candy and now held, as best I could tell, an artfully arrayed exhibit of Ginger's handmade soaps, most in various religious symbols and personages—crosses, goblets, Elvis, Jesus, and Buddha—the big three—and so on. No sign of John or anyone else.

I heard some voices behind the curtain leading into the theater. It had been a small movie house with maybe a hundred wooden seats, ten to a row. At some point the seats had been unbolted from the floor and stacked in their rows against the walls. The white screen was in tatters. The high house lights were mostly burnt out and it took my eyes a moment to adjust as I threaded all the card tables loaded with Ginger's whatnots, glass, used clothes, a whole table dedicated to more religious figures, dishes, and enough homemade soaps to keep the entire town of Rockmuse clean for years. John was on a gigantic four-poster bed that took up most of the stage. It occurred to me he was lying in state; I hoped not. Ginger and an old man were standing next to the bed.

I hopped up onto the stage and joined them. There had been a lot of bleeding and the green flowered comforter had large stains where the blood had pooled. I half expected to find John looking like a piece of raw meat, which wasn't the case. A plastic bowl of pink water sat on a table next to the bed and I assumed Ginger had been cleansing his injuries. She had cut off his jeans and shirt and they were in a nearby pile. He was still wearing his worn-down army surplus combat boots. He appeared almost serene, dressed only in his underwear beneath the stage lights. He didn't seem to be breathing.

"Did he die?" I asked.

Ginger kept her eyes on John as she answered. A gold crucifix, only slightly smaller than the one John hauled, dangled from a chain around her neck. "No, thank God." Though we had never actually met, she acknowledged me by name. "You're Ben."

I recognized the old man and assumed he was the desert rat who had found John and brought him to town. Over the years I had only delivered to him a few times and couldn't remember his name, if I ever knew it. He remembered my name, though, and slowly shook his newly trimmed beard.

"Hell of a thing, Ben. Hell of a thing. The preacher got knocked maybe fifty feet off the shoulder. Would have missed him completely if I hadn't seen the cross layin' there. That old jeep of mine only has two gears and I was just pokin' along as usual."

"Coming into town for supplies?" I asked.

"More important. Dancin' lessons." He winked at me. "With Ginger here."

He was old but he wasn't dead. Maybe he didn't weigh more than a hundred pounds soaking wet and skinny as a rail and with his best days in his rearview mirror, but things hadn't changed that much. Dancing was just an excuse for him to be close to a woman. His hands were clean, and so was his denim work shirt, except for a few spatters of what I assumed was blood. An aroma of cheap aftershave and talcum powder hovered like a hopeful cloud around his narrow shoulders.

"I don't know if he should be moved," Ginger said. "I was up on my ladder when George drove up. All he's got for a bed at his place is an old army cot. I thought this would be a better place for him. I think I've done all I know how to do. Life Flight should be here soon."

"It won't be here soon," I said. "It won't be here at all. Not today. It's at an accident two hundred miles away and Price is about to have a snowstorm."

"What about an ambulance?" Ginger asked.

"And no damn ambulance either," I said. Hearing my harsh tone, I added, "It's too far, especially with a weather front coming in."

I leaned over John. There were a lot of gashes in his head and upper body and blood was still oozing from under his beard, which was rapidly turning from white to pink. His left leg had an ugly protrusion just below the knee. A break, I supposed. There were also some bruises coming up beneath his rib cage that indicated, at least to me, there could be some internal bleeding.

"But he needs a doctor!"

"There is no doctor," I said.

"Then what do people do out here?"

"They die," I said. "Or they get better. John would probably recommend prayer. I think you'd get a better response from Elvis, but if it helps pass the time then go ahead."

My remark made her sputter. "You!" she shouted. "You're supposed to be his friend."

"I am," I said, and I hoped truthfully. "That doesn't mean I share his love of Jesus. John knew something like this could happen. The only miracle is that it took this long. I tried to give him a ride into town just this morning. The crazy son of a bitch turned me down." Soon as the words left my mouth I knew I was angrier with John than with whoever had run him down.

"Shut up," she said. "Just shut up. You have a truck, don't you? Why not take him to the hospital? Even with a storm it's worth the risk, isn't it? Or maybe you'd just like to stand here and insult the man and his ministry until he dies."

The desert rat thought she had a point. "It's worth a try, Ben. You usually get through."

That was true, though I might get stuck along the way. Two days was the longest I'd ever been stalled waiting for the weather or road to clear. It seemed like forever then and it would be forever with a gravely injured passenger. I was seriously considering it, knowing John could die at any time on the way to the hospital. It wouldn't be the first time I'd hauled a corpse. I knew I would need someone to go with me and see to John while I drove.

"I don't know," I said. "If that's our only option."

Lenny joined us on the stage. He asked me if we could speak alone for a moment.

I followed him off the stage and out among the tables. "I'm going to need someone to ride along to care for John," I said. "Probably inside the trailer is best. We can set up a bed. You volunteering?"

"Sure," he said. "But I have another idea first."

The second fifty percent of the Rockmuse population boom that had occurred during the summer was a man I had never seen, though I delivered water and propane to him. Delivering him propane was technically against the law, but technically I did it all the time for others and I technically didn't care. The man lived in a small Terry trailer tucked under the lip of the mesa just a couple miles out of town. He paid in cash that he left under a rock near his door. Lenny, who delivered his groceries and booze to him from the Mercantile, which included lots and lots of vodka, and only at night, by the man's request, had set up the arrangement with me. Lenny had never actually seen him. He paid the Mercantile by check and the checks were always good, which for Rockmuse was an oddity in itself.

"The name printed on the checks says his name is Rupert

Conway, MD. Maybe you should stop by and see if he could take a look at the preacher."

"Why me?" I asked. "You're the one that knows he's a doctor."

"He scares the shit out of me, that's why." It was obvious that Lenny was not joking. "I'm used to the hardcore desert rats, Ben. But he's different."

I knew there was something Lenny wasn't telling me. "Let's hear it all," I said.

"He always holds a weapon on me. A shotgun. Maybe that's why I've never seen him clearly. All I see is this big damn Remington over-under. I get the impression he doesn't want visitors."

I admitted that was a logical assumption. "He's a fucking alcoholic," I said. "I'm not sure he'd be of any use anyway."

"Don't you think a drunk doctor is better than no doctor at all?"

"No. Besides, maybe he hasn't practiced in years. His medical license is probably no good, if he ever had one."

Lenny sheepishly admitted he had Googled the doctor. "That's what I was doing. Up until five years ago he was with Doctors Without Borders. Then something happened. Not much on exactly what that was. There must be a hundred entries for him. He's the real deal, drunk or not. It's worth a try, Ben. At least he might be able to tell us if it's safe to transport Preach."

It wouldn't be the first time I had been confronted by an antisocial armed drunk. Such events didn't qualify as commonplace, though, given the nature and location of my clientele, it wasn't uncommon either. As far as I knew none of them had been doctors, not that that would make a difference. An eighty-year-old former nun once greeted me wearing nothing but her habit headgear, a smile, and an ancient Luger. It wasn't my charm that kept them from shooting; it was the realization that shone through the alcohol or crazy cloud that if they shot me there would be no one to deliver to them. While I hated to breach a man's privacy, especially one who seemed dead set on being left alone, I agreed with Lenny that it was, for better or worse, worth a shot. Maybe needing water and propane would allow me enough consideration to make my pitch and leave alive.

I asked Lenny to unload my trailer as best he could and get the vegetables into the Mercantile. One way or another I wanted to be prepared to transport John. "If I'm not back in an hour," I said, "do not come looking for me. Understand? But you might mention it to Trooper Smith when and if he makes it to town."

Lenny went to offload my trailer and I walked up to the stage and addressed the old man. "Any objection to me borrowing your jeep?"

He said he had no objections and asked no questions. "What's your name?" I asked. I was slightly embarrassed for not remembering and said so.

For some reason that seemed to tickle him. "It don't matter, does it?"

I agreed it didn't, but I still wanted to know.

Over the years I had run across a certain reticence on the part of some desert dwellers to let loose of any information no matter how harmless. Then again, some had good reason to want to keep their identities to themselves.

"George," he said.

17

The crowd outside the theater had grown. As I headed for the desert rat's jeep, I heard someone call my name. There were four men and two women, none of whom I knew well, all residents of Rockmuse. "How's Preach doing?"

"He's not dead," I said. "Yet."

"Can we count on you to get the sick bastard that did this?"

"What sick bastard is that?"

"The one driving the red semi."

I got the whole picture in a second. Not one person standing before me had been in the Mercantile when I brought up Trooper Smith's interest in the candy-apple-red White Freightliner. In less than two hours word had spread and now that there was a tragedy the driver of the semi was not only the lead suspect but about to be lynched. Within an hour he would probably be blamed for everything from the high unemployment rate to daylight saving time. I made a note to myself to be more careful about what subjects I brought up in order to change the subject. In the very near future pickups filled with the heavily armed and vengefully righteous would be tear-assing around the desert looking for a phantom red semi and, failing that, anything that appeared at all red or suspicious. This was my fault. I vaguely hoped that the driver and his truck were hundreds of miles away. If the vigilantes met up with him there would be dying, and that might well include a few of the jaspers arrayed in front of me.

Since I felt responsible, even though I was in a hurry, I thought a bit before I spoke. "I see you're all prepared to get the person responsible for running the preacher down," I said, "but I've got it on good authority that rig wasn't within a hundred miles of here."

No one bothered to question exactly what "good authority" I was citing. My comment had the intended effect. The violent party spirit quickly disappeared and was replaced with something more useful: silence, which maybe included some rational thought.

A man I didn't know by name said, "Well, it had to be a stranger. No one from around here would hit Preach and just leave him to rot on the side of the road."

There were nods of enthusiastic agreement.

I realized now that I had only removed the red semi from the list of possible perpetrators, allowing suspicion to fall on any stranger who might have recently and unfortunately wandered into town. This struck me as a consequence of a population with too much time on its hands, or just a pure streak of human nature. Either way there wasn't much I could do. For my own part, I considered how much of a stranger is present in every person we think we know. When and if the driver who hit John became known, everyone, maybe even me, could be unpleasantly surprised.

It was a short drive out to the crazy doctor's place, though it took a long time in the desert rat's old Willys jeep. The jeep had a top speed of twenty miles an hour, not that it mattered much. It took almost the entire two miles to get up to its cruising speed, and even at that it registered not only every bump in the road but also bumps that weren't even in the road. I had to wonder if John wouldn't have been better off being left in the sand and weeds rather than jostled around balanced on the hood of the Willys. As for its brakes, it didn't really have any and I finally brought it to a complete stop by dragging my left boot out the door. An anchor to throw over the side would have been a nice option.

The old faded blue Terry travel trailer rested alone in a sea of sand and rock on a dirt-and-gravel side road that dead-ended up against the towering mesa cliff. If I'd been in a charitable mood maybe the trailer could have been referred to as "vintage." Judging from the rust spots on the door and front panels that had been sloppily covered over in white fiberglass patch, "old" was more accurate. The small louvered windows had been duct-taped over. His backyard was about ten feet of sloping talus and then the sheer wall of granite rising nearly two thousand feet that lorded over the small trailer like a menacing frozen tidal wave of stone. Off to the right side some kind of large vehicle was protected by a fitted tarp. I waited well back from the front door, as is the custom in the desert. Given the known proclivity of the residents for violence, or at least the threat of it, I gave my arrival a good couple minutes before approaching, pausing every few steps to shout a "hello."

I didn't expect much in the way of pleasantries and I didn't get any. From behind the door a gravelly voice said, "Get the fuck out of here."

I told the voice my name and that I delivered his water and propane. This softened him up a little. "Are you delivering?"

I told him I wasn't. Before I could say anything else, he said: "Then you have no reason to be here."

"There's been a bad accident," I said. "I know you're a doctor."

He didn't argue and I thought he was listening. It turned out he was filling his hands with his response. Like most travel trailers the door opened outward. When he kicked the door open from the inside I was standing just far enough back it missed me. Years of experience dealing with such types had taught me a thing or two. Out of the interior blackness I saw the shotgun barrel come forward into the light. Lenny knew his guns. It was indeed a Remington over-under and, though I couldn't see his finger, I didn't doubt it was on one or both triggers, though at that range one barrel was enough to blow me in half.

"I asked you nicely to leave. Don't make me ask you again."

"Ben," I said.

"Ben," he said. "Now get the hell out of here."

I studied the figure still veiled in the darkness of the trailer. He was wearing wraparound sunglasses and a black hoodie and from the way he held the shotgun up against his groin I guessed he hadn't ever fired it. This was not good for me. I didn't want him to learn the hard way on me that if he fired the recoil would cause him considerable discomfort. As for me, my discomfort would be quick and final.

"If you're really a doctor, then you have to come. That's a rule, isn't it?"

This seemed to amuse him a little, or maybe he was just clearing his throat. "I'm holding the only rule you need to be concerned about."

I didn't move. At that moment I was thinking about John dying and maybe his only hope standing there with a shotgun pointed at my waist. I offered to deliver all the propane and water he'd need for a year, for free. When he didn't respond I offered him all the money I had in my pocket, about a hundred dollars.

"Just look at the preacher," I said. "If you can't help him then tell me if I can safely transport him to the hospital in Price. Take my offer or pull the trigger." Part of me was telling him the truth. The shotgun moved a little and I wished I had perhaps phrased my last words differently to allow some room for negotiation.

His next comment surprised me. "The preacher? The old man that hauls the cross?"

"That's the one," I said. "You know him?"

He didn't respond. He appeared to be thinking, which meant he wasn't going to shoot me just yet. Not being able to see his face, especially his eyes, was a hindrance. All I had to go on was the way he held the shotgun. He'd lowered the barrels an inch or two but that only meant my knees could wave goodbye to my ass on its way to the Willys parked thirty yards behind me. The longer he hesitated the better my chances were. I just had to grow roots in the sand and allow the silence and time to work their magic.

"He got hit." This was an expression of fact and not a question. I nodded. "And then left on the shoulder of 117 to die."

"Are you a friend of his?"

I nodded, again.

As far as what constitutes friendship in the desert, we probably qualified as friends, separated sometimes by weeks and months with no more in common than imaginary cigarettes and the road and the sky.

"Is he conscious?"

"No," I said. "A woman in town who's living in the theater cleaned him up some. That's where he is." I mentioned what I thought was a head injury, broken leg, and probably internal bleeding. "Maybe spinal cord." To that I added, "The old guy who found him brought him in on the hood of that jeep I'm driving. Tried not to move him too much, but—" I shrugged.

"I'll examine him," he said. "First, you should know I haven't practiced in a long time. I no longer have a license to practice medicine, nor do I want to. Who else knows I used to be a physician?"

"Just Lenny," I said. "The young man who works at the Mercantile and brings your groceries."

"Your friend is probably going to die. That's what people do, they die—and most of the time they die badly—the preacher knows that better than most. I might be able to make him more comfortable, that's about all. Just so you know, if he's suffered head or spinal trauma and he's bleeding out in his gut only a first-class hospital trauma unit can give him a chance. You said you might try to transport him. I'd probably advise against that. How long until he can be medevac-ed?"

I explained the situation with the Life Flight helicopter and the storm. While he listened the business end of the shotgun slowly lowered until it was pointed at a spot in the sand midway between his door and my feet.

"If there are people around him I want them cleared out. I'll come on my own in my own time. I don't want an audience of any kind, and I absolutely do not want anyone to think this town has found itself a doctor. Is there a back way into the theater?"

I told him there was and that we'd block open the emergency exit in the alley. "I'll stand guard in the front," I said. "Lenny can make sure no one enters from the alley. That's the best I can do."

"I want you there with me. I might need your help. You need to witness what I do and maybe time of death. When I'm done I'll leave the way I came. Don't come back here and don't ever ask for my help again. For now, let's be optimistic. How's your short-term memory?"

"What?"

"Here's my list. See if you can round up some saline bags somewhere, preferably with an IV kit. If not, as many sterile syringes as you can find. Some alcohol and latex gloves. And adhesive tape. Or any kind of cloth tape. And five or six bath towels. Can you remember that?"

"Yes," I said. "What if I can't find the saline or syringes?"

"If you can't, then you can't."

"Why me?" I asked. "I don't have any medical experience. Ginger might be better."

"I won't need anyone with medical training. I don't want to meet anyone new or shake any hands or have a conversation. Just you." He paused, then added: "You know, I might have killed you a few minutes ago."

I said I didn't think so. "You've never fired that shotgun before. I can tell by the way you hold it. The recoil would send your gonads into your backbone."

He let go with both barrels. The sound was deafening. Sand

and pieces of rock flew up from the ground and into my face and set me to blinking and spitting to clear the debris. The explosion echoed off the cliff behind us and lingered in my ears, though not so much I couldn't hear what he said next.

"You're wrong."

I stood corrected.

18

When Conway showed up almost an hour later I was still arguing with Ginger, who had her back to him. He'd come in the rear entrance and was standing offstage in the shadows. Twice I'd been successful in getting her to leave and twice she returned while George, the desert rat, seemed content to listen from the theater floor as he absently perused the tables of junk. I figured he'd leave when I told him to and without any discussion. My argument with Ginger was apparently what passed for high entertainment in his world.

"Why do I have to leave?" she asked. I had answered the question several times before and what little patience I had was gone.

"Because he doesn't want anyone here."

"Why?"

"Because that's the way he wants it."

It had seemed like an odd request to me too, not that oddness commanded much attention from me anymore. As I stumbled back to the Willys, still spitting sand from my lips, I was thinking how lucky I was and how fatal it could be to misjudge someone in the desert. Whatever his reasons were, I was fine with them. People, like the desert, were full of mysteries and my motto was "Leave the Mysteries Alone." I did what I had come to do and left under my own power. There was a big simple truth about the doctor: for whatever reason, he was willing to make an exception for John. If it had been anyone else he would have said no and if I had pressed the issue he would have shot me.

Doctor or not, he was a man who no longer cared about consequences, for himself or anybody else. A man like that was dangerous and only a fool would fail to take proper precautions, number one of which was not asking questions. Ginger was new to town. The desert and its people hadn't yet weaned her of curiosity. For her, there was an answer to every question and she thought that she was entitled to ask questions and worse, felt she deserved answers that made sense to her.

"Okay," she said. "I agree. If that's the way it has to be."

George walked up to the stage and addressed Ginger. "I brought my two dollars for my dancing lesson. I'd hate to drive all the way home with nothin' to show for it but the preacher. How 'bout you and me cut a rug out here and let Ben do what he has to do?"

George's true intention, to distract Ginger, was transparent to all three of us. He offered up a sunburned and callused right paw to Ginger and bowed slightly. "Out here is good. If necessary we can move a few tables to make room. You'll still be close. Think that'll be okay, Ben?"

I said I thought it would be and glanced toward the doctor to see if I could get a read on him. He didn't speak or move.

To my astonishment, Ginger accepted George's hand and, with surprising grace for a large woman, hopped off the stage. The two of them retreated toward the back of the room.

As the "Merry Widow Waltz" scratched over the theater's old speakers Rupert Conway, MD, walked out from behind the curtains, his body hunched forward like a question mark, taking short, awkward steps that had him pitching from side to side as if undecided about which way to tumble—but no cane. I fought the impulse to reach out and catch him. He stood at the end of the bed for a few seconds and stared at John. He glanced inside the cardboard box that contained most of his supply list. Lenny had somehow managed to scavenge some of it from the Mercantile and

then in a resourceful lightning strike raided the school infirmary.
There hadn't been money for a nurse for years and he didn't know
how old the supplies were.

Conway produced a pair of scissors from a large plastic sandwich bag and dumped rubbing alcohol on them before putting on
the latex gloves. He began cutting away the rest of John's clothing,
including the laces on his boots. In less than a minute John was
shoeless and naked. As Conway worked I got a whiff of stench from
a mixture of body odor and alcohol, both rubbing and drinking
varieties. I'd noticed his hands were red and appeared to have
been freshly scrubbed through at least one layer of skin—mostly
black skin, packed with threads of dense white scars. Some of the
latex fingers drooped and flapped aimlessly against his hands. The
fingers that might have filled them were missing.

He still wore the wraparound sunglasses, held in place on the
sides by a black stocking watch cap. Most of both ears were gone
and wide scars ran the length on each side of his face. The scars
dwindled into a sparse, mangy black-and-white beard. Branches of
smaller pink scars climbed upward from his throat like tributar-
ies of a great river and petered out in the hair under his jawline.
I hadn't realized that he was so short, maybe five feet, and would
have been shorter still if not for the irregularly elevated soles of his
dusty work boots. Black denim jeans hung from his legs and ass
like sails. The right-side sole was elevated perhaps as much as six
inches and still he moved quickly and with precision around John
though occasionally he leaned against the bed to steady himself. I
chose to look away rather than at John as he lay unconscious and
naked on the bed.

How long is the "Merry Widow Waltz"? Four minutes? Five?
Ginger and George glided in and out and between the tables. She
towered above the old man and though they kept a puritanical
distance between them, even in the dim light I could see his chin
gravitate to her sizable breasts as if drawn there by a magnet. She
would correct this by almost lifting him off his feet and resetting

him at a proper angle, all without either of them missing or mis-timing a waltzing step.

When I returned my attention to John, Conway was busy pok-ing, prodding, and peering into every inch of John's body from head to toe. After a long look into his ears he folded up two towels until they looked like loaves of bread and wrapped them with ad-hesive tape. He placed one on either side of John's head and taped them in place, I guessed to stabilize John's neck.

Conway said, "Give me a hand turning him over."

I did as I was instructed as the waltz began to play again. Though I wouldn't recommend it as a fitness regimen, dragging a crucifixion cross for months out of every year had muscled John to a point that might be the envy of any garden-variety body builder. With a height of maybe six foot four and all the lean muscle, he had to weigh every bit of two hundred and twenty-five to two hun-dred and fifty pounds. He needed every bit of it to haul that cross, even with the wheel. Conway didn't have much strength and the actual turning of John's heavy body was a workout in itself. I bal-anced John on his side while Conway continued his exam.

I felt obliged to keep my attention on what I had been in-structed to do, which left me nowhere else to look but at John. His right arm slipped behind his back and interfered with Conway. As I lifted it out of his way my eyes took in John's bare wrist and the jagged vertical scars extending up his thick forearm. If I were a betting man, I would have bet the other arm told the same story. Conway asked me to hold John's head and neck steady.

A chapter in John's life had made itself known. Thick braided scars encircled his neck into an upward spiral that disappeared into his beard. I'd seen scars similar to those on his wrists before, on a woman I had gone with for a while when I was young. Hers weren't like John's, they were thread thin and horizontal and she laughed when she referred to them as "love letters to myself in braille." John's scars were in caps and bold and testified to the fact that at one time in his life he had been damn serious about taking the fast lane to the next life. When I looked away Conway was staring up at me.

"You can lower him onto his back. Gently."

Conway was breathing heavily but trying like hell to control it. I could see beads of sweat trickling down from his forehead and beneath the sunglasses.

"You holding up okay?" I asked.

"No."

I asked Conway if I could do anything for him and he responded by ignoring my question.

"Here's my opinion, though it's really a guess. My biggest concern right now is kidney failure from rhabdomyolysis—muscle deterioration. Common in untreated injuries like this." Conway pointed to the protrusion I had noticed earlier on John's left leg. "He has a tent fracture, probably where the bumper of the vehicle made contact. It might not make any difference in the long run but that needs to be set. Without antibiotics he could lose that leg. Good thing he's unconscious otherwise it would hurt like hell." He paused and added, "I'll need your help with that if you're up to it."

I nodded. "Anything else?"

"The immediate-term worry is dehydration. The saline IV will help with that. I'll get that going right after we set the leg. As for the rest, my expert medical opinion is he'll either live or die. Sooner or later. Don't try and move him. If he regains consciousness within the next twenty-four hours, that would be a good sign. I could give him a more complete neurological exam. If he doesn't regain consciousness—" He shrugged. "Then infection and rhabdo and dehydration and God knows what else will probably kill him before the head trauma. Getting him medevac-ed out of here as soon as possible would be best, but . . ."

"What?"

"You say you know this man?"

I nodded.

Conway said, "I met him. Just once. Based on that I'd say he wouldn't want to go to a hospital, that he'd prefer whatever is going to happen happens right here. You understand?"

I said I understood, though I wasn't exactly certain I did.

"Think about it."

Setting the leg didn't take long, though it was hard work, mostly my muscle, made easier by Conway's experience. Conway took one of the larger towels and wrapped one end around John's foot and taped it in place. He secured the other end of the towel to the end of the bed and inserted another towel in between and began turning while I held John at the waist. It took a bit to get the tension going. Conway asked me to pull John's torso back as hard as I could and hold it and I heard him wheezing followed by a loud grunt. When I looked at the leg again the protrusion was gone.

With no wasted movement Conway wrapped the leg in a bandage and splinted it with another towel. A minute after that he had the saline bag hanging on a bedpost and the needle inserted and taped down. No doubt about it, messed up as he was, probably both drunk and hungover, missing fingers and maybe a laundry list of other body parts, he knew what he was doing.

Conway stood sweating and huffing at the end of the bed while I covered John with a blanket.

"Thank you," I said.

I didn't expect him to say anything and he didn't. He didn't have a chance. His knees buckled and he collapsed on the stage floor.

Conway was a pitiful ragbag of a man, no more than clothes over bones. The fall had knocked his sunglasses askew and his one good eye wobbled in its socket. The other was a milky white. I gently straightened the sunglasses. Conway's breathing was labored and he was drenched in perspiration from the exertion of tending to John. He wasn't unconscious, just totally exhausted, with barely enough energy to speak. In a hoarse whisper he asked me to take him home. He felt like next to nothing at all draped over my shoulder.

I half expected Conway's collapse to draw in the dancers. The music had stopped. Ginger and George were whispering in the back and focused on their conversation. If I had to guess, they were covering the same topic that's been discussed between men and women since the beginning of time. One of Ginger's whispered words was clear enough, even at a distance: "No." I glanced one more time at John stretched out in the bed and made my way off-stage and down the steps of the back entrance.

The vehicle that had been covered by the tarp next to Conway's trailer was parked in the alley. I felt almost giddy and a bit guilty at the prospect of driving it, if only for two miles and with a broken recluse of a doctor slumped in the passenger seat. The old Mormon couple who raised me had taken me to a local car show in Spanish Forks when I was a teenager and there had been twenty or thirty old cars, all American makes, surrounded by small crowds and owners who seemed more ancient than their cars. There were a handful of DeSotos, all convertibles, and they captured my attention to the exclusion of everything else.

Unless I missed my guess, the one squeezed into the alley was most likely a 1957 or '58 black DeSoto convertible, a beast from another time, another world maybe, when people thought God was in his heaven keeping them safe and the bigger the tail fins the better and the measure of a car was how close it came to being the length of a football field. It screamed of a future that was never to be, except maybe for a short time in the mind of the person lucky enough to be behind the steering wheel on a '50s summer evening.

The white ragtop was up and fine flakes of snow spun in the light wind and skittered over its contours as if afraid to touch down anywhere on its huge, sleek body. The massive passenger-side door was unlocked and there was barely enough room to open it. I lowered Conway onto the red-and-white leather bench seat that took his smallness like a miniature poodle floating in a chrome and leather swimming pool. How Conway came to own such a vehicle and why he still had it given his circumstances was probably a story I would never hear, another mystery happy to stay that way. His head slumped backward and his upturned sunglasses reflected the view of the metal stays supporting the canvas ceiling.

The keys were not in the ignition, not that I expected them to be. I flipped down the visor. They weren't there either. Going through an unconscious man's pockets is not something I'd done much of in my life; in fact, never, and it wasn't something I wanted to do now.

Conway was snoring in small gasps, and rather than disturb him I decided to check his pockets. The keys were there, along with the warm plastic of what I assumed was a colostomy bag. What wasn't there sent a current through me like an electric shock straight from my hand into my brain and back down to the pit of my stomach. There was a damn good reason why the recoil of the shotgun into his groin hadn't bothered him.

19

I closed the car door and stood for a moment in the alley.

The sky was clear and the sun was low and well toward the west and glowed red against the upper edges of the alley walls. In the couple hours I'd been inside the theater the expected weather front had begun to move across the desert and toward Rockmuse. The trifling spray of flakes didn't come from the cloudless sky but instead blew off the high stone lips of the mesa two thousand feet above and then filtered downward into town through the crisp air. I didn't need to see the top of the mesa to know that one hell of a snowstorm was already raging on the plateau and in an hour or maybe less it would descend to the desert floor with an icy vengeance.

Somewhere in the back of my head I'd been thinking that Conway's injuries were the result of birth defects or disease or an accident of some kind. Without knowing exactly why, I didn't think that anymore. There was an almost diabolic pattern to them that suggested they were the consequence of a grim purpose. I now knew with an unexplainable certainty that whatever misfortune had befallen Rupert Conway, MD, it hadn't been any goddamned accident. It was difficult to imagine what manner of black-hearted demon would do such terrible deeds to another human being that would result in the kind of physical damage and suffering for which he was a walking billboard, the product of a blind God or an indifferent one.

I didn't say it, but I thought it: *You poor son of a bitch.* And I thanked him again for what hadn't been just a favor but an act of death-defying courage.

The big V-8 caught on the first try and the exhaust pipe crackled with power. I goosed the accelerator a few times just to hear the roar and then let the RPMs drop into a civilized growl before idling down the alley and out into the empty street. As I turned the corner Conway's head slumped against my shoulder and I just left it there as I drove to the front of the theater. The Willys was still at the curb but the crowd was gone and no one was on the street. I touched the horn to alert Lenny, who I hoped was still around. I needed a ride back to my truck. The blast startled me and bounced off the storefronts from one end of Main Street to the other.

Lenny poked his head out of the theater entrance. I pointed at Conway next to me. He gave me a thumbs-up. I drove the two miles back to the doctor's place as slowly as I could, savoring the ride despite the circumstances.

Out of respect I parked the DeSoto where I had seen it earlier. The tarp was folded and tucked under the hitch of the trailer. The inside of the car was warm and the cold wind ate at the hairline spaces between the side windows and the canvas top. The high squealing sound of the wind unnerved me a little. The engine popped as it cooled.

Conway's eyes were closed and I gently righted him on the seat. "You're home," I said.

His breathing was regular if not easy and it seemed a shame to wake him and carry him into the little aluminum cave where he lived, not that I could imagine what he had in there was much of a life.

I got out and stretched and stared back down the gravel road to see if there was any sign of Lenny. There wasn't. It was darkening fast and a few distant lights in town flickered, dimmed, and disappeared beneath the approaching clouds to the north. Tilting my head back I stared up at the mesa cliffs and watched the snow and fog tumble over its face like a creeping waterfall of rose-colored light bringing with it a freezing downdraft that swirled at my feet and crawled up my pant legs like phantom snakes.

If I didn't get going to Price I might not make it to the junction with US 191 by nightfall—and I still had to pick up Annabelle and the girl. There was a damn good chance I might not make it at all and the very real prospect of being stalled for a day or two somewhere on 117 with two kids in my cab drained what was left of my energy and left me bone tired and not a little concerned about what I should do. A whole day was gone and I had nothing to show for it that might be counted as paying work.

Conway awakened and began to scoot across the long bench seat toward the passenger door. When I opened it he tumbled out into my arms. He pushed me away and demanded to walk on his own. He took a few steps in the direction of the trailer and his knees buckled again. He sat down hard on the cold ground.

"How about now?" I asked.

He shook his head and began to pull himself up by my belt. I let him climb until he was standing. "Don't fuckin' carry me."

With my arm under his we made our way to the trailer door. Once inside he immediately dropped into a surprisingly nice leather recliner. The trailer might have looked like a shithole from the outside but the interior was clean and sparsely furnished to make it seem almost spacious. It was pleasantly cozy and warm— and dark. I switched on a floor lamp near the recliner and it illuminated a pile of books that supported an open bottle of Jack Daniel's and several pill bottles. No sign of the shotgun, which I found idly reassuring. On the wall behind the recliner were a couple framed photos, one of an old man leaning against the same car, or one like it, parked outside; the other was of a tall young man in a cap and gown.

There was a resemblance between the two men. "Your father?"

"My father," he confirmed. "The whole time I was growing up he was restoring that DeSoto in our garage."

"Brother? Son?"

Conway removed his shades and the brown eye and the white eye both stared up at me. "Those saline bags won't last the preacher too long. If we can't keep him hydrated his guts and brain will cook. Nothing else will matter. See if you can locate some more."

"I'm going to try to get back to Price tonight," I said. "I'll pick some up and do my damnedest to get back tomorrow. I know you said you didn't want to be bothered again. If that's still the way you feel then I respect that and won't let you know if John's condition changes. But—"

"Did you give some thought to what I said about how the preacher might feel about going to a hospital?"

I hadn't, but I didn't need to think about it too much. "I can't let him die."

Conway nodded.

"If you make it back tomorrow—and he's still alive—come out and get me. We'll see what kind of shape I'm in."

I turned to leave. "I appreciate everything."

"Me."

"Yeah," I said. "I appreciate you. What you did was a bigger favor than I realized."

He sighed. "The young man in the photo you thought was my brother or son . . ."

"Which is it?"

"I just told you." He let his answer sink in for a moment. "Now, leave me alone." As I opened the door he added, "Replace that car cover. Please?"

"Planned on it," I said, and left.

Lenny pulled up in his aunt and uncle's old Ford pickup just as I secured the last bungee strap on the car cover. Even as tight as I could stretch the cover the rising wind was tearing at it and flapping the few loose wrinkles in the soft canvas. Before I got inside the pickup I looked back at the small trailer and the covered car huddled at the shadowed foot of the mesa. The trailer's power came from a utility box mounted on a four-by-four fence post. There were several other junction boxes dotting the landscape around me and I realized the area had once been an RV or trailer court years ago, a remnant of temporary housing for workers at the coal mine. Something in me wanted to do something else. There was nothing I could do.

20

Lenny wasted no time in asking me about John's condition and I told him what Conway had told me, which wasn't much. The big picture was unchanged: The preacher would live or die and all the doctor could do was buy him time to see which it would be. This information didn't seem to do much for Lenny. It didn't do much for me either. The only difference between Lenny and me was I had built a small business out of buying people time while they waited and I'd pretty much given up on the idea of caring too much—at least when I could help it. Of course, sometimes, especially since Claire died, I had trouble shaking the notion that my customers and me were one and the same.

"You aren't really going to try and get back to Price tonight, are you? That's over a hundred miles."

"I am," I said. No one knew better than I did how far it was or the potential risks involved. "John needs more saline bags." I thought about the kids. "And I need to get the cargo door on my trailer fixed." I decided that moment I also just wanted to get the hell out of Rockmuse. There was a certain claustrophobic desperation floating around town along with the bad weather and it was a toss-up which one unsettled me more.

My stated reasons for hitting the road didn't seem to sit any better with Lenny than the news about John. "You could stay the night with us. The sofa is pretty comfortable. The weather could be better tomorrow."

"Or it could be worse. But thanks all the same."

My truck was backed up to the loading dock of the Mercantile. Ordinarily I didn't like anyone driving my truck. Under the circumstances it didn't seem worth mentioning, not that I liked it any better. I opened the door to the pickup and Lenny caught my arm.

"I offloaded everything except the water containers. I couldn't budge them, not even with the hydraulic dolly. Sorry."

I responded with a shrug. "Check in on the preacher as often as you can," I said. "I think Ginger will take good care of him but she'll need a break now and then. I'll get back as soon as I can. Don't bother the doctor if you can help it. He's—" I thought about how to describe him and said, "unpredictable. Letting him be might be considered a healthy choice."

Lenny nodded his agreement and said, "What if you don't get back?"

"Then you and Ginger and the town can switch to plan B."

"What's plan B?"

"Same as plan A," I said, "only with more enthusiasm." I slapped him on the shoulder. "Do the best you can with what you've got. Keep calling Life Flight."

PHYLLIS WAS STANDING on her porch waiting for me by the time I got down her long driveway. I'd been gone a hell of a lot longer than the couple hours I'd told her. She wasn't smiling and her arms were folded. The moment my boots hit the gravel I launched into my explanation about John getting hit and was starting on my apology.

She cut me off. "I know. I had to go into town to the Mercantile to get more formula for the baby. No need to apologize. How's the preacher doing?"

I hit the high points, which were actually the low points, all without mentioning the doctor, as I followed her inside. Neither the girl nor the baby was anywhere to be seen or heard and the big house was quiet except for the wind.

She got right to the point: "I know you're going back to Price. I'm begging you, Ben, please leave the children with me. I promise you I'll take good care of them for as long as necessary."

I hadn't wanted to ask her and now that she was offering—insisting—I considered how Ginny would react if I showed up without her baby. I didn't know a lot about mothers, or fathers for that matter, though it seemed safe to assume the babysitter should be able to produce the kid when the mother showed up. It was small comfort that I had warned Ginny that morning about forcing Annabelle on me for a bad day of driving 117. As for the girl, that decision was easier. I didn't even know her father's last name or how to reach him except for asking Cecil at the truck stop. I had a choice to make a smart decision and I was sure enough going to make it.

"Okay," I said. The single phone lines from Rockmuse, which for some reason hugged the base of the mesa for two hundred miles instead of following 117, often went down during the winter. The phones went out during the summer too. "Is your phone working?"

Phyllis nodded. "It was an hour ago."

I asked for a piece of paper and a pen. "I'm going to give you Ginny's cell phone number. Soon as my taillights hit the end of your driveway, give her a call and tell her who you are, that you're keeping her baby safe, and I'm on my way back."

Phyllis rolled her blue eyes. The sternness in her face evaporated into a toothy, wry smile. "Why, Ben Jones," she said, "you are a coward!"

I hadn't thought about it that way. Maybe I didn't know much about mothers, but I damn sure knew Ginny. "Yes, ma'am," I said, "I am. Nothing brings out a cowardly streak in a man like anticipating the wrath of a woman."

Phyllis produced the paper and pen and went into the kitchen. When she returned she held a thermos and a large sack she said contained sandwiches. "It might be a long trip."

There was something else on her mind and I was willing to let it remain there and get on my way. I had my hand on the doorknob when she said, "How well do you know that girl's father?"

I'd decided to try out the name I'd given her. "You mean Manita?"

Phyllis smiled. "Yes," she said. "Manita."

"Hardly at all," I said, hoping that would be all there was to it. It wasn't.

She touched my arm and lowered her voice. "Have you ever heard the saying 'old soul'?"

I had heard it.

"But it's more than that. It's way more than that. She hasn't said a word the whole afternoon. Hasn't tried to communicate verbally or otherwise with me at all. She was wearing clean new clothes but she was filthy beyond description so I gave her a bath. You said you thought she and her father were in the country illegally—maybe that's what it is but . . ." As eager as I was to leave, I waited for her to continue. "Do you know why I was sent to prison?"

"You kidnapped your grandchildren."

"Do you know why?"

"I guess you had your reasons and I always guessed they were damn good reasons."

"I thought so. Still do. Both my grandson and granddaughter were being abused. My daughter had her trust fund and all the drugs and the life that went with it. She still fought me in the courts and finally just taking them was all I could do to protect them. She never married their fathers and neither one was ever in their lives or wanted to be. Some men die in childbirth. There was no way to know who in Sheila's sick little entourage was hurting her children. She died of a drug overdose when I was in prison and I brought them with me back here when I got out."

"Are you saying you think she's being abused?"

"Maybe. I'm over sixty and when I look into her eyes I get this feeling. It's hard to explain. That child knows more and has seen more than I can imagine. Maybe more than I could stand to imagine."

"What do you want me to do?" I asked. "If I don't get her back to her father the INS will probably deport her. Or at best she'll end up with Social Services. Maybe, if she's lucky, in a foster home for a while. I didn't want to take her in the first place. I had to get on the road this morning and I didn't have time to call the cops. It's none of my business."

"I don't know," she said. "For right now just let her stay with me as long as you can. And don't be in a hurry to return her to her father. After all, he dumped her on you, practically a stranger, at a truck stop."

"And your husband?" I asked. "Did he die in childbirth too?"

"No," Phyllis said. "He couldn't wait that long."

She followed me out onto the porch. "I'll keep the dog too."

I'd forgotten all about the dog. "Thanks."

"No choice. That dog isn't going anywhere without the girl. I have always loved dogs and I've had a few over the years. I like cats but I love dogs. If you have a dog you have company. With a cat you're still alone. I can only guess about the girl." She corrected herself. "Manita. The dog on the other hand is an open book. You try to separate him from the girl and that book will turn you into raw meat."

"You're not wrong," I said. "And thank you again." I leaned over and kissed her cheek. "Make that call, please. If I had to choose between crossing that dog and crossing Ginny I'd choose the dog. When the blood and crying were done there'd be a sight more left of me."

"You know, Ben, you can explain all day about why you took that little girl this morning. I think you're full of it. I think you took her because you just couldn't bring yourself to leave her there."

When I didn't respond Phyllis returned inside and closed the door. The click of the deadbolt being turned hit me like a slap and left me nowhere to go but out on 117. Even with what I knew was waiting for me in the desert, there was no escaping the truth: I was filled with a guilty joy to get behind the wheel again and just drive.

21

For the living, there is only one way out of Rockmuse: State Highway 117. I had one hundred miles ahead of me that could take a few hours or a few days. Fortunately, leaving Rockmuse meant I had to pass the Rockmuse Shell, and it seemed prudent to top off my diesel tanks to accommodate what could be some long periods of idling.

I was done being social and I used my Visa at the pump rather than go inside and get the locals' discount. No one else was at the pumps, and Eckhardt was alone inside, consumed with some remodeling project that involved dismantling the counter. Since his wife had left him a few years earlier he spent most of his time at the station. Without the countertop I could see the La-Z-Boy recliner through the front window. This was where he sat and rocked through most of the night nursing a beer and growing bitterness. I could hear the saw and the hammer pounding and hoped he was busy enough he wouldn't notice me. I almost made it.

He waved through the glass and I ignored him. He waved again and finally peeked out the front door and yelled my name. I waved back and ignored him some more. His voice was almost happy and enthusiastic. "Ben Jones! Get your ass in here, I have something to show you!"

I unhappily complied as soon as my fueling was completed.

With my head only halfway inside, I said, "I have to get on the road, Eckhardt. What's up?"

"This," he replied, tipping the front of the counter up so I could see it. There was a hole about twelve inches square about waist level for anyone standing in front of the counter and register. The hole was covered with black screen-door wire.

I had no idea what "this" was and didn't care. "Nice. I have to get going."

Eckhardt turned the piece of counter so I could see the other side, or what would be the inside when it was all put back together again. What he was showing me seemed to be the perfect ending to a full, sad, and unproductive day. He had mounted a sawed-off shotgun on angle iron. The screen-door wire hid the barrel from sight. I couldn't remember ever seeing him so damned happy.

"Get in here and take a look-see!"

I told him I was in a hurry and that I could see fine from where I stood in the door. I was in more of a hurry with every passing moment.

"Suit yourself," he said, and began to give me a detailed description of his plan, which was unnecessary. He had anointed himself the Thomas Edison of death. "The trigger will be wired to a dead man's floor switch. I can fire with my foot. Or if the son of a bitch shoots me it will go off the second my foot moves. Someone tries to rob me they'll get what-for damn quick."

My forehead dropped against the cold glass of the door and I took in his fiftysomething potbellied righteous Christmas smile. At least Roy's tire doghouses weren't going to kill anyone. Knowing better, I felt compelled to give Eckhardt a history lesson.

"Eckhardt, you've only been robbed once," I said. "And that was seven years ago."

"Don't matter. It could happen. I know it will again. I'll be ready."

There was no doubt in my mind that Eckhardt would be rewarded for his faith. If you're looking for trouble you will almost always find what you're looking for, because it is also looking for you.

The question of what Eckhardt was thinking about all the lonely night hours and years in his recliner at the Shell station convenience store was now obvious and it wasn't really about getting robbed—it was about the opportunity to kill someone. There isn't a damn thing you can say to someone like that but I said it anyway.

"It's illegal," I said. "And what if you have a heart attack or something and your foot slips off and you kill an innocent person? That shotgun will blow them all the way into the cooler."

"Illegal my ass!" he shouted. "The government can't take away my right to protect myself and my property." Then he perked up. For a second he actually seemed to think about what I said. "You're right, Ben. I'll need something like a safety. I don't have so many customers I can kill one." He thought that was funny.

"That's the spirit," I said, and let go of the door and practically ran to my truck.

I pulled out on the highway so fast my truck fishtailed a little but I kept my foot down all the way out of town, shifting up through the gears as quickly as I could. The thermos of coffee and sandwiches flew off the passenger seat onto the floor. Not far from the City Limits sign I roared into a thick sheet of blowing snow backlit by the setting red sun lingering over the Wasatch Mountains. It was like disappearing behind a peaceful pink curtain and I could feel myself being closed off from civilization as the town and my day faded into my side mirrors. The clock on my dashboard read 6:20.

There was always a chance Eckhardt would shoot himself before he managed to kill someone. We are the trouble we seek. His big robbery had been nothing more than a teenage boy who had stolen a relative's pickup and was hell-bent on getting into Price to see a girl he had just learned was pregnant with his child. Fear, youth, and stupidity shouldn't equal a death sentence. The kid didn't even really want money; he wanted gas because he had stolen a pickup with an empty tank. At first he didn't even have a gun. When Eckhardt told him no way on the gas, he went back to get the .22 rifle that happened to be hanging on the gun rack of the stolen pickup. The two just stood there and glared at each other until the boy broke down and started crying and eventually took off hitchhiking down 117 under a broiling sun.

Highway 117 is the main reason why there is so little serious crime in Rockmuse. The escape route is a hundred miles of desert highway with plenty of time to alert the county sheriff or Highway Patrol, who could just have a Fraternal Order of Police picnic while they waited for your criminal ass to show up at the junction with US 191. Odds were that if Eckhardt had his shotgun booby trap back then the kid would have died right where he stood and the baby would have never known its father. As it turned out, he got a deferred judgment on the vehicle theft when it was reduced to trespassing. Some community service and counseling were ordered.

Seven years ago Eckhardt was a more reasonable if not kind man and allowed the judge to dismiss the attempted robbery. Maybe his former wife had a hand in convincing him to let the boy off easy. The next boy or man or woman or unlucky pet wouldn't have a chance. I made a note to myself to never stand in front of old Eckhardt's convenience store counter as long as I knew that shotgun was pointed at my privates. Shit does, in fact, have a way of hitting the fan, and the chances of getting sprayed with it only increase if you stand in front of the fan. Unfortunately, this was a lesson I was still in the process of learning—that and minding my own business.

22

It was a beautiful night in hell. More or less, I got exactly what I expected. Around daybreak I was approaching The Well-Known Desert Diner and I glanced at the clock. The hundred miles had taken me about twelve hours.

Once the sun had set, the wind and snow kicked up in earnest and the horizon disappeared, sometimes for long periods, with visibility all the way to my front bumper and a shining darkness my headlights often only seemed to make worse with the icy glare of the road and the crystal white of the blowing snow.

This was what it was like for days on end when a FedEx and a UPS driver got lost and died. It took Search and Rescue three weeks to find their trucks. The desert snow, which tends to be fine and powdery, drifts and piles itself against anything remotely stable, usually sage and dwarf juniper, tufts of prairie grass, though occasionally even mounds of gravel shoulder rub.

Without cell phones or GPS or even stars, when the blacktop is as white and flat as the miles of desert on either side, a driver can't tell the difference between right or left, the desert from the highway, and it's possible in places to drive for miles without knowing you've left the road.

When they found the frozen drivers they were huddled together for warmth like reconciling lovers in the FedEx delivery truck, the Romeo and Juliet of warring corporate tribes, which explains why when the Big Brown camp tells the story the drivers were found instead in the UPS truck. What always amazed me was that in that cold, dark desert wasteland, when they couldn't find their way home, they somehow managed to find each other.

I'm not a praying man, but I always nod my thanks to them when I'm driving, especially in the winter desert. Their deaths were enough that UPS and FedEx both came to me with an offer to deliver for them on 117 by special contract. In my heart I knew no one was coming to rescue me in the desert if I got as lost as they had, and I understood and accepted that hard truth. Sometimes I felt as if I wouldn't want it any other way. As terrible as it was, it was a life and a death I knew well and small comfort that it was, it was still a comfort.

Everyone has a lucky star. Though I was big on telling myself how smart and experienced I was at driving the desert, I knew the difference was luck, pure and simple. At one point during the night the road merged with the desert just as I knew it would. Conventional wisdom dictates that in zero-visibility driving conditions the driver should follow the tracks of the vehicles ahead, or the taillights, if you can see them. On 117 there was rarely anyone ahead of me to leave tracks to follow, and I wasn't the following sort anyway. A couple times in the past up on Soldier Pass a line of vehicles had followed the leader right over the high side. If I was going over a cliff I didn't need someone to show me the way. I prefer to do stupid alone. It's more efficient.

I set my emergency flashers and put on my cold-weather gear and walked to the end of my headlight beams, probably no more than ten feet. From there I walked along with my flashlight sweeping the shoulders, or what I thought were the shoulders, searching for natural markers to follow with the truck.

I found what over the years I had begun to call the Headless Men: tall grasses and twisted junipers that had gathered the snow around them so they appeared like an army of torsos poised for battle. There were intermittent stretches of the army along 117, and since the highway didn't have mileage markers or guardrails they had served me well. Full of Phyllis's coffee, I stepped a few feet in among them and relieved myself, my head tipped back peering into the blowing snow above me and hoping for a little break that would reveal the stars or the moon. When I turned back the Headless Men were gone.

I knew the boys were there and laughing at me—the Indian-Jew half-breed trucker—from their headless mouths. A few steps and a few steps more and nothing but darkness and snow and no sign of the highway or of my truck. My heart began to beat in my ears and I took a few more steps while swinging my flashlight in every direction. Then I turned the flashlight off. In popular lore, given my mixed heritage, I could expect a vision from an old Native American chanting and leading me in the right direction. Or perhaps an ancient Jewish Rabbi chanting and offering me a matzo-ball sandwich and advice phrased as a question. I would have settled for the ghost of Joseph Smith in drag. No one appeared and as usual I was on my own.

The thing to remember about a lucky star is that you have to trust it, and such stars shine brightest when it's darkest. I trudged slowly through the snow for several minutes trying not to think of anything. A few times I stopped and listened hard for the sound of the diesel engine of my truck. It wasn't that sound, or even the headlights, that found me in the night. It was the smell of the diesel fumes trapped in the dense falling snow. I damn near bumped into the rear of my trailer.

The Headless Men directed me as I crept along, always keeping them to my right, and I drove almost five miles with them for company before the sky cracked open with enough moonlight for me to see ahead without their help. Oddly, I was sorry to see them go and as I picked up speed I rolled down my window and shouted, "Thanks, boys!"

It was less than an hour later that I dropped down onto the straight stretch that I recognized as leading to The Well-Known

Desert Diner. From there onward, even in darkness and the worst weather conditions, I could find my way to the junction with US 191. I ate the last sandwich to celebrate as dawn began to peek over the unseen mesa in my rearview mirror and chase my rig the final few miles to the diner.

The wind was steady and the cloud cover lifting as the silhouette of the diner's roof and Walt's Quonset workshop came into view. The cheap exterior thermometer attached to my driver's side mirror told me it was a balmy eight degrees. A fragment of moon was pinned in a shred of inky sky over the diner and its light glared up off the apron of black ice that served as highway. The fatigue of the previous day and the long night of driving hit me all at once and I began to downshift and slow to pull into the diner's parking lot. All I wanted to do was close my tired eyes for a bit before heading into Price to begin my day's chores.

There was movement in front of The Well-Known Desert Diner. I backed off the accelerator, slipped into neutral, and began to coast. Anything going on at the diner was rare, and at roughly six in the morning it was unknown. In twenty years I'd never seen anyone at the diner at that hour of the day. My rig came to a rolling stop about a hundred yards from the parking lot while my eyes sorted through the sunrise shadows cast by the gas pumps and eaves. Someone was on the phone in the old phone booth outside the diner.

It had to be Walt. He was dressed in his usual faded blue jeans and white T-shirt and with his white hair it was hard to distinguish him from the snow that stretched in every direction. Why that phone was still there and how it made and received calls in a digital world was a mystery in itself. Unless you had a pocketful of change you couldn't even get a dial tone. I knew Walt used the phone once in a while but I had never personally seen him. To my knowledge he had no friends and his nearest relatives were buried in the nearby grotto behind the isolated model house in Desert

Home. But Walt was a tight-lipped sort and he had his secrets, though I thought I'd disposed of the last of them when I buried his decorative commode-hugging corpse a few months earlier.

Clouds of breath billowed out of the phone booth as Walt talked. It was a long conversation. A minute would have been a long conversation with him. There was no particular reason why I couldn't pull forward and onto the gravel apron in front of the diner. Walt probably knew I was nearby anyway.

I pushed in the clutch and was ready to shift into first when he slammed the receiver into its cradle. I stayed where I was and watched him leave the phone booth and walk out into the white desert maybe fifty feet. He just stood there, facing northwest, his back to the phone booth and me, staring into all that silent, beautiful nothing. Any minute I expected he would turn and look down the road to where I sat in my truck. The wind was blowing lightly toward the southeast, taking my diesel fumes out into the desert and away from Walt and the diner.

He continued to stand in the snow—back straight, hands on his hips—for several minutes. Standing alone in that endless field of white was as emotional and accurate a portrait of the man as I could have imagined. The Emperor of Solitude surveying his kingdom. When he finally started walking again it was to the rear of the diner and probably into his Quonset workshop. I waited a few more minutes before getting under way. My need to close my eyes and rest had passed.

There is no use in denying my curiosity was piqued, especially on the heels of my visit the previous day, though with all that had happened in between it felt more like ten years. Still, though I suffered from occasional relapses, I knew how to mind my own business, especially when it came to Walt Butterfield. Walt's antisocial streak was the stuff of legend. Since the diner closed in 1987, some known reported incidents of Walt's behavior had risen to prominence in the Carbon County Sheriff's blotter and by comparison made Dr. Conway and his shotgun seem about as noteworthy as a visit from the ladies of the local welcome wagon. That said, Walt was my friend and I nursed a certain concern for him all the way into Price, though not so much concern I would ever risk asking him.

23

The junction of State Highway 117 and US 191 was clear both ways, though I could see a line of semis in the distance coming down the slippery grade from the north. To the south, the rest of the straightaway was as empty as I had ever seen it and I guessed that most of the long-haul drivers had held up outside of Price during the night waiting for the weather to break. Now they were getting on their way to Denver and probably a few to Moab. I was a touch skittish pulling out onto 191 given my experience the previous morning. Part of me half expected that red cab-over to suddenly appear out of nowhere.

I had the road to myself as the Stop 'n' Gone Truck Stop came up on my right. As I expected, the lot was filled with trucks of all descriptions waiting to enter the steady stream of traffic leaving Price. It seemed as good a time as any to see if Pedro was around and arrange to return his daughter.

The huge building behind the truck stop that housed the tire center was locked up tighter than a drum. I peeked in the window with the hope someone might be inside at such an early hour, possibly Pedro. No luck. The place was dark and quiet. I had no choice but to go to the office and talk to Cecil to see if I could get a line on Pedro.

Cecil was nowhere to be seen. Ana was at the register finishing up with a driver. I waited until he was gone and approached her.

"Cecil around?"

Ana had worked at the Stop 'n' Gone for a few years. If you were an attractive woman working nights at a truck stop you had to be of the strong, no-nonsense variety. Ana was every bit of that. She was somewhere in her late thirties, on the tallish side, made taller by black cowboy boots. She looked Latina to me, or maybe Indian, or both, with a touch of Elvira, Mistress of the Dark. Everything she wore was black. Always a long black dress, tight black blouse, long black hair piled high on her head, with dark-colored hoop earrings. She always wore the same wide belt low on her hips, black leather studded with small opaque gems with one large one set in the center of the buckle. Opals would have been my guess. No matter what they were, that belt was expensive, especially for a truck-stop clerk. Even her lipstick was a dark red. If she dressed in white Ana would still be, without a doubt—formidable. Black was merely the color of the exclamation point.

Ana did smile on occasion. It was a good smile and it communicated a temperature about the same as what it was outside at the moment, though I always thought her big coal eyes promised a slightly warmer soul. It was that kind of wishful thinking that sometimes got me mistaken for a romantic. At one time I'd entertained the idea of asking her out. Before that could happen I watched from behind an aisle of snacks as one of my poor brethren truckers took a run at her. She never did answer him in words. She simply stared at him until his manhood retreated between his legs and he followed. I'm not shy, or a coward, but I'm not suicidal either.

"Haven't seen him," she said.

"Just as well. I'm really looking for Pedro."

She raised her thick eyebrows. "Pedro's gone."

"Gone?"

"Last week Cecil suddenly shut down the whole tire department. Overnight he emptied it out right down to the floor jacks."

"You have a number or address for Pedro?"

She said she didn't. "Cecil probably has that."

I asked her when Cecil would be in.

"He should be here now." There was a note of frustration in her response. I waited for more. "It's the first of the month and I stopped by yesterday morning to get my paycheck. The office was locked and there was a note on the door saying he would be back in ten minutes. He never showed. I have a key to the door. Except for a quick shower last night, I've been here ever since."

I wondered if the note she found had been the same one he'd left for me. "Cecil pull this shit often?"

"Not often," Ana said. "Never this long. He'll turn up. I called some of the other clerks and someone is coming in to relieve me at two."

Whatever was going on with Cecil was none of my business. Pedro, at least temporarily, was my business. Soon as I got his kid back to him that business would be over. A driver came in and we paused our conversation long enough for them to transact their business. When he left I asked if she'd do me a favor and look in Cecil's office for anything that might get me in contact with Pedro.

"File cabinet is locked. Cecil has the only key. I'll see what I can do if you do a favor for me."

Not knowing what it might be, doing a favor for Ana would be worth it if she could help me locate Pedro. "Sure," I said. "What?"

Ana handed me her paycheck. "Drop this by the bank? I haven't had time and my rent check is going to bounce if I don't get it deposited before noon." The check was endorsed. She gave me the name of her bank.

How many times had I been in the same situation?

"I know that tune," I said. "Been humming it all my life."

"Ben," she said, and leaned over the counter toward me. My heart kicked me in the chest as I wondered if she might be planning on giving me a thank-you kiss. She didn't. What she gave me was probably better, or at least more useful, given the situation.

"An INS officer was here last week. There's a good chance Pedro has left town. If he didn't, they might have picked him up. You understand? If he's still in Price, he's going to be hard to find."

I understood. "I hope the hell not," I said. "He needs me to return something."

"One more thing. Lately Cecil has been making a lot of trips to Las Vegas. Says he's been sick some, nursing an infection. Maybe—"

I waited for her to finish. When she didn't, I said, "Maybe what?"

"A lady friend. Maybe a lot of them. Who knows, maybe not everything that happens in Vegas stays in Vegas." The implication was not lost on me. The line of her lips parted a little, which I took for a smile. "I'm curious. Just what did Pedro loan you?"

For a moment I actually considered telling her about the girl. Instead I asked: "Is Pedro married? Kids?"

"Who knows." She shrugged. "He's your friend, not mine."

Phyllis's suspicions about the father came back to me. "I wouldn't say that."

A husband-and-wife driving team walked in and I took the opportunity to leave. I paused at the door. The husband was saying something to Ana. She might have been listening but she was watching me as if she thought I'd been shoplifting. She didn't trust me. At least we had that in common. I waved her paycheck over my head. "Soon as the bank opens."

The morning was cold but had turned clear and bright and the waves of diesel fumes from all the trucks tinged the air. It wasn't clean desert air, and yet I inhaled it deeply as if it were because it was familiar and almost comforting. Sure, it was poison, my personal brand of poison for twenty years, and its smell was the stuff of work and it filled me with a sense of purpose. I had a lot to do in a short period of time and the rumble of truck engines and diesel made me eager to get to it.

For the first time since emerging from the long night I took a moment to organize my day. If I did it right I could be back on the road to Rockmuse by midafternoon and with luck I could be there before dark. Saline bags for John were the priority, followed by getting my cargo door repaired. Maybe I could squeeze in a visit home and a shower. What there wasn't much time for was tracking down Pedro. If I had time, I still wouldn't know where to begin. Taking on fuel first, since I was already at the truck stop, made sense. That way I could hit the road running as soon as my errands were done. Sandwiched in somewhere in the morning I had to find time to deposit Ana's check.

Island 6 was clear. Filling up I could see the trash can of Island 8—the girl and the dog, the darkness and Cecil's shit-eating grin—and the note. I pulled it out of my pocket and read it again. Maybe Phyllis was right about Pedro. Maybe she was wrong. He went out of his way to make me believe his daughter was his son and the only conclusion I could draw from that was Pedro was trying to protect her.

I didn't know Pedro. Hell, like most people, I couldn't say I really knew the people I thought I knew.

There was something in those dark eyes of hers and I saw it the minute I laid eyes on her, though I didn't, or couldn't, recognize it. John saw it. So did Phyllis. "Abuse" was one of those small words that took in a lot of territory, none of it good, and I still carried some of that ugly country left over in me from foster homes, usually from the older kids, and one adult in particular.

Whatever was in that little girl's eyes was more than abuse, if that were possible. Phyllis was probably right about one thing: I couldn't leave that kid—not to the cops and certainly not with Cecil. When it came down to it, maybe not even her father. My choices hadn't improved much over the past twenty-four hours. I hoped Cecil was enjoying his infection. He deserved it.

When I left the truck stop I knew exactly where I was going first—Los Ojos Negros.

24

Los Ojos Negros was the worst-kept secret in Price, a Mexican restaurant unlike any other in just about every way. To call it a *taqueria* was an insult. For one thing, you never knew where to find them. They and their sand-blasted green trailer had first shown up in the parking lot of a chain big-box building supply store and that's where I met them, dispensing food to customers coming and going all day and sometimes into the night past when the store closed, rain or shine. After several months people started coming to them to eat whether or not they needed anything in the store, filling up parking spots. This pissed off the store manager and some bigwigs from corporate. The ladies were asked to leave—unpleasantly and publicly—including some racial insults. Maybe the manager was ordered to get rid of them, but no one forces someone to be an asshole.

The ladies of Los Ojos Negros weren't just cooks, they were witches with food and, according to rumor, other things. The rumor began when the store manager, a short young guy with an old big attitude, demanded they get off the premises immediately. Not long after that he had a heart attack between the walls of toilet seats and bathroom vanity mirrors. He died where he dropped. His last views were of himself surrounded by expensive "whisper close" and "radiant heated" butt buckets, probably with Made in Mexico stamped on them. A year after that, when so many big-box stores were closing, it closed overnight, bankrupt, leaving a lot of folks out in the cold, financially and otherwise.

Since then the ladies were always on the move. They had set up beneath underpasses, the city park, and a long string of vacant lots. From one end of Price to the other, Los Ojos Negros would show up overnight like a miniature Mexican boomtown. At one time or another everyone from cops to construction workers visited the ladies.

One night on my way home I decided to get dinner and their pickup had broken down. I dropped my trailer in the street and hooked up theirs. The four of us crammed into my cab and drove around Price for three hours looking for another spot. Nothing is more fun and satisfying than doing something harmlessly illegal for a good cause. I had cramps in my cheeks the next day from all the laughter.

They usually opened by six a.m. Fortunately, they were at the last place I'd seen them, under the sloping canopy of a closed discount gas station off of 191 on the west side of Price. The place had been closed a long time, judging from the faded signs advertising gas at $1.59 a gallon. There was a small crowd gathered at the window of the trailer, including a city councilman. A few times I'd seen both men and women, their arms loaded with foil-wrapped foods, get into pickups with bumper stickers that said things like BUILD THE WALL; DON'T BREED 'EM IF YOU CAN'T FEED 'EM; and one that looked like a hunting permit that declared it to be an IL-LEGAL IMMIGRANT HUNTING PERMIT. In smaller print it added, NO LIMIT—NO TAGGING REQUIRED.

It takes a special kind of brutal hypocrisy to eat someone's lov-ingly prepared food and get into a pickup spouting that kind of violent bullshit. The ladies of Los Ojos Negros were dependable. No one hungry was ever turned away for lack of money—or brains.

The moment I stepped onto my running board I smelled the food and heard their shouts of welcome. The crowd turned briefly to see what the fuss was about and, satisfied I wasn't worth the fuss, returned their attention to the window. Collectively, I called them "ladies." Individually, they were Michaela, the oldest; Josefina; and Tiffany, the youngest, whose real name was Julieta. As a teenager she had idolized the '80s pop singer of the same name, even dyeing her hair for a while, and insisting the whole family call her Tiffany. The family, out of loving cruelty, kept calling her that long after her infatuation ended. The other two still liked to tease her about it. They would call her "Teefanee."

I didn't know their exact ages, though Josefina and Tiffany had streaks of white in their thick black hair, while Michaela had streaks of black in her white hair. They were all related, though I had no idea how. They were all of varying height, married, happily I supposed, Catholic, and had what I could only charitably but accurately call substantial builds, though each had a proud beauty that in the past must have been a pure, breathtaking loveliness.

There were deck chairs circling a portable propane fire pit next to the trailer. Josefina and Michaela stood on their boot tips and kissed me on the cheek while Tiffany stayed in the trailer tending to customers.

Michaela offered me a chair and said, "We thought you didn't love us anymore!"

Josefina gripped my biceps and said something in Spanish I didn't understand. She laughed and made a growling sound. In English she said, "Oh Ben, I'd leave Lico in a minute."

Tiffany yelled to her from inside the trailer, "You'd leave Lico for any *malo caballero* with his own teeth! Besides, he's mine!"

I'd be lying if I said I wasn't enjoying their good-natured attention. They sensed I wasn't there just for the breakfast burrito, which Tiffany handed me when she joined us. The ladies didn't need language, English or Spanish, to communicate, at least not with one another. When they were all seated across from me they glanced at each other, nodding and angling their heads as if listening. They were having a conversation about my visit, and then they all focused on me and calmly waited for me to speak.

I began to unwrap my breakfast while I got straight to the point. "I need to find a young man named Pedro. I don't know his last name. Up until last week he worked as the tire man at the Stop 'n' Gone Truck Stop."

They exchanged looks and Michaela spoke. "You think we know everyone?" All three were solemn. "We're just old women, Ben."

"I don't know," I said. "I think you might know people who do know everyone. I have something very valuable he loaned to me. I need to return it to him." I felt the need to be honest with them, but only to a point. "He might be in trouble," I added.

This launched a burst of silent chatter between them. Josefina and Tiffany got up from their chairs and took seats on either side of me and Tiffany spoke in almost a whisper. "We don't know him. We can't get involved in any trouble, Ben. Especially immigration trouble. It's immigration trouble?"

I nodded and began to rewrap the burrito in its foil wrapper to take it with me. I apologized for putting them on the spot. "I don't know what else to do and I don't want to make his trouble worse. He trusted me with something very special to him."

Tiffany took my hand and held it in her lap. *"Muy especial?"*

"Sí," I said. *"Muy especial."*

All I could see were their dark eyes darting back and forth between them, punctuated by eyebrows and squints and twitches in the corners of their mouths. Two Hispanic men wearing cowboy hats and quilted jackets had arrived and were waiting at the window of the trailer maybe twenty or thirty feet away. None of the three women acknowledged the men, and the men glanced toward the ladies, and me. I nodded at the men and as I did one of the ladies, I wasn't sure which one, said quietly, *"Los niños del desierto?"* When I turned back to them all three had their heads bowed, praying or in deep thought, I didn't know. Maybe both. I started to repeat what I had just heard, not certain if I'd heard correctly.

Suddenly all three were laughing and they stood up at the same time. Tiffany shouted to the men in Spanish. The most I could make of it was that I had just told them their food was made in heaven. The men grinned and nodded as if the compliment was meant for them. Starting with Tiffany each hugged me and went to the trailer to serve the waiting men. Michaela was the last and she lingered a second longer while she kissed me on the cheek. As close to my ear as she could manage, she whispered, "We think you're the one in trouble. Don't come back here. We'll find you."

"Thank you!" I said, loud enough for everyone to hear, and waved the burrito above my head and started toward my truck. The ladies threw big theatrical kisses after me from inside the service window of the trailer.

Inside my cab I gripped the steering wheel for a few seconds before giving my air horn a blast. I thought I had an idea what had just happened, only an idea, though mostly I felt as if I had just been swimming under the surface of a dark Hispanic pool and hadn't come up for air yet.

I didn't really believe the ladies were telepathic. They had just been together for so long and knew one another so well they had developed a kind of shorthand. The ladies didn't appear to be frightened. Maybe they were leaving that to me. I was the one they thought was in trouble. It might have been an easy guess that the loaned item was a child, except the word that they used meant children. Not male or female. Not one, but two or more. *Niños.* Not just *niños*, but *desierto*. Desert children.

They didn't seem to know Pedro, though I doubted they would have come right out and let me know if they did. The moment I said what he loaned me was very special, something happened between them and the presence of the men at the window ended any further conversation. Michaela said they would find me and I was convinced they would—the sooner the better. When I'm told I'm in trouble I usually know why, or I can narrow down the list of reasons to a top ten. The fact that I didn't know why worried me.

I was glad I left the girl with Phyllis, though trouble has a way of spreading like a stain.

JOHNSON'S TRUCK SUPPLY AND REPAIR had mostly empty bays when I arrived. They'd run an all-night crew to handle as many trucks as they could for the drivers who figured they'd use the weather downtime to catch up on light maintenance. Most of them had already moved on, leaving the remaining trailer techs with nothing to do but my small job.

Rather than sit in the waiting room I walked the half mile to Ana's bank and back. It was a brisk and slippery walk. By ten I was on my way to the local hospital to see about buying saline bags for John. If my morning continued the way it was going I would have time for a shower and, weather permitting, be in Rockmuse before dark.

My walk gave me a chance to get the blood pumping into my head again. By the time I returned to Johnson's to retrieve my truck I was feeling better and less concerned about what had happened, or didn't happen, at Los Ojos Negros. They were just old women with strange ways. Their community, the Hispanic community, was guarded and a little insulated, and the ladies were protective. Like a lot of immigrants, they had a tendency to think just about anything coming from the outside meant trouble for them—not that they were wrong. There just wasn't any good reason why I would be in trouble over babysitting the little girl. As for the mention of children and the desert, who knew? No, the ladies weren't scared; they were simply cautious old women whose powers extended only to creating magic with food.

25

The Southern Utah Regional Hospital was a compact cluster of buildings that sat on a small hill a couple miles from the center of town. It was relatively new and well staffed. If you were sick or injured on the southeast side of the Wasatch it was your only chance. I'd been treated in the emergency room a few times for the side effects of a bad temper, drunkenness, and poor judgment—stabbed, shot, and beaten—dealer's choice.

There was a heliport behind the hospital, where the one Life Flight helicopter was dispatched. It covered the entire southern Utah desert from Soldier Summit to Moab, about a thousand square miles, which meant it was frequently landing and taking off, sometimes several times a day due to highway accidents, injured four-wheel drivers, ranch mishaps, and mountain biking and hiking tourists who were so busy enjoying the desert and rock formations they left their common sense in their travel trailers or hotel rooms.

It isn't often I get a view from the opposite direction. The hospital parking lot looked out over Price and to the southeast across the desert all the way to the mesa that loomed above Highway 117 and Rockmuse. My view didn't go that far. Somewhere out on 117 a dark haze blocked the horizon. It was either snowing, or maybe raining, or simply socked in with fog. Or all three at once, plus the incessant wind. Whatever the weather was out there, it didn't bode well for Life Flight taking off to get John, or my return trip.

The waiting area of the emergency room was almost empty. The place brought back memories I couldn't remember, since I had been drunk or otherwise semiconscious when I was admitted for most of them. A young woman with two small boys fighting and holding back tears sat near the reception desk. The boys had streaks of blood on their faces and patches of blood-matted hair on their scalps. Their mother gave me a weary smile as I passed them.

"Some things never change," I said. "Let me guess, rock fight?"

She nodded and the boys began to cry anew. I pointed to my head. "Threw a few myself. I've got the scars to prove it."

The receptionist watched me speak to the mother and was poised to ask me the nature of my injury. A female doctor was sitting at a small desk in an open cubicle behind her. Without getting up, and without actually looking at me, she said, "Mr. Jones, what a nice surprise to see you." There was nothing in her voice that would give anyone the impression that it was either a surprise or nice.

She was the head doctor of the emergency ward. Her name was Wanda Stafford and she had treated me on a few occasions. On at least one of them, I had asked her out for a drink, though she was pushing fifty and her blond hair was pulled back so tight it made her face look as if she were a pale sun-dried tomato caught in a wind tunnel. I still recalled her reply: "Not on your life." I asked her why and she said there wasn't enough time to give me all the reasons. I could guess a couple dozen of them right off the bat— starting with drunk and in police custody.

I said hello to Dr. Stafford and, thinking she had warmed to me, I said, "I'm glad it's a nice surprise."

As it turned out, I was mistaken about the warmth. "What I should have said is, it is a nice surprise to see you without a police escort and handcuffs."

The young mother suddenly decided she needed to keep her boys closer.

There was no use denying our past encounters, so I didn't. "I found Jesus, Dr. Wanda," I said. "I'm a changed man."

She swiveled around to face me but she wasn't about to get out of her chair for the likes of me. "My condolences to Jesus," she said. "As much as I'd like to believe that, I highly doubt it." I did my best to appear changed, though since I didn't know what that would actually look like, I shrugged my acceptance.

I told her I wanted to buy some saline bags for an injured man in Rockmuse.

This got her out of the chair. "You mean the victim of the hit-and-run?"

I nodded. "Life Flight couldn't get there yesterday and maybe not today either, from what I can see of the weather out that way. I drove all night to get here. I'm going back soon as I get the saline."

Dr. Stafford and the receptionist, who might have been all of eighteen, exchanged glances. "Was the victim a friend of yours?"

I answered yes before it hit me how the question was phrased. "He's the whack job who hauls the cross up and down. . . . 'Was'?"

"He didn't survive." There was just a hint of kindness in Dr. Stafford's voice and that threw me as much as anything else. "I'm sorry," she added. "When did you leave him?"

"Late yesterday afternoon."

"The call came in last night. The main switchboard took it. I only know because I review all the Life Flight calls first thing in the morning when I come in."

Whether it was the expression on my face or the fatigue in my shoulders, Dr. Stafford told the receptionist she'd be in Exam Room 1 and invited me to follow her. She poured two Styrofoam cups of coffee on the way and handed me one as we sat down in the small room.

"I really am sorry. This happens more than I'd care to admit, but it comes with the territory. Small budget. Big demand. We can't be everywhere at once, or anywhere when this weather hits."

I sipped the coffee and discovered my lips were quivering too much to take in any coffee. I was embarrassed. "Dumb son of a bitch," I said. "Twenty years he's been out there spring to fall. He used up all his miracles. You can see that damn cross bobbing on the shoulder for miles. People just don't pay much attention. They get lulled by the road. The scenery is monotonous. They go too fast. It had to happen." I made another attempt to sip the coffee and succeeded. "It had to happen," I repeated, and saying it again made it real.

"The driver left the scene?"

"Yep," I replied. "An old desert rat found him and brought him to town on the hood of his WWII Jeep."

"Was the victim—"

I interrupted her. "His name was John."

"Was John conscious when he was found? Ambulatory?"

"I don't think so."

"Was the driver alone?"

"Why?"

"Then the old desert rat who found him must have been in great shape. I didn't know—John," she said. "Unless he was a small man, and I doubt that if he carried a cross, lifting or moving dead—" She caught herself and began again. "Lifting an unconscious person of substantial size and weight is hard work." She thought for a moment. "It's possible. People in extreme situations sometimes manage to do what might be considered impossible. It doesn't matter, really. I don't imagine the Highway Patrol has been out there to investigate yet."

I told her that Trooper Smith hadn't made it out and might not for a while. "When the weather gets bad he's busy. He tried though. Chances are whoever hit John will be just another mystery. It will have a lot of company in the desert. We did our best to save him, and that's all that matters now."

"Who's 'we'? You must have had someone with medical experience if you knew you needed to keep him hydrated."

I didn't want to say too much. Conway made it clear he wanted to protect his privacy and I understood. "There was a retired doctor visiting in town. He did what he could."

"Who?"

"You probably wouldn't know him," I said. "Maybe he could have done more if we'd had some medical supplies on hand. A long time ago there was a small clinic. It closed a few years after the coal mine closed. Nothing since."

"Wait here," she said.

A few minutes later Dr. Stafford returned. "We usually have a few prepackaged emergency medical supply chests. Not much. The basics. When Life Flight can't land or extract the victims due to terrain or weather, the kits are dropped into the accident scene and used to stabilize the patient. I thought we had a few extra kits ready to go."

I told her I appreciated the gesture. She took a moment and studied me as if she was making her mind up about something. "Are you really a born-again Christian?"

"Nope," I answered. "I wasn't a Christian the first time either." I raised my Styrofoam cup in her direction. "But I've been sober for a few years now."

"I'm happy to hear that." She sounded genuine enough. "I'm not a Christian myself, born-again or otherwise. It was Rupert Conway, wasn't it?"

Her question startled me, coming as it did out of nowhere. When she said his name my face answered her question. Maybe she planned it that way.

"You know him?"

"No, I know *of* him. I'm surprised he's still alive."

"Don't cause any trouble for him. Please," I said, "he's got enough."

"Trouble?" She actually smiled. "No, Ben. I promise. He grew up right here in Price, you know. I wasn't surprised when I heard a rumor that he'd returned. That was a few months ago. I guess he came home to die."

"What happened to him?"

"Humanity, Ben. Humanity happened to him. Worked over-time on him. From what I know, it's a miracle that anyone could convince him to practice medicine in any capacity, and candidly, I don't blame him. If any part of what I heard is true, it's also a miracle he was able to be of any assistance. Modern medicine can heal and prolong life but every physician has seen patients die when they should have lived. In Dr. Conway's case, there wasn't any medical reason why he shouldn't have died from his injuries."

"That's it?"

"That's it. If you want to know what happened to him you should ask him yourself. I treat a lot of ranchers and desert folks, outdoor adventure types, all tough men and women like you. Or think they are. If you have the guts to ask him, and he decides to tell you, all I can say is, I hope you've got a strong stomach. I don't know all the details. I've been an ER physician for almost thirty years and I've seen physical and emotional trauma that would make a corpse turn away. If just a small part of what I heard was done to him is true, then even I don't have the stomach to hear about it."

"I doubt I'll get around to asking him," I said. "No reason. I probably won't ever see him again. If it hadn't been an emergency for a friend, I wouldn't have asked in the first place. He greeted me with a shotgun. The man would have used it too. I was lucky."

She didn't seem surprised. After a deep sigh, she said, "Can you come back in a couple hours? I'll get one of those emergency medi-cal kits made up for you to take back to Rockmuse. It might come in handy next time. Trust me, there will always be a next time."

I asked her how much and explained I didn't have much cash, though I did have a credit card.

"No charge, Mr. Jones. I'll add a few more items that might come in handy." She actually winked at me. "But let's keep this between us."

I thanked her and we parted ways. There was no longer a big rush to return to Rockmuse and I felt like a long, hot shower, followed by a lingering memorial imaginary cigarette to say my goodbye to John. Highway 117 wouldn't be the same without its resident religious wing nut. Neither would I. Maybe I would wait and have that cigarette out in the desert halfway between nowhere and nothing and pretend he was there with me.

26

My duplex is in east Price, on a narrow street with a few anemic trees and a broken sidewalk and older, small houses with dirt yards. The neighbors didn't like it when I parked my big rig on the street. I understood, though a lot of them parked their vehicles in their front yards, which also served as open-air storage units for used appliances, yard furniture, gas barbeques, and swing sets. The fact that I kept my weedy, mostly dirt yard free of cars and junk made me the uppity one in the neighborhood.

I knew my neighbors' vehicles, running or not, and there was a late-model Cadillac Escalade pickup with Nevada plates parked in front of my duplex. Seeing those useless pieces of machinery always made me laugh, because their beds were too small to carry anything of real importance and their gear ratio didn't allow for a decent towing capacity. They were a joke to any real workingman, which is why I often heard them referred to as cowboy limos, and the disdain extended to those who drove them. Of course, if I had the money to afford one I probably would have been less critical. Maybe not. Either way, that particular vehicle was out of place on my street. People on my street worked, or were trying to find work, and their vehicles had a job to do, even if that job was serving as a semi-mobile storage unit.

I passed by the Cadillac pickup and parked on the next block.

Ginny was sitting on the steps of our shared front porch wrapped in a quilt. My attention was on the vehicle or I would have seen her when I drove by. She watched me as I walked up the sidewalk. Even from a distance I could tell she had been crying. Ginny was not prone to crying. I'd only seen her cry once before.

She waited to speak until I was right in front of her. Returning home without her baby, however justified, filled me with guilt.

She opened her mouth and I beat her to it. "I had no choice, Ginny!" As much as I hated hearing that bullshit excuse from others, I hated it even more when it came from me.

Ginny buried her red face in the frayed edges of the quilt and began to sob in heaves. I kept my mouth shut and waited for the courage to comfort her without making excuses. The courage deserted me and I went straight to the apology and excuses.

"I'm sorry, Ginny," I said. "The weather was terrible. I didn't know how long it would take me—117 was an ice rink, zero visibility, wind—" After a quick breath, I finished up. "I just couldn't take Annabelle. It would have been too dangerous. Forgive me?"

Ginny stood up on the step and threw her quilted head into my shoulder and went on crying for a minute before answering. "I gave my baby to you!" she wailed. "What kind of mother am I?" She composed herself and without lifting her head from my shoulder, she said: "I can't do this anymore, Ben. I just can't. I had to. I had to."

I rested my hand on her shoulder. "I know," I said. "You had work and college and no sitter. You made the only choice you could. Phyllis is taking good care of her, I promise. She's safe and warm and I'll have her back to you as soon as I can."

Ginny raised her head. "No," she said. "That's not what I meant."

The front door to Ginny's side of the duplex opened behind her and I saw what she felt she had to do. I hadn't seen Nadine, her mother, since we dated ten or more years earlier. Even then I hadn't really seen her. What I saw was her backside riding a married UPS driver down the home stretch in the cab of my truck while it was parked overnight in the terminal lot. I saw them and they knew and the silence that passed between us was the only goodbye. Ginny was a little girl at the time and already wise in the ways of the world, especially the part of her world that had to do with her mother—a lot wiser than I was. Even as a child, Ginny was the adult in the family.

I'd lost track of them until I stumbled across Ginny, seventeen, homeless and pregnant, while shopping for cello CDs after midnight in the Price Walmart. That had only been five months ago, though it seemed like years. Ginny had been seduced by her mother's current boyfriend and her mother sided with the boyfriend, who denied everything, and abandoned Ginny, still in high school and three months pregnant, to move to Salt Lake City to "start over" with the boyfriend.

Everything Ginny had done since—getting her GED, having and raising the baby, working two jobs and going to night school—she had done on her own, including saving my little trucking company with her grit and quick wits. Without exaggeration, what she'd actually done was save my life. In the final month of her pregnancy a girlfriend from high school, without Ginny's knowledge, had contacted Nadine for help. Nadine hung up on her.

The full extent of how overwhelmed Ginny was with life had come down to this—her mother, who had never really been a mother except in name only. For my two cents, and mostly what she'd done to Ginny, a number of words came to mind, and none of them were "mother," though one of them started with it. Maybe the biggest surprise was that Nadine had come at all. I suspected there had to be a reason, and that reason had little to do with caring about Ginny and Annabelle.

Nadine was a couple years older than I was, which put her at about fortysomething or so. She knew her best qualities, and where and when to apply them, and her trim, coiffed, high-heeled, short-dressed self was on full display—though not for me. At her shoulder was the shadow of a white Stetson tipped low over a pink brow.

"Where's my grandchild!"

It was a perfect opportunity for me to count ten before I spoke, think about the situation and the emotions and the people involved—take the high road. "Shit!" I said, though discreetly. No one on the next street overheard me—probably.

Ginny kept her head against my shoulder. "They just got here a few minutes ago. I haven't had a chance to really talk to my mom yet."

"Here's your chance."

Ginny lifted her head and looked at me. A dribble of snot ran from her nose onto the tip of her silver nose ring. Oddly, it reminded me of her as a little girl, a bit of a tomboy, a sharp tongue and a tough sense of humor. At eighteen she still had those qualities, along with a strength that I had come to take for granted. That call—asking her mother for help—must have taken more courage than I could imagine.

With a strained calm, she turned to face her mother. "Let's talk inside, okay?"

I got a better look at Nadine and the new boyfriend once we were inside. Nadine stood with her hands on her hips champing at the bit to get started on me. She was the well-known piece of work. She had her strengths though. Not many women can manage to be both overdressed and underdressed at the same time. The boyfriend, who introduced himself to me as Rod, a "rancher," no handshake offered, perfectly fit the role of a Cadillac cowboy—middle-aged and pink, huge biceps available for viewing—and wearing enough cologne to get the attention of the EPA. If Rod was a rancher, and I knew a bunch of real ones, it involved wrangling cats and little dogs and a spread that was fenced by sidewalks and required a lawn mower.

Ginny took a shallow breath and steeled herself. She quickly explained about her sitter being sick, the tests, work, and how I *offered* to take Annabelle for the day. Doing her a favor.

I was amazed Nadine held her tongue as long as she had.

She cut Ginny off with "I bet he does lots of favors for you—and himself."

Ginny ignored her and continued through Nadine's interruption. The weather. The smart decision to leave the baby in Rockmuse with a friend.

Nadine huffed. "So he left my grandbaby with a *friend*? A *friend*? I can only imagine what his *friend* is." She let her words burn in the air a minute. "Oh God!"

I was clenching my jaw so tightly I could feel my teeth cracking. If only to relieve the pressure and make a contribution to the conversation, I said, "That grandchild you're so concerned about has a name. It's Annabelle."

"I know her name!"

Nadine teetered on her heels for a second and I could see her tightening her right hand into a fist. Rod put a beefy arm around her shoulder. "Settle down, honey." He let us all see a big white-capped grin. "My little filly does have a short fuse."

"Just when," demanded Nadine, "are you planning to get—" She took a breath she didn't need to cover not remembering her beloved granddaughter's name. "Annabelle back?"

"Tonight," I said.

"You mean right this damn minute, don't you?"

"Sure," I said. "Right after I take a shower. I'll be back with her this evening, depending on weather."

Ginny lowered her head. "Thanks, Ben."

Rod said, "I think that's the smart thing to do, pardner."

There was the color of both reproof and intimidation in what he said and how he said it. Rod wanted to let me know he was a tough guy. More than that, he wanted his "filly" to see him being a tough guy. I looked him over and let him see me look him over. Who calls a woman a filly? *Pardner?*

"Careful," he warned. "Womenfolk are present."

He was right, of course, and I counted to ten at least five times in the few seconds it took me to back out of the door.

Ginny followed me out on the porch and closed the door behind her. "I'm sorry, Ben. The important thing is she came when I called her. They're getting married. I've asked to live with them for a while in Reno. Just until I get on my feet."

"I understand," I said.

"Do you?" She started to cry again. "I hope so. You've been my best friend. Annabelle and I couldn't have made it through the past few months without you."

"I didn't know you were staying in touch with your mother."

"She phoned me a couple months ago."

"Well, she's trying," I said, not believing a word.

As it turned out, I was wasting my time.

Ginny let out a sour laugh. "She called me to borrow money."

I pulled her close to me and hugged her. "I'm still your best friend." I kissed the top of her purple-and-red spiked head. "Five hundred miles doesn't change that." It was not my place, nor was I inclined to try to talk her out of her decision. "You've thought this through? Quitting college. Everything?"

Ginny nodded.

"When are you leaving?"

"Probably tomorrow. They're staying at the Holiday Inn while I pack and tie up some loose ends at work and school."

"I'll miss you," I said, and went inside my side of the duplex.

27

oodbyes to people you really care about don't happen all
at once. Maybe the words get said, but the goodbyes go on.
I stood in my duplex and thought of her a few months ago
asleep in my old brown recliner, her dress hiked up and holding
her belly to relieve the weight, one baby wrapped inside another.
For someone I'd known as an adult for such a short time, she was
everywhere I looked. The duplex I now owned, my rig, my company, a few thousand dollars in the bank, taxes filed and paid,
bookkeeping up to date—on a computer program no less—all this
I owed to Ginny.

And I owed the long nights lying awake in my bed missing
Claire being gratefully disturbed and somehow comforted by Annabelle's crying from the other side of the wall. I would be saying
goodbye to Ginny often and for years.

The small-capacity hot water heater in my duplex kept me from
wasting water and taking long showers. I usually waited until the
water turned tepid before I got out—five minutes or ten minutes
tops. The hot water had gone to cold and I just let it run. The
previous day and the slow, cautious drive back had taken up residence in my shoulders and bloodshot eyes. When I finally turned
off the water I could hear knocking at my door. I pulled on the
dirty denim work shirt I had been wearing and wrapped a towel
around my waist.

By the time I opened the door Rod was pounding instead of knocking. "The women are off shopping. You and me need to have a man to man."

He reached down to open the screen door and I got there first and set the flimsy hook. I knew it wouldn't necessarily keep him out, but at least it sent him a message. I was thinking we were a man short for that conversation and I didn't feel like talking.

"I'm not in a talking mood," I said.

Rod pulled on the screen door handle and the lock held. "I'll be damned if you're going to keep me on your porch like a mongrel dog."

"Then get off my goddamned porch."

"Nadine told me the whole story," he said. "We all know whose baby that is. Don't try to deny it. You're a sorry son of a bitch for taking advantage of a naïve high school girl." With every word his voice grew louder. "Nadine and I are going to do right by her and the baby, even if you won't. Aren't you a sweetheart, letting her live next door. I bet you're liking that arrangement just fine. But it's over, and you're going to at least take some financial responsibility."

This was familiar territory to me. An almost forty-year-old single man cannot be friends with a single teenage young woman with a baby without a few tongues wagging. I usually let it go, except this wasn't just a tongue wagging. True to form, Nadine fed him a lie to excuse herself and avoid telling him the truth. She probably fanned the flames and pointed him at me just before she left with Ginny, hoping he'd pull some wrongheaded macho bullshit just like this. Rod's pink face had turned to a bright red. It wasn't all Nadine's doing. Rod was the kind of man who could whip himself into a frenzy with nothing more than his own words.

Behind Rod, just coming into view, Earl and Imogene, a couple in their seventies, were taking their daily noon walk, arm in arm, something they did seven days a week. I didn't know them well, just enough to say hello. Their house was a couple blocks away. The sun had come out and melted the snow off the sidewalk. Earl had been a heavy-machinery operator for the coal mine; Imogene had been an elementary schoolteacher. Earl was pulling his miniature green oxygen tank.

My loud conversation with Rod was exactly the kind of sordid domestic disturbance that I hated and that happened too often in my neighborhood. Calming Rod down wasn't going to be easy. I had to try. "Let me get dressed."

My offer at least had him thinking for a moment. "All right," he said. "Open up."

I wasn't going to let him in. If something was going to happen I wanted it in the open. Calling the police occurred to me—for a second. It wouldn't make a damn bit of difference if I had been the one to call. Rod could be holding a gun on me, or I could be dead on the ground, and they would arrest me. Simply going inside and closing my door would only result in more pounding and yelling. For all I knew he'd kick the door in anyway.

"No, Rod," I said, as calmly as I could manage. "That's not a good idea." If I'd stopped right there maybe things would have been different. Unfortunately for both of us, I didn't. "You need to cool down."

Telling anyone, especially a man, to cool down, usually has exactly the opposite effect. It sure as hell did on Rod. For some damn reason being told to cool down seemed to be interpreted as weakness, and weakness was opportunity to press the advantage. He reached for the screen door handle again and I could see he was going to put his back into it this time.

"Stay the fuck out of my house," I shouted.

"I'm coming in!"

Rod did put his back into it and the lock gave way all at once, so quickly it threw him off balance. In that instant I did what I had been trying to avoid. His left hand was still wrapped in the door handle when I hit old Rod as hard as I could through the screen door wire, my right fist to flesh, from the end of his nose to his jaw. The screen door separated from its hinges and covered him.

He stumbled backward off the steps of the porch and I followed. Once the backward momentum started he was helpless to stop. He tried to push off the screen door and I punched him again, harder, through the wire.

By the time he fell, he was on his back on the sidewalk with just part of the aluminum screen doorframe over his face and his white Stetson pushed up revealing his bare scalp. My knuckles were a shredded bloody mess from the wire. I straddled him and with my left hand I threw what was left of the frame aside. I pulled his hat off his head and held it over his face while I punched him again. He was barely conscious beneath his rumpled and now bloody hat when I stood up.

Earl and Imogene were standing a few feet away. Earl said, "Afternoon, Ben."

I apologized. "He tried to force his way into my home," I said between breaths. "If the police get involved, remember what you heard and saw."

Rod began grunting and moaning from under his hat. He was the type to have a gun in his vehicle. I looked to the curb and the Cadillac was gone, probably taken by Nadine and Ginny. Truth be told, he was probably lucky mine was in my cab a block away.

When I turned back to Earl and Imogene, Earl had a smile on his face. I repeated what I had said about remembering. Imogene raised her eyebrows with a wry smile of her own. "Oh, believe me, Ben, I'll remember."

I felt the chilled draft between my legs and realized the towel was lying on the ground halfway down my walk. It was only about ten feet, but it was a long, cold ten feet until I reached it and covered myself. Imogene stepped over Rod. Earl could have gone around if he'd wanted. Instead he stepped over as well and pulled the wheels of his oxygen tank across Rod's chest. Imogene waved back at me as they continued down the sidewalk.

28

I couldn't hear sirens. Yet. That could mean my neighbors hadn't called the police. Yet. I grabbed some clean clothes and dressed as quickly as I could. In my stocking feet and carrying my boots, I walked out my door. Three minutes or less. The street was empty. Cadillac was still gone, and so was Rod. But not far. He was sitting on the steps of Ginny's side of the duplex, his mangled and bloodstained hat in his hands.

"You sucker-punched me," he said, the fight if not the anger gone from his voice.

"Yes," I said, "I did. You wouldn't back off. And only a sucker can be sucker-punched. You might want to keep that in mind for next time."

Screw John Wayne westerns. I'd been in enough fights to know that when men get into it as Rod and I just had, they don't just get up and laugh, shake it off, and have a beer together. Rod and I were not going to have a beer together, then or ever—and no laughs, either. He was hurt, and hurt badly. My right hand was throbbing and torn to hell. The only thing both of us could be thankful about was there hadn't been any guns readily available.

I listened and still didn't hear any sirens. "You want to talk now?" I asked.

"No."

"Then maybe you'll listen." I sat down next to him and pulled on my boots as I spoke. "You're not going to believe me. I know that. But there's another story about Ginny and Annabelle and it's a sight different than the one you were told."

"You calling Nadine a liar?" He made certain he made eye contact with me. "Because if you are, I can go again. It might turn out differently."

I ignored him. Whether or not it turned out better for him, I didn't want to fight. I didn't want to fight the first time. "This is what I think," I said. "I think you're a decent man—a good man. And if you actually knew me, you might think the same about me. Maybe not. I've got a long history of poor decisions, and one way or another every damn day I answer for them. But bedding a teenager isn't one of them."

"Still sounds as if you're calling the woman I love a liar."

"If you love Nadine and you've offered her and Ginny and Annabelle a home, then good for all of you. If you get a few months or a year down the road and you still think I'm a piece of shit, then you give me a call and I'll let you do whatever you want to me."

This got him thinking. "The three weeks I've been with Nadine have been the happiest of my life. She's been good to me and like a mother to my three kids. My wife died a couple years ago and they've missed the hell out of her. So have I."

And there it was, upfront and clear as a bell. Nadine couldn't seem like a good mother and wife if she turned away her own child. This was all about appearances, until she married him. After that the truth would come out and it would be too late, for Rod, his kids, and Ginny would be worse off than she was now. Nadine had to make herself and her daughter the victims and me, the bad guy. There was no use trying to get that through to him.

I stood up. "Remember what I just said. You know where I live."

"I'm set pretty good for money and I don't mind supporting Ginny until she gets settled on her own. If you have an ounce of honor you'll send some money here and there to help out."

I said I would, but not because of honor or out of guilt. "I'm going to go get Annabelle now. It's a fair piece of driving and the weather could be bad. But I'll deliver her to Ginny as soon as I can. Guaranteed."

"You do that," he said.

The skin on his face was weeping blood from the wire mesh I'd driven into it. His nose was near the size of a lightbulb and there was a three-inch gash over his right eye that was still bleeding. He needed stitches, but I wasn't going to recommend he get them. I was way past any more talking. We were both alive and that was something—no thanks to Nadine. I walked over and picked up the pieces of my screen door and tossed them on the porch without another word.

IT WAS ONLY a five-minute drive to the hospital from my place. I thought I'd pick up the medical supplies from Dr. Stafford before she changed her mind. A quick side trip wasn't going to amount to much in what was going to be a long round-trip to Rockmuse to get Annabelle. The emergency waiting room was empty when I arrived and she was standing in the admission area.

I was nearing the reception desk when she saw me. "Meet me outside around back," she said.

It was a bit of a walk to get to the rear of the hospital. I had to go to the parking lot and then a block or so along the side of the building. She was standing just off the empty helicopter pad waiting for me. She held a small white chest with a red cross on it. When she handed it to me she said, "Technically this is stealing. Hospitals in general shouldn't be confused with charities."

I reminded her I had offered to pay. The offer was still on the table.

"I had to sit through three fund-raising receptions this year. I feel like I've already paid for this myself."

Her eyes immediately went to my bloodied knuckles. "Christ,

have you relapsed in two hours? I guess it's true, leopards don't change their spots."

"Maybe not," I said. "Spots don't matter. There's always someone who won't ever let you forget you're a leopard."

She got my meaning. "Well, leopard, you should get some ice on those knuckles. Then some antibiotic." She examined my face and seemed surprised there wasn't a violent mark on it. "The other guy must be in bad shape. It was a man, wasn't it? Should I call the police?"

I wasn't sure if she was serious. It stung to hear the accusation that I might have hit a woman. "I wish you wouldn't. It wasn't my fault and the other *man* is fine."

She tipped her head in the direction of my knuckles. "He's probably alive but judging from that I'd say he's far from fine. I won't call them this time." She added, "But I won't forget in case it becomes an issue later."

I thanked her and started back to my truck. She caught up with me in a few feet. "By the way, how's Walt Butterfield doing?"

I stopped. She said she treated him when he had his motorcycle accident. Only Walt and I knew he hadn't had a damn motorcycle accident; that's the story he told when he was admitted. The truth was he got caught in the same flash flood that had killed Claire and her former husband. I'd carved Walt out of an arroyo wall and the churning water of sand and rocks beat him near to death. It must have been like being caught in a commercial washing machine. Still, he waited a week to go to the hospital, and when he did he rode his vintage Vincent motorcycle there. His choice.

"Okay, I guess. How'd you know I knew Walt Butterfield?"

"When we treated him this past June he listed you as his emergency contact and next of kin on the admissions form."

Articulate as ever, I expressed my shock that Walt would do such a thing. "No shit?"

"No shit," Wanda repeated. "I thought it was odd too."

I knew why I thought it was out of character for Walt—and I was oddly touched he'd do such a thing. I was curious why she thought so and asked her.

"Usually people list a family member."

I'd known Walt for twenty years and he had no family, or friends, unless I counted myself, and that was probably just unbridled optimism on my part. "Walt doesn't have any family," I said. "He doesn't have any friends either, unless you count me. I'm surprised he did."

"That explains it then."

"What?"

"The commotion when his son visited him. I wasn't there, though I understand it wasn't a happy reunion. Hospital Security had to escort the man out and Mr. Butterfield had to be sedated."

I just stood there.

"Next time you see him, tell him we'd like for him to drop by for some follow-up. No one ever answers his phone."

I walked away without thanking her and got in my truck and drove almost all the way to the junction of US 191 and State Highway 117 before I could take a regular breath. I was wrong; Walt still had secrets. At least this one wasn't a corpse. A son? Walt had a son.

29

The road ahead wound into a brilliant sunlight and the snow-capped hills threw back mirrorlike flashes into my eyes. A shrouded red haze was all I could see of the mesa cliffs in the distance. It might be snow, but my guess was fog from the warmer air on the ground rising to meet the cooler, shifting currents coming down from the plateau. Out of habit I began to slow to make the turn into Walt's diner. It wasn't a turn I felt like taking and I quickly shifted back up and pressed the accelerator down—hard.

The Well-Known Desert Diner, The Never-Open Desert Diner, began to recede in the distance behind me, swallowed up in the glare and rise and fall of the road. I'd had a love affair with the place for twenty years and once referred to it as a junkyard, and Walt as its guard dog. Now I wanted to leave it behind as fast as I could, and the faster I went, the harder I pushed my truck, it stayed in my mirror—its white adobe walls and green trim, its pale gravel driveway and antique bubble gas pumps—following me, keeping pace with me, as if the two of us were tethered by an invisible towline. Somewhere on a straight or a turn or on a bridge over a nameless canyon, it stopped being a diner and I saw it for what it really was, the museum of a life that no longer existed.

I could have used ten thousand miles of bad and crooked road to try to sort out Walt and his diner. Maybe a hundred thousand. And after that I'd probably still feel as if it were a tangled mystery. I was a visitor to Walt and his museum—nothing more. Every damn thing in the diner dated from before Bernice's rape—the Wurlitzer jukebox, lime-green stools and booths—time stood still there. Even his motorcycles were from another time. This was Walt's carefully preserved world. But the visitor only saw what was on display, and that included Walt himself. If you asked questions, your ticket was torn up and you were thrown out. Most of what I knew, I knew by accident. The Never-Open Desert Diner was closed for a reason; and it looked open, welcoming, for a reason. But God help you if you tried to enter. There were more rooms than you knew. Claire was a room. The corpse of one of Bernice's rapists was a room. And now, by accident, I learned of another room—a son. I was tired of all the rooms. It felt like the end of the love affair.

I WAS MAKING good time getting to Rockmuse, and I hoped I made equally good time on my return. There was no reason to think I wouldn't. Steam rose from the warm asphalt on a short straight stretch. John's cross came into view, its weather-worn brown wood standing out on the shoulder among the prairie grass and scrub junipers. This had to be the scene of the hit-and-run and I wanted to take a look for myself, not that I expected to learn anything.

I parked fifty yards ahead and walked back to the cross. Snow still clung to John's knapsack of camping supplies, though its contents had been scattered—a couple cans of chili, canteen, pan, and miscellaneous items. I stepped carefully around the cross, which sat upright on one of its corners, probably held in place by the bracket and tire from the wheelbarrow. Unless George righted the cross, which I doubted—why would he?—the impact knocked John cleanly out from underneath it. I walked out into the middle of 117. No skid marks. This stretch had been clear yesterday, probably sunny. From where I stood I could see the knapsack and its contents strewn in a line pointing beyond the shoulder and out into the desert. A plane had crashed at the small airport in Price. It left what they called a debris field. This was John's debris field and it wasn't much.

There, standing in the middle of the highway, I thought again of Walt, and his debris field. He had put me down as his next of kin.

About ten feet from the end of the debris field some branches of a scrub juniper had been torn off its slender trunk and I supposed that was where John's body had landed.

I knelt on one knee and looked out past the tree and shoulder grasses into the desert. When I stood, I saw downtown Rockmuse, floating in the foggy distance, maybe a mile or two southeast, though the road itself at that point continued due east for a few miles before a long, sweeping right turn to the south that led to the City Limits sign.

I took a few more steps and tripped over a discarded old tire half-buried in the sand. Next to it was a black plastic trash bag, also partly buried. It had been there long enough that the plastic had begun to deteriorate, exposing its contents—fast-food garbage. Welcome to the desert. Throw your shit anywhere you like. It's the desert.

A little farther on I saw a faded pink piece of paper, and then another, caught in some dead brush. I knew what they were before I picked them up—some of the Abandoned Vehicle warnings that Trooper Smith had stuck to Ginger's broken-down old Subaru. Wind had blown them all over the place. They'd practically blown away even as I reached for them. There wasn't much to see, and what I saw wasn't much help.

Back at the highway I guessed at where George had come to a stop in his jeep. There were tire tracks everywhere and could have belonged to any vehicle, though not George's. The tires on his jeep were as smooth as river rock. Almost everyone's vehicle in Rockmuse was running on bald tires. By the time Trooper Smith got out to investigate, John would be buried and mostly forgotten and the desert would have blown away and buried anything useful.

I got back in the cab of my truck and released the brakes. I didn't go; I just sat there. I set the brakes and again walked back to where I thought the jeep had been parked. While there weren't any tire prints to speak of, there also wasn't any sign of how George got John on the hood of his jeep. If it had been me, at six foot four and two hundred pounds, I would have picked up John in my arms, or put him over my shoulder, to carry him. Even with my strength, Dr. Wanda was right, it was tough, awkward work to dead-lift an unconscious person.

So what would George have done? He might have driven the jeep up next to where John lay and pulled him by his wrists over the hood. Except to get that close, there had to be some sign he drove the jeep way off the shoulder. There wasn't. That left the same tactic, but meant he had to have pulled John maybe twenty feet or more to his jeep. And what wasn't there was any sign of John's heels dragging. With his weight and bootheels, and a small man struggling, it seemed to me there would have to be. Of course, I wasn't a cop, or a trained investigator. I was just guessing.

Ginger's old Subaru had become the new Rockmuse City Limits sign because once you passed it you knew Rockmuse was just around the bend. I confess that I often laughed when I saw the JUST DIVORCED painted across the back window. The message was hardly visible anymore after months of rain and dust plastered to the car. And now snow, which had melted, leaving dried muddy rivulets from the roof down the doors. The wind had managed to take most of Trooper Smith's pink warning tags. It made sense that at least a couple had blown back up the highway and joined the rest of the litter skittering along the shoulder.

I had one job. Get Annabelle and take her straight back to Price and Ginny. I could have stopped on the way to deliver the water to Dan Brew. It didn't even occur to me. If he was really pressed for drinking water he could melt some snow, though I did leave him two five-gallon cans. That should last him a couple days for drinking and cooking. These were excuses. I didn't do what I said I'd do, come back on my return and deliver his fifty-gallon container of water. Maybe I felt a little guilt. What I felt most was the sting of not delivering on a promise.

I drove straight through town and out to Phyllis's place. My route took me past the theater and I considered stopping, if only for a minute. There was no reason. John's body wouldn't be there. The town didn't have a morgue, or a funeral parlor, and just like all the other businesses that had teamed up and merged, the Rockmuse Mercantile had the largest cooler and it pulled double-duty. When someone died, that's where he or she was taken, and like the others, John was probably napping on cold cuts and fresh vegetables or across crates of milk. That's where he would stay until the county sent the wagon out for him, and they'd be in no hurry. From there, I thought with some sadness, he'd go into a pauper's grave at the cemetery in Price.

I wasn't much for socializing with the dead. Not once since the old couple that adopted me had died had I visited their graves. The one exception was Claire. And I didn't talk to her. I just stood over her grave in silence and engaged in the Trickle Down Theory of communication, which probably worked as well with the dead as its economic counterpart did with the living. All she had was Walt and me, in death as well as life. There was room near her for John. Maybe, if the county had no objection ... I didn't even know his last name. As far as I knew, no one did. If George hadn't brought him in he'd just be roadside litter, and unlike a tire, only for a while until the desert and the animals got to him.

30

The white fog was tinged with a soft pink from the low sun in the west reflecting off the mesa. The fog wasn't all that thick—at least, not yet—and I could see the horses still in the pasture and Phyllis's two-story ranch house. Coming up the driveway the pink mist made it all seem dreamlike. Twenty-four hours without sleep is not something I would recommend. It would be close to forty-eight by the time I delivered the baby to Ginny. My right hand ached, my shoulders ached, and there were places in me that held Ginny, Annabelle, and John that ached as well. Sleep alone wouldn't heal them. If I hadn't needed to turn right around and head straight back to Price, I would have asked Phyllis if I might spend the night in a comfortable bed. If she'd said no I might have fallen asleep in my cab. Instead, I would ask her to refill the thermos with coffee and head back out with the baby.

Phyllis didn't know when to expect me. I stood on the wide porch and knocked on the door and waited for what seemed a long time. When she opened the door she looked as tired as I felt. Though it was late afternoon, she was in her robe and slippers.

"Long night?" I asked.

She tightened the belt on her robe and ran her fingers through her unkempt hair before she answered. "You don't know the half of it," she said. She sighed and let her chin drop to her chest. "I had all night to remember why women my age don't have babies! Grandparents get to give them back after a few hours."

"Well, the baby won't keep you up tonight. But I haven't had much luck in finding the girl's father. Would you mind keeping her a little longer?"

"And that's the other half," she moaned. "Between the two of them, I was up and running all night. And I mean running."

Phyllis leaned with her back against the door while she gave me a summary of her evening, night, and day and why she was still in her bathrobe at four in the afternoon. I'd be lying if I said she didn't look as pretty as she was tired. Or maybe it was the laughter that bubbled out from time to time as she spoke. Yes, she was exhausted. She was also obviously happy as she recounted her adventures with the children in what had been, before their arrival, a big, quiet, empty home.

Annabelle must have been on her best infant behavior with me during the ride to Rockmuse. According to Phyllis, the baby hadn't slept more than an hour at a time and wanted to be fed every moment she wasn't sleeping. And she was very vocal about it. As for the girl, Phyllis had not been joking about the running. After the bath and a much-needed nap, she hit the ground running. Literally. I'd gotten a small taste of that across from the diner when she suddenly bolted and started off down the trail to Desert Home.

"The first time," Phyllis said, "I was standing in the kitchen feeding the baby. She was right at my side. The next thing I knew I heard the back door open and she was running across the field toward the desert. Not walking. Not jogging. She was running!"

"Did she see something?" I asked. "Where was the dog?"

"Nothing to see. There's nothing but sand and rock and snakes all the way to Moab. Which is where she'd be right now if I hadn't managed to catch up with her. And that dog! Just loping along behind her. I think he was wondering how long he could keep up." Phyllis shook her head. "Wherever she goes, he goes. He sat next to the tub when I gave her a bath."

I thanked her. "You were lucky you saw her. You must be in pretty good shape to catch her."

"Luck? You have no idea. I had just enough time to put the baby in the sink. It was all I could think of. But I would have never caught up to her if—"

"If what?"

"If she hadn't stopped. I'd been shouting for her to stop. Maybe she didn't understand me, but she didn't even slow down. Or turn around. I swear she was the Energizer Bunny. Then she just stopped. When I reached her she wasn't even breathing hard, just standing and staring out into the desert. Not a hundred-yard stare—a hundred-mile stare."

"She came back willingly?"

"Not until I offered her my hand. Thank God she and the baby are both sleeping right now. I didn't know when you were returning."

"I guess I better take her with me," I said. "Though I don't know what I'm going to do with her. I've gotten nowhere finding her father. It's probably best to take her to whatever government agency takes abandoned children. A couple days more of looking might not change anything. There's a good chance the INS picked him up."

"But it might?"

"It might," I said. "It might not."

"Then let's give it another day or two. She's a strange one, but such a sweet girl. Manita fits her. And she's a long way from home, wherever that is. Maybe Mars." Phyllis laughed then—a tired, sleepless laugh. "As long as I keep her close and the doors to the outside locked, she's safe. I taped an old walkie-talkie on to use as a monitor."

"Likely she's worn out," I offered. "She'll probably sleep."

"She'll be fine, Ben. Don't worry. Find her father if you can. I'll have plenty of time to rest later. Besides, this is good for me."

"The exercise?"

"Well, there is that. But I haven't had a moment or the energy to make myself a drink. I'm fast becoming a member of the 'I Don't Give a Damn What Time It Is Anywhere' Club."

I asked her if she had enough strength to make me some coffee. Twenty minutes later, with a warm thermos in the console, fresh diapers and four full bottles of formula, and Annabelle sleeping off a milk drunk in her car seat, I pulled out of the turnaround.

The fog was now glowing pink and pulsing from the setting sun beating itself against the mesa walls. We had peeked in on the girl while the coffee was brewing. She lay on her stomach, arms out, no more than a small brown boat adrift at sea on the enormous four-poster bed. The dog, curled up next to the bed, registered our intrusion with only an ear twitch. The red lights in her shoe heels blinked on and off in the dim bedroom.

In the hallway, Phyllis whispered, "It's funny, when I finally caught up with Manita and the dog out there in the desert—she was just staring—I got this feeling she knew where she was going."

I imagined myself at her age, loose in the world and alone. I always knew where I was going too—somewhere else—as fast as I could get there. These days I only went back and forth between no place and nowhere, though for a while it had looked like Claire might change that. I wondered if that was where Manita was headed. I hoped not.

ROCKMUSE HAD NEVER seemed like more of a ghost town as I pulled onto Main Street. Most of the streetlights had burned out years ago. Even the stores that were open looked closed. A steady wind brushed the wispy pink fog across my headlights. It hadn't been my plan to stop in town, except for a fast fuel top-off at the Shell station on my way out. Ginny was waiting on Annabelle and I aimed to get her there as soon as possible. Lenny was in front of the theater smoking a cigarette. He saw me at the same moment

I saw him and he waved. There was no longer any reason for him to be there. What the hell, Lenny deserved to be thanked and I doubted anyone else would get around to it.

I pulled over and set my flashers on the small chance another car might appear. Lenny jumped up on the running board and I lowered the driver's side window. "Damn, it's quiet," he said. "Sometimes this town gives me the creeps."

"Surprised to see you here," I said.

"You told me to stay. I've been here almost 24/7. The good news is he sort of came out of it early this morning. Mumbled a bunch of religious stuff. Sounded like names. Freaked Ginger out."

The fatigue had taken its toll and I hadn't really been paying close attention. All I wanted to do was thank him and I had just been waiting for him to take a breath so I could.

Several long seconds passed before I spoke. "Are you telling me John is still alive?"

"Yeah," he said. "But that was ten minutes ago. I'm kind of amazed myself. He's hanging in there. We're down to the last saline bag. Did you manage to find some in Price?"

The emergency medical chest was on my passenger-side floorboard. I set the brakes and used the minute walking around my truck to think about what Lenny had just told me. The cold fog was a welcome slap in the face. As soon as the sun set, the temperature would fall and the road surface would freeze.

I handed Lenny the small chest.

"I thought you'd be happy John's made it this far," he said.

"I am happy," I said. "Just tired."

Both were true. What was also true was that someone had canceled Life Flight. The only assumption I could make was, other than that the message had been misunderstood, which was far and outside, whoever made the call wanted John to have a better chance to die. There were conclusions I could draw from that. John might have recognized something or someone in the moment before impact. The problem was, I couldn't focus on what they might be from the lack of sleep. My thinking wasn't any clearer than Main Street.

Annabelle woke up and began to cry. Lenny asked: "Is that what it sounds like?" He didn't wait for a reply. "You delivering babies now?"

"Lately, it's about all I am managing to deliver," I said. "And don't ask." I told Lenny to keep staying with John and not to let anyone near him. "No visitors. You or Ginger need to be with him every minute. Both of you would be best."

Lenny nodded. "Okay, Ben. No one's come around anyway."

"Don't tell anyone you saw me."

"Even Ginger?"

"She's going to know anyway when she sees the saline bags and medical supplies." Between squalls from Annabelle I asked if Trooper Smith or a county deputy had made it into town.

Neither had. Lenny wore a *What's up?* expression, though he wisely didn't ask any more questions. He took the chest and went inside the theater. Annabelle's screams livened up the deserted downtown until I closed the door. One thing was for sure, that kid had a pair of new lungs and she knew how to use them.

The fog was a welcome screen at the Shell station. Eckhardt couldn't see the pumps from inside, and all I could see was the hazy light from the windows of the convenience store. If you've seen one hidden, counter-mounted, foot-operated shotgun, you've seen them all. One is too many.

While I topped off the tank, I decided to also top off Annabelle, one hand on the diesel nozzle and one holding the bottle. I wanted to get on the road as soon as possible and while there was still some daylight left. Attending to the baby and diesel at the same time seemed like a time-saver. The asphalt around the pumps was getting slick when I carried her back to the cab. She was already dozing when I settled her into the car seat. It was 6:47 when we left the station and headed into the desert.

31

The freezing fog stayed with us all the way on 117 and onto US 191 into Price. The drive had been slow but steady and I would have arrived in Price sooner if not for Annabelle. Highway 117 could have hosted the Stanley Cup Playoff. The temperature hovered at fifteen degrees. Keep the wheels turning on ice and you'll keep moving. Stop and you'll likely stay where you are while the tires spin trying to get enough traction to pull the trailer. With the dense fog and the icy road it was too dangerous to stop as often as she would have liked.

Most of the trip was spent listening to her cry, though I did manage to find safe places to pull over a few times and feed her. One wasn't as safe as I thought. I needed to stretch my legs and figured I might as well feed her at the same time. I paced back and forth in front of my headlights holding the baby in my arms, a blanket covering her face and the bottle from the cold. The headlights began to drift toward the shoulder. My whole rig was slowly sliding off the road without me. There was nothing I could do but watch. After a foot or so, the tractor angled slightly away, pointing the headlight beams out into the desert. Cautiously, I opened the door and got Annabelle and myself safely inside just as it began to slide again. For the better part of a mile, balancing Annabelle and the steering wheel, I feathered the accelerator in second gear and gradually regained traction.

Sweat was dripping off my forehead. Annabelle did her part. She slept through it all.

It was a few minutes after one o'clock when I parked my rig in front of the duplex. The Cadillac was gone and there was a light burning in Ginny's living room. She appeared at my shoulder as I was lifting the car seat out of the cab.

"She needs changing," I said. "If she doesn't, then I predict she'll explode like a water balloon any minute. We went through four bottles of formula in six hours."

Ginny didn't say a word. She put her face close and stared at Annabelle in the car seat. Annabelle stared back and then grinned up at her mother and reached out her little fingers for Ginny's nose ring. It was a touching moment I supposed, and I was happy to have the two of them together. On the other hand, it also occurred to me that one day soon those little fingers would grab ahold of the nose ring and give it a tug. I kind of wanted to be there for that, though I knew I probably wouldn't be. I hated piercings, especially that nose ring. I'd pay to be present for such a magical moment.

Ginny took the car seat and I carried the diaper bag and together we went into her duplex. She'd been packing. The front room had stacks of cardboard boxes already full and some open and partially filled. Annabelle began to cry and Ginny produced a bottle before the baby could get her back into it.

"You beat up Rod pretty bad, Ben. He seems like a good guy. Better than most my mother hooks up with. Jury is still out though. You want to tell me why?"

"You don't know?"

"No. But I bet it had something to do with my mother."

I was tired to the bone. I didn't want to discuss Rod, or Nadine, and my guess was neither did Ginny. Bringing up Rod was a way to put off saying goodbye.

"That's a safe bet," I said. "I think he is a good guy. The problem is he is in love with your mother and the poor man doesn't know who she is."

"That's why you beat him up?"

"No," I said. "That's why I didn't kill him when he came after me. I hope he gets wise before it's too late. I hope you get what you need and away from her before it's too late for you and Annabelle. You'll find out sooner or later why Rod and I tangled. But not from me."

"They were arguing when they left for their hotel. Rod wanted to talk about what happened. My mother didn't. Not in front of me. Don't argue in front of the kid, or some shit like that. She wanted to call the police. He refused."

"Good for him," I said. "Did she call them?"

"No. Rod said if she did he wouldn't file a complaint. What happened to your screen door?"

I ignored her question. "What time do you leave tomorrow? I'm hoping we might have another chance to say goodbye when we're both conscious."

"How many goodbyes do we need?"

Damn, I loved that young woman. There were moments when I was sure she was indeed my daughter. Who else could be so proud of her when she said something like that?

"Okay," I said. "I'm sleeping in a little tomorrow. If we have another chance, then we will. If not, we won't." I kissed her on the forehead. "You need anything, anytime, you get in touch with me. Drop me a line once in a while, huh?"

Ginny gently pushed me out and closed the door softly behind me. I could hear her crying on the other side.

After checking for phone messages and finding there weren't any, the last thing I remembered was brushing my teeth. Around four, my usual time to start the day, I was awakened by Annabelle's crying. I lay in bed awhile savoring her cries, and then held on to them in the silence afterward. I went back to sleep and slept a deep, dreamless sleep until a bright desert sun shredded its way through my bedroom curtain.

My first thought was not of Ginny, but of George, the desert rat who had brought John in. My second thought was to phone Trooper Smith. My third thought was Ginny, and I decided she was right. We'd had enough goodbyes. No matter how many times we tried they were never going to be good.

For five seconds I stayed in bed ignoring the silence coming from Ginny's side of the duplex. Then I ignored the silence while I took another shower and dressed, slathered antibiotic on my knuckles, and continued ignoring it all the way to my truck and then to Tractor and Farm Supply, where I bought two hundred-pound sacks of 9 percent textured equine sweet feed, the heaviest sacks available. I'd decided to postpone phoning Trooper Smith until I had thought through what I was going to say.

MAYBE I'D ONLY had five hours of sleep, but it was enough to renew my energy. It was a gorgeous high desert day in the sixties, only a light breeze and clear for miles in every direction. I'd spent two days doing absolutely nothing for which I would be paid. In the interest of survival, if not work ethic, I drove to the transfer station and surveyed the cargo stacked up and waiting for me on the loading dock. The late start wouldn't hurt me too much, and in thirty minutes I had taken on a crated rebuilt John Deere tractor engine, two pallets of cinder block, ten sections of prefab vinyl fencing, and various cases of this and that. The heaviest cargo paid the best.

The loading and organizing might have taken me longer if not for the discovery that a change in schedule introduces you to a whole new world. Transfer-station workers I hardly knew would stop and say, "A little late, aren't you, Jones?"

I'd say I was and it was a good story and then ask them to help me sort this or lift that. Some actually stayed and helped for a few minutes until they figured out I wasn't going to tell them the story. I felt a little like Tom Sawyer getting his friends to whitewash Aunt Polly's fence for him. By ten I was at the Stop 'n' Gone fueling. Ana was at the register. I stuck my head in the door and asked if Cecil had shown up. She shook her head and I was on US 191 by 10:20.

32

A few hardy colorful desert flowers popped back up along the roadside. The grasses that were beaten down from the snow and ice greened a little and reached again for the sunlight. The desert was always a showcase for resilience.

I had left behind a carton of motorcycle parts on the dock waiting to be delivered to Walt. Usually I put Walt's deliveries on the truck regardless of when they arrived or my delivery schedule. Not this time. I roared past the diner with barely a glance at the place. I knew I would eventually have to stop, with or without a delivery, just not now—not for a while.

My first stop was Dan Brew's sod house. He didn't show. I left his drum of water just off the drive. The portable hydraulic lift I used groaned under the weight and its metal wheels sunk into the soft ground until I couldn't move it any farther. The thought of knocking on Dan's door and asking for help disappeared quickly when I realized his help meant seeing Dan, probably in boots and underwear.

The lift properly stowed, I stood on my lift gate and gazed around the yard. Something was slightly off, as if the ground was somehow tilted in places and sunken in others. Rain could do that sometimes, except it hadn't rained. Whatever caused the earth to settle didn't bother me enough to stick around. Today was going to be a payday and I was a man on a mission to get a paycheck—and try to answer a question that must have been nagging me in my sleep.

Down rutted, nameless side roads, bouncing over holes and across dirt bridges and arroyos, one by one I ran through my delivery schedule without a hitch. Hellos and farewells were nods, which was the way desert folks preferred to conduct their business, both professional and personal.

I saved my call on George for last, and the sun was to the west of high when I pulled onto the shoulder to try to recall exactly where the turnoff was to his place. It had been a few years or more since I'd made a delivery to him. Since I began driving 117 I probably hadn't delivered to him more than two or three times. He did have horses the last time I was there. Even if he no longer had them, I'd improvise. Of course, he was a crafty old man and there was a chance he'd see through my ruse. If he did, no harm done, and I'd be back where I started.

My delivery days were generally spent without the luxury of man-made signs and addresses, no numbers or arrows, or mailboxes, or even fences or mile markers. My customers liked it that way and lived the roadless, dead-end life with a kind of fierce passion for isolation that few would want and even fewer would survive for very long. For the most part their philosophy was "Make do or do without," and even some essentials, especially water when and where it was needed, were considered luxuries. Desert trees that go without water for long periods develop a rock-hard, stringy grain that resists death with a grim and tenacious attachment to survival. Old desert rats like George thought such trees were pretty things, but a bit too fragile to truly respect. As a result, in my opinion, the desert rats rarely died from doing without. If and when they died, it was usually from an accidental overdose of stubbornness.

I left my truck idling on the shoulder and walked several hundred feet up a small brown hill of burnt rock. My signs and addresses and arrows were natural: gullies, stone pillars of various shades of red, a bend in 117, a clutch of gnarled bushes creating a distinctive pattern, and sometimes unique shadows, depending upon weather and time of day. I saw what I was searching for about a mile away to the northwest—a crumbling spire of granite leaning against an upheaved striated sheet of white sandstone.

George's place was behind me, and I had to backtrack west a couple miles and drive slowly to find the dip in the highway that signaled the broken shoulder and entrance to the dirt road that led to his house. Most of the desert rats didn't live more than a mile or two off of 117. George's place was a good five miles of driving on a surface that refused to be dignified by calling it a road.

The last mile was flat as a board and his collection of hovels was visible while my truck banged and rocked along. It is unwise to simply drop in on a desert rat, and I knew George had to see me coming. This gave him plenty of time to think about why I was coming to visit and be ready. How he greeted me might give me a sign about what to expect.

Over the years George had strung together various old travel trailers and wooden structures into a kind of compound. A twenty-five-foot '50s-era trailer had been expanded by welding two smaller travel trailers to its ends in the shape of an I. Nearby was a lean-to built up against a small hill that served as a garage for the Willys, and off of that another outbuilding made of scrap wood with a sloped, corrugated steel roof that served as a barn of sorts; and behind that, a corral that was really just a circle of odds and ends of junk metal and rusting farm machinery. I was relieved to see a couple nags in the corral. The overall impression was that a scrap train had derailed and dumped its contents in the middle of the desert.

I parked about a hundred feet from the trailers and sat in my cab waiting for George to acknowledge my presence. Several minutes went by before he appeared bareheaded in the doorway of the longest trailer, jean jacket, and jeans tucked inside a pair of tall black riding boots that reached to just below his knees. He held a rifle slung across his left arm. Another couple minutes went by while he just stood there in his open doorway squinting across the dirt-and-sand expanse that was his front yard. He motioned with the barrel of the rifle for me to approach. The rifle didn't bother me. Considering George and the etiquette of the desert, it usually was as close to a handshake as you could expect.

I stopped about fifty feet from George. He raised his chin an inch or two and bluntly asked why I was there.

"Just to say thank you for bringing John in. If not for you, he'd've been a buffet for the carrion eaters in no time."

George's grip tightened around the trigger guard of his rifle. "You drove all the way out here for that?"

"No," I said, and watched as his elbow dipped and the barrel angled toward me. "I had a couple bags of good-quality horse feed I overordered. Can't return them. Thought maybe you could use them, along with my appreciation."

"Free?"

"Yep," I said. I decided to get a little salty with him. "You want 'em or not? I haven't got all day to talk."

That did the trick. "Sure," he said, "I'll take the feed off your hands. Let's put them in the barn."

When he joined me at the rear of my trailer I had already unchained the lift gate and had hopped up to open the door. He was still carrying the rifle, a pristine lever-action .30-30, pre-WWII, and just as lethal as it was then. I ignored it as much as I could and went straight to the back of my trailer and dragged both hundred-pound bags to the lip of the gate and jumped down.

I hoisted one onto my shoulder. "Dammit, George, you going to shoot it or carry it?"

Reluctantly, he leaned the rifle against my rear bumper. As I turned, my sack bumped the remaining one, which I had managed to balance precariously, and it landed on the ground in front of the gate. I started walking, my back toward George. "In the barn?"

I might not have been looking, but I was listening. After a few grunts, I heard exactly the sound I expected—the sack being dragged. I dropped mine and said, "Let me help you with that, George."

I grabbed one end and he grabbed the other. Together we carried it to his barn and returned for the other. He was a cagey, poker-faced son of a bitch, I'll give him that. Nothing moved on his face either going or returning. I didn't see it coming and was half-bent to grab the sack I'd dropped. Pure quickness was all that saved me. George flew by the second sack like lightning, nimble as hell, and reached the rifle a second ahead of me. He had his hand wrapped around the chamber and I was just able to stamp my boot on it and knock it to the ground and out of his grasp. It went off and the report echoed across the desert.

George jumped back a step. I kept my bootheel on the rifle. Somewhere along the way to the barn he figured out what I was up to. As we stood there, I could see anger but no fear, and certainly no sign of surrender.

"You're not as smart as you think you are, Jones."

I shook my head, feeling both weary and lucky, careful to keep both my eyes on him. "George," I said, "I'm not smart at all. In fact, I'm dumb as dirt. I only seem smart standing next to an idiot."

"I didn't run down the preacher," he said.

I relaxed and leaned my back against the trailer, keeping the rifle under my foot. Maybe if I seemed to lower the situation a notch, so would George. "I don't think you did," I said. "My guess is you're not a coward, or a killer." I tapped my foot on the rifle. "Of course, if I'd been a touch slower you might have had a chance to prove me wrong."

This struck him as amusing. "Well, thanks for that, I guess."

"You're welcome," I said. "Now, back up."

George took a couple steps backward.

"A little farther, please. Your dancing has made you a bit too light on your feet for my taste."

My comment burned through his smile. He backed up a few more steps.

I lifted my heel and bent over to pick up the rifle with my left hand. He didn't surprise me. In an instant he covered the distance and lunged forward, stretching for the gun. I backhanded him hard across the cheek with my right. He stumbled and sat down hard on the ground, which he used to his advantage by scrambling on all fours toward the rifle. By the time he got to where he was going I'd chambered another round and he was eye to eye with the barrel.

Slapping an old man around wasn't something to be proud of and I confess to feeling a bit ashamed. Underestimating old men like George and Walt, and a few others who came to mind, could leave you proud and hurt, if not dead. Dealing with a smudge of shame was a small price to pay. If anything, old men were more dangerous. Despite appearances to the contrary, the ones I usually came across in the desert didn't give much away to age. You sure as hell didn't want to count on infirmity. Old men got older when young men got cocky.

He skittered backward on his hands like a spider. "I told you I didn't hit the preacher. What's this all about?"

"It's about whoever helped you lift John onto the hood of your jeep. You in a sharing mood?"

George stood up and dusted himself off. "I got nothing to say. You're not the law. If you were I still got nothing to say."

I believed him, but pushed anyway. "Come on, George. It was an accident. I'm not in the justice business. I wouldn't be here at all except now whoever did it seems hell-bent on finishing what was started. You don't want any part of that, do you?"

What he said next surprised me. "Could be a job that needs to be finished."

There was no use asking him what he meant; he wasn't going to say another word. The set of his jaw and squint showed me his mind was made up. He knew I wouldn't shoot, not that he cared. I could have beat on him awhile except, in the end, all I'd get was a fist that hurt worse than it already did. And it already hurt plenty.

I jacked out all the remaining rounds onto the ground, including the one in the chamber. "I don't want to see or hear that your bony old ass is anywhere near Rockmuse for a while."

"Or what?"

He had me there. It was a beautiful old rifle. A classic. Well cared for. Worth serious money. After a moment spent openly admiring it and caressing the bluing with my fingertips, I spun it around and gripped it by its barrel—and swung it down hard as if I was pile-driving a railroad spike into the cast-iron lift gate. The polished wooden stock splintered and the fine old metal magazine shattered into pieces. What was left in my hands, mostly the now badly dented and slightly bent barrel, I tossed onto the ground between us. I hated to do it. On the other hand, it saved time and my voice, and George deserved as clear an answer as I could give him.

My truck tires kicked up a fair amount of dust as I hastily drove out of George's little compound. He didn't watch me go. From my rearview mirror I could see him in the haze standing over the pieces of the Winchester, head down and forlorn, as if in mourning beside a fresh grave.

I didn't feel as bad as I thought I might. Maybe it was George going for the rifle—the second time. Or his refusal to tell me who had helped him carry John—or Ginny's departure. Or my morning exercise with Rod. Or Nadine's nasty scheming.

Busting his rifle to hell was a meaner thing to do than if I'd slapped him around or just shot him. Maybe my spots had faded a bit, but I was still a leopard, especially when I was up against another leopard, even an old one. George would not forget what I did. He would not forget what I knew. As long as he was alive, even if and when the hit-and-run was sorted out, I'd have to watch my back if he was nearby—even when he wasn't. The good news was, unless he was getting a dancing lesson from Ginger, I'd smell him coming. Maybe he might think twice before going into Rockmuse or warning whoever blindsided John. Maybe not.

33

When I finally got back on 117 it was a forty-five-minute drive to Rockmuse and the adrenaline rush had faded. George wasn't even on my mind. Turning south put the mesa square in my eyes, its towering red, mica-flaked walls stretching for miles, always there and always a background, even when I couldn't see it. I'd done a day's work and it felt damn good. Seeing the mesa on a clear day felt good. Having an open road in the sunlight felt good, and I just drove for a while with nothing but the mesa and the desert and the setting sun at my back for companionship—until I reached the cross, which had become a natural formation of its own, growing up out of the shoulder as if it had always been there.

If George hadn't gone for his rifle the way he did—the first time—then there was no need for what had just happened. I would have gotten what I came there for and left him with a hundred dollars of free horse feed. Of course, the only logical assumption was that George was protecting someone.

Logic doesn't always apply with a man like George. Or me, sometimes, if the truth be told. George might have just stubborned up on principle, which usually means that the principle itself is stubbornness and reason and common sense shrivel and die in its shadow. He didn't care about justice, or right or wrong, except his version of them, and right and wrong would always come second after "Fuck you." Looking back on my life, there were plenty of times when I'd felt the same way. Hell, I wasn't even all that angry that George might have killed me.

From the beginning I had assumed it was an accident. We all did. The driver got frightened—understandable—and left the scene of the accident, out of fear, probably, maybe fear and something else ... not decent or humane, but still understandable. Perhaps what made the visit to George worth it was getting him to lose his temper. Being unable to carry a hundred-pound bag of feed didn't mean a thing. His unwillingness to tell me who helped him carry John, unimportant, really. "Maybe the job needs to be finished." Not an accident, a *job*—intentional. That was a game changer. The driver wanted John, a harmless religious nut who never bothered anyone, dead, and still wanted him dead. And George thought John should be dead too.

Timing. On Monday George did try to do his best to save John, even with help. He seemed genuinely upset at the sight of John's broken body when the two of us stood beside Ginger's bed. A day later, George had experienced a change of heart—far in the other direction—and that change of heart must have taken place after he took John into town. Based on his changed heart, if given another chance, he wouldn't bother to try to save the preacher.

I passed Ginger's abandoned Subaru. Soon the JUST DIVORCED in the back window would completely disappear. A lot of people who wandered down 117 were not on their way to anywhere in particular; they were leaving somewhere, or someone, particular, and nowhere always seemed the best place to start, and nowhere is a destination only found by the lost. The desert is the country of "you," and if you stay long enough you lose track of where you end and where it begins.

My attention had been on my side mirror as the Subaru receded in the distance and the sight of a group of people on the shoulder ahead startled me enough to hit my brakes. Three men were standing in front of the City Limits sign and a fourth was off behind his truck taking a leak. Another pickup and a car were parked across the highway in the desert. As I approached I slowed enough to see they were some of the same people I'd sat with over lunch at the Mercantile, the unofficial Rockmuse city council and chamber of commerce.

They heard my truck and turned to wave. None of them seemed to be doing anything, so they were doing what they usually did—probably talking about doing something. Near as I could tell they were all just standing there looking up at the City Limits sign like it was a big-screen television in a sports bar. Refreshments had been served. Everyone was holding a can of beer. They picked a nice day for it, whatever "it" was. I pulled to a rolling stop next to them and lowered my passenger-side window.

"Did you guys get kicked out of the Mercantile?"

All but one of them ignored me. The one who didn't jumped up on my running board with a big grin. I'd seen him around but didn't know his name. "We're going to do it!"

I appreciated his enthusiasm without much caring what the enthusiasm was for. "Sounds good," I said, the truck still rolling. Whatever they had decided to do didn't interest me very much.

"We took up a collection for a new City Limits sign. The new one will be bigger." He liked the word "bigger" and said it with such exuberance he almost lost his balance, and his beer. "When people drive into town they're gonna know something about us besides our population."

If I didn't stop he'd be in downtown Rockmuse with me still hanging on to my door—and still talking. "Glad to hear it," I shouted. "Progress." If I stopped he'd still be talking. I felt as if I'd picked up a sticky piece of chatty sagebrush. "Have to get into Rockmuse." I revved the engine to emphasize my intention. It didn't do any good. "You best get back there before they make a decision without you," I suggested.

We'd traveled maybe two hundred feet. He glanced back down

the highway. "You're right! How about a contribution to the sign fund? Whatever you can spare."

To make a contribution meant I'd have to stop and take out my wallet. If I didn't stop he might ride all the way into town trying to convince me. A small investment to scrape him off my running board seemed worth it. The brakes squeaked and grabbed and the jolt threw him forward and then back and his left-handed grip on my door slipped. If he hadn't been trying so damn hard to hold on to his beer he would have been fine. Down he went on the shoulder.

I set the brake and ran around the front of my truck to see if he was all right. He was, but the beer had met an untimely and unfortunate end under one of my tires. He was a decent-sized guy with an indecent-sized gut, and an ass to match that had contributed to a soft landing. I was relieved it was the beer and not him, though the expression on his face as he surveyed the crushed can told me he didn't necessarily see it that way.

His hat was a few feet away. I picked it up and offered him a hand. It took both to get him off the ground. I asked him if he was okay.

"Lost my damn beer," he said, and began to sway on his bootheels. Judging from his breath, the beer he'd lost to my tires was the last soldier in a dead platoon. I steadied him with one hand while I reached into my back pocket for my wallet. Most of my customers paid me in cash and I was flush with ones, fives, and twenties. More out of guilt than civic pride, I handed him a $20 bill.

The twenty fluttered in the light breeze. He was looking back up the road, squinting into the sun, at the others I thought, until he said: "I wish that damn woman would get her car off the road."

In the far distance, beyond the men and the City Limits sign, Ginger's old Subaru was barely visible. "Maybe one of you should tow it into town for her?"

He took the twenty without looking at it and stuffed it straight into his jeans' pocket. The sign fund was probably really a beer fund, at least for him, and my twenty would probably lubricate additional planning meetings once they returned to Rockmuse.

"It's an eyesore," he said. "Every one of us has offered to tow it in for her. There's no reason now, and still it sits. Gives the wrong impression of our town, don't you think?"

I thought it gave exactly the right impression of Rockmuse, though I refrained from telling him so. "Why isn't there any reason to tow it?"

He started wobbling in the direction of the other unofficial, and probably drunk, council members. "No need," he said, slapping his hat against a meaty thigh to remove the dust. "Cowboy Roy rode his bike out here last week and fixed it in exchange for dance lessons and a bar each of Jesus, Buddha, and Elvis soap." He continued weaving up the shoulder. He was mostly talking to himself and that was fine with me. "I'm divorced too, you know. Twenty-two years down the toilet last year. For christsake, I don't plaster it on my goddamn pickup for everyone to see."

Whoever he was, he might be sore tomorrow with no memory of why. I got back in my truck and headed straight for Ginger's theater to check in on John.

So that's what they called him, "Cowboy Roy." I hadn't heard him called that before, and I hoped to never hear him called that again, certainly not if he was present to hear it. If you live in a small town and the locals give you a nickname, you can bet it isn't out of respect or affection. Nothing brought out cruelty mixed with poetic cleverness faster in some folks than someone afflicted with a long streak of bad luck. That's all it was. Most of the time it was only slightly worse luck than your own and the proximity scared the shit out of you. Nearly everyone in Rockmuse was just a half tank of gas and an unpaid utility bill from being Cowboy Roy. I thought again of Ginny, that pierced and pregnant teenager. If not for her, I wondered what my nickname would have been.

34

The theater entrance was open and I found Lenny onstage dozing in a tattered recliner next to the bed. The air had an aroma of freshly burnt grass. He heard me jump up on the stage and opened his eyes but didn't get up. "He's come to a couple times," Lenny said. "Gibberish. And he's running a fever."

"Where's Ginger?"

Lenny pointed to a small window on the second floor above the lobby. "Projection room. Fixed herself a cot up there. It's got its own bathroom."

"How she doing?" I asked, taking a look at John, who was now clean-shaven. His long wild hair had been trimmed on the front and sides around his ears. Thin locks of silver hair still dotted the white sheets around his head. In twenty years it was the first time I'd ever really seen his face. Without the beard his chin looked like a squared-off block of granite. Barefaced he looked completely different and familiar at the same time. The cuts on his face were beginning to scab and showed sign of fresh antibiotic. "She shave him?"

Lenny nodded and joined me beside the bed. "You'd think John was her best friend the way she's been taking care of him. Crying half the time. Always praying. Or chanting. Smell that? She's been burning homemade sage sticks. Claims it has medicinal properties."

"Maybe it does," I said. "But so does the hospital in Price." I touched my fingertips to John's forehead. "He's got a fever all right." I gently pulled back the quilt that covered him. Two things had changed. A towel had been wrapped like a diaper around his groin and the faint odor of piss filled the air. The second change was shocking. The broken leg below the knee was a deep purple and swollen to twice its normal size. I thought for a moment and then made up my mind. "The weather is clear. You up for riding in my trailer with him? You can spend the night at my house. I'll bring you back tomorrow."

"Right now?"

"Right now."

"You think it's safe to move him now?"

"I think it's unsafe not to."

"I can't believe Life Flight never came."

Part of me wanted to tell him why Life Flight never came. I chose not to tell him because it wasn't a conversation I wanted to have at the moment. For the time being, it seemed best to leave Lenny thinking it was just one of those things that happened when you lived in the desert. Folks rarely asked why. They knew why. What didn't kill you didn't make you stronger, or even wiser, it waited patiently for another chance. I could have called the hospital and tried to get John on the schedule again. I wasn't sure why I hadn't, other than I just didn't think of it with everything else. Perhaps I just didn't want to hear the helicopter was booked solid with traffic accidents or maintenance, or any one of a hundred reasons that added up to John's life being less important than someone else's.

I covered John up. "It's going to be a long, dark, bumpy ride in my trailer." There were a couple overhead lights inside, though, with the door closed, they wouldn't provide much if any light. It was a lot to ask of Lenny. "You a praying man, Lenny?"

"Sometimes," he said.

"Then let this be one of those times."

In five minutes we had a spot in my empty trailer outfitted with bedding and as comfortable as it was ever going to get. Lenny and I had made knots in the corners of the bottom sheet in order to use it as a kind of stretcher. It seemed the best way to move John without jostling him too much, though just carrying him in my arms might have been easier. On the count of three we both lifted and the weight was more than either of us expected. We lowered John back down on the bed and took a minute to fortify ourselves for another attempt. If it was tough for me to lift my end it had to be even more difficult for Lenny.

"Shouldn't we let Ginger know we're leaving?" he asked. "It's going to give her a coronary if she comes back and John's gone."

"Let her sleep," I said. "We'll leave her a note."

"What's going on?" Ginger was making her way through the tables and across the theater floor. She wasn't curious, she was angry, and she was being none too careful about bumping into tables and upsetting her knickknacks as she rushed toward the stage. "It's too dangerous," she shouted. "You can't."

Lenny let go of his end immediately and looked at me for some sign about what to do next.

"Get up here, Ginger," I said. When she got up onstage, I pulled back the quilt and pointed at John's swollen and discolored leg. "Can and will."

Ginger looked away from John's leg and covered her mouth with her hand. She knew what the leg looked like, she just didn't want to see it. She shouldered me out of the way and squeezed herself against the bed, forcing me to let go of the knotted ends of the sheet. "Life Flight could still come."

"You think so, Ginger?"

She didn't answer immediately, instead she lowered her head and closed her eyes and prayed, silently. I thanked God for that—silently. Ginger's long red-and-gray hair was in braids. The braids, together with the high-necked sleeping gown she wore, and the movement of her lips as she prayed over John, made me as uncomfortable as I could ever remember feeling. Ginger was the girl on *Little House on the Prairie* who hit middle age with a vengeance. When she was done she took the quilt and covered John again.

"The Lord will deliver assistance in his own divine way," she said, as much to herself as to Lenny and me. The way she said it didn't necessarily sound as if we were all on the same page when it came to divine intervention.

Lenny burped out an "Amen."

When I glanced at him he gave me an embarrassed shrug as if to say he couldn't help it. I understood. I almost said it myself, or anything that would have ended the proceedings and gotten us on the road before dark. If I was wrong about Ginger, then no harm done. The single best thing I could do for John's health was to get him the hell away from Ginger, and the hospital in Price served both goals. Learning about her car being in running order got everything else stacking up—George, the call to cancel Life Flight, and the red Abandoned Car stickers.

John's pale eyes suddenly opened. Ginger sucked in an audible breath and took a step back from the bed. We all waited for whatever came next. We didn't have to wait long. John sat bolt upright in bed and the quilt slipped over his bare chest to his waist.

In a booming voice that echoed around the theater hall, he said: "And Barabbas was chosen! Barabbas shall go free. We, the guilty, inherit his freedom and his guilt! And so it shall always be, the guilty must walk freely among us!" John closed his eyes and collapsed again on the bed without another word.

"Amen!" I shouted, and grabbed my end of the sheets.

Lenny did the same.

Ginger backed away from the end of the bed and began to pray again, this time in whispers that quickly turned into sobs. With the spirit of the Lord in us we managed to get John across the theater and into my trailer without dropping him or banging his head against any of the doorways.

When John was settled, Lenny sat down next to him on the floor of the trailer and wrapped a soiled packing blanket around himself. "What do you suppose that was all about in there?"

"Hell if I know," I said. "We learned one thing, though."

"What's that?"

"His spine and neck are in working order. Praise the Lord!"

I started to pull the cargo door closed. Lenny shouted for me to stop. "Hold up a minute, will you, Ben? Please?" I did as he asked. Lenny blinked a couple times and looked past me down Main Street as if he might suddenly bolt from the trailer and make a run for it, not that I would blame him if he did. "Once you close this door I'm locked in, right?"

"Afraid so," I said. I reassured him as best I could. "You'll be okay."

Lenny gave me a game smile. "I hope to shit he doesn't start preaching on the way to Price."

I told him if he needed me to stop, to pound on the back wall as hard as he could. Lenny nodded and I lowered the door and slipped the heavy latch hook in place. I rapped softly on the door. "You okay in there?"

His voice from the other side of the door was muffled but unmistakable. "Fuck no, Ben. I'm not okay. I might never be okay again. Let's get going."

35

I couldn't help myself. I had to laugh. It felt good, and I felt lucky to have Lenny to count on. John had more blessings than he knew. Outside of that time in Salt Lake City I hadn't spent much time with or around Lenny. We really hadn't spent much time then. John and I never discussed his view of homosexuals—an odd word, since I'd never heard anyone refer to an entire group of people as heterosexuals—but I could guess. He might surprise me, though. With some luck we actually might get to have that conversation someday over an imaginary cigarette.

I topped off with diesel at the Rockmuse Shell. Eckhardt was busy with a customer who was blissfully unaware a shotgun was aimed at his groin. As we left town and picked up speed I saw Ginger's Subaru coming up on my left. The town council had adjourned their meeting at the City Limits sign and there were no other vehicles coming or going, not that I cared one way or the other. I grabbed a hammer and a screwdriver from the tool kit behind my seat and whacked the side of the trailer with my open palm and told Lenny I'd be a minute.

I stood in the low western sun next to Ginger's car. Maybe for the first time in my life I regretted not becoming a car thief. Of course, I didn't want to steal the piece of shit, only disable it. Ginger had to know I was on to her, and praying over John wasn't going to change my mind. Who knew what was going on inside of her?

She was upset and she had taken pretty good care of John, though for what reason? It was possible John had seen who had run him down. I aimed the hammer at the driver's-side window and then thought a moment. There was a possibility I was wrong—a strong possibility.

I walked around the Subaru to the front right fender. There were dents and scratches in every quarter panel of the body and they were all covered in dried mud and dust with a sugarcoating of sand that sparkled in the sunlight. Kneeling, I examined the front bumper and right headlight. The headlight was broken and there was a crease in the fender, though when and how they were damaged was impossible for me to know. It was enough. Maybe not a smoking gun, but a gun in the right place at the right time. This time I tried the door and found it unlocked. I pounded the screwdriver into the ignition switch and twisted it back and forth until the metal broke into pieces.

As I got out of the Subaru something caught my eye in the flat stretch between the car and Rockmuse. The way 117 curved around to Main Street, walking across the desert into town would be a shortcut, cutting the distance by more than half—maybe a quarter mile. Five minutes at a good pace. Ginger had used it. I knew that because I could see her coming across the desert from the direction of Rockmuse. She didn't expect anyone to be standing at her car and so she didn't see me. I waited until she was a hundred yards away before I gave the roof of her car a good loud rap with the hammer. She froze. I waved. Her long braids lashed out at the air as she turned on her heels and began walking back the way she had come.

A minute later I was gaining speed into the late-afternoon light. I confess that woman scared me, and the more I knew along with what I guessed, the more scared I was. Old desert rats like George would come at you straight-on, more or less. Ginger seemed to be the kind to zig and zag, say a prayer and throw a nice smile and Jesus soap your way, and wait until you were alone before she aimed her car at your backside. Breaking the hell out of the Subaru's ignition might not stop her from leaving town, but it would slow her down a little. All things considered, I'd rather have another dance with George than a moment of prayer with Ginger.

WE MADE GOOD time. We passed Walt's diner just as the last rays of a red sun were flaming upward into the stars behind the silhouette of the Wasatch Mountains far to the west. Lenny only pounded once. The truth was I'd forgotten about him and my thoughts were happily wandering with Claire out in the fading desert light. For one startled second I was certain my diesel motor had thrown a connecting rod. I stopped as soon as I could and raised the door. Lenny was already standing, eager to get out.

"Is he preaching?"

"No," he said. "I have to pee."

With Lenny in the desert doing his business, I looked in on John. If anything, he seemed more comfortable and at peace in the trailer. I wondered if that meant he was about to die, and if only to put a good face on it, I figured he'd rather die in the back of my trailer on 117 than in a poster bed on a theater stage in Rockmuse.

It was full dark when we pulled up to the emergency entrance of the hospital. I hit the horn three times and then hopped out to free Lenny. His exit was more of a burst and he landed a good ten feet from the trailer and rolled across the asphalt, scrambling for even more distance.

"Is he still alive?"

Lenny stood but still kept his distance. "Oh yeah, he's alive. Damn, is he ever."

A male nurse and a doctor appeared in short order and got in the back with John and began checking his condition. I told them he had been the victim of a hit-and-run on Monday outside of Rockmuse. They were only partially listening, going about their work with an efficiency I admired and that John deserved. When they put John on a gurney I followed them in after asking Lenny if he was coming. He shook his head and huffed starlight.

Dr. Stafford met me coming in. "Is this the hit-and-run we were sending Life Flight for?" When I told her it was, she said, "What the hell?"

"Yeah," I said, "what the hell. He's semiconscious. Fever. Sure glad you sent that emergency supply chest with me anyway. Someone didn't want him to survive. At least, that's my guess."

"The police will have to be called."

"Fine by me," I said. "They've known about this since it happened. Weather," I added, as if that might explain everything. Wanda's expression told me she didn't seem to think it explained anything, and I was inclined to agree.

"When I have a chance I'll check and see if there's a recording of the call. Don't leave." This was not a suggestion. She said this with the complete confidence of someone who has no doubt that her commands would be followed. I assumed she wanted me there when the police arrived, and she was certain they would. I didn't share that certainty.

She walked quickly back to the exam rooms and I left, though only to move my truck out of the turnaround and into the parking lot. Lenny was sitting on a bench along a strip of grass smoking a cigarette. I thought of asking to bum one from him. I didn't. Quitting cigarettes was harder than quitting drinking. I quit them both at the same time and ever since I'd been afraid if I took up one again I'd take up the other. Like most addicts, I made the decision to quit several times a day.

A young female admission clerk took what little information I could provide about John. I really didn't know a damn thing about the man I knew, including his last name. Family? Drug allergies?

Address, phone? Employer? I answered, "God." She didn't write that down and slapped the pen against the clipboard signaling the end of our interview. "Oh," I said, "and he's not a smoker or a drinker."

After an hour of cooling my heels in the waiting room reading WebMD and *National Geographic,* I visited the vending machines that, thankfully, catered to the impatient and nervous and were filled with snacks guaranteed to keep you that way. The machine sucked in my dollar bills and gave me nothing in return except a blinking red light, which I thought was probably good if not fair. I peered through the outside window to check on Lenny. He was stretched out on the bench beneath the stars, relaxed and relieved to be anywhere outside. I was still standing at the window looking down at the city lights of Price when Dr. Stafford came up behind me.

"I can't tell you anything," she said, "except that he'll probably live. HIPPA privacy laws. It's even odds we can save his leg."

I imagined John hauling his cross on one leg, hopping really. When that didn't work I imagined him with an artificial limb. The one thing I couldn't imagine was that he'd stop pulling that cross up and down 117.

"You look tired," I said. "Long day?"

"You too. Slow days are my longest days. I spent most of it doing paperwork. Stayed late." She looked past me out at the lights. "You saved his life, you know. The infection was spreading fast. It was down to a handful of hours and then . . . We'll see."

I sighed, exhaling all the events I'd been holding for the last few days. It was only Wednesday. "I thought you couldn't tell me anything."

She squinted into my eyes. "I didn't."

"I assume I'm waiting on the cops," I said. "You must have not told them it was me they needed to talk to. If you had I'd have been wearing cuffs by now."

"You can go. They're not coming. Big night—bigger fish to fry."

I told her I didn't mind not being fried until later and we stood in silence for a couple minutes. "Your work here must be tough on your family," I said.

"Would be," she said, "if I had one. Never wanted a family. I was close to my dad when he was alive." She reached into the pocket of her blues and handed me her card. "Your friend Walt Butterfield reminded me of my father. We got along well when he was here."

Knowing Walt, and a little about Wanda, I said, "I'll bet you did."

She had a nice laugh and I was glad to hear it, as weary as it was. "That generation, my dad's, Mr. Butterfield's, only dying wish was that if they were dying you didn't talk them to death."

I held the card up. "What's this for?"

"Give it to Mr. Butterfield. Tell him I want to see him here or by God I'll see him there."

I put the card in my back pocket. "I'll do that. Since you're not telling me anything, can you not tell me when I cannot visit John?"

"You cannot visit him until he gets out of ICU. We'll keep him there twenty-four hours and then move him into general. He won't be going home for a week or so. Longer if we have to amputate his leg. Go get some sleep."

"You too," I said. "Thank you." I stepped toward the automatic sliding doors and they opened with a hiss. "Tell the cops my name when they show up. They know where to find me."

"It's going to be a while." She yawned. "They have a suspicious death. A body, and like all small-town departments, everybody gets to go to the party."

The door went on hissing while it waited on me. "That's usually what they call it when they don't want to call it a homicide."

Wanda turned and began walking across the lobby. "True," she said. "I met this one a couple times. I'm betting on homicide. Cecil was an asshole. Good night, Ben."

I stepped back and the doors closed. "The manager of the Stop 'n' Gone Truck Stop on 191?"

She kept walking. "One and the same. You didn't hear it from me. Make sure Mr. Butterfield gets my card."

36

enny could tell there was something on my mind during the short drive to my duplex. Among what seemed like a long list of admirable character traits was Lenny's ability to sense when to keep his mouth shut. I couldn't locate Pedro and now Cecil was dead, probably murdered. Of course, it was possible he died from natural causes that, for him, included venereal disease or losing too much brain tissue out of his ass. One could only hope. It would be a rare and elegant demonstration of cause and effect.

My problem was, no matter how he got that way, Cecil was dead, and he was my only real lead for returning the girl. Without Cecil to help me locate Pedro, I would have to turn her over to some agency, and I really didn't want to do that; in fact, I hated the idea. I would, though, if it came to that—unless a miracle happened and the ladies of Los Ojos Negros came through for me.

Ginny's side of the duplex was dark and until it was rented it would stay that way. Lenny followed me into my duplex and headed straight for the easy chair and put the footrest up. In the time it took me to tell him he could have the bed and I would take the chair, he was asleep.

When I was his age I had already begun my life's work. I didn't know then it would be my life's work and I thought it was something to do until I knew what I wanted to do for the rest of my life. That's how it is sometimes. You keep doing what you're doing until you don't know anything else. Change was eating at the edges of my desert. Maybe it always had been. My customers came and went, died, disappeared, along with a few friends and lovers and time killers, like Nadine, and I got up every weekday morning and drove my truck into the unchanging desert. Until Claire. Until Ginny. Now their absence was everywhere, as if the red mesa had evaporated overnight leaving nothing on the eastern horizon but a pink glow.

Not yet ready for sleep I went to Ginny's side of the duplex. The key was in the door. It was pitch-black inside and still seemed that way even after I hit the switch. She'd left a few pieces of garage sale furniture, a sofa, table, and lamp. She'd re-covered the shade in a fabric patterned with cut-outs of devils and pitchforks. A cheap kitchen table and two chairs had been shoved against the wall near the kitchen counter.

There was a note on the table. Pure Ginny: "Dear Ben—You know. Love, Ginny." I ran my hands along the Formica counter and went into the bedroom and then the bathroom. The whole place was not only clean, it was spotless. I walked out and closed and locked the door and stood there a moment. I said to the closed door, "Dear Ginny, Yes, I know. Ben."

I went back inside and moved the end table in front of the window and put the lamp on it and turned on the lamp. The shade threw silhouettes of devils and pitchforks against the bare walls. I liked what it did to the room, though I knew there were real devils, real evil, in the world, and Ginny and Annabelle would run across them in time and they wouldn't always look like demons or carry pitchforks. They would look like friends, husbands and wives, and lovers and cops and grocery store clerks and foster parents. It would be nice if they carried pitchforks so you could identify them. Or you had a true friend to help you decide which is which—then be there when you made the wrong choice.

I locked up Ginny's duplex again and leaned against a porch roof post trying to decide which I wanted most, a drink or a cigarette. The street was empty and quiet and a light breeze moved in and out of the scrawny trees. A dirty crumb of waxing moon was fighting hard for its place in the heavens against a thin band of high clouds while the stars retreated into the background. I wasn't looking at anything in particular, just taking it all in and deciding on sleep instead of alcohol or tobacco, knowing once again I'd found the resolve to stay sober. My thoughts began to drift and I closed my eyes for a few seconds and felt the cool wind brush my face and tasted the smell of the desert.

Across the street on the other side of the sidewalk in the shadows were three plump shrubs swaying with the wind. I began to stare at the shrubs, trying to remember if I had ever noticed them before. They seemed to separate slightly and then lean in together against the wind. The longer I stared, the more certain I became they were not shrubs but dark figures in long dresses. Figures but no faces, the distinct outlines of hips and breasts, but no shoulders, as if they were one. I waved. They remained as they were and I began to slowly walk down the porch steps and into my front yard toward them—the ladies of Los Ojos Negros.

My foot hit something in the yard and I bent down to see what it was. I'd missed a piece of screen door, or it had blown off the side of the porch where I had tossed the broken pieces. I left it where it was and continued toward the ladies, calmly happy to see them even though it was late. I waved again and they seemed to dissolve in the shadows as I approached. When I got to where I thought they had been standing beneath the trees, they were gone. Why they had left was anyone's guess, if they'd been there at all. I'd hoped they were there to tell me something about Pedro or the girl. There were no shrubs in that area. It seemed to me there was the delicate aroma of tortillas and carnitas and a thousand unknown spices.

An engine started up around the corner and down the next block and I made it to the intersection as quickly as I could. At the other end of the block, through a haze of oily exhaust fumes, two small red taillights were fading into the darkness.

If they hadn't come to help me, I couldn't think of any other reason for them to be there. I wasn't surprised they knew where I lived. It wasn't exactly a secret, and even if it was, my sense of them was that they knew secrets, or knew how to find out whatever they wanted to know, and I hoped that extended to finding Pedro.

Lenny was snoring away in my easy chair, his head tilted back in an awkward way. I took a small throw pillow off my only other piece of furniture, a broken couch, and slipped it under his neck. The snoring stopped. He didn't wake and his head flopped lazily to one side. I covered him with an old wool army blanket. The only other person who ever slept in that chair, other than me, had been Ginny.

I brushed my teeth and went to bed hungry and slept until my alarm went off at its usual four a.m. Awake and with a few hours of sleep behind me, I was convinced my imagination and fatigue had gotten the better of me the night before, perhaps fueled even more by Ginny's parting gift of the devil lamp and a hunger I was too tired to feed, though it all fed my dreams.

My dreams were filled with old women and a few younger ones, and the two youngest, Manita and Annabelle. It was a relief not to dream of Claire, though Bernice, her mother, made an appearance at the window booth of the diner, brain damaged, staring vacantly into the desert. The ladies of Los Ojos Negros hadn't been watching me. Maybe that was what I wanted them to do—come and take the desert child. Perhaps I wanted them to watch out *for* me? When old women tell you they think you're in trouble it sticks inside you somewhere and all the logic in the world won't shake it loose, and probably shouldn't. It was nice to think that the ladies were looking out for me in some way. It wasn't a luxury I'd had much experience with, and it didn't have to be true for me to enjoy it.

Lenny was still sleeping when I got out of the shower. I peeked out my front window at the dark street and then quickly dressed and drove to where I'd last seen the Los Ojos Negros food trailer. Instead of their faded green trailer under the slanted awning was a Price police patrol car. No other vehicles were on the road at that hour and as I passed by the patrol car his headlights came on and the cop followed me for almost a mile. Talk to anyone and they'll tell you seeing a cop car in your rearview mirror makes you wonder what you just did wrong. With my history it didn't matter.

When the street that led up the hill to the hospital came up on my right I turned and the patrol car continued. At the top of the hill I had decided he wasn't following me. Everyone knew the ladies opened early, and he probably hadn't known they had moved. Just a hungry cop and nothing more. My bet was he called in and found out where they went and if I'd followed him he would have led me straight to them. Just in case I was wrong and he doubled back, I drove all the way to the hospital and parked in the rear at one of their loading docks.

I gave him a couple minutes and then on impulse decided to go in and check on John. Dr. Wanda said he would be in ICU for at least twenty-four hours and no visitors until they moved him into general. It was something to do and maybe someone would tell me how he was doing. If not, then I'd be on my way.

No one was at the front desk. The place was void of any human activity. The apocalypse had come and gone. I found ICU on the second floor and the janitor was coming out of the door that would have required me to use the intercom and be buzzed in. I slipped my foot into the doorway to keep it from closing.

"It's okay," I said. "I'm a doctor."

He was an old black man whose tired eyes had stories going back a thousand years. Those eyes took in all of me with one glance, from dirty roper boots and jeans and denim work shirt to unkempt long black hair. "Me too," he said, and pushed his squeaky cart down the hall.

A male nurse was on duty sitting behind a tall counter staring intently at a computer screen. He took no notice of me for a minute and when he did, all he said was, "What?"

I was amazed I had gotten as far as I had, and I was pretty sure this was the end of my early morning raid on the hospital. "You have an old guy here, first name of John. Victim of a hit-and-run. Just curious how he's doing?"

He put on his official face and asked me how I got in and told me there were absolutely no visitors in ICU without a doctor's permission or presence. I told him the truth and as the truth often is, it was appreciated, and it amused him.

"I've known him for twenty years," I said. "I don't even know his last name. He doesn't have any family or relatives that I know of. I might be it."

"You the one that brought him to the hospital in the back of your truck?"

I nodded. "I just want to know how he's doing. Then I'll get out of here."

"You Ben?"

The surprised expression on my face answered his question. Before I could ask him how he knew my name, he said, "He's sedated and in bad shape—in and out—but he's been asking for you."

I gave him my thanks and turned toward the door. "I'll come back."

He came out from behind the counter and asked me to follow him. "His condition could go either way at any moment. I believe you when you say you're probably all he's got. He's lucky. Some of the old-timers we see in here don't have anyone." He stopped a short distance down the hallway. "You know how to say goodbye without saying it?"

I told him I'd had a lot of practice lately. If I'd thought about it, the truth was more like my whole life.

"If he's conscious, you have two minutes. I'll be in the room with you." He handed me a mask from a dispenser mounted on the wall. "Put this on." He pointed to a large window. John was on the other side hooked up to so many tubes and wires and machines I figured he'd strangle before anything else had a chance to kill him. We went in and I pulled a chair up to the side of the bed and waited to see if he'd open his eyes. He did, and managed a smile and croaked out my name.

"Preach," I said, "you stupid son of a bitch." The nurse registered his disapproval of my observation and language with a cough. I ignored him. "I told you to be careful."

"You did," he said. "And I was. God has his own plan." His eyes brightened. "I feel like a smoke. I'm all out of papers."

This brought the nurse to attention and he rushed to my shoulder. "Absolutely not!"

I shook my head at him. He relaxed and retreated and watched me as I rolled an imaginary cigarette and placed it between John's parched lips and lit it. John inhaled deeply and coughed. I took it back and lowered the mask and puffed quickly before returning it to John.

The nurse raised his eyebrows. "Time's up."

I held up my index finger and the nurse nodded.

I took the cigarette from John's lips and crushed it with my fingertips and put the butt in my shirt pocket. "Who's Barbaros, John?"

John closed his eyes. I thought that was the end of our visit and then he asked, "You mean, Barabbas, from the Passion of the Christ?"

I didn't know if I did or not, but I said, "Sure."

"The guilty man Pilate set free instead of Jesus." John opened his pale eyes and gazed at me for a few seconds. "As it was and needs to be."

The nurse tapped me on the shoulder and I left. At the exit from ICU, he said, "Thanks for not throwing that cigarette butt on the floor."

"You're welcome," I said.

37

It was just past dawn by the time I arrived back at my place. Lenny was still in the recliner with the blanket pulled over his head. I began making breakfast—eggs and toast and coffee—and he lowered the blanket long enough to tell me he was starving. We ate silently and quickly and headed back out within half an hour.

There was no reason why I couldn't load up at the transfer station for a normal day. Lenny earned every calorie of his breakfast helping me take on cargo, organizing it—moving items around to one side then the other in the trailer, tying down—based on the order of deliveries I kept in my head. He knew how to work and we both had a nice rolling sweat going by the time we were done.

He was quiet, resting his head against the window, when I pulled in to get diesel at the Stop 'n' Gone, as was my habit before heading out for a day of driving 117. I had my eyes on the pumps and he had his on something else that I wished I had noticed before I made my turn.

"Wonder what happened?" he said, craning his neck to see to the far side of the truck stop.

Two Price police cars, a Carbon County Sheriff's cruiser, and a Utah State Public Safety van were blocking the driveway that bordered the building that once housed the tire department. A length of red crime-scene tape was fluttering in the morning breeze in front of the cars. I'd forgotten all about Cecil until that minute.

"It's none of our business," I said, and hoped to keep it that way. I would have only drawn attention if I'd pulled through the pumps and left.

From where I stood pumping diesel I could see Ana inside at the register. I turned my back to the window and the spinning numbers on the pump seemed to slow down to a snail's pace. Just as I turned back and hung up the nozzle, I saw her pointing at me. Two Price cops were staring through the window following her finger. I hopped in my truck and had it in gear and moving forward when both cops stepped in front of my truck, motioning with their open palms for me to stop.

With my eyes on the cops, I said to Lenny, "Stay in the cab unless they say otherwise. If they do, answer yes, sir, or no, sir. Not another word if you can help it."

I set the brakes but left the engine idling. The lights were on in the empty tire building and I could see people moving around inside. "Morning, Officers."

They were both young, not much more than Lenny's age. Both tall and lean and all business. One began to walk alongside my truck while the other said the woman inside told them I was a regular. "Did you know the manager? Cecil Boone?"

I said I did. I assumed Ana had mentioned I had been looking for Cecil, but I wasn't going to answer any question that wasn't asked. He requested my driver's license, which I took as a lucky break. Our paths hadn't crossed in the past. It might mean nothing would come of a brief, informal interview. He looked over my license and then motioned for Lenny to join us. Any fool could see Lenny was nervous. So was I. He missed the running board getting out and tripped and came down on one knee and then limped over to us.

The officer asked for his license as well and attached both of our licenses to his clipboard. He said to Lenny, "You're both commercial drivers?"

Lenny shook his head.

"Just me," I said.

He addressed Lenny. "How about you? You know the manager, Cecil Boone?"

Lenny shook his head and was told to answer verbally. "No."

The other officer joined us but stood back a couple yards behind my left shoulder. The first officer, the one who had taken the lead, addressed us both. "You know why we're talking to you?"

Lenny and I both said no.

The officer behind me said, "Were either of you here on Monday morning?"

Lenny said no and I said yes.

A Utah Highway Patrol pickup pulled in and parked at the pumps on the other side of my truck. Andy got out and set the nozzle and then got back in his truck and turned his attention to paperwork, not five feet behind the officer who was now asking the questions. Both officers ignored Trooper Smith and I kept my attention on them. Lenny was trembling and I didn't blame him. He still had some of the sweat on his forehead from loading and raised a flanneled shirtsleeve to daub it.

The officers had their guns out of their holsters before Lenny's sleeve touched a drop of sweat. The officer behind us shouted, "Hands up!"

Our hands flew up. Lenny started to explain and was told to shut up. Big rigs were rumbling, coming and going, and vehicles buzzed both directions on the highway. None of that mattered. The Stop 'n' Gone Truck Stop suddenly became the quietest place in Utah.

I heard Andy's nozzle click off and his door open. When I looked over my shoulder he had reached onto his front seat and was putting on his hat. When he had snugged down the brim, he calmly strolled over and stood to the side of the officer in front of us.

Andy nodded at the officers and then to me. "Morning, Ben."

I returned the greeting, careful to address him as Trooper Smith.

"Mind if I check you two for weapons?"

Andy patted us both down and, finding nothing, he said, "I think we can all relax now." When neither of the officers lowered their weapons, Andy said, "Please holster your weapons, Officers." They did so, slowly and with extreme reluctance, and with, I noted, what seemed to me something akin to disappointment.

The lead officer said, "Mr. Jones was here Monday morning. He has an arrest record going back several years."

"I know Mr. Jones's record as well as the names of my children," Andy said. "Maybe better. Monday afternoon he was a hundred miles away in Rockmuse. I know. I spoke to him by radio from my patrol vehicle." Andy reached over and put his hand on Lenny's shoulder. "You doing okay, Lenny?"

Lenny said that he was and with that small gesture, he obviously was.

Trooper Smith said, "How about you let me talk to these two, since I know them?"

The officers glanced at each other and our driver's licenses were given to Andy. They walked off and approached another driver a few islands over. He had been watching because he looked none too happy to see them coming his way.

"Thanks, Andy," I said, and never meant it more.

"You notice anything about me, Ben?"

Lenny's head bounced back and forth between us, wondering what was going on. I knew. "Trooper Smith," I corrected myself.

"I heard you brought in the preacher last night. You come along to help him, Lenny? Ride in the trailer and tend to the preacher?"

"Yes, sir."

Trooper Smith thanked Lenny and added, "I'll wager that was a long ride."

"Yes, sir," Lenny answered. "The longest ride of my life."

Trooper Smith said he needed to speak with me and then suggested Lenny get back in the cab. Lenny didn't hesitate a second. "Say hello to your aunt and uncle for me."

"How's the preacher doing?" Andy asked.

"Could go either way," I replied. "If he lives, he might lose his left leg."

"Too bad," he said, and changed the subject. "You know what happened here?"

"I was waiting at the hospital to be questioned about the hit-and-run. When no one came, a doctor told me to go home. Said the police were investigating a suspicious death." I left out that she had told me it was Cecil.

"That's it?"

"That's it. I assume the suspicious death was Cecil's. Great guy. Everyone loved him."

"Jones." Trooper Smith angled his head in the direction of the two Price officers. "Maybe I should invite my law enforcement colleagues back over here and let them finish this."

"Cecil was an asshole. If you find someone who didn't think so, they're either lying or never met him. Was he murdered?"

"Go on," he said, not answering my question, not that I thought he would. "You're here between five and six every morning five days a week. You and Cecil get into it?"

"No," I said. "Not even words," I said. "We might have. When I went back to the office he was gone."

Trooper Smith pointed to my right hand. "You got into it with someone."

"Not Cecil." I thought about telling him about the little girl and decided to risk asking him a favor first. "Take off your hat, Andy. Just for a minute?" He took off his hat. "If I tell you something and it doesn't mean anything, will you keep it off the record?"

"Depends on what it is. No promises."

"It has to do with a little kid. Little girl. Probably Mexican. Probably in this country illegally."

He said he was listening and I took a chance and told him what happened on Monday morning, about Pedro's note, and Cecil putting the girl and her dog out in the freezing weather, and the note Cecil left on the door. "I took the girl with me and never saw him after that. I've been trying to find Pedro ever since. I'd like to try for another day or so. I just don't want to turn her over. She'll be deported, right?"

Andy was solemn. "I don't know. If she's in the country illegally, probably. You and Pedro friends?"

"Not really."

"Why would he leave his daughter with you?"

I told Andy I didn't have a good answer. "I just figured he was telling the truth about being in trouble. He knew my schedule and about me driving 117 every day. I bought tires from him a couple months ago. Had to be desperate or he wouldn't have left his daughter with someone he hardly knew." I mentioned that Pedro had even tried to get me to believe his daughter was a little boy. "Referred to her in the note as Juan. Dressed her like a boy."

Andy asked if I still had the note. I found it wadded up on the floor of my cab and brought it to him. He took longer than necessary to read the short note.

"Where's the girl now?"

I told him I'd left her with a good person in Rockmuse. "She's safe and well cared for."

"No doubt in my mind, Ben. I think sending her off with you wasn't quite the long shot for Pedro you might think." I knew what was coming and wasn't surprised. "Bring her in, Ben."

"Now? Give me another day or so to find Pedro. Come on, Andy."

"Now," he said. "We've got Pedro."

"He's in custody?"

"He's in a body bag."

38

Five minutes later Lenny and I topped the grade leaving Price. I didn't say anything after my short conversation with Andy, unsure what to say, or if I should say anything at all. None of it needed to be any concern of Lenny's.

Andy didn't know much and couldn't say much, especially since the Major Crimes Section showed up early in the morning and took over. We agreed that Pedro's intention was to get his daughter out of town and safe for a while. Sending her out into the desert with me was a gamble, and maybe not all that safe. Pedro was desperate and I was definitely headed out of town and he could be reasonably certain I would return at night.

Cecil had been badly beaten, though that wasn't what killed him—preliminary news was that honor probably went to heart failure. The closed tire building was where he had been beaten, and his body had been dumped in a ditch behind the truck stop. While they were checking out the tire center they found Pedro, also beaten and then shot. Andy was nice enough to emphasize that the phone call I made to him from Rockmuse was the best-timed call I'd ever made. It kept me from being on top of a very short list, if only for old times' sake. Though Andy didn't say so, I assumed the time of death was sometime after I'd arrived in Rockmuse.

It didn't appear to be robbery. No witnesses. There were cameras, though just monitors, no recording. No leads yet, unless the girl was somehow connected. I hoped not. Andy wanted me to bring her into the Utah Highway Patrol Headquarters. She had been there Monday morning with Pedro and Cecil. There was a small chance she'd seen or heard something. I didn't tell Andy she hadn't said a word since she came with me. It occurred to me that might be why she wasn't talking. That was their problem. Still, he said he'd do what he could, which we both knew was damn little. Any investigation of John's hit-and-run would have to wait. Get the girl. End of discussion.

I left the truck stop quickly. Once Major Crimes knew about the girl, they'd want to know exactly where she was and might want to send one of their own for her. Andy probably knew that too, and was sticking his neck out a little by allowing me to get her. I couldn't do much for the kid. At least she wouldn't have a team of investigators swooping down on her at Phyllis's. We'd have a nice ride back to Price together and when we got to headquarters I'd stay with her as long as I could. Andy was pretty sure Major Crimes would want to take a statement from me. So was I. Sometimes the fun never starts.

From the top of the hill we looked out over a steady stream of semis, pickups, and cars ahead on 191 as they started out across the desert toward Green River. Though the temperature was dropping, the weather was good and visibility at least ten miles. Clouds were rolling in from the north that would probably bring high winds and snow.

Lenny hadn't said a word since the truck stop. Now that we had a little road behind us, he was ready. "I don't mind telling you, Ben, I almost shit my pants when those cops drew down on us." Lenny spoke to the windshield in front of him. "I've never had a gun pointed at me before."

"I have," I said. "The feeling never gets old. Those two were young and jumpy. Not your fault, Lenny. You handled it damn well."

"Why were they so touchy?"

"This might come as a surprise to you," I said, "but I have not always been the kindhearted, civic-minded, cross-dressing Mother Teresa you know today."

Lenny made a show of banging his head against the passenger window, and then laughed. "Hard to believe."

"Isn't it, though?"

There was more on Lenny's mind and I knew if I was patient he would get to it. We had turned onto 117 and had already passed the diner when he found the courage. "You're hard to read, Ben. And you don't like questions, but—"

I finished for him: "'What the hell is going on?'"

"Something like that, yeah. I'm kind of scared and I don't know why. Or even if I should be. And that scares me even more."

Part of me was always scared too; scared of myself, what I'd done and what I might do, could do. Every day was a balancing act and most days I stayed on the wire. Lenny had a right to feel afraid, though I couldn't point to any one thing. Maybe it had nothing to do with him or me. Maybe it was Price, or Rockmuse, the desert, the mesa looming over everything, the heat and the cold and the winds, always the wind. Out here we all were in the middle of a balancing act all the time without ever really knowing if we were falling until it was too late. Cecil had gone over. George had tipped. John was leaning, maybe for good. Walt for damn sure was being blown by something. Ginger too. For some unknown reason, she'd aimed her Subaru at John. When it came right down to it, I didn't care why. I planned on having a talk with her when I finished up my day's work.

I wanted to answer Lenny and do what I could to put his mind at ease. "Makes sense to be scared," I said. "If we're not scared some of the time then we're not paying attention."

"You don't seem scared."

"Don't let my sunny disposition fool you, Lenny. Maybe I'm used to it, and that's not good either. You had cops pull their guns on you. The last few days someone you knew was the victim of a hit-and-run and it probably crossed your mind more than once that the driver was someone you knew. Maybe liked. You lost sleep taking care of John. That was followed by a long, dark ride in my trailer. That's far from the usual stocking shelves at the Mercantile with your aunt and uncle. You're bound to be jumpy. If you weren't you'd be an idiot." I'd been watching 117 as I talked and I made eye contact with him. "And you're a good guy, Lenny, and you're no idiot. John might be dead if not for you."

Lenny looked away into the passing desert. "Thanks, Ben."

"Just telling the truth," I said.

"I don't think the preacher would care much for me if he knew what you know."

"Don't be too sure, Lenny."

Lenny was cautiously curious. "What makes you think so?"

I'd been giving some thought to why Ginger showed up in town out of nowhere. John had a past. We all did. If Ginger running John down wasn't an accident, and I didn't think it was, then it was possible she knew him in his former life and held a grudge. Over the years I'd often mused on what compelled a man to move to a dying town in the high desert of Utah and take up hauling a cross up and down an isolated highway six months a year. Sure, it was crazy, but most of the time if you can look behind the crazy you'll find a reason. The reason might be crazy too, though it will be a reason that helps you understand.

"Just a guess," I said. "Doesn't matter. Think about this, though: knowing that one thing about you doesn't tell anyone anything important about who you are any more than me driving a truck tells people anything important about me. I know John well enough to say underneath that cross he's more than a religious whack job."

At least since morning I was reasonably certain John knew it was Ginger that hit him. He probably knew why, though if he lived he wouldn't be the one to talk. Andy could investigate all he wanted, perhaps come to the same conclusion I had about

Ginger. John would not cooperate. I knew John pretty well, his biblical way of thinking. During his feverish outbursts he'd made his wishes known: Barabbas must go free. Ginger must go free. I was fine with that, as long as she didn't want to pick up where she left off.

Lenny voluntarily pitched in as I made my deliveries. We made a good team, not that I needed help, and not that I could afford it. He had the ability to know what to do and when, and wasn't slow to get into the rhythm of the work. And no chatty bullshit. While this was something that could be taught, some men never learned, or never wanted to learn. Lenny came by it naturally. Whatever he ended up doing for a career I was certain he'd be a success at it.

We passed by John's cross, still standing on one corner. The winds out of the north or off the mesa should have knocked it down. I'd witnessed those winds take down things a lot bigger and heavier than that cross. Ginger's car was also right where I made sure it should be, though that didn't mean Ginger hadn't found a way to leave town. Part of me would be relieved if she were gone.

Lenny's help had us in Rockmuse by two thirty. I dropped him off outside the Mercantile and got two twenties out of my wallet. He didn't want to take them. "Really, Ben. I was glad to help. I can't take money for riding with John."

"It's not for your help with John," I said. "It's for your help at the transfer station and with my deliveries. Not a handout. You were worth every penny."

He took one of the twenties and thanked me. "Maybe you'll let me come along again sometime?"

I said I'd think about it.

He closed the door and I could tell by the way he walked to the entrance of the Mercantile that the work and his recent adventures, if you could call them that, had taken a toll on him.

I drove straight to the theater to talk to Ginger. At least, I hoped it would be nothing more than talking—and it would suit me just fine if there wasn't much of it. I still needed to get the girl from Phyllis and drive back to Price and Highway Patrol headquarters— and the weather was due for a change. It was going to be another late night.

39

I parked my rig on the street in front of the theater and sat in the cab for a moment listening to the engine idle. There was something calming to me, even comforting, in the regular soft churning of the engine and sitting up high in the cab—an illusion that I was in control. We all have our lies. I needed time to consider what I would say and, maybe more important, how I would say it.

It was only midafternoon and Ginger had the Closed sign up in the ticket window. The entrance door was unlocked and I walked into the dim lobby and waited for my eyes to adjust. While sitting in my truck I'd spent a second thinking about tucking my gun in my shirt, and another second asking myself if I would really shoot Ginger, even if I was forced. The answer was no. I was the messenger with the Get Out of Jail Free card. As long as I could tell her that and she believed me, there was no reason why our conversation couldn't be civil and brief.

I listened hard for sounds of movement or voices and heard only the sound of the wind pushing at the entrance door. The theater hall was dark. The lights were turned up on the stage. The bed had been stripped to a bare mattress. Ginger was sitting in the recliner sewing and gently rocking, intent on her work. I wasn't trying to sneak up on her, and walked at an easy pace toward the stage, careful not to disturb the tables of soaps and knickknacks and other junk.

At the foot of the stage, I said, "Ginger, we need to talk."

She looked up from her sewing. "About what?"

"About you and John."

"How's he doing?"

"He's alive. No guarantee he'll stay that way. Might lose his leg."

Ginger seemed way too relaxed for my taste. It made me nervous. I turned and looked back into the theater hall and saw nothing but tables and shadows and a thin streak of light leaking out from behind the lobby curtains. She rocked and sewed.

"We both know you're the one who hit John," I said. "I'm only here to tell you what you've already guessed."

"And what's that?"

"There probably won't be an investigation. No charges. John won't cooperate. No one's going to be prosecuted or go to jail."

"What if John dies?"

"Nothing changes, except, of course, for John."

"What if he lives and changes his mind? What then?"

Ginger wasn't just relaxed, she was emotionally flatlined. There was no remorse and no relief in hearing she was in the clear. I had to be missing something, and I was baffled about what it might be.

She stopped rocking and set her sewing down in her lap. "So, you're saying he forgives me?"

Not exactly what I was thinking, though I answered yes and watched Ginger's face slowly contort until she threw her head back and began to laugh, full-throated, her body shaking in the chair and then explosive convulsions that turned to a long, high wail.

"He forgives me!" she shouted. "Hallelujah! Praise the Lord!"

Ginger worked for a few moments pulling herself together and I could see tears gathering in the corners of her eyes. She resumed her sewing as the tears rolled across her cheeks and pooled at the edges of her lips. She started to speak, stopped, and patted her mouth with her sleeve. "Thank you for that," she said. "My life is complete." She raised her voice and called out beyond me into the theater. "George, dear, quit standing back there. You're not going to shoot anyone."

The steady rhythm of footsteps began behind me as George walked out of the shadows, probably holding a rifle, one of several he owned I supposed. I didn't turn, choosing to keep my eyes on Ginger. When he was close enough, I felt the barrel against my back. "Ben," he said.

"George," I responded, acknowledging him.

He sounded calm enough and, oddly, between the two of them, George, even with the rifle in my back, was the one I trusted. "If you've been listening, you know I'm not here to hurt anyone."

His voice caught when he tried to speak and I realized the old desert rat was having a tough time holding himself together. He spoke in a whisper. "There's no one left here to hurt, Ben." He asked me to join him in the lobby. Ginger began rocking again, nodding and mumbling to herself. I turned and George followed me out into the lobby, the rifle still bouncing against the small of my back.

George leaned the rifle against the display case. He wasn't perfumed and powdered like he was the first time I'd seen him, or dressed down and stinking as he had been the day before. The black string tie he wore was pulled low around the collar of a white shirt that was tucked into new jeans. Same high riding boots, clean if not polished. It seemed to me he was dressed for something special.

"You mean what you said in there?"

I said I did. "I'm not in the justice business, George." Angling my head toward the rifle, I added, "I don't want to be a target either."

George spoke to the display case. "Sometimes people come down this road and end up out here and find what they're looking for, even if it's not here."

I wasn't sure what he was talking about and said so. "If Ginger was searching for crazy, she found it. You saying she brought it with her?"

"A little of both, I guess."

He asked me to wait a minute and went upstairs to the projection room. When he returned he was holding a heavy photo album, old and worn, crammed full with dog-eared edges sticking out. He held it out to me. "You should take a look at this."

I gently pushed it back at him. "Not interested," I said. I assumed it had something to do with John, who he was before he came out to the desert. "I don't want to know. I already know too much about things I never wanted to know in the first place."

"Suit yourself," he said, and placed the album on top of the display case. "I just thought it might help you understand how she ended up in Rockmuse and why she ran down the preacher. She's a good person, Ben."

I allowed as how that was a possibility. Good people sometimes do bad things, out of stupidity, thoughtlessness, or simply because in the moment, for whatever reason, it seemed like a good idea. I opened the album.

The first photo was the cover of a glossy magazine, a man in his fifties, fit and powerful, with the straight back and bearing of a military officer. His iron-gray hair was buzzed short. He wore a dark suit with a large gold crucifixion cross on his chest like a war medal. He was standing on a runway in front of a private jet with bright crosses painted in gold on its fuselage. The caption read: Thaddeus T. Monroe, the General of God's Christian Soldiers. The general did have a passing resemblance to the preacher, though that was it. I would have bet my life that John was not the general.

George repeated that he thought Ginger was a good person. I

told George I'd withhold my opinion on that, though I thought that someone could be both good and crazy at the same time. "I don't care why she hit the preacher," I said. "No doubt she had her reasons. John probably had it coming to him. We've all got some kind of shit coming due. My only part in this is to see she doesn't take another run at him—if he lives, that is."

George asked me to consider taking a look at a few more pages.

I thumbed through the album, articles and photos, most of the general, a few of young women in pink uniforms. The women might have been related. I recognized what could have been a teenage version of Ginger. One photo was an aerial view of maybe thousands of people in black marching in formation with rifles on their shoulders with a skyscraper-sized golden cross looming in the background.

Then the articles and photos changed as the general began his fall. Seemed he had a taste for a better life than suited Jesus. And an even greater taste for young women, the younger the better. Young men and boys too. Photos of him with his attorneys. Fierce denials. Countercharges of religious persecution. On the last page was a newspaper article announcing that the general had jumped bail. Disappeared like piss into sand, leaving behind a spreading, dark stain while it trickled down the strata of generations.

I didn't recall reading about the general. Some of the dates in the scrapbook were from the 1970s and early 1980s. A little before my time, if I would have paid any attention at all. No more than I would now. It didn't matter. Just another version of the megachurch variety tragedy, of which there were many, before and since. Men and women, though mostly men, who confused serving God with being God, followed by folks who couldn't tell the difference, or simply didn't want to.

I closed the album. George permitted himself a weak smile. I'd never really looked at George's face before, except for the part that registered me. I studied it now, the blotches of red and the deep wrinkles, some still with specks of sand buried in them. Up until that moment it hadn't occurred to me that his interest in Ginger amounted to any more than a chance to cheat on his right hand. George was in love with Ginger, crazy or not.

"Crazy might be the most contagious disease there is, George."

George told me the scrapbook was about the man, the monster, Ginger had been searching for, had devoted her life to finding and punishing. John was not that monster. "I came along right after she'd run the preacher down," he said. "She was kneeling next to him, wild with guilt. I couldn't get a straight word out of her. I think she realized John was not the monster she needed him to be. I didn't know that then. I couldn't leave him out there. Or her."

"But now she thinks he is?"

"She's in and out. When she first showed me the scrapbook, I believed her. I wanted to believe her. That's why I called in and canceled Life Flight. I bought into it all. She showed me the scrapbook and told me what that man, their preacher in Missouri, where she's from, had done to her and her sisters. Like you said, crazy is contagious. Then her car breaks down out here and all the years and the bad memories along with the desert went to work on her. I came back after my little run-in with you and looked through the scrapbook again. Came to my senses and saw what's what and what isn't."

"What now?"

"I asked her to come out with me to my place for a while. Took her out there a few weeks ago. She liked it. Not many women would. If you'll let this all go like you said, in time she'll be okay."

"And what if I hadn't?" I asked. "Were you going to kill me when I showed up?"

"Maybe," he said. "I thought of it as reasoning with you."

Bringing a gun to reason with someone was a little like bringing a can of gasoline to preheat your electric oven. If there's a gun around, reason has left the building, or is on the way out the door. Fortunately, thanks to John and my ambivalence toward the law and justice, I'd brought enough reason to keep George from trying to reason with me.

"How old are you, George?"

"Seventy. Give or take."

"I'm not trying to change your mind. You'll do what you want anyway. I just think you might be overly optimistic about Ginger getting her mind right out at your place. She might decide you're the monster next. You think of that?"

George had thought of that. It showed in his eyes as he thought about it again. "Maybe," he said. "Doesn't matter. What have I got to lose?"

We both knew what he had to lose, and we both knew he was prepared to lose it.

"I wish you luck, then. And I wish Ginger luck too. In her own way she's as much of a religious nut as John. You a religious man, George?"

He laughed and shook his head. "No, not really. At my age I think about it more. My guess is I'll be a true believer about one minute before I take my last breath. Until then I'll go on believing in desert sunsets and silence."

I knew what he meant. "No preachers needed for that," I said. "Cuts down on the monsters too."

George picked up the rifle. "That's why I'm thinking she might get better with me out there. You know, when she visited we spent the day and the night together and hardly said a word. Didn't need to. She held my hand all day."

George said it and heard himself say it as if he couldn't quite believe his own words. There was a simplicity in the image of the two of them together holding hands that made me hope he was right. Just a few months earlier Claire and I had sat naked holding hands on the porch of the house in Desert Home. We sat in silence watching the desert slowly surrender to the dawn. I didn't want to think about what it might mean for them both if he was wrong.

I left the theater considering John and Ginger and the way their pasts collided with each other in the middle of nowhere. In John's case, it came speeding up behind him. What is it called when the past catches up with you and it isn't even your own past? I fired up the diesel and listened to the RPMs settle. Maybe it was karma that was blind. Justice sure as hell wasn't.

40

It was almost four in the afternoon when I arrived at Phyllis's. Manita was standing alone in the center of the horse pasture with the horses grazing on nubs of grass nearby. The western sun threw their long shadows across the brown earth toward the fence-lined drive. The dark girl and her shadow might as well have been a human sundial. Phyllis was reading a book on a swing chair hanging from the porch while the dog sat on the steps watching the girl. Even as my brakes squeaked to a stop in front of the house, none of them took any notice. With the reflecting sun tumbling off the red mesa behind us, I felt as if I had been given the chance to walk into a painting of a life I had never known.

The dog was right in the middle of the steps and wasn't about to move, so I stepped around him. My boots clunked against the old wooden planks of the porch and Phyllis looked up from her book. "She's been standing out there for almost an hour. I've never known a child who could stand so still for so long."

"At least she's standing still," I said. "Maybe she's done running off for a while."

Phyllis lifted herself out of the swing and stood next to me. "Look at her, Ben. I don't think she's done running at all." The girl was facing north and slightly west where the horizon was turning gray with clouds. "I think she's like a prisoner making a plan. There's something or someone out there, a home maybe, or the promise of one. Who knows? Next time she runs, she'll know where she's going."

"It won't be from here," I said. "Found her father."

Phyllis took the news as a mixed blessing without knowing just how mixed it was. "Oh," she said. "You're taking her with you."

I told Phyllis that Pedro had been murdered, roughly where and when. "The kid's part of a murder investigation now. No idea who killed him or why. I'm supposed to bring her into Highway Patrol headquarters in Price."

"That's terrible. The poor girl," she said. "Part of me wants her to start running right now."

"I wish there was something I could do, Phyllis. I'll stay with her as long as they'll let me. No telling how long that will be."

"You think there's a chance the police can locate her mother? She must have family in the area."

I shrugged and said, "They'll try."

I didn't say I doubted they would have much luck. If her mother or any other family members were around, Pedro wouldn't have sent her off with me. I didn't see anything in the child's near future that amounted to more than standing alone in an empty pasture staring at the desert.

Phyllis went inside to put together a few things for Manita and for our drive to Price. I walked out into the pasture and, seeing where I was headed, the dog followed. She hadn't moved, and I stood next to her for a few minutes tracking her steady gaze into the desert on a line that skirted Rockmuse and ran past the coal pit site. The tire dump was in that general direction and, beyond that, only hundreds of square miles of sand and rock all the way into Wyoming.

I tapped her on the shoulder and she looked up at me with her black eyes. "Time to go, Manita," I said, and offered her my hand, which she took, though as we walked toward the house her head was turned and she looked back into the same darkening nothing she'd been staring at for an hour. We waited on the porch for

Phyllis, who came out with a sack lunch, water, and a tiny stuffed animal—a purple dinosaur with a green belly.

Phyllis handed me everything but the stuffed animal. Kneeling, she held out the animal to the girl, who first took it and then handed it back. The two exchanged it back and forth a few times until the girl finally accepted it. "Barney," Phyllis said. The dog gave it an approving sniff and then the girl did the same. I didn't think the girl had the slightest idea of what it was or what it was for. She took it only because Phyllis offered it to her. When Phyllis reached out to hug Manita, the girl did not return the hug. The hug was acknowledged only by a slight leaning of her body toward Phyllis. Then she looked up at me.

In a flash she took off running and I cleared all the stairs to try to grab her and missed. It happened so quickly, Phyllis only managed a grunt as she reached for the girl, who by that time was already halfway to my truck. From there she walked to the passenger door and stood there. The dog ambled up to her side and together they waited there for me.

"I'd say she's eager to get going."

Phyllis brought herself up and straightened her shoulders as if steeling herself. "I guess so." She pointed at my boots. "You might want to consider investing in a pair of good running shoes. Until then, don't take your eyes off her."

Once I had everyone settled, I climbed up behind the wheel and rolled down the window and glanced over at Phyllis in her jeans and flowered work shirt. She would always seem somehow out of place, or maybe she made the world around her seem out of place. I thanked her, and added, "Why do you stay here?"

It must have been a difficult question, and one that she found slightly amusing. "I don't honestly know, Ben. Waiting for Godot, I guess."

I didn't know who Godot was, and asked her.

"No one knows," she answered. "It's just a reason to be where you are."

Oddly, that made sense to me. I thanked her again and rolled up my window. She chewed her lower lip and turned and went inside before I had the truck in gear.

THE CLOCK ON my dashboard blinked 4:30 as we made our way down Main Street. With no stops and decent weather we would be at the Highway Patrol in two hours, seven o'clock at the latest. Maybe it was just me, but the girl seemed almost happy to be back in the cab again and moving. I certainly was. There was no reason to rush. The weather shouldn't hit until long after we made the junction with US 191. We could all enjoy the drive through the desert. As long as we drove, whatever was waiting for us could go on waiting—forever, as far as I was concerned. Ginny was gone, John was in the hospital or dead, and Pedro was dead. No one was waiting for us, except the cops. Manita smiled at me and wiggled her butt deep into the seat, making herself comfortable. I took that as a sign of agreement, maybe even contentment.

41

I slowed and debated whether or not to take on diesel at the Rock-muse Shell. The islands were all empty and there was only one car parked in a spot near the doors. It was the kind of vehicle you don't see much of in Rockmuse, even during tourist season—a lowered Honda Civic coupe, primered dark gray, deep-tinted windows, with oversized chrome spinners and low-profile tires. The Honda's trunk sported a high aftermarket chrome spoiler that screamed out-of-towner. In winter, such a car was a sure sign that whoever was driving it had taken a wrong turn and had no idea where in the hell they were.

I had a clear view inside the convenience store and what I saw made my blood run cold. I jerked the wheel to take an abrupt left-hand turn into the station. The force of the turn had the girl and the dog fighting to keep upright.

Eckhardt was standing ramrod straight behind the register watching a young Hispanic or black man in a sleeveless shirt and baggy pants near the cooler at the rear of the store. This was one of those times I could see the potential for tragedy unfolding right before my eyes. The seconds were counting down until the shotgun blast splintered through the plywood.

My first impulse was to honk and run as fast as I could into the store. Instead, I pulled alongside a row of pumps and hopped out and waved at Eckhardt. He didn't wave back. I'm not sure I strolled, but with every step I was sure as hell trying. The window on the driver's side of the car was partially down, and inside was a young woman holding a fussing baby. She had her eyes glued on the interior of the store.

When I came through the door the bell rang. The young guy at the rear glanced at me. Eckhardt didn't move a muscle.

"How you doing, Eckhardt?"

I hoped my greeting didn't sound as hollow to him as it did to me. His hands were flat, palms down on the counter, out front and visible, almost like an invitation.

I picked up the first item I saw, a package of Hostess Sno Balls, and then continued down the aisle eyeing snacks and cans of motor oil. The guy had the cooler door half-open but he was watching me move toward him in the glass.

"That your car outside?" I asked.

He was a powerful guy, medium height, shaved head, with tattoos on his muscled arms and neck. He didn't answer my question. I had to get him out of the store, though I had no idea what I would do or say if I succeeded. Maybe he was just what Eckhardt wanted, someone to try to rob him. Maybe he wasn't. My gut told me it didn't matter.

"You might want to check with your wife or girlfriend," I said. "She's got some problem with the baby or something and asked me to tell you."

It was the only thing that came to mind. It worked. He bobbed his shiny head at me and went straight for the door. As he came near the register I saw Eckhardt stiffen and I sucked in a breath. The bell rang and the guy was safely outside.

Eckhardt started to say something and I cut him off. "Don't!"

I stepped outside holding the cupcakes and a can of motor oil. The door was open to the car and the guy was bent over talking to the woman. I made it about ten feet toward the pumps when I heard the car door slam and footsteps behind me and an angry voice shout, "Hey, you! What the fuck is your deal?"

In that moment I asked myself what the fuck my deal was and realized I had no good answer. I faced the guy and for some silly reason made a show of the cupcakes and motor oil in my hands. "I can explain," I said, though I wasn't sure I could, or that he would listen. "Don't go back in there."

I didn't hear my truck door open. Manita and the dog were standing next to me and all three of us were staring at the guy who had raised his shirt up just enough to reveal a handgun against his brown belly—and a brown hand on its butt. The girl reached up and put her hand on my right elbow. I had no idea what the dog was doing. This was a record, even for me—a gun aimed at me three times in one day, though technically the guy in front of me hadn't pointed his at me . . . yet. Though with guns, like a game of horseshoes, close counts.

He spoke to Manita in Spanish asking if I was her father. She responded only by tightening her grip on my elbow. I answered for her. "Close enough."

After a long silence, I spoke again, knowing silence wasn't going to change the situation no matter how much I wished it would. "That old man in there," I said, "he's been robbed. He's jumpy."

The man glanced back over his shoulder. Eckhardt was still behind the register staring out the window at us. "You need to check yourself," he said.

"I'm trying as hard as I can."

"Try harder."

The woman got out of the car and the baby's fussing turned to crying. She stood by the door, half in and half out, gently bouncing the baby against her shoulder. The man told her to get back in the car and she shook her head.

"Whatever you need," I said, "I'll go in and get it and bring it out to you."

"You will, huh?" He lowered his shirt but kept his hand on his gun. "I look like I need help?"

From where he stood I could see him reading the side of my

truck. He read it out loud. "Ben's Desert Moon Delivery Service. You Ben?"

I said I was.

"That old man got a problem with people like me?"

I answered as truthfully as I knew how. "He's old and bitter and lonely. He's got a problem with everything and everyone and he's just waiting for a chance to express himself. Brown works fine." I realized I was maybe giving Eckhardt too much benefit. "Anything different works fine too, even white—in a pinch."

This drew a hard smile from him. "Food," he said. "Good food, none of that snack shit. Milk. Lunch meats. Bread."

"I don't think he stocks formula."

"She's got that going," he said. "Diapers?"

"I'll see."

I went into the store and the girl and the dog followed closely. There were only four aisles and I picked up everything he asked for and had the door to the cooler open when Eckhardt found his tongue. "What the hell are you doing, Ben? That spic was going to rob me."

He was probably right. I set everything on the counter. "And now you get to rob me and you get to save a shotgun shell and the trouble of replacing your counter. Not to mention cleaning up the mess."

Eckhardt rang everything up and I paid him. He tossed me a plastic bag. "You need to mind your own goddamned business." He motioned toward Manita. "Who's that belong to?"

Not child, not kid, but "that." I finished bagging the groceries and diapers. "Eckhardt, you need to mind your own goddamned business."

Outside I handed the bag to the man. "And you'll need some gas too."

"I've got money," he said.

"I'm sure you do." I was sure he didn't. "But unless you've got a credit card you'll have to go back in to pay."

I walked over and stood by a pump. He drove over and I swiped my Visa card. While he was filling up I got Manita and the dog back inside the cab. Maybe I could have tried to reprimand her for getting out. On the other hand, I was glad she did, and she wouldn't understand me anyway. It seemed to me that she understood a lot of things that words can't or won't say.

I rejoined the man at the pump and pointed to 117. "Turn left and stay on the highway for about a hundred miles. When you get to the junction with US 191, left for seventy-five miles to the interstate, right for twenty miles to Price. Another hundred or so to Salt Lake City."

"And what if I don't want to leave town? I'm beginning to like it here. Free food and gas." He swiveled his head around, taking in Main Street and the desert and mesa in the distance. "Paradise."

"Sure," I said. "You should stick around. I'll be back next week for the funeral."

His expression told me he didn't like what I'd just said and that he understood. "Is there a hotel in town?"

"Nope," I said, and then told him that was the truth. There was the Rock Dock Bed and Breakfast, but Mildred was closed for the season and she wasn't going to open for him. No use mentioning that. "You have to stick around for a reason?"

No response.

"Okay, then," I said. "None of my business."

"We'll car camp out in the desert."

"You'll die in the desert. And that's a guarantee. All three of you."

"More bitter old white men?"

"Hell, yes," I said. "More than you can count. Not all white, not all old. Not all men. But it's the desert that will kill you. Storm is coming in. Once it's here, your car, with those tires and ground clearance, will be the fastest sled in town."

"Hector," he said, and extended his hand.

I took it. "I know a place out in the desert. It's empty but it's got the basics. Maybe even some canned food still in the cupboards. If you're set on staying, I'm going that way. It's not pretty and it's isolated, but it's warm and decent for a while. Has its own putting green."

He asked me to give him a minute and stuck his head in the car while he talked to the woman. I heard him tell her it had a putting green.

He popped his head up. "You're joking about the green, right?"

"Truth," I said. "But the place is no resort."

After another brief conversation with the woman, he said, "She says we'll do it." He lifted his shirt so I could see the gun, again. "This says you better not be fuckin' with me."

My crew settled in, I turned back onto 117 for what I estimated to be a thirty- or forty-mile drive. The dog stayed on his haunches watching the girl. When her eyes began to drift with sleep he curled up on the floorboard and did the same. Hector stayed a safe distance behind and I dawdled at an even fifty-five. Sometimes, unlike Sammy Hagar, I can drive fifty-five, when I have nowhere to go and no one waiting but cops with lots of questions and no good answers.

The wind was starting to gust. The first one hit my trailer a full broadside that momentarily pushed me dangerously close to the shoulder. Even when you're expecting it, a crosswind will throw you, especially in a high-profile vehicle. I checked my rear-view mirror just as another rocked us. Against the empty trailer it sounded like a wave crashing against the shore. Hector weaved and braked and straightened out nicely. The high chrome spoiler on his Honda was nothing more than a sail making the worst out of a bad situation.

A short way before we were to turn, I slowed and pulled over. Hector pulled up behind me and waited until I walked back to his car. He lowered his window and I said, "Just making sure you want to do this. I'd recommend you follow me on, at least to the junction with US 191. You could spend the night in Price."

"If it doesn't feel right I'll scramble."

"If you can," I said. "You got a cell phone?"

"Yeah," he said. "But it's broken."

"It's not broken. There isn't any signal out here. Not one you can rely on."

He picked up his cell phone and stared at its screen as if checking to see what I said was true. Convinced it was, he tossed it over his shoulder into the backseat.

"Cheer up," I said, "your gun still works."

Hector looked over at the young woman. She nodded. "Let's do this."

"The road is rough—bumps, ruts, the usual. Go slow or you'll seed the desert with your drivetrain."

My truck crept along 117. Hector followed as I made the turn down the narrow dirt road that led to what used to be the Lacey brothers' place. The place wasn't ever theirs, their last name wasn't Lacey, and they weren't brothers either but sad old bank robbers, father-and-son killers who had managed to evade the FBI for thirty or more years by living alone in the desert. It was a life that was maybe only a little less confining than prison and perhaps, as it turned out, only a bit preferable to execution.

I hadn't been to the Lacey place, which was really only two boxcars welded together and set on a cinder-block foundation, since early that summer. Fergus Lacey had asked me to take both halves of his son Duncan's body into Price. Duncan had been caught in an accidental garrote while stringing barbed wire. The wire cinched him clean through just above the waist. Fergus committed suicide there only days after his son's death, which was when everyone found out who they were and what they'd done. It was old news and forgotten before it even made the local papers. It was a hell of a place to take Hector and the woman and baby, but it was the best I could think of on short notice. It was better than car camping and a damn sight safer than shopping at Eckhardt's.

It took a little while to get to the boxcars. Hector was going slow and often it wasn't slow enough to navigate around and over the rough road. We pulled into the dirt-and-sand turnaround and came to a stop in front of the heavy-gauge cable spool and milk crates the Laceys had used for yard furniture. I asked Manita to please stay inside and she began to pet the dog, which was as close to a yes as I was likely to get.

All I wanted to do was show Hector the place and then get back on the highway. I figured sunset would begin in an hour or so. The sun was already low and the light was skimming the desert floor like a yellow stone. Neither Hector nor the woman said anything as they followed me to the back entrance.

The small putting green was sprouting weeds and brown spots from months of neglect. Before going in they paused on the deck and squinted across the miles of flat nothing into the northern horizon. Dervishes of sand and dirt swirled on a low hillside where the Laceys had built a small windmill.

A decomposing strip of crime-scene tape fluttered in the wind between the door and the deck railing. Hector rubbed the remnants of it between his thumb and forefinger. He shook his head. "Just like home."

They seemed to like the inside better, with its cozy woodstove and twin beds, two easy chairs, and small kitchen. I was right, there were still canned goods and jugs of water. Since the place was solar-powered, with a backup gasoline generator, the fridge and the lights still worked. The cops had been nice enough to take the rope that Fergus had strung from a steel ceiling beam to hang himself. Crime-scene ribbons aside, the worst crime committed in the boxcars was their wasted lives.

The woman, a slender Latina, sat down in the recliner and began nursing the baby. Hector and I stepped outside. He asked if I had permission to let them stay there. "It doesn't belong to anyone," I said. "I have as much right to grant permission as anyone else. Trust me, no one will ask. Hardly anyone even knows this place exists. Of the few who do, none care. Leave or stay. It's up to you."

"I feel like thanking you. So, thanks. But I have to ask—"

"Why?"

"Yeah. Why?"

I didn't need to think about my answer, though I hadn't really thought about it. "Because I've been threatened with a gun three times today and I'm fuckin' tired of it." Just saying it aloud made it seem unreal, though nonetheless true. "And three times, no blood: not mine, no one's. I think you're lost. Maybe you're a bad man. Maybe not. The daddy of the little girl with me just got himself murdered. If you're the one that did it, I hope not. If you did and I find out, you'll see a whole new me." I thought about telling him about Eckhardt's shotgun and decided against it. "That baby in there yours?"

Hector worked up a smile. "Close enough."

"That baby gets one more chance to know you. An old man told me today that sometimes people come out here searching for something, and sometimes they find it even when it's not here. Whatever brought you here, I don't want to know. I just don't want you to find what isn't here, or shouldn't be. Like I said, maybe you're up to no good out here. Either way, you're still lost."

"That's it?"

"That's it," I said. "I'll stop by in a few days. If you're still here, alive, then I'll drop off some more food and water." I counted out fifty dollars in small bills. "If you have to go into Rockmuse, go to the Mercantile. Healthier food—and environment—and since it's winter, you might want to buy the rest of those pants."

"I didn't kill the girl's padre."

"If you say so," I said.

"I say so." Hector moved closer to me, closer than what is comfortable, and whispered, "How about you? You ever kill anyone?"

"No," I answered. "But not for lack of trying."

"You think you could kill me?"

I didn't answer that. We both knew the answer. I was pretty sure it cut both ways. From the moment I'd lured him outside I had been wondering if I'd made a poor decision. It was done now, and if he was running from the law or something worse, as I suspected, all I'd accomplished was a respite from what was sure to come. If he hurt or killed someone because of my actions, I'd have to live with that, along with everything else.

Hector went inside and I joined my crew to begin the rest of the drive back to Price and what would be our goodbye. The dog was going to be a problem if the Major Crimes investigators tried to separate him from the girl. My money would be on the dog, though in the end, they'd shoot him or have Animal Control come and get him, and that would mean putting him down. Manita and I exchanged looks and she began scratching the dog's ears.

Out on 117 again I picked up the pace a little, though not much. We were still more or less on schedule and the wind seemed to have died down, though the sun was in our eyes and glaring up off the asphalt. I lowered my visor. She stared out the window at the passing desert with the same intense focus that some kids watch their computers or television. I wished we could exchange a few words, anything that might lessen the distance between us during our final hours together. Maybe sharing the desert and the hum of the tires on the road did all that better.

On a short straight stretch I saw a vehicle moving up fast on us. It came on so quickly I didn't have time to do more than check my mirrors. An easy S-turn up a slight hill came at the end of the straight and I slowed to make sure the other vehicle would be back in the right lane after passing.

It was the circus train from Monday, the big black Ford dually pulling the Airstream and trailer. Long streaks of dried red mud fanned out like earthen flames along the sides of the truck and trailer. The driver honked several times as he blew by us, the Airstream and trailer once again twitching dangerously behind him. The boy in the passenger seat barely had enough time to stick out his tongue and flip me off. He didn't seem to be shy about what he was doing and that made me think he'd done it a lot, and maybe with some encouragement from his father. I slowed down even more to put as much distance as possible between us. At that speed they'd make the junction in less than an hour. With luck Manita and I would never have to see them again.

Our luck was bad; theirs was worse.

42

Bright chrome flashed in my eyes as we emerged from the S-turn. I locked up the brakes and wrestled my truck over to the shoulder. Another short straight of a few hundred yards ended with a low rise and a gentle right-hand turn. Both lanes of the highway between us and part of the rise were scattered with what remained of the circus train and, though I didn't spot them, its ringmaster and circus boy.

This was the textbook definition of a debris field, in living color and chrome, spreading everywhere like a metal nightmare. The pickup was a twisted piece of expensive junk. It had separated from the Airstream and rolled several times before coming to rest on its side a hundred feet off the left shoulder, its engine releasing an acrid smoke that drifted across the highway. The Airstream had gone right, rolled, and broken in two like a stainless-steel egg. The trailer with the ATVs was nowhere to be seen, leaving its contents strewn in every direction. No sign of the man or his kid that I could see, though any pile of wreckage could be hiding a body, or parts of one.

I grabbed a handful of road flares and hopped out of the cab. Manita had slipped out from beneath the seat belt and she and the dog were both standing on the passenger seat staring out the front window, hands and paws on the dash. I jabbed the air with my index finger to tell them to stay put and hoped to hell they got the message.

I walked back down the road a couple hundred yards and lit flares, placing them near the center of the highway where the S-turn became the straightaway. Little by little I made my way up the highway dodging pieces of jagged metal, chunks of spidered safety glass, coolers, bedding, wheels and miscellaneous shit that was so damaged I couldn't even tell what it was. I couldn't go five steps without having to go around or step over something. At the top of the rise, I lit two more flares and figured that was enough to get anyone going east to slow down or stop. Coming back the way I had come I saw the legs of the guy protruding from beneath the chassis of one of the ATVs that had come to rest on the southbound shoulder.

Not knowing what I would find, I pushed the ATV to the side. His body was intact, eyes open. He blinked blood flowing from a gash in his forehead. Both legs had been snapped at the knees and were tucked at a cartoon angle beneath him. So much for seat belts, if he had even been wearing any. Airbags only worked if you're where you're supposed to be. In a continuous roll, as they must have been, the man and his son were as loose as two ball bearings in a tin can.

His lips moved. I got down on one knee and bent over him. These were probably his dying words. In a hoarse whisper he repeated, "My son, my son."

"You mean the brat?"

He blinked his eyelids.

"I don't know. Haven't found him yet. Let's just hope I don't need garbage bags to bring him to you." Even as I spoke, I was regretting what I said. "Maybe he's okay," I added, though I didn't believe there was a chance in hell that he was. Kicking a man when he's down had never been my style, but in the moment I was running short on style, and forgiveness.

A deep moan rumbled up from his throat and I stood and surveyed the debris all the way back to where my truck was parked. Flames were licking upward from beneath the pickup's hood and I ran over and looked through the broken windows. No boy. Off to my left, not far from my truck, I saw Manita and the dog in the desert near a stand of dwarf juniper. They weren't moving.

Up closer I saw they had found the boy. She was sitting cross-legged in the dirt with his head in her lap. Manita was busy brushing wisps of wind-blown blond hair from his face. Before I could get over to her an old flatbed honked and skirted the wreckage by going out into the desert. A man got out and I recognized him and his wife, residents of Rockmuse, though I didn't know them or their names. He knew mine, or saw it on the side of my trailer as he passed by. Manita looked fine to me where she was. There was nothing I could do about whatever horror rested in her lap. I walked over to the man.

He stood by the door. "Jesus H. Christ, Ben. Anyone left alive?"

"One, at least," I said, "probably not for long."

His wife leaned over and said, "What can we do?"

That was always the big question when something bad happened on 117. No houses. No cell phone reception, if you had one, which few, myself included, bothered to own. Someone needed to go for help, either back to Rockmuse, where there was no help but you could find a phone; or ahead to Price, or use the old pay phone at Walt's diner. Help, if it ever came, was almost always too late.

"I'll stay," I said. "You go ahead and call the Highway Patrol from the pay phone at the diner."

The man got back inside his truck. "I'll get there as fast as I can."

"Be careful," I said. "You don't want to end up like this."

He nodded. "Wind?"

I told him that would be my guess. "And speeding without a

brain. Get going. If dispatch wants to know how many victims, tell them two."

The flatbed took off and disappeared into the glare of a low sun. The highway was impassable and he knew it would be easier to bump around in the desert for a half mile or so until he could get clear of the mess and rejoin the road. It would be dusk within ninety minutes or so. I could already feel the temperature dropping and the wind rising.

How does a child express sorrow? The boy didn't seem to have a mark on him that I could see. He was conscious and in shock, and I knew he had to be busted up inside. His eyes were open but unfocused and he seemed somehow comforted by the presence of Manita, and maybe the dog too, whose big head hovered over him, snout lowered as if in mourning. I didn't know the girl and would never get the chance, but the kindness in her dark eyes and her gentle way with the boy told me both who she was and who she would become. I looked back toward the father and then at Manita again. I wondered if I'd ever grow up to become a child like her.

The sound of a gunshot startled me. I wheeled around trying to locate where it had come from. The thought that someone might be shooting at me occurred only when the dog lifted his head and the girl turned. It wasn't until that moment that I threw myself on the ground and tried to shield them. We stayed that way for a couple minutes. Even the dog seemed grateful to have some cover. Suddenly I knew where the shot had come from—and who had fired it. I remembered the open-carry handgun the man had been wearing and jogged as fast as I could up the road, afraid of what I knew was waiting for me.

The gun was on the pavement inches above his head. He was straining with his fingers to reach for it and finish what he'd started. I kicked the gun away and it clattered across the highway and into the sand shoulder. His tears mixed with the blood and

rolled a dark pink as they slipped over his face. He'd almost succeeded. Only his injuries and the odd angle he was forced to use
caused him to miss his right temple. A deep, bloody furrow ran
from his forehead into his shaved scalp.

His eyes blazed up at me. "Let me—"

I didn't kneel and spoke to him from where I was standing.
"Your son is alive. Badly injured. Help is on the way." That was all
the kindness and comfort I had in me; the remaining room was
rising with guilt.

I left the gun where it was and walked back to my truck to pull
out some cheap thermal blankets I always carried. I covered the
boy first and then the man before returning to the girl. No vehicles appeared from either direction. There wasn't anything else
we could do.

We waited as the sun hovered over the peaks of the Wasatch
Range and dusk came on in stages of lavender and gray and the
evening wind kicked up brown clouds of dirt and sand and sent
them swirling in and out of the wreckage. Some of the lighter debris skittered and scratched against the rough pavement and then
tumbled and went airborne out into the desert, some catching in
the grasses and sage like sad ornaments.

At first I didn't quite believe I heard the siren, its wail muted
by the shifting winds. Perhaps only as long as ten or fifteen minutes had passed. The red and blue lights of Andy's Highway Patrol pickup appeared on the rise and steered cautiously into the
wreckage a little ways before he stopped and positioned his vehicle diagonally across both lanes. His headlights and their blue
flashing grille markers stayed on, strobing the whole stretch of
highway.

A hatless Trooper Smith and I approached each other. He was
covered from head to toe in sand and dirt, some of it still wet
and muddy. I didn't comment and we walked in silence to where
the man lay. Trooper Smith introduced himself and dispensed
some brief, vague encouragement, for which the man attempted to

whisper his thanks. Andy anchored a red whip flag with a flashing light. We continued on to the boy, where he did the same. Marking the locations of the injured or dead at an accident scene made evacuation easier and faster, especially in darkness.

When Andy knelt by the girl and the boy and introduced himself she remained solemn and ignored him. The boy only gazed upward into the face of the girl, almost at ease, the white corners of his eyes beginning to redden with blood. This was part of Andy's job, and he'd done it too many times in all kinds of conditions.

I gave Andy and his dirt coat the once-over. "Long day?"

"Long week," he answered.

He motioned for me to join him several feet away. "Life Flight is en route."

"Figures," I said, thinking of John. I asked Andy how in the hell he managed to get to the scene so quickly.

"I was just down the road turning onto 117 from Dan Brew's place. The old couple flashed their lights. Pure luck. My radio was even working—just one of those things. That the girl?"

"That's her," I said. "She was out of my cab and next to the boy before I could stop her. Calm as she could be, so I let her stay. Damage done, if any. I get the impression the kid has seen worse. If he dies, at least he won't be alone."

"Wind?"

"Of course," I said, and mentioned that when the guy passed me I estimated his speed at eighty or better. "I suppose you'll want to take the girl with you from here."

"Can't." He tipped his head in the direction of his pickup. "I got Dan Brew's fiancée with me. Or maybe she's his widow. Doesn't matter."

Andy briefly filled me in on Brew, which also explained why in his present condition he resembled a bigger version of a rain-soaked prairie dog. Brew had thought his sod house sat on a gold mine and had honeycombed the entire area for the bits of gold that had washed down from the mesa over hundreds of thousands of years. What little he had found only drove him harder and crazier until one of his tunnels collapsed on him and the woman. It hadn't been my imagination when I noticed during my last delivery there that the ground seemed sunken. Brew had been partially buried and crushed and eventually died. The woman had been trapped with him until Andy heard her cries for help and dug her out. She was half-naked and wrapped in a blanket sitting on his front seat.

"Damn good luck for her," I said.

"Not so much for him."

"Where's your hat?"

"Buried under a ton of dirt and sand."

Andy returned to the man to see if he could make him more comfortable. The next time I caught sight of him he was on top of the rise taking photos of the scene. Within a few minutes the helicopter, lights flashing, came in low from the north, pitching and yawing as it fought the gusting wind before setting down in the desert nearby. Everyone had their job to do and they did it.

Two tow trucks even made the scene, another miracle, and began spraying the pickup with flame-retardant foam. After that they began pushing and dragging heavier pieces and generally clearing the highway. I helped out as I could, careful to keep an eye on the girl. It all went efficiently and quickly, the result of too damn much practice.

By the time two EMTs had the man and the boy stabilized and on board, one wrecker had already winched up the carcass of the pickup and left. The other was clearing the last pieces of wreckage from the road. Andy had his head in the open door of the helicopter talking to the EMTs. When he pulled his head out, he scanned the road until he saw me. The helicopter rose and wobbled and then disappeared into the twilight. Andy walked to where the man had been and started searching the roadside for something. He picked it up. "Jones!" he shouted. "A word."

I was in no hurry as we walked down the centerline of 117

toward each other. He started talking when we were still several feet apart. "Please tell me what I just heard is not true." He tucked the man's handgun into his belt. "Well?"

"He was an asshole," I said. "And a stupid asshole at that."

"So you told him you had to collect his son in a garbage bag?"

I hadn't said that, exactly. Close enough, I guessed. There was no use in denying it. Part of me wasn't all that sorry.

"You bet I did, Andy. He damn near forced me off the road on Monday. When we caught up to each other in Rockmuse I told him to slow down. Warned him of crosswinds and high-profile vehicles. He basically told me to fuck myself. He was stupid."

Andy just gave me a long, weary stare. "He was stupid, huh? That's it? Jones, you take the prize. Stupid? I don't even know where to begin with you. You win stupid. Worse than stupid—mean stupid."

I shrugged and started to defend myself, not that I had a damn thing to say in my own defense. He closed the distance between us. "Shut up, Jones." I did, and he continued. "I spend most of my days dealing with stupid, just like most cops. Stupid is our stock-in-trade. Murder, drugs, and worse get a pass because of days busy with stupid. If I could give citations for stupid, I could paper the desert with them, not that they'd do any good. But you, Jones, what you did to that man, that was felony cruelty in the first degree. It's no wonder he tried to shoot himself. If he'd succeeded you'd have been the one responsible. Think about that."

"So give me a ticket," I said.

I could say it was getting dark. I could say I wasn't ready. Both true. I just didn't see it coming because I didn't expect it. Andy's fist connected with my chin and the impact lifted my heels and down I went, my ass hard against the pavement. I'd been punched before, and by men who knew how to do it and where, and what had just hit me deserved an award of some kind. I rolled to my side and tried to get my feet beneath me.

"There's your ticket, Jones."

"Goddammit, Andy," I said, trying to shake my eyes back into their sockets. "What kind of Mormon are you? You learn to punch like that at temple?"

I managed to get to my knees, my fists tightening.

"Don't even think of getting up, Jones," he warned. "Stay right where you are, you cruel asshole." He was angry enough he was shaking. "Report me if you've got the balls. I'll gladly take a suspension. I could use the break. And considering who I punched, there might be a commendation in it for me."

My head was clearing, though I wisely took his advice and stayed down and wiped a trickle of blood away from a split lip.

"I'm going to get in my pickup and head into Price. You just stay in the middle of 117. Take your time. Maybe a truck will come along and hit you and knock some simple common decency into you."

I stayed put and watched him march to his pickup and leave, and followed the blue and reds as they went spinning west behind the rise and faded into the early evening dusk. I got up. Andy was right, and I didn't need a truck to hit me. That short Mormon trooper's right hand was almost the same thing.

I'd only taken a couple steps when I started to run. The girl and the dog were gone. The driver of the second wrecker was just getting into his cab to pull out.

"Did you see a kid and a dog?"

He pointed northeast, into a wall of shadowed desert. "I'm pretty sure I saw them go that way."

I asked him why in the hell he didn't stop them.

"Fuck you," he said, "not my kid."

With that he drove away and left me in silence staring north into the absolute last rays of sunlight fading into a roiling bank of gray clouds. I took off in the direction the girl went and quickly stopped. This was my fault, all of it, and beating myself up about it was just using up precious time. There was no question I had to go after her, and as soon as possible. The only question was how.

43

I broke every traffic law in the book getting to Rockmuse in record time, thirty minutes or less. Laying on my horn and flashing my high beams, I roared up the drive to Phyllis's house and skidded to a stop in front of the porch. I cleared the stairs in one leap and pounded on the door. A light was on in the living room and I tried the knob. Without waiting I came through the door just as Phyllis was opening it. The force of my entry knocked her to the floor. I apologized and offered her a hand up.

She guessed at what had happened. "Oh God," she said. "You lost her."

"I sure as shit did." There was no use in saying any more than that. It was a waste of time. "I need that Kawasaki UTV Mule you have."

Two years earlier I had delivered a used utility task vehicle to Phyllis that she'd bought cheap at a ranch liquidation sale. It was nothing more than a small four-wheel-drive motorcycle with a tiny truck bed. Ranchers and hunters used them to get around and carry light loads quickly and inexpensively. It fit in my truck and would allow me the speed and capability to cover a lot of rough desert terrain. Using it would compensate for the time it took to go to Rockmuse to retrieve it.

Phyllis shook her head and moaned. "I don't have it anymore, Ben. I couldn't get it running."

I had planned on using that UTV, and the news that it wasn't an option drained me of hope. I didn't have a backup plan. "I'll have to go on foot," I said. "She already has an hour head start on me."

We both knew waiting until morning would be too late. I turned to leave and Phyllis grabbed my arm. "Can you ride?"

"A horse?"

"No, a bicycle—yes, you idiot, a horse."

I'd been called an idiot before, though never with such affection and beguiling enunciation. It was like being called a peasant by a no-nonsense and kindhearted princess. This princess was in white tube socks, blue jeans, and a snug black ranch blouse embroidered with red roses. In that moment, I confess, I smiled and was slightly ashamed, as I thought of Phyllis in a new and altogether inappropriate way, especially given the circumstances. Perhaps, for men, there is no time such thoughts cannot occur.

Her suggestion caught me off guard. Most of my life had been spent wrangling horsepower and not horses, though as a teenager I'd worked as a ranch hand one summer and even tried rodeo—once: a Brahma bull—on a dare. That had been going on twenty-plus years ago, and my millisecond ride on the bull put my gonads in places they were never meant to be. My eight seconds were reduced to less time than it takes for a fastball to cross home plate.

"I have," I ventured, then added, "Hell, it's better than nothing, but it's been a long time, Phyllis. I'll need something to transport the girl if I'm lucky enough to find her."

She sat down on the sofa and pulled on her boots. "You'll need some supplies too. I've got just the horse for you—short and surefooted."

Phyllis left immediately for the barn to saddle the horse while I went to my truck and began dressing in every bit of cold-weather gear I owned. Within fifteen minutes she had the saddlebags filled with food and water and other miscellaneous necessities and was handing me the braided leather reins. I extended the ramp tucked beneath the lift gate and together we walked the horse into my trailer and tethered him two ways. He turned his head and gave us an unhappy, brown-eyed snort, raised his tail, and unloaded a pile of steaming shit at our feet.

Phyllis laughed and I said, "I think the horse speaks for all concerned."

"His name is Riley," Phyllis said. "Got him as a rescue a few years ago and we've had several rides. He's a desert horse and knows his way and doesn't spook easily."

After I closed up the trailer, I said, "I would have made a lousy father."

Phyllis kissed my cheek and seeing my now swollen and split lip, lightly touched it. I winced. "That looks sore—and fresh."

I told her both were accurate. "Sometimes my face gets mistaken for a suggestion box."

"You might have made a good father, Ben. It takes practice. And you wouldn't be the first to misplace his child. Now, go!"

My return to 117 was a bit slower to allow for the horse tied up in my trailer. One quick turn could result in a broken leg. While Phyllis was saddling and packing the horse I had taken a few minutes to draw a rough map of the area where the girl had gone. Search and Rescue needed a place to start, and that wouldn't be until daylight and, depending on weather, maybe not even then. There was no sense gambling more life in a search. Given the terrain and the time of year, a search would be dangerous from the air or on the ground. If the odds were that the object of the search was already or might well be dead, body recovery didn't warrant high priority. If I didn't make it back or contact her by morning, Phyllis would make the call. I was responsible for what happened to the girl, and I didn't want to be responsible for anyone else's misery or death but my own.

As I drove I thought about the map I had drawn for Phyllis, the spot on 117 where the accident occurred, and the direction the girl was heading—northeast. My plan had been to go where she'd last been seen and follow her in more or less a guess that she'd keep going in the same direction. Though it made no sense, she seemed to have an idea where she wanted to go.

That afternoon, in the pasture, she had been staring northeast, as if sighting in her destination. There was not a damn thing in that direction but hundreds of square miles of shallow canyons, dry washes, and flat, rough ground of mostly rock and sand—and eventually, Wyoming, which was more of the same. Long before that, traveling in a diagonal path, she would run up against the northern edge of the vertical mesa cliffs—and long before that, Manita would be dead. I had some life-and-death decisions to make, mine as well as hers, and no matter what, they were going to be based on guess and hunch. I figured I had eight to ten hours to have a decent chance of finding her alive, and by the time I got under way, it would be a couple hours less than that.

I decided to place my biggest bet on the girl, which was also my biggest hunch: She knew where she was going, or thought she did, and that meant she'd stick to a northeasterly course. My intuition told me she was determined and fearless, and motivated—though by what exactly was unknown. In a way, I was placing my faith in her. Instead of returning to the scene of the accident, I stopped a few miles east, before the turnoff to the Lacey place, where I'd taken Hector. If I took a northwest heading, I would pass north and a few miles behind the Lacey place; our paths might intersect somewhere in the dark desert night, maybe close enough to find each other. Close? I would still be searching for a needle in what I optimistically estimated was fifty square miles of darkness and freezing wind—and probably snow and God knows what else.

I parked the truck well off the shoulder of 117 and unloaded the horse and tied him to the bumper while I buttoned up the cab. Riley seemed eager to get the hell out of the empty trailer, and I didn't blame him. I'd started to untether the horse when I did a quick review of what I had and might need. There would be no chance to return in the event I'd forgotten something important.

I returned to the cab and got the revolver from beneath the driver's seat, a Smith & Wesson 586 with a six-inch barrel, and spun the cylinder. Six chambered rounds. For the first time I was grateful for the idiot who had tried to rob me with it. It was reliable but heavy as hell. Animals—coyotes, maybe cougars and wolves— even in the dark and cold, would stalk her if they picked up her scent, and this time of year they were hungry and opportunistic and just as motivated as she seemed to be. The dog had saved her from the cold once, and he might be able to keep her warm and the predators at bay for a while, but sooner or later, they would win. The only question was whether or not their meal would be warm or cold.

I turned on the Coleman hurricane lantern and glanced at the flush-mounted compass in the saddle horn. A compass was often unreliable in this part of the desert due to the iron deposits and weird magnetic fluctuations. The wind stirring up the sands might increase the inaccuracy. In a mile or so I'd have only my gut and the direction of the wind to tell me north from south. For the moment, I knew where I was on 117, the mesa to my right and nowhere everywhere else.

I patted Riley on his nose and asked him if he was ready. His answer was unbecoming a horse but honest enough. I wrapped a scarf around my neck and face and pulled up the hood on my cold-weather overalls. We took off into a razor north wind speckled with icy snow, walking to save the horse and, truth be told, my tender ass, which hadn't been in a saddle for a very long time.

44

My estimate was thirty minutes equaled one mile and I could have been off by 50 percent as I trudged into an unforgiving wind. Just to tease me, the clouds would part every once in a while and provide a momentary sliver of starlight and present me with a short peek ahead into silhouettes of rock and scrub vegetation.

If not for the wind and the horse's occasional snorting, silence was the rule, and in the rare seconds when the wind died, the quiet made my heart race with desperation. I had no name to shout except the one I had given her and that alone intensified the silence until I realized it didn't matter. Wailing my own name or Riley's, or Ginny's, or even Claire's, had an equal chance of finding the ears of the girl, and that was assuming she wanted anyone to find her.

How fast was she moving? If she started out running, she might cover two or three miles in a couple hours, though she'd have to slow down eventually. The map in my head kept a steady chart of what I hoped was our mutual progress toward each other. There was no use in second-guessing my route or hers, no *What if she stopped?*, or *What if I was slower and she was faster?* All of it was luck, either good or bad, and as the wind roared in stronger and colder gusts, I knew we could pass each other without ever knowing we were perhaps only a few feet apart. What lay behind and what lay ahead fused into another step and another shout, a waving of the lantern and an increasing fatigue that forced me to mount up to keep going.

The night went by one step at a time, mine or the horse's, until my throat was raw and the condensation had frozen and the scarf was a piece of slick rock. I walked, I rode, and Riley remained surefooted, his own steaming breath becoming labored. My face and hands and feet were numb. After several hours I stopped to rest us both and take on food and water and admitted to myself my gamble had failed and the girl and I were equally lost but unequally stumbling toward death: she was wearing only what she had on the morning I found her at the truck stop, the blinking tennis shoes, white shirt, and jeans.

It was time to admit she could be dying, huddled with the dog beside a rock or in an arroyo. Or dead. What I did or didn't do was not going to matter one way or another, except to me—and that made a difference—to me. My legs were so stiff from walking and cold, it took several attempts to get my foot in the stirrups. I began to laugh and made a kind of peace with freezing, an easy death as deaths go, and an end somewhere in a desert that was as close to home as I had ever known. I was feeling content that my life had come to this, which was a sure sign I was reaching the limit of my physical and mental endurance. The lantern flickered and went out. I dropped it on the ground, tired of its weight, and continued, comforted by the simple sound of our steps.

In the hour before dawn, when the sun was a distant promise and the temperature was at its lowest, we entered a glowing fog, apart from the darkness, stretching in incandescent layers, drifting and settling with thin bands of pure night sandwiched between the odd strata of weightless light. Inside the vaporous glow the wind ceased and the air began to warm slightly and I did not question the luminous fog that seemed to rise from the ground like a smoldering grass fire. There was a place like this that I'd heard of once but never seen, and I tried to concentrate on that memory as the white fog turned to a milky pink.

A small rush passed by overhead. A flash of red bobbed and floated out of sight—then another, and another—blinking, rising, and falling in the stillness. I unwrapped the scarf and lowered my hood and stopped, watched, and listened. The horse saw them too, and raised his long nose and tracked the lights with circular motions of his head as if trying to follow the erratic path of silent bees.

I fought the overwhelming desire to sit, or fall, down, and I didn't much care which it was. If this were the beginning of death, I was resolved it would find me standing—and moving. I forced myself to continue and let the reins slip from my hands and thought of Claire and making love in the desert sunrise on the porch of the isolated house and the long, sweet notes of the cello I'd never heard her play except in dreams. It all returned to me then, that small life and hope, and she returned to me, and the ache of her death fell away. The long night had come to this and I was grateful.

The swooping light show ceased and the silence was replaced with the sound of fast running water, or a coarse broom over stone. I glanced down at my feet, though they were obscured by the fog. I had the sense of a gentle slogging, as if through sand or ash. The horse whinnied behind me. I took another step and the ground beneath me gave way. I tumbled downward, rolling to a stop. I just lay on the hard sand for a few moments, uninjured and glad for the unexpected rest, and listened to the horse breathing somewhere above me. I knew I'd fallen off the bank of a shallow arroyo. Smart horse. I should have listened to him. The scraping sound was louder. It engulfed me and swirled around me as if I were a rock in a current, and I closed my eyes and was happy to be a rock, for just a little while, or so I told myself.

The horse had found his way to me and nudged me awake with his cool nose. The strands of pink light were fading as the first glimmers of dawn infused them with needles of yellow penetrating the ground fog above me. The sunlight was straight ahead of me and the meaning of it struck me like a slap: During the night I had wandered way off my northeastern course and had turned west, as impossibly far from the search area as I could have gone. I didn't need to see it to know that the red mesa was hovering on the eastern horizon, maybe only a few miles away, a beacon of my ineptitude, and failure to find the girl.

I reached into the sound, pouring, scraping around me and produced a handful of round, paperlike discs dotted with black beads. I recognized the fruit of the noxious Siberian elm and knew there must be trees and some form of water nearby. These invasive elms were the by-product of the early settlers in the Southwest and forced out nearly everything once they gained a foothold. They were almost impossible to kill. The amount of seeds they produced was staggering and I'd seen them blow and drift like lakes of snow. The black beads glistened as I held them out into the weak light and I knew what they were; dead flies. I was sitting in an ocean of Siberian elm seeds and large, dead flies, perhaps hundreds of thousands. The realization spurred me into pulling myself up by the reins. I tried to mount the horse and discovered my legs were as flexible as tree stumps. I gave up and began walking as the slanted sunlight filtered through the fog.

Dawn has probably saved as many lives in the desert as water. Sunrise is a luminous source of strength and renewed hope, and I felt its effects as I moved forward down what I knew now was a dry riverbed, shuffling through the elm seeds and dead flies blowing over the hard, sandy surface beneath my boots. With every step the diffuse light increased and radiated around me without ever actually allowing me to see anything except the light itself. I was wading in light.

A little way ahead I saw what appeared to be the fractured lines of some kind of structure. As I neared it loomed up out of the milky light—a small travel trailer, the kind used for temporary offices on a construction site—floating in the fog. It was a gift, and a sign, probably dumped and long abandoned in the desert by people long dead whose names will never be remembered. I moved toward it as quickly as I could, grateful to find anything, any remnant of human presence. In less than a minute that changed.

Winds had rolled the trailer end over end down the riverbed like aluminum tumbleweed, contorting its frame, rounding its corners and smashing dents into its soft skin. The side with the door was facedown, pressed into the sand. I pulled myself up on top where there was a window. In the soft light I could see the smear of small bloody handprints around the broken window. I kicked at the battered frame with my bootheel until it gave way and fell inside. It was a tight squeeze but I managed to lower myself into the dark interior of the trailer.

45

It was a short drop into a stinking pit. I called out for Manita not expecting to get a reply—and, thankfully, I didn't. Some small animals skittered at the rear and then nothing. The smell of feces and urine was overwhelming. This was not a travel trailer; it was a mobile construction site office, or had been. I kicked out a couple more windows to allow in some more light. I wished I hadn't.

Piles of dirty bedding and clothes lay strewn on the floor, along with food wrappers. This might have been a trailer once; it was a coffin now, though the dead had escaped to die elsewhere—perhaps nearby. I used the toe of my boot to push over a mound of rags and two fixed red eyes of an animal stared back at me and then blinked. I knelt and stared back, not into eyes, but into the heels of white athletic shoes, small shoes, children's shoes, covered in dead flies with a tiny gold crucifix on a chain stuck to a matted sock. Too late, I reached for the empty window above me and doubled over and heaved upon the clothes—the tiny shoes, and the cross.

I threw myself at one of the low windows I'd kicked out and rammed it several times with my shoulder before realizing it was too small to allow me to fit through. My head was spinning as I jumped and slapped at the opening above me, struggling to grasp its edges and pull myself out. For a moment I felt trapped, the space too small for me to bend my arms to lift myself out the way I had entered. Everywhere I looked—the floor and walls, shattered cupboards—I was besieged by the red eyes of little shoes. A built-in table had torn loose from the wall and I used it as a ramp to boost me the extra foot to the overhead window and squeezed through and out into the clean morning air.

I half rolled, half fell off the top of the trailer and landed on the fog-shrouded ground and rested my back and head against the exterior aluminum. For a few minutes I sucked fresh air in and out of my lungs and tried to spit out the bitter vomit still left in my mouth. My breathing returned to normal and I turned to gaze upward through the clouds toward the hidden mesa. A dark head bounced just above the ground fog in my direction, skimming and sinking and bobbing below the pale surface.

Seconds passed as I watched the raven's silent approach, its huge black-feathered body gradually emerging until it stopped just a few feet away. I didn't have to guess, I knew. There, before me, as a dark gift, a marker, a desert buoy to tag this terrible and desecrated place, the raven dropped the empty white shoe, its red-lighted heel beating like a small heart. The raven's wings opened and the bird held itself motionless for a moment before pounding the air into flight.

I am not a crying man and the tears I wanted, the tears this piece of children's hell deserved, refused to flow, not because I would not allow them, but because I was beyond them, exhausted and driven inside myself where horror and grief settled into muscle and bone. This was where Manita was headed, filled with the dead-reckoning knowledge of what was here, or perhaps with the hope her friends, maybe her brothers or sisters, had already escaped as, somehow, she had. I understood, and even in the darkness and fog, if necessary, I knew I could lead the authorities here. She had accomplished this. People would know what happened here and maybe, in time, who was responsible. It was unimaginable, and I hated myself for being capable of the very tip of imagining their captivity and slow deaths over what must have been days, maybe a week or more.

The sky was clearing. The sun rose and its warmth against the cool sand vaporized the moisture into writhing fingers of rising fog that reached upward around me. The mesa would appear soon and I would walk out of the desert and eventually find my way to 117 and Rockmuse. The horse, sensing I was ready to begin again, waded through the fog toward me. I picked up the blinking shoe and put it in my pocket and took the reins. We began to walk down the white-veiled riverbed in the direction of the mesa.

I wasn't hungry; I was thirsty. The riverbed wound in lazy turns gradually westward and I just wanted to walk, skirting the wall of the southern bank that rose in shadows ten to fifteen feet above us. We'd gone perhaps a half mile and my pace had slowed to the point that Riley was nudging me forward and my right leg became entangled in some deadwood or brush beneath the ground fog. Whatever it was dragged me to a stop while I tried to shake it loose. It seemed to tug at my pant leg.

Bending over to free myself, I looked into Manita's black eyes. She was covered in a man's coat and nestled with her back against the sandy embankment, her fingers still grasping my pant leg. I fell to my knees and reached out for her. She leaned into my chest and wrapped her arms around my neck—without a cry or a whimper, or any sound at all, from either of us. I'd given up hope of finding her, alive or dead, and her small, frail body felt like no more than a shadow of rain. There was movement next to her, which I assumed was the dog.

As my eyes adjusted, I saw a man next to her, the familiar outline of Stetson and the faint, acrid odor of burning rubber. Roy. He was snoring softly, his head tilted, chin on his left shoulder. I shook Roy's shoulder and he started, then winced as his eyes opened and focused on my face.

"Hello, Ben," he said, with no more surprise than if he'd bumped into me on the street in Rockmuse.

"Hello, Roy," I said. "I see you're taking good care of our girl here."

"No. It's more like she's been looking out after me." It pained him to do it, but he reached out and stroked the dark hair on the back of Manita's head. "I'm messed up, Ben. Bad, I think—snake bit and shot—in that order."

I was just then reminded of the FedEx and UPS drivers who jumped-started my little trucking business when they managed to find each other during a whiteout in a couple hundred square miles of desert, and all the accidents between the only two vehicles within miles of each other. If there were only two people left on Earth I was convinced that sooner or later their paths would cross in the middle of nowhere, as if humanity came equipped with homing beacons and home was always another human being. If Roy lived, there would be time to hear how he and the girl stumbled across each other and how he came to get himself shot. My guess was we were somewhere in the vicinity of Roy's stash of used tires. Roy's transportation was a bicycle, and I doubted he could roam too far off his range. For Roy's part, he didn't seem interested in talk either. For now, I needed to get them both to safety.

I carried Manita to the horse and wrapped her in a blanket and then I went back for Roy and asked him where the gunshot wound was. He angled his chin toward his left shoulder. "Right here," he said. I pulled back the lapel of his leather vest and could see the dark blood oozing through his shirt.

Bending him forward I checked his back for an exit wound and found one hell of a hole. There was nothing I could do for him where we were.

"Who did this to you, Roy?"

"Never saw him," he said. "But I think the girl knew him. She came out of nowhere, Ben. If not for her—"

"I think the bullet went through," I said, then asked him where the snake struck him and how many times. Roy pointed to his left leg. He had removed the boot.

The same snake could strike one person multiple times with each strike carrying a lethal load of venom. I was relieved to hear Roy answer just the once. He added, "Thanks to the girl—" I didn't know what he meant by that and didn't ask.

There was already swelling and discoloration in his calf. "Can you stand?"

It took a lot of grunts and moans as I got him up. With his good arm draped around my neck, I led him to the horse, whose presence seemed to amuse him. "You have a horse?"

"Yeah," I said, "love 'em." The mention of the horse made me think of the dog, who was nowhere in sight. "She had a dog," I said.

Roy glanced up at the girl and shook his head. "Not anymore," he whispered. "But it saved us both first."

I didn't doubt that for a moment, though I couldn't quite imagine that brute dead.

It immediately became clear there was no way Roy could mount the horse from the ground. He suggested we try it with him a few steps up on the sloping sand along the riverbank. That worked. I gave each of them a little water, some to the horse, and some to myself. The two of them huddled together under the blanket, slumped forward over Riley's mane, and we began our journey with me leading the horse, plodding forward as the fog slowly dispersed and a hard yellow sun burned its way across the upper lip of the mesa cliffs.

Roy was right; he was in bad shape. Either wound could kill him. It seemed to me that his biggest problem was blood loss from the gunshot, though that might actually be an advantage to surviving the rattlesnake bite. What did I know? I wasn't a doctor, just a truck driver, and all I knew was to keep him calm and the bite below his heart and get him medical assistance as soon as possible.

We hadn't gone far when the winding ridges of tire mountains appeared ahead. I knew exactly where we were and how to get to town more quickly. We cut through the towering rubber canyons and turned south on a heading that would intersect 117 a mile or two from the city limits.

The horse needed to rest. After a long, cold night and now burdened with the weight of two riders, my fear was the poor animal would go down and strand us with no way to get into town—terrible for the horse and worse for Roy. If it came to that, I knew I would leave Roy and continue on foot carrying Manita, who I was certain was too weak and exhausted to move under her own power, and if she could, not for very far. How she'd gotten as far as she had—what?—thirty miles?—more?—would always be a mystery to me—more than a mystery, a miracle of sorts. If Roy died, I would be sorry. Under no circumstances was I leaving Manita, a decision I believed in my heart would meet with Roy's blessing.

It was still morning when we crossed 117. I did what Ginger had done, traversed the desert in a shortcut to town, both the horse and me weaving and stumbling the last several hundred yards between buildings to the junction of Main Street and 117.

I took Manita in my arms and led the horse with Roy's unconscious body slumped dangerously to one side. I kicked at the door of the Mercantile. Whoever opened it yelled or screamed, my name maybe, and that was the last thing I knew for sure. I dropped to my knees fighting to keep Manita from hitting the floor as I fell forward.

46

I awoke with sunlight in my eyes and a terrible weight on my chest, which turned out to be blankets. The light was broken in odd shapes as it streamed in through lace curtains. I lay quietly on a sofa as the room became familiar—a chair, a table, the high ceiling and the staircase leading to the second floor. A grandfather clock in a corner ticked and tocked rhythmically through the silent room. Phyllis was sitting in a plush blue wing chair, wearing her robe and reading a book, her bare feet resting on a matching hassock.

The girl. I started, fully awake, swinging my legs to the floor and tossing the blankets aside, and attempted to stand. The blood in my head throbbed behind my eyes and I collapsed backward onto the sofa.

Phyllis put down her book. She guessed at what had suddenly driven me up and calmly answered my unasked question. "She's upstairs sleeping, Ben. She's safe now."

Phyllis excused herself. The sound of the clock began to pound its way inside my head. She returned a moment later with a full glass of what looked like cloudy water and sat down next to me on the sofa. I suddenly became aware that I was dressed only in underwear. My head hurt too badly to care. She handed me three capsules. "Drink this," she said. "Doctor's orders."

I held the glass up to the light. "It's not Long Island tea, is it?"

She parted a small, thin smile that held no humor. "No." The water was warm and slightly salty. "Among other things, you're suffering from mild hypothermia and a few spots of frostbite on your nose and ears. I wish I could tell you to go back to sleep, but I can't."

There was something on her mind and I studied her eyes and waited. She started to speak and then left the room. When she returned she was carrying a plastic sandwich bag and placed it on the coffee table in front of us. Phyllis sat down beside me again. Inside was a child's shoe, a red light blinking in its heel, dulled into pink as it passed through the plastic.

Her eyes closed and she took a breath. When she opened them they had filled with tears. "I found that in your pocket."

The long night and the trailer in the desert returned to me then. I stared at the shoe as the red light seemed to beat in time with the ticking of the clock. Long minutes went by as I tried again and again to speak, each time choking back a word, until I gave up and managed to break my eyes away from the plastic bag. The shoe still held the bloody remnant of an anklebone, matted with tissue and dried blood. Phyllis laid her head against my shoulder and I put my arm around her while she cried and the sunlight shadows inched their way across the room.

It was Peggy who had opened the front door of the Mercantile and Peggy who screamed as her husband and Lenny and a few morning customers rushed in behind her. Search and Rescue was already on its way. It was a scene I could only vaguely remember, flashes of faces, voices, as people tried in vain to pry the girl out of my arms while she kicked and tore at them with her teeth like an animal. Eventually they gave up and left us on the floor until the rescue copter landed in the vacant lot behind the Mercantile. The horse died as the response team approached. It had probably given the last of its courageous heart, fetlocks buckling a moment before it staggered and dropped on the sidewalk in front of the store, pinning Roy's unconscious body beneath it.

Roy was dying and they had only minutes, if that, to get him to the hospital in Price. There was no time to wrestle with the girl and me. We didn't seem critically injured, so they left without us. Lenny and Phyllis, along with the help of others, carried us, still clinging to each other, to the bed of the pickup. I remembered carrying the girl inside the house and falling on the sofa. Only then, after I had passed out, inside the safety of the house and with the woman she knew, did Manita allow Phyllis to separate us.

Phyllis could not bring herself to touch the plastic bag again. Neither could I. Its presence in the room drew our eyes and every breath toward it. She retrieved the book from the end table, opened it, and placed the pages gently over the shoe. It was out of sight though it might never be out of mind.

"I phoned the Highway Patrol and told them what I'd found. I wrote the officer's name and number down. It's in the kitchen." She glanced down at the book and what was beneath it somehow became more terrible as the pulsing pink light reflected off the glass tabletop. "He told me to use the baggie. Said it was probably animals."

I agreed and kept what I was thinking to myself. "Roy was shot by someone," I said. "I don't know who or why." I asked for my clothes. "I found Roy and the girl and the"—the book wasn't helping much—"in the same place."

"I promised I'd have you call as soon as you woke up. They want you at Highway Patrol headquarters as soon as possible."

"You'd think they could wait till tomorrow," I said.

"Ben," she said, "it is tomorrow. The county sheriff and Highway Patrol were here yesterday afternoon. All those men stood right here in this room and stared at you and the girl."

"The girl?"

"She was sleeping on your chest for a long time. Wouldn't move. Trooper Smith convinced them to let you and the girl be. It was kind of sweet, really. But time's up, Ben. I promised you'd be there by tonight."

The clock chimed four o'clock as she handed me my clothes, freshly washed and folded. "Late yesterday, after they left I finally managed to get you out of your clothes. That's when I found—it." She apologized. "The cold-weather overalls are double-sacked in a garbage bag behind the barn—along with hers. I had to, Ben. The—"

"Smell?"

She nodded and fought to keep the tears back.

My whole body ached for what she knew, for what I knew—and for what I didn't and couldn't stand to know. I only pulled on my jeans and went in the kitchen to phone the Highway Patrol station in Price. Phyllis wisely chose to stay in the other room during the brief conversation. There were no words to describe what I'd seen, and I couldn't begin to conceive of what Manita had experienced, during the night or the previous week—or perhaps her entire life. Whatever there was to say, I only wanted to say once. I explained my thoughts on the matter to the trooper using exactly those words. When he started to ask another question I told him to have Trooper Smith call me and hung up.

A few minutes later Andy called, patched through from his radio. He was over a hundred miles away from the junction with US 191 in Moab, wrapping up an accident. The connection was filled with static and a frustrating echo. I'd never really asked Andy for a favor before. I just wanted to have a few minutes with him before Manita and I showed up for questioning.

"No hat, Andy."

"No promises, Ben."

Andy suggested we meet at Walt's diner. It would take him at least two hours to get there from Moab, and about that long for the girl and me to get there if we left immediately. With luck we might meet up on the gravel lot before dark and have a bit of time alone.

I was bone weary and then some, the kind that seeps into every nerve and muscle, like a dark water coming from a deep well. My head felt better and I asked to take a quick shower and hoped it would chase away some of the ache, though I suspected the real ache could not be washed away by hot water and soap. I was right. In some ways I felt worse, as if the cleansing left behind a residue of the sorrowful night, of the week, that only settled deeper into raw crevices.

As the water ran over me I kept repeating "But not like this" to myself. I'd been living in and driving the desert for twenty years and thought I'd seen it all—but not like this—and I wondered why I could detach, step back, and go on after the grisly accidents, the lunatic stupidity and craziness that ended in suffering and death, as it always did, not just in the desert, but everywhere. This was different. George's words came back to me, about bringing your own trouble out here. Most people brought their own trouble—the idiot circus train master, Ginger, even Claire and, if I was honest, even me.

The difference was these were children, however many of them there were, and they had been brought out here by someone for some reason I would probably never know. They paid the full price, probably alone, except for one another. Knowledge of this was the real smell and weariness, and the realization that if not for the old couple that had adopted me, I could have been one of those children. Manita survived as I survived and the beautiful truth was that survival wasn't an accident. We didn't do it alone.

What did I really want to tell Andy? And if I knew, could I find the words? I was no cop, and no one wanted to hear what I thought, except maybe Trooper Smith, the lowest man in the law enforcement food chain. I'd always believed in the randomness of things— the "shit happens" school of philosophy. "But not like this." Cecil was dead. Pedro was dead.

The girl was connected to them, just as the light reflects off the mica-flaked mesa, and onto the trailer in the desert and the white shoes with the blinking red lights in the heels. All the children had been dressed the same, or at least had the same shoes, uniforms, like a collection of interchangeable dolls, their uniqueness, maybe even their names, and their humanity, erased on purpose.

Phyllis took us in her Rolls-Royce pickup out to where I'd left my rig on 117. Manita rode in my arms, mute as always, watching the desert roll by our window. Phyllis had clothed her in leftovers from her grandchildren, a red gingham dress and jean jacket with cowboy boots. Her grip on me tightened as Phyllis pulled in behind my truck and trailer, covered in dried dirt and crusted with sand. The blue horizon of late afternoon reached in every direction and wary stars had already begun to sneak in to harvest the dark sky beyond. There was no joy or relief in my return. It seemed like a hundred years since I'd left my rig two nights earlier, which made perfect sense, since I felt a hundred years older.

My thought was to leave Manita with Phyllis for a few minutes while I warmed up the truck and cleaned the windshield. A crowbar and dynamite were not going to separate her arms from my neck. Once I got out of the pickup she even managed to wrap her small legs around my waist in a scissor grip that would have made a WWE wrestler pound the mat. And I was more than fine with her decision.

When we were ready to get on the road, Phyllis hopped up on my running board and handed me a small brown paper bag through my window, delicately pinching its top between her thumb and index finger—a sack lunch of nightmares. I didn't want it. I didn't want Phyllis to have it either. I placed it behind my seat and waved farewell. To my surprise, Manita waved too.

Within a couple hours we would be at Walt's diner to meet Andy. I felt as I did the first time, in no hurry, oddly content to have the silent girl in the seat next to me as we aimed ourselves west into the sun. The fanned warmth of the heater and steady hum of the tires became her usual lullaby and, rocked by the gusting winds of early evening against the cab, she drifted into sleep and what I hoped were dreams filled with nothing more than ice cream and starlight.

47

We crested the hill that led to The Well-Known Desert Diner just as the sky entered the precious golden moments between sunset and twilight, when the light was losing its battle against the shadows. Dawn and dusk were usually the times I stopped at the diner, and it was in those gentle, turning seconds the diner was transformed into a rare, timeless dinosaur that was both vanishing and appearing in the distance like the ghost it was. I wanted her to see it as I saw it, in that insubstantial phase.

All that was missing was a full moon. Manita was sleeping so soundly.

What I thought were the last slanted stabs of sunlight did not diminish as we approached the diner. The habit of seeing what I always saw delayed the truth of what lay before us: the interior lights of the perpetually closed diner were on and cut across the antique bubble gas pumps and pale gravel parking lot. The old neon sign that sat on top of the roof suddenly flashed its purple and pink news—COOL DRINKS! GOOD EATS!—which was a first. In twenty years I'd never seen that sign lit up. No one had, probably since the '80s or earlier.

My shock was so complete my foot slipped from the accelerator and the truck came to a rolling stop on the highway a handful of yards before the gravel apron of the parking lot. I dropped into neutral to keep the engine from stalling and just idled there in the middle of the road.

Walt was crazy, but his craziness was consistent and oddly predictable, if that's possible. As far as I knew, I was his only regular contact with the outside world. Lately, even that small interaction had been missing. He had been acting strangely, though that word took in a lot of territory when it came to Walt, except for this, which was far beyond his established limits of strange and crazy. It was like coming upon an empty carnival ride at the edge of the world, a beacon for respite in a darkening wasteland—and it was anything but welcoming.

I put the truck into gear and lurched and crept onto the gravel apron as if stalking a well-lighted desert apparition. The dull crunch of rocks beneath my tires came through my partially open window as we drove toward the diner. I stopped with the nose of my rig facing the pumps in front of the diner and set the brake. The headlights traversed the light escaping from the windows. No one was visible inside. I got out and stood on the running board, watching, listening, and hearing the faint melody of some old record playing on the vintage Wurlitzer jukebox.

I glanced at Manita. She was still asleep.

On Monday morning, when I'd last seen Walt, he was lying on his single bed with the revolver by his side. I'd wondered then if he'd been toying with the idea of suicide and dismissed it just as quickly. As I took in the diner, all its lights ablaze and the jukebox playing, maybe I shouldn't have. Maybe this was exactly as Walt would have wanted it, the diner alive again for a while as he put the gun to his head. I walked to the door and peered through. Everything, the stools, salt and pepper shakers, spit-polished linoleum floors, even the ticket from the last paying customer hanging in the stainless-steel pass-through, was perfect, untouched, preserved as they always had been.

The song ended and the machine clicked and then came the sound of static and the needle settling on vinyl. A new song began, a song I recognized—"Blue Moon." It was playing the night I showed up at the diner and found Claire and Walt dancing. To my left, hugging the corner of the diner, sat the phone booth. The heavy black receiver was missing. The Closed sign on the door and been turned over. It now read Open. I tried the door. It was locked.

I stepped several paces back and stood just outside the light and listened to the soft music and the crackling of the neon lights on the roof. I was stalling and I knew it. Walt was in there, somewhere. I could almost feel his presence. I walked to the east side of the diner, steeling myself for what I would find in the bedroom off the kitchen or in the Quonset workshop.

The flashing neon light of the sign fell across some long, rough gouges in the dirt and I knelt to run my fingers along them. A heavy vehicle of some kind with deep treads had recently driven over the moist ground. There was another set of tracks inside those, a smaller vehicle, a pickup or car. The one time I had parked on the side of the diner Walt and I had almost come to blows. He was particular in the upkeep of his frozen world.

I followed the tracks past the flagstone patio between the diner and the Quonset and continued all the way to the back. Snugged up against the rear wall of the Quonset was a semi-tractor, a cab-over, painted a dark blue. The passenger-side mirror had recently been replaced, and I ran my hand over the puckered metal of the door skin where the mounts had been jerked clean. The paint was fresh and hastily done. From the running board I reached across the windshield to the fiberglass visor. The sharp edges of the words that had been removed allowed me to trace them out in a braille of sorts—not "Red Hell." The two words were "Red Heaven."

I knew of Red Heaven. It had been the original name of the town of Rockmuse, though that site was several miles away from where the town was now. I'd never been there—until that long night searching for the girl.

I was so intent on the truck I almost missed the other vehicle parked nearby in the darkness: It was a Utah Highway Patrol pickup, the hood still warm and popping softly as it cooled from the drive in from Moab. Andy was nowhere in sight. None of this was Walt's doing, and my guess was that he and Andy were already dead. If I didn't get the hell out of there, the girl and I would be joining them.

At the corner of the Quonset a friendly male voice said, "Welcome to the party, Mr. Jones."

I glimpsed a tire iron as it swung out of the shadows and caught me just above the waist. The impact folded me like a cheap deck chair and I fell forward, my face in the sandy dirt, gasping for breath, and feeling the all-too-familiar sharp pain of broken ribs. I heard the iron spin through the air and land in the brush. He checked me for weapons and shoved a gun barrel into my mouth and knocked a tooth out in the process. The pain was so intense I almost passed out.

The jovial host whispered, "You're the last guest, but that's okay. You're the most important. You can stand up now. Slowly."

I couldn't stand. He decided kicking me a few times would help motivate me. Having to hold the gun so close to my face hindered the force of his kicks until he gave up and simply raised the barrel against the roof of my mouth and used his free hand to lift me by my belt. He had all the strength he needed to do it. From there he walked me backward down the flagstone patio. My tongue fought to keep the gun barrel from going down my throat and choking me. When we reached the fuse box he pulled the main breaker, and the lights of the diner, including the sign, went out.

"Closing time," he said.

48

He walked me backward through the door of the Quonset. Inside, he gave me a quick knee in the groin and I fell. He jerked the barrel free. The only light was the bare bulb swinging over Walt's workbench. I scooted myself away from him and across the floor and leaned my back against a metal leg of the workbench. I spat a wad of blood onto the concrete floor.

"Where's the girl?"

I allowed my head to flop from side to side, trying to speak, drooling blood down my chin. It was an act, though not by much. Out of the corner of my eye I located Walt, bound head to toe in gray duct tape and tied with rope to one of his motorcycles. He'd been badly beaten and I wasn't sure if he was alive or dead. The blood on his face seemed to have dried. I spat another mouthful of blood on the floor, this one carrying pieces of my teeth, and managed a look up at my attacker.

He saw what I was doing and grabbed ahold of the cord and held the light to his face. "Is that better?" He turned the light on Walt. "Take a good, long look at my daddy over there." I took another, longer look at Walt and still couldn't tell if he was alive. "Tell me where the girl is or I'll make you look just like him, only worse." He whistled. "He was game, though. Quite a scrapper for his age."

I mumbled.

"Where's the girl?"

I stared up at him and saw the resemblance, the thin nose, white head of hair and muscular forearms, and put his age in his forties, all hard years judging from the scars on his face and a drooping left eyelid, the common nerve damage of professional and garden-variety brawlers alike.

"You're going to kill me."

"No," he said, "you're killing you." He was as quick as I'd ever seen. In one move he leaned down and rapped me on the side of the head with the gun. "One more time—where's the girl?" The blow wasn't meant to knock me unconscious. It was just enough to make me wish I was, and I was close.

"What's she to you?"

"She's my *mija*, asshole. My daughter. She made my whole operation work."

"I thought she was Pedro's daughter."

He rapped me alongside the head again. I figured I only had a few more words left in me before he either hit me too hard or decided I wasn't going to tell him where she was and just shot me, though after I was dead he was certain to find her anyway.

"Pedro is nothing to her, just a meddler like Cecil. If not for those two—" He spit on me and the saliva ran down my cheek. "*Putas!*" he said quietly. "Tires, children? What does it matter? I lost a whole crop because of them. There are more where they came from—but not her." This time I saw it coming and flinched in anticipation. He grinned, changed his grip, and hit me across the bridge of my nose. My eyes clouded and more blood ran into my mouth.

He was the better man, stronger, meaner, faster—and that was without the gun. I had one chance, and it was almost no chance at all. I would have to be something I'd never been before: smarter—and lucky. He could just shoot me and go outside and retrieve her himself. I was betting he wouldn't.

"She's in my cab. Asleep."

He squinted at me, slow to take the bait. "If that's true, it's too easy." He laughed. "Okay, Ben Jones. Why don't you go get my little girl. I'll wait here."

I pushed away from the leg and made as if I was going to stand and do what he suggested. "No!" Using his boot tip, he pushed me back. "Let's go to her together."

He let me get up and we walked out onto the dark patio. He paused and sniffed the air and pushed the muzzle of the gun against my head. "I grew up in this desert, you know. Smell that?" For a moment I sensed he was looking up at the faint stars. He inhaled and exhaled loudly. We began to move as he talked.

"Red Heaven. Left when I was a toddler. That old man in there, he bundled us up and sent us south. I didn't know he was my father until my mother died last summer. Told me on her deathbed. The whole time I was growing up in East L.A. she would cry when she spoke of leaving Red Heaven. I thought my father died in Vietnam. Too bad we can't hang out for a while and catch up on life."

We stood beside the cab's passenger door. "You open it," he said. "Easy. If she's not there I will kill you where you stand." I knew he would. In fact, I was planning on it, a couple seconds after I killed him.

He stepped back a few feet on the gravel in case I had a surprise for him. The girl was still sleeping and I moved aside so he could see her, still buckled in the seat. He ordered me to get her out, keeping the gun on me, as I knew he would. Up on the running board I leaned over the girl as if undoing her seat belt. Just over the console, beneath the seat, I felt for the Velcro'ed bag with my gun, slapping at the empty space. It wasn't there. I'd taken it with me into the desert and not replaced it. My chance, my one chance, had passed and in a minute, maybe two, he would kill me. It's tough to be smart without any practice.

My time was up. I knew because he told me so. I cradled the sleeping girl in my arms and backed out of the cab. Anything I attempted now might get her shot by accident. She put her arms around my neck and wiggled her nose into my shirt and I silently said goodbye to her, knowing what was to come next, just not exactly when. She would live a life of some kind, perhaps eventually a good one, though judging from the man who claimed to be her father, and what I understood about what he had her doing, that life might as well be no life at all. It was all I could do to keep my legs under me as I carried her toward the darkness at the rear of the Quonset.

He jabbed the barrel hard into my back. Manita began to awaken, yawning, shaking her head sleepily, and I pressed her warm body closer to mine. We walked past his truck and into the rolling desert, where we were surrounded by small hills dotted with rocks and scrawny, dwarfed trees, and hesitant tumbleweed rocking back and forth in the night breeze.

Manita stiffened in my arms. She was looking over my shoulder at the man following us. In all the time we had been together, in the truck, through the long, cold night, even when the folks at the Mercantile had tried to separate us, I had never heard a sound from her. In one second, all that silence, the holding back, the abiding muteness, exploded from her tiny body in a series of gulping, wild screams that shredded the cool air and echoed in every direction.

The man spoke softly to her, cajoled her in Spanish, and his efforts only caused her to scream more loudly and writhe in my arms and lock herself to me in a death grip. His words and his tone changed and he began to swear at her and shouted at me to put her down.

He rapped me on the back of the head again, hard, and I stumbled forward, doing my best to untangle the girl's arms from my neck. He hit me again and again while the girl cried and wailed, her hot tears flowing from her eyes and streaming into my collar and down my back. He hit me again, trying to drive me to the ground, and I refused to fall as the darkness and the shadows around us began to move and spin. He had only one choice left and we both knew it. I turned to face him. I'd be damned if I would make it easy.

The barrel of the gun rose and I stared straight into his eyes and began to back away. It had to be a perfect shot to miss the girl. We were only a few feet apart and I fought wildly to free myself from the girl one more time, twisting my shoulders and prying at her arms, doing everything to shake her loose and throw her to the ground if possible.

The shot came just as she raised herself higher on my chest and Manita's small body jerked. I felt the bullet enter us both. She went limp. I fell backward, her head slamming into mine, and the weight of her body came down on me, driving all the air from my lungs.

Her hair was matted into mine, intertwined by tears, and I supposed blood, and in that silence I heard him shout and two more gunshots. As I lost consciousness I heard running footsteps and the soft rustle of fabric and whispers and felt the desert wind tugging at the girl and the tugging turned to a gentle drawing away and in my last seconds I used what fading strength was left in me to try to hold on to her—*Manita, Manita*—until I had nothing left and she rose above me and my fingers loosened and my hands dropped into the sand. I struggled to open my eyes and thought I had and saw only shadows and dark stars gleaming inside passing clouds of white and gray silhouettes.

Minutes or maybe hours later a cloth lightly covered my face and the ground beneath me changed, becoming colder and harder and the weight on my chest returned and my eyes hurt from a light that passed back and forth above me. Someone was saying my name.

Andy was leaning on me, his right arm across my chest for balance. My eyes were slits and the light and Andy's misshapen head seemed as if I were seeing them through the slats of a red picket fence. "Ben," he said. The bare bulb of Walt's workshop light burned above us. "Ben!"

I knew I had been shot, though I didn't know exactly where and was beyond caring. Everything from my waist up pulsed and burned. The most intense pain came from my face and mouth. When I tried to speak all I could produce were gags and a mumble. Andy's eyes closed and he collapsed on top of me. I thought of her, Manita, and cradled the back of his head and caressed and held him until I passed out. That was how they found us.

DR. WANDA WAS holding my hand when I woke up in the hospital in Price. A Utah trooper was standing at the door behind her. I knew I was alive but I wanted to be dead, at least until I felt well enough to die.

"I've got good news and better news," she said.

Forming words was impossible, but I tried anyway.

She shook her head. "We got the bullet out. Your mouth is full of sutures and gauze. Bad concussion. No brain damage so far, except what you were born with." No smile, though I recognized some sad entertainment in her eyes. "The back of your head looks like a road atlas of Africa. That's the good news. The better news is"—she raised my wrist up a little higher so I could see it and I grimaced—"Look, Mom, no handcuffs!" The trooper coughed and she added, "Well, not yet anyway."

I closed my eyes and was in and out for three days, though I could speak with great effort, after a fashion, on the second day. The cops wasted no time in beginning their interrogations. I asked about the girl and was told, simply, there was no girl found at the scene. The authorities had received an anonymous tip about trouble at the diner. When they arrived there were only the three of us. Walt was still in a coma, and Andy had been Life Flighted to Salt Lake City, where he was in the ICU at University Hospital.

Each session continued until I lost consciousness or the doctor on duty called a stop to it. They got everything I could tell them the first time, which wasn't much, and it became less and less every time they arrived and began again. They weren't much interested in my dreams, though it was in those drugged and dull episodes that the events unfolded in layers, the real and the imagined equally true. I wasn't allowed visitors, though, according to Dr. Wanda, it wasn't that much of a problem. Lenny was the only visitor who was turned away. It was Lenny who came to take me home when they released me ten days later.

It was also Lenny who brought John home from the hospital. Later, I told Lenny I assumed the ride with John back to Rockmuse was better than the long night ride to Price in the back of my trailer. Lenny took a minute to answer, as if reliving both trips, then laughed. "About the same, Ben."

A few nights after I returned to my duplex, I lay in bed fighting my way through a fitful sleep and listening to the wind gust against the walls. Off and on the wind was interrupted by a baby's muffled cries. The cries mixed with the wind and the screams of Manita in my arms and I squeezed the pillow to my chest until my arms ached and I returned, as I had so many times, to that night in the desert behind The Well-Known Desert Diner. Early in the morning there were footsteps on the other side of the duplex and I knew Ginny and Annabelle had returned. The ordinary noise of life next door chased the nightmares away and I began to sleep soundly.

49

A pleasant autumn came to the high desert of Utah for a few days in late December. I sat in the cab of my truck on the eastbound shoulder, just outside of Rockmuse, a warm, northwestern breeze coming through my window. I stuck my head out like a dog on a car trip to the grocery store. They had to shave my head to clean and stitch all the wounds and the air felt good on the thick bristles of short hair. A cold, foil-wrapped burrito lay on the passenger seat next to me.

My jaw had been wired for weeks after I left the hospital, and then the dental work began, thousands of dollars in oral surgery, caps, and implants. I was glad to be alive and it seemed as though I'd be making payments for the privilege for a couple years or more. I picked up the burrito, planning to eat it while I waited. The afternoon sun was already reflecting off the red cliffs of the mesa and snow streaked the edges of the plateau, splintering the distant light.

Walt was in a rehab facility not far from downtown Price. The doctors had told me the week before that he remained unresponsive, even though his most serious injuries had healed. By that they meant he wasn't talking much, though he seemed to understand the questions of the police and doctors just fine. My weekly visits there were almost the same as my twenty years of visits to him at the diner. Unresponsive was pretty much how he had always been. The medical staff just didn't know it.

Walt was changed, thinner, gaunt-faced, his pale eyes always fixed on some private world as he sat in the wheelchair in the dining hall. We didn't speak of that night. The cops tried and got nothing but grunts, and it wasn't for some time that I remembered the man saying he was Walt's son. When I asked him about it, he was extremely unresponsive.

There were lots of things I remembered later, and the more I remembered, the more I questioned how accurate those memories were. Like so much of my life and the lives of people I knew, living and dead, I kept most of it to myself. None of it really mattered anyway.

The question of who ran John down remained a local mystery and curiosity eventually went the way of the wind. What happened at the diner and in the desert came and went so quickly in the news and disappeared as a topic of local conversation that, as usual with tragedy, only those with scars cared, and like Walt, we gradually became unresponsive, except perhaps in our dreams.

I saw the cross in my side mirror, bobbing toward me along the shoulder a hundred yards away. I got out of my truck. It seemed to me I had forgotten something and then I remembered the burrito. I wasn't ready to eat it, but I was far from ready to leave it behind.

John said he was just fine with leaving the cross on the side of 117. The unofficial Rockmuse City Council wanted it moved off the road, and it would be several months at least until John was strong enough on his new leg to even attempt to haul the cross into town. I'd offered to transport it in my trailer and he was adamant that the cross should never leave the ground. It had to be carried.

There was the implication that hell was a possibility if his wish was ignored, and, publicly at least, that suggestion brought some laughter, except from the few of us that knew a bit of hell firsthand. We could have lied to him—in fact, the consensus was to lie—but when it came right down to it, no one wanted to be a party to lying to a preacher, especially John. A relay of volunteers became the only solution, followed by a community potluck dinner at John's True Value First Church of the Desert Cross.

The squeak of the wheelbarrow axle signaled the impending arrival of the couple who had the leg of the relay ahead of me. I recognized them as the two who had come upon the accident and had gone up ahead and sent Andy.

The relay had begun at dawn and it hadn't taken long for folks to realize that hauling that cross was more strenuous and weighty labor than anyone anticipated. Roy solved the problem, as he solved all problems, by fashioning a yoke of sorts out of a used tire. With some foam rubber and an old quilt for padding, two people could harness up and carry the cross for the prescribed mile. To my knowledge no one had been able to carry the cross alone.

Roy had mended well and quickly. He never saw who shot him, or the dog. He did see the snake—after it had struck him, and would have struck again if the girl hadn't come out of nowhere and grabbed the snake and thrown it back into the mountain of tires. For a week or two after he returned to his garage, people from Rockmuse, including Phyllis, brought him food. He must have liked her food because little by little he began taking his meals at her place, where, as rumor has it, he now occasionally eats breakfast. The two of them shared an early leg of the relay.

The couple, perspiring heavily, huffed up to me and I put the burrito inside my shirt and hefted the cross on my shoulder. The makeshift yoke dangled behind me. I thought I was big enough and strong enough to carry the cross all by myself and declined offers of a partner. Less than a hundred yards later, when it was too late, I reassessed that glowing estimation of myself and increased my admiration of John—and Jesus, in that order.

The bullet the surgeon dug out of me had not penetrated very far, slowed considerably by first passing through the girl. It had lodged in the dense muscle of my neck, barely missing the carotid artery. If it had hit the artery, someone else would be carrying the cross in my place. The pressure of the cross brought back the pain, and as I walked I switched the weight back and forth between shoulders. It didn't help that much and my mile stretched out end-lessly ahead. I knew if I stopped to rest I might never get going again and I concentrated on putting one foot in front of the other, my eyes on my boots, and willing myself not to look too far down the road. My relief was to meet me at the Rockmuse City Limits sign.

Ginny and Annabelle were coming to the potluck, which sur-prised me. She would be late and moving fast, as usual. Two days went by after their return before she knocked on my door. I needed those two days. The distance from my bed to my front door seemed as far as the night's journey searching for Manita, and a lot less fun. I assumed my visitor was Ginny and made the effort. She just stood there for a moment looking at me, unable to disguise the shock. When she recovered she said, "I see you've started dating again."

Annabelle was napping and I invited her inside. She stood while I gently lowered myself into my tattered old recliner. I didn't ask her why she had returned. I could guess. Besides, talking was painful. I was just glad she and Annabelle were back. She volun-teered that it hadn't taken long for Rod to discover the truth about her mother, and the truth about Belle's real father.

"Rod even told me I could stay. He gave me the money to come back to Price. Said to say hello." She reached into her pocket and pulled out a $50 bill. "Rod told me to give you this to repair your screen door." I took the fifty.

"After Rod got a clue, it was all downhill in a hurry from there," Ginny said. "I said goodbye to her at the coffee shop at the Reno Greyhound bus station. She wasn't even listening. She was batting her eyes at some guy a few tables over. My guess is she got on some-thing after I left, and it wasn't a bus."

After a long pause, she concluded by telling me that Belle

missed me. I asked her if Belle was talking now. Ginny went to the door and wiggled her pierced eyebrow. "Better than you."

A few days after her visit, Ginny took me for a follow-up visit at the hospital. On the way back I asked if she'd stop by the Price cemetery. She stayed in the car with Annabelle while I did something I hadn't ever done: say "Thank you" to the childless old Mormon couple who had adopted me when I was six. They loved me as best they knew how, and I didn't make it easy. More important, they kept me safe. My visit didn't take long. Saying thanks never does. It's the excuses that eat up time.

50

The potluck had two guests of honor, John and Trooper Smith, who was attending in a wheelchair, along with his wife and two kids. Andy survived the ordeal less well than John and me and had only recently been released from the hospital in Salt Lake City. I'd visited him there several times and each time it hurt me to see him so broken.

Only minutes before I arrived at the diner that night he'd been badly beaten with the tire iron and dragged into the desert and shot twice, once in the chest and once in the face. The Kevlar vest absorbed most of the chest shot, but the shot to his face took a big chunk of his left cheek and ear. He had months, if not years, of plastic surgery ahead of him, and his wife began crying when she told me he was planning to return to the Highway Patrol. For her sake, I hoped he changed his mind, though a lot of people, me included, would miss him.

Every time I saw Andy in the hospital I concluded our visit by looking him in the eye and saying, "Thank you." He always replied, "Jones, try not to do anything stupid today."

I was trying harder than he knew. What I said was, "That would put you out of work, wouldn't it?"

His was a busted, contorted smile, and the pain it caused him was obvious. That smile tore at my heart and mended it a little at the same time. If he hadn't been a Mormon, he would have told me to go fuck myself. But he was thinking it. I knew he was.

The last time I'd visited Andy was a few days before the relay. I'd brought him a present—a new Smokey the Bear Utah State Trooper hat to replace the one he'd lost in the tunnel at Dan Brew's. The Cop Shop refused to sell it to me until I told them why I wanted it. When I did, they insisted I take it free of charge. With all the care I could muster, I set it gently on his shaved head. It slipped to an angle over the missing ear. He asked me how he looked and I searched for a few seconds for an honest response. Andy seemed pleased with my answer: "Like a good cop," I said, and meant every damn word.

I was surprised to see who was taking the next leg of the cross relay. The good news was George was not carrying a gun. I hadn't seen him or Ginger since that afternoon at the theater. As far as I knew, she was still living with him out in the desert.

I waved and said hello, straightened my back and forced myself to control my labored breathing, doing my damned level best as a member of the "This Is Killing Me But I'll Never Let It Show" Club. I carried the cross past the City Limits sign and lowered it right at their feet.

George said hello. I returned his hello.

Ginger glared at me and I offered her a friendly, measured "Ginger."

I helped them yoke up and then stood back out of their way. Ginger whipped her gray-and-red pigtails around and said, "I don't much like you, Ben Jones."

I didn't say anything, though there were days I agreed with her.

George chewed on his lip whiskers and lowered his head. Off they went. I waited until they were a good fifty feet away before turning and walking, sprightly, I thought, back up the highway. I didn't make it far before I collapsed on the roadside and drug my hand across my sweaty face and scalp and gulped for air.

Some folks had volunteered to drive others back to their vehicles after they'd completed their leg of the relay. When mine
showed up, I waved them away, telling them I would walk the mile
back to my rig. They shouted for me to suit myself and I returned
to gulping air like a drowning victim.

When I finally stood the sun was at my back and I was facing
the newly revamped and installed Rockmuse City Limits sign. It
hurt my eyes just to look at it. The posts were uneven, one side
sloping toward the shoulder. To correct this imperfection they had
raised the upper right-hand corner of the sign even higher. Only a
drunk could look at it and not become disoriented. I wasn't drunk
and hoped I never would be, at least not that drunk.

The boys had added a new metal strip to the bottom of the
sign, aligned crooked, with its tip overlapping the sign above it as
if trying to compensate for its own imperfection. It read: "Gateway
to." Maybe they hadn't yet decided exactly what Rockmuse was
the gateway to. Or maybe there had been another strip of sign that
completed the declaration and had been blown away by the wind
and was now vacationing somewhere south. Maybe they thought if
the sign asked a question sooner or later someone might provide a
good answer. I hoped not. I kind of preferred the idea that motor-
ists and residents alike could routinely continue to fill in the blank
with whatever they wanted.

I turned my head north and took in the desert view, the mesa
cliffs tapering off to a point in the distance and the horizon clear
all the way to the Wyoming border.

I'd shown the authorities where the battered trailer was before
I'd even been released from the hospital. I was driven there in a
Utah Highway Patrol Suburban, my jaw wired shut and my head
aching so badly I could hardly sit up straight. They took the route I
had come with Roy and the girl, across the desert, the SUV bumping and slamming into every hole and over every rock every foot
of the way.

In fairness, they'd tried several times by helicopter to spot the upended trailer that had held the children. The rugged terrain and weather always interfered. When we reached the area I knew why. The trailer had caught or likely been set on fire and had burned to a puddle of melted aluminum. Crime-scene investigators, aided by volunteers and Explorer Scouts, combed ten square miles on and off for weeks and found no trace of the children except a few small bones and articles of clothing.

I was told to stay in the vehicle and I got out anyway. Though the area was littered with used tires, this was the place once known as Red Heaven. Back then a small pink river had bubbled out of the mesa and across the desert where it joined with the Price River. Crystals tinged with radium that had washed out of the mesa lined the sandy riverbed and gave the water its pink glow. At the turn of the previous century it was known as one of the most beautiful spots in Utah, with a hot springs, a couple tree-lined streets, houses, and the finest hotel south of Salt Lake City.

Then gold was discovered. The rush didn't last long and the brief mining operation, hydraulic mostly, bored into the mesa and tore up the land, eventually diverting the fragile river deep underground. The place dried up and blew away, except for a few small ranches that survived into the 1970s, until they were abandoned.

The man, who called himself Manita's father, must have been born on one of those ranches, a place Walt had visited when a young wife's husband was away at war, and while Bernice was waitressing and going to night school and trying to make the development of Desert Home a reality. I thought I might have met the woman's husband, one of Bernice's rapists, during the previous summer. He was a corpse by then, hanging from the wall above the commode in the tiny restroom of Walt's Quonset hut. Only Walt knew if that was him or not, and he was more unresponsive than ever—with more reason than ever. Walt's past had begun coming home and the fortress he had built to keep it at bay, his perfect, closed desert diner, was beginning to crumble.

I haven't had a reason to go back to The Well-Known Desert Diner, or the area of Red Heaven. Walt will eventually return to his diner and when he does, I expect he'll commence ordering motorcycle parts again, and I will deliver them. The diner had lost its allure for me. It had become a home to loss—the loss of Claire, the loss of the girl, and maybe a lot more I don't know about and hope I never will. The same goes for Red Heaven, a place of beauty once, and now just a dry riverbed that glows pink at night from the crystals, those that aren't hidden beneath used tires.

When the cops arrived at the diner, the cab-over was gone. There was no trace of the man or the girl. A week later the truck was found at a huge truck stop in Toole, Utah, maybe 150 miles away at the edge of the Great Salt Lake. He's somewhere in the top ten Most Wanted, with little doubt that he murdered Cecil and Pedro, and no doubt at all that he beat Walt and me nearly to death and beat and shot a State Trooper. There were official and strongly worded press releases for a while that they would get their man and bring him to justice. I didn't think so. I liked to think justice had already found him and no one and nothing would ever find him again.

I had visited John in the hospital not long before he was released and the subject of vengeance came up. John, predictably, quoted the Bible. "Vengeance is mine sayeth the Lord."

"Yeah," I said, wondering if Walt's son had met the end I had to imagine. "But wouldn't it be nice if once in a while the Lord let us be there to see it?"

Andy told me the investigation uncovered records at Cecil's home itemizing a tire-smuggling operation bringing counterfeit rubber in from Mexico that was sold at the Stop 'n' Gone Truck Stop and others in the west. Cecil was even greedier and also pocketed the fees collected to dispose of the used tires at recycling plants and dumped them at Red Heaven. Somewhere along the line, Walt's son added children to his tire smuggling. Or maybe the other way around. That was their working theory and they were sticking to it. For all I cared, it made as much sense to me as all the other senseless shit in the world.

I took another look at the City Limits sign and couldn't help myself—I began to laugh. Laughter had not made an appearance in my world for a long time and I hadn't seemed to miss it. The burrito in my shirt made me laugh too. That burrito was evidence of a sort—proof of life, the life that mattered most—and proof the cops could look for the man until hell had frozen over. They conveniently, at least publicly, hadn't got around to addressing how Andy and I ended up in the Quonset, or the anonymous call that sent them out to the diner. They didn't know. I knew. There was only one reason why all three of us were still alive and not murdered— and it wasn't because Walt's son, if that's really who he was, got scared off and ran with the girl.

When I was first released from the hospital I was a little crazy, consumed with pain and memories of Manita and that night. I'd begged Lenny to drive me to Los Ojos Negros. While Lenny stayed in the car I told the women I knew, for whatever reason, it was them in the desert behind the diner. I never really saw or heard them, or the other women I assumed were present that night, who rose up out of the shadows and sand in their long dresses like a crowd of vengeful feminine spirits. The ladies were sweet and sympathetic and listened to me, shook their heads and spoke to each other in that secret unspoken language of theirs.

All I really wanted to know was what they did with the body of the girl. I had no way of knowing for certain Manita had died, but I couldn't imagine her surviving what had come so close to killing me, and would have if not for her small body shielding me. In my grief I wanted to bury Manita with Claire, the cello, and Bernice in the grotto graveyard of Desert Home. I wanted Manita with them, with me. The ladies sent me away with food and quick kisses and sad expressions on their faces.

My visits continued and as time passed eventually I gave up and convinced myself I was wrong, that I had imagined it all, conjured it from the dark desert, the screams of the girl and the pain and certainty of death. If they had taken her body, she was in good and loving care, and that was enough for me, though the sadness dogged my days and nights.

I visited their food trailer early in the morning the day before the relay. No other customers were there and as I waited for my order I idly scanned the business cards and flyers posted on the side of the service window. They were all in Spanish—ads for junk hauling, yard care, special meats, car maintenance. There was a grainy Xerox copy of a flyer for a missing girl. I only glanced at it. There were several, all faded and largely ignored by everyone.

The girl was five or six, wearing a red gingham dress and cowboy boots. Her left arm was in a sling and in her hand she held a small, stuffed animal. She wore a beautiful smile, though it was her large black eyes that caught my attention. Tiffany handed me my order and I walked back to my truck and then returned. In the photo the missing girl was standing next to the edge of a faded green trailer. Behind the girl stood a tall woman in a dark dress, visible only from her waist down. The belt the woman wore seemed to be decorated with oblong stones—maybe opals—reminding me of someone.

When I returned the morning of the relay to look again at the flyer of the missing girl, who I had begun to suspect was my Manita, the poster had been taken down. I asked and the ladies all squealed at once. Michaela spoke for all three. "Good news, Ben! She was found!"

Indeed, she had been. The missing girl had been found by maybe the one person left in the world still missing her. I was handed a free celebratory burrito, which I had kept with me untouched all day, afraid to let it out of my sight. Who knows how long that flyer had been up? Weeks? A month or more? Once the right person had seen it there was no longer any reason to keep it up.

The sun felt good on my back as I stared up at that crooked

abomination of a sign. It would take me fifteen or twenty minutes to walk back to my truck and then maybe ten minutes more to drive to the potluck. There was even a rumor that Rupert Conway might make a rare appearance, which was beginning to occur more often—with and without his shotgun.

Maybe the biggest surprise, at least to me, was the revelation that somehow Cecil was not the complete asshole everyone thought he was. The girl had a chance because Cecil drew a line between greedy, petty criminal and monster. The dog had belonged to Cecil and those that knew him better than I did wondered what had happened to that huge, mean devoted mongrel that was always with him. I don't know how he got the girl away from the man, only that he must have been pressed for time, and he judged that maybe there was someone, a local trucker who drove the desert every day, who might take her if he had no choice.

Cecil probably didn't even know the child was female. He and Pedro were trying to protect a kid. If Cecil didn't survive, the girl would be returned to Pedro. As it turned out, neither one of them made it. I've come to think that the only thing you can count on with people is that they will always be human—good and bad—usually both, and occasionally at the same time.

A car went by on its way into Rockmuse and honked. I recognized the lowered Honda Civic. Hector and his family had decided to stick around for a while. I waved as they passed and he waved back. The Rockmuse City Limits sign caught my eye again, framed against the distant, sprawling red mesa cliffs hovering over the desert. The foil-wrapped burrito felt good against my chest and I guessed it would keep for another day.

I shook my head. If the Roman soldiers who built the cross upon which Jesus was crucified had the same carpentry skills and split a case or two of beer like the boys in the unofficial Rockmuse City Council, Jesus might still be alive today. Maybe things would be different. Maybe not. I wouldn't know. I just drive a truck.

ACKNOWLEDGMENTS

The process of writing a novel is done in solitude, and if you're lucky, inside a circle of love. My circle is filled with literary Zen Masters, high priests and priestesses of nature, students of life, and laborers in the fields of ordinary miracles. To all, my sincerest gratitude. First among these is my editor, Nate Roberson, who guided me past each mile marker. Thanks to my immediate family for listening and excusing my hundred-yard stare of inattentiveness. To all the poets, especially Laure-Anne Bosselaar, Ira Sadoff, Dzvinia Orlowsky, Gary Miranda, Steven Huff, Sam Hamill, Michael Simms, Aliki Barnstone, Kathy Fagan, Peter Meinke, Mary Jane White, Henry Carlile, Christopher Merrill, Meg Kearney, Sandra McPherson, Major Jackson, Jonah Bornstein, and Ana Castillo, whose poems were daily companions. To dear friends whose faith never wavered: Bruce Berger, Ann Rittenberg, Jaime Manrique, Lisa Parmenter, Alicia Griffin, Alison McLennan, Gloria Estela Gonzalez, Migs Muldrow, James Cleveland, David Yoo, Joan Macri, Kerry Beckford, Shawn, Tracy, and Ramona Smith, Michael and Elaine DeLalla, Rich and Pam Larsen, and Jon and Dally Ingersoll. A very special thanks to the writers and faculty of the Writers in Paradise Conference in St. Petersburg, Florida. To my agent, David Hale Smith, and always to my mentors from the Pine Manor/Solstice MFA Program, Sterling Watson and Sandra Scofield, whose wisdom and stern affection are always present.

ABOUT THE AUTHOR

JAMES ANDERSON was born in Seattle, Washington, and grew up in the Pacific Northwest. He is a graduate of Reed College and received his MFA in creative writing from Pine Manor College. His first novel was *The Never-Open Desert Diner*. His short fiction, poetry, essays, and reviews have appeared in many magazines, including *The Bloomsbury Review, New Letters, Solstice Magazine*, and others. He currently divides his time between Colorado and Oregon.